Part 1

H.Gwyne CHO

YULLIM COLLECTION

Published by **ATELIER H**.

ISBN: 9791198584816 (Paperback)

ISBN: 9791198584809 (EPUB)

ISBN: 9791198584830 (Audiobook)

First Edition: Dec 2023

Printed in the United Kingdom.

Contents

Prologue

A modéliste in the French fashion industry is essentially a pattern-maker, whose mission is to create an actual body-size construction based on the designer's sketch.

In those days in Paris, independent designers had their own modéliste, employing them either as in-house staff or as third-party contractors.

In the case of in-house employment, they typically had two types of modélistes, one to create the initial construction, known as the '(main) modéliste', while another to copy and modify the senior's work, called the 'assistant modéliste'.

Chapter 1 : Behind the Black Door

One afternoon in Paris, Jindo was en route to a job interview for an assistant modéliste position, scheduled a mere hour after submitting his application. He was thrilled about the company's location in the Marais district, a well-known area for its trendy and artistic atmosphere.

Jindo had prior work experience, but the French industry was uncharted territory for him yet. Nonetheless, he had a confident attitude, which stemmed from his successful completion of training at a local institute. On his own, he labelled himself with such keywords as 'hardworking', 'skilfully competent', 'detail-oriented' and 'polite with a sense of humour'.

He also prided himself on his linguistic prowess, boasting a London English accent, a charming lilt of Italian, and a smidgen of Parisian-French. Though not fluent in the local language, he remained undaunted, aware that English was prevalent in the industry. On this basis, Jindo considered himself an appealing candidate, which might explain the prompt response he had received that morning.

Following Google Maps, Jindo reached the destination. Before ringing the bell, he phoned the office to confirm the location but received no answer. He rang the bell, yet still no response. He tried calling again but to no avail.

Checking the time, he realised he was ten minutes early. Supposing people might be on a break, he decided to wait. Five minutes later, a tall French guy in a feather-adorned fedora, arrived and inquired about Jindo's intentions.

Filled in by Jindo, the guy seemed puzzled as to why no one had answered the door. Regardless, he entered the door code and ushered Jindo in with him. Once inside, Jindo immediately felt a sense of claustrophobia. The windowless space was painted in matte black and poorly lit, and there seemed to be several doors but all were closed.

Meanwhile, the place appeared to be in the midst of remodelling, with various objects haphazardly strewn about. Jindo stood modestly, and at that moment, the fedora guy shouted upstairs for Gabrielle before vanishing through a door in the corner.

A few minutes later, another door opened, revealing a weary-looking French girl.

"Bonjour..."

Greeting Jindo like a lifeless zombie, she walked directly into another room, leaving Jindo momentarily bewildered before he followed her into what seemed to be her office.

At first glance, Gabrielle appeared younger than Jindo and rather forlorn, clad in dusty black leggings, a t-shirt, and quite unprofessionally customised flip-flops with hole-ridden socks. Her dishevelled hair and slumped shoulders only added to her pitiable appearance.

Sensing her exhaustion, Jindo instinctively decided to keep conversation to a minimum, not wanting to burden her with unnecessary energy expenditure. He waited for her to settle down, and then they finally made eye contact. Jindo quietly gestured towards a chair in the corner, asking if he should sit.

"Oh, yes please..."

Gabrielle seemed to suddenly register the situation, offering Jindo a feeble, apologetic grin. Meanwhile, when her facial muscles lifted to form a smile, Jindo couldn't help but notice her nose hairs poking out.

In addition to the unmistakable dark circles beneath her eyes, the unexpected emergence of sharp, pointy black hairs against her pale face was indeed rather conspicuous.

Trying not to gawk, he averted his gaze and pretended he had not seen anything. Settling into his seat with an innocent smile, Jindo was now facing Gabrielle, and the interview was set to begin.

So far, Jindo was not too perturbed by Gabrielle's dishevelled appearance, as it implied, she had been too preoccupied to attend to her personal grooming. Particularly, her nose hair issue seemed to indicate that she was a committed worker in the dusty atelier environment, rather than just someone lounging in a cushy office, being a finger-wagging director.

As with any typical fashion job interview, Jindo introduced himself while Gabrielle browsed his portfolio and prototypes. After Jindo's brief presentation, a Q&A session commenced.

Being of a similar generation, they seemed to communicate effectively, and their conversation quickly became casual. A positive vibe for Jindo was that Gabrielle appeared impressed by his prototypes and also intrigued by his English accent.

"By the way, you have a British accent Jindo."

"Thank you Gabrielle, as you saw in my CV, I lived in England and learnt English there. That might be why... Having said that, I don't think I've got the accent. I appreciate it though because that's a big compliment to me..."

Jindo replied modestly, but in fact, he had consciously cultivated his accent. This was likely because he wanted to project himself as a well-rounded individual who had not only lived in England but also experienced and understood the local culture.

Indeed, from that point on, he put even more effort into his accent to convey his immersion in English culture. Sadly, he was unaware that his accent did not sound so natural.

"So Jindo, you don't speak English before England?"

Gabrielle's command of English appeared less advanced than Jindo's, and he also noticed that she often observed his facial expressions after speaking English. Indeed, Jindo found this endearing, recognising it as a common habit among those who lack confidence in their foreign language skills.

"No, not really Gabrielle. Well, I learnt English in school but never spoke it much. So, when I arrived in England, it was like starting from scratch. I'm still learning the language, though..."

Jindo endeavoured to portray himself as a constant learner who was already competent enough, and Gabrielle seemed to appreciate his attitude. Meanwhile, she appeared somewhat intimidated, and it might be due to Jindo's unnecessarily loud voice and unflinching gaze.

"I think... your English is... very good."

Gabrielle complimented him but couldn't maintain eye contact.

"Thanks very much."

Jindo replied nonchalantly, and Gabrielle steered the conversation in a new direction.

"These prototypes... you did everything by yourself?"

"Yes... is that... okay?"

Jindo feigned confusion at her question, though he indeed suspected she was impressed by the quality of his work.

"Because... this is... very good quality. I think there aren't many people in Paris who can make this level..."

"Thank you Gabrielle, but I feel a bit guilty just accepting the compliment. I've actually redone these pieces a lot of times, so it's not like I can produce this quality at any time... Having said that, I don't mind reworking as long as it makes the quality better..."

Jindo presented with calculated honesty of him, and Gabrielle seemed to value it. He continued.

"By the way, I come from a small, family-run boutique in Korea. My mother is a designer, my father is a modéliste, and my uncles and aunts handle all the production work... I mention this because I want you to know although I might not have innate talent, I'm naturally familiar and comfortable with the fashion-making environment. For instance, long hours of hard work in a small atelier wouldn't bother me much..."

"That's great Jindo."

Gabrielle seemed to be growing more interested in Jindo and asked a follow-up question to clarify a practical concern.

"Okay then, if I give you a sketch now, just a piece of the sketch... do you know how to make everything by yourself?"

"One question please... are we talking about a designer's original sketch or an industrial technical drawing with measurement information?"

Jindo sought clarity, as he did not want to dive into the task without knowing the specifics.

In fashion, sketches typically come in two forms: a designer's original touch, like those by Karl Lagerfeld, and a flat drawing, which is an outlined version of the garment shape. From a modéliste's perspective, original sketches require personal interpretation, while technical drawings necessitate objective analysis.

"Of course, an original sketch!"

Gabrielle quickly replied as if she had discovered a weak link in Jindo. She smiled, but it seemed somewhat teasing to him.

"Gabrielle, do you also mean to sew the entire piece... all by myself?"

"Yes, construction, pattern drafting, cutting fabric, sewing, ironing, EVERYTHING..."

Gabrielle appeared to be testing Jindo's confidence rather than his competence. Unfazed, Jindo calmly took a moment to think before replying, then slowly spoke up.

"At first, it may take a bit of time to interpret your sketch, as it's my very first time to see your original touch... but yes, all in all, I think I can show you something..."

In fact, he had hesitated to consider any better answer for later. It was because he believed that not many modélistes would respond positively to such questions, as sewing might not be their primary role or forte.

"Can I test you?"

Gabrielle continued to doubt Jindo while smiling.

"Yes, certainly. Actually, I have my tools with me. Maybe today won't be my finest performance, but I'm sure I can show you something. Shall we do it now?"

Jindo displayed a ready-to-go attitude, and Gabrielle seemed taken aback by his confidence. Indeed, it was a rare case for a modéliste to bring their tools to a job interview as no chef would bring their knife to a job interview. Nonetheless, it would certainly not be a minus point.

"No no, it's okay..."

Gabrielle returned to Jindo's portfolio, then peeked at his face, back and forth. Jindo, puzzled by the multitasking expectations for an assistant modéliste role, sought clarification.

"Sorry, Gabrielle… I'm a bit confused. Do you not have a main modéliste? I thought the job position was for an assistant modéliste."

"Yes, I have but she went back to her country."

"Her country? She's not French?"

"No, she is Japanese."

"Japanese?"

Jindo was chuffed to hear this, as he had always held Japanese modélistes in high regard. Meanwhile, he wondered if the Japanese lady would return. It was due to that Gabrielle's phrase was mixed with the present and past tense.

"So, when is she coming back from Japan?"

"No, she's not coming back."

Disappointed by the confirmation, Jindo found himself increasingly befuddled. It was because there was no main modéliste, yet Gabrielle was seeking an assistant modéliste. Furthermore, her probing questions about his proficiency in various tasks led him to ponder if she saw him as a potential candidate for the main modéliste. Hoping to gauge the previous standard, Jindo asked a question.

"How was the Japanese modéliste, though? They're quite detailed and precise, aren't they?"

"She was very good, and we're like friends. We worked together and had fun together after work…"

"That's… great."

Gabrielle's response wasn't what Jindo was fishing for, but she carried on regardless.

"I like working with Asians. They're hard workers, and I'm also like that…"

It appeared that Gabrielle was steering the conversation towards her ethnic preferences now, and Jindo politely refrained from engaging in the topic. Instead, he asked a question to casually prolong the conversation.

"Interesting… By the way, do French people not work hard?"

"No, never."

Gabrielle clearly did not seem to favour local employees, but Jindo tried to offer a positive perspective on French.

"Well, I think they do. I know there's a stereotype that French people are lazy. But in my opinion, it's just that they know how to enjoy their break. It doesn't mean they're not hard workers…"

"NO, FRENCH PEOPLE NEVER WORK HARD. They're always lazy. I don't like working with them, EVER…"

Jindo's words seemed to hit a bit of a raw nerve with Gabrielle, as she suddenly tensed up, furrowing her brow. He wondered if he had overstepped, and Gabrielle continued to stare at him in uncomfortable silence. She then moved her face closer and firmly stated once again.

"I like Asians."

As an Asian himself, this preference of his potential employer was supposed to sound positive, but Jindo was being careful not to make any reaction yet. Instead, he posed another question.

"Have you worked with many Asians?"

"Yes, many many… I also have many Ai-sian friends."

"Great…"

Jindo replied with a grin but refrained from adding any further comments. His instinct probably alerted him to something not quite positive about the French designer.

In fact, Jindo had encountered diverse people during his decade in Europe, and he believed he had developed an intuition, for those who seemed open to other ethnicities, but revealed their stereotypical ideologies when caught off guard.

Regardless, Jindo moved on.

"It's great you have many Asian friends. By the way, Gabrielle… just to let you know, not every Asian is as hard-working as you think."

"NO. ASIANS ARE HARD WORKERS."

Gabrielle was adamant; this time, she raised her pitch like a cat hissing. Jindo was embarrassed, as he had only meant to temper her overly positive image of Asians. The French director seemed unyielding in her beliefs.

An awkward silence followed, and Jindo, feeling uncomfortable, opted to change tack, remembering he was conversing with a potential employer, not a friend. Jindo steered the conversation back to the Japanese modéliste, intrigued about her departure.

"By the way Gabrielle, can I ask you why the Japanese modéliste has left?"

Gabrielle commenced with a shake of her head.

"She messed up her life. Her mother was dead, her family was fighting, and she was depressed… She came to work late every day, always with a sad face, making mistakes all the time… She was weak and stupid. I never really liked her anyway…"

Jindo was surprised by Gabrielle's steep change in tone, contrasting with her initial description of the Japanese woman as a friend. Even so, Jindo did not dwell on it, understanding that other factors might have influenced her decision as a company owner.

"Okay, so you had to let her go…"

"No, she just stopped coming to work."

"Really? That's… not quite professional."

"She left without saying anything, and I was sad because I treated her like family. It even happened during Paris Fashion Week when we were busy like crazy… Anyway, I was left alone… AGAIN…"

Gabrielle suddenly seemed to become melancholic, and Jindo sighed, feigning empathy.

Meanwhile, though her last word, 'again', piqued his curiosity, he brushed it aside for the time being. Instead, he sympathised with the Japanese modéliste, knowing how losing a close family member while living abroad felt.

Gabrielle appeared moody, just staring at her desk floor for quite a moment. Meanwhile, she appeared to steal a glance at Jindo's face, as if checking if he was keeping up with her. After a moment of further grieving, she slowly switched the topic.

"Anyway, let's talk about work. So, you know how to make menswear and womenswear, both?"

"Yes."

Jindo bounced back with a ready-set vibe, and Gabrielle appeared to be chuffed. He then unexpectedly piped up further.

"But to be honest Gabrielle, I don't see a big difference between the two areas."

Jindo seemed to have a bee in his bonnet about it, and Gabrielle followed suit.

"Why?"

"Well, because I think modélisme is ultimately about garment construction with sewing instructions… In my opinion, whether it's men's or womenswear, there're a lot of crossover elements… As far as I know, Stella McCartney, for example, when she was younger, worked at a men's tailor boutique in Savile Row, London, and now she uses the menswear tailoring techniques for her womenswear jackets... I'm sure there are many other designers mixing methods in a similar manner. I think, these days in particular, womenswear is becoming like menswear and vice versa…"

Jindo expressed his opinion, and Gabrielle still seemed to be following along. Meanwhile, Jindo did not forget to portray himself as humble.

"Well, surely though… my knowledge isn't deep enough yet, so… I'm probably generalising a big topic too simply. The main point is that I don't like distinguishing the two ideologies of menswear and womenswear. I want to be open to all possibilities for creation. So, I may say… I know how to make a piece of a garment when there are fabrics, body measurements and design."

Gabrielle was quietly nodding, and Jindo quickly lobbed a question to let her talk. This was probably because he felt embarrassed for talking too much about something that was not asked.

"Gabrielle, do you do menswear though? I thought you specialise in womenswear only."

"No, I don't do menswear yet, but many guys like my collection, so I want to do men's one day… Actually, some guys already wear my pieces as they're oversized…"

Gabrielle tried to say it proudly but looked somewhat unconfident. Meanwhile, Jindo did not catch the moment as he was too preoccupied with pondering how to flaunt his knowledge.

"That's great, Gabrielle. I think the menswear industry will grow, and with young male celebrities experimenting more, it's already expanding. Even CHANEL might start menswear soon…"

Jindo passionately demonstrated his vision for future menswear, but Gabrielle seemed to be getting a bit miffed. It was likely because Jindo seemed to consistently dominate the conversation with his loud voice, talking about something not even asked.

Gabrielle then said something, and it seemed like the French designer wasn't keen on merely being a bystander in the situation.

"Well, I'm not sure if CHANEL will do menswear…"

Gabrielle tentatively proffered her view, but the tactless man commandeered the moment once more.

"Can I ask why you think so, Gabrielle? You know many male celebrities already enjoy their CHANEL wear. Look at Pharrell Williams…"

"…"

Gabrielle was quiet, evidently irritated by Jindo. Meanwhile, the irritating man continued.

"Who knows if they already have their menswear department in progress…"

"They don't."

Gabrielle curtly stated it, and Jindo found her nuance a bit off. It was because she seemed oddly certain about her claim. Jindo picked up on this.

"They don't? Can I ask how you know that?"

"Because I was at CHANEL."

"Pardon?"

Gabrielle's unexpected revelation left Jindo speechless.

Chapter 2 : Unveiling Ambitions

Jindo was utterly gobsmacked, and his voice quickly turned into a mere whisper.

"Ah... you were... at CHANEL? Sorry, I didn't know about that..."

Gabrielle's sudden revelation certainly embarrassed Jindo, and he quietened down. Sensing the shift in dynamics, Gabrielle seized the opportunity to take control.

She fixed her gaze on Jindo with newfound confidence, and her voice grew louder. She proudly reiterated her statement.

"YES, I WAS AT CHANEL."

For Jindo, it was undeniably exciting to meet someone from the famous fashion house. However, he could not shake the feeling of intimidation; Gabrielle was younger, seemingly not even speaking fine English, and yet had worked at one of the top labels in the sector when he had not even been to the doorsteps yet. Moreover, it was not just any 'luxe' label, but arguably one of the most prominent names in fashion history.

"Why? You like CHANEL?"

Gabrielle's tone was somehow teasing, reminiscent of a cheeky girl asking a shy boy if he fancied one of her best friends. Jindo felt more intimidated, realising they actually came from different worlds. Despite their previously friendly and casual conversation, there now seemed to be a clear division in their professional records.

Nevertheless, Jindo attempted to establish his own stance.

"Well… I wouldn't say I like them, but I just acknowledge their excellence."

"Ah, yeah? Why?"

Her speech quickened, her tone oozing confidence as if she were certain she held the upper hand. Her posture in the chair even became laid-back now. Jindo still attempted to establish his stance, but it was evident he was rather intimidated.

"Well… I mean, it's… CHANEL… I don't think anyone would deny that it's one of the most prestigious labels in fashion. The reason I can't say I'm a fan is simply that it's mainly a women's label yet and… I admire menswear or, well, total fashion if I may say…"

Jindo cautiously explained, his voice losing its earlier strength. He continued.

"Having said that, I'm well aware of their greatness. I'm sure I don't know as much about CHANEL as you do, but I do know that, their pieces are of exceptional quality, including their hand-tailored manner of construction…"

Jindo was exceedingly careful with his words, aware that it would be risky to reveal any superficial knowledge, in front of someone who had just claimed to have worked at the place.

Instead, he tried to shift the focus.

"For me, the one I like is Hermès. I really admire them because…"

"I WAS AT HERMÈS TOO."

Gabrielle interjected, a pleased smile on her face. She seemed surprised that Jindo had mentioned the very brand she had worked for.

"Ah… were you also… at Hermès? Wow, I'm speechless now."

Jindo was further impressed with Gabrielle and decidedly more intimidated.

"Why?"

Gabrielle inquired, making her already laid-back position more relaxed.

"It's because… it's actually been my dream to go to Hermès and experience their savoir-faire (know-how). I may not know as many designers or brands as you do but I do know that… the reputation of Hermès has been top-notch in the industry for as long as I can remember and I think it's their product quality that speaks for itself…"

Jindo expressed his opinion with a touch of confidence, perhaps because he believed no one would dispute the quality of Hermès. He continued carefully.

"As far as I've heard, they have their particular system to achieve this. Of course, the creative DNA and its universe are important but for me… my respect lies more in the systematic know-how of a brand…"

Jindo delicately articulated his admiration for Hermès. However, Gabrielle did not appear to be listening to his words.

Instead, she seemed to be enjoying the sight of him desperately making an effort. It was likely because Jindo had been loud and confident earlier, but now quietened down, painstakingly choosing his words to illustrate his opinions.

Gabrielle remained silent, merely staring and smiling at Jindo in a somewhat patronising manner.

Feeling uncomfortable under Gabrielle's gaze, Jindo was to summarise his thoughts quickly.

"CHANEL… It's absolutely an amazing brand but for me… I see myself more suited for Hermès if I may say…"

By this point, it appeared that an impression had been made; Jindo seemed skilled, but perhaps immature and inexperienced within the industry.

Gabrielle continued to stare wordlessly at Jindo, prompting him to try and alleviate the awkward atmosphere by asking her a question.

"By the way Gabrielle, may I ask how your experience at Hermès was?"

Jindo asked with intrigued eyes, and Gabrielle calmly responded.

"Hm… there are so many rules for employees at Hermès. You would… just stay at your place and work with the given materials only… and that's why I quit because there was no space for me to be creative… Also… it was just too strict for me. No high heels, no makeup, no hair dye…"

Gabrielle briefly listed her dislikes about Hermès, although her tone seemed somewhat unsure. However, Jindo was too engrossed to notice, possibly excited to hear an insider's perspective on his ideal workplace.

"Great, that's exactly how I imagined it would be. What you mentioned wouldn't be a problem for me by the way, because it's just part of their office culture and I think that contributes to their ability to produce such exceptional quality… Sorry Gabrielle, I'm talking too much again… Anyway, my point is I'm quite envious of you, Gabrielle…"

Once more, Jindo spoke about his admiration for Hermès, unprovoked, probably to ensure that Gabrielle was aware of his strong preference for the label.

In fact, Jindo had heard many times that those prestigious luxury fashion houses frequently hired individuals through their private networks, relying on recommendations or references from current or former employees.

Therefore, this effort of his might have stemmed from deep-seated self-consciousness, that if he established a fine rapport with Gabrielle, she could help him secure a position at those luxury fashion houses later on.

From that point on, Jindo regarded Gabrielle with respect, all the while subtly hinting at his admiration for Hermès by occasionally touching his 'chaine d'ancre' bracelet.

Even so, he wanted to confirm his understanding of her career path.

"So Gabrielle, you were at CHANEL and also at Hermès?"

"Well, I was at many brands but CHANEL was the last company I worked for…"

Gabrielle responded with a faint sigh as if the question was too naive. Perhaps it was because she now ran her own company and no longer worked as an employee.

Nevertheless, her story seemed perfectly aligned with Jindo's expectations; someone progressing through various brands, reaching one of the top names in the industry, and ultimately establishing her own label in the heart of Paris.

"That's amazing, Gabrielle. I mean... you're amazing, Gabrielle."

Jindo directly expressed his admiration for Gabrielle and encouraged her to share more of her story.

"Really sorry, Gabrielle, but... may I ask you why you decided to quit CHANEL and start your own label? Excuse me, but CHANEL? It's just such a big name for me…"

Gabrielle appeared pleased to be asked and willingly replied.

"Okay... Firstly, I never had any plan to start my own label but one day, my CHANEL colleagues saw my personal accessory collection then introduced me to an exhibition manager. He offered me a booth for free, and after that, it just became BOOM…"

She narrated her story fluently, and Jindo listened with rapt attention, like a child engrossed in his favourite bedtime story. It was evident that Jindo was genuinely captivated by Gabrielle's tale.

"That's fantastic Gabrielle, so... you basically started off with your accessory line, then expanded to prêt-à-porter (ready-to-wear), correct?"

As Jindo continued to ask questions, Gabrielle seemed more validated in speaking about herself.

"Yes, but I already knew how to make clothes anyway. I did my training at Chambre Syndicale de la Haute Couture, from garment making to accessory designs... I was also a fitting model for LANVIN when I was a teenager. So, I was already familiar with stylisme and modélisme. I learned a lot from their studio discussions... Maybe that's why I finished my training early because I was so faster than the others..."

Gabrielle exuded confidence about her background, and this revelation was another surprise to Jindo, as he had not seen any of this information on her website.

"That's... incredible, Gabrielle."

Gabrielle's additional accomplishments only served to enhance Jindo's respect for her. He was well aware of the prestige associated with her institute and the complex curriculum they followed.

Moreover, her early graduation made her seem even more exceptional. At that point, Jindo realised that Gabrielle was both academically and professionally outstanding.

With this in mind, Jindo re-evaluated his impressions of her, concluding that Gabrielle was a consummate artist who prioritised her craft above all else.

After this brief reflection, Jindo returned his attention to Gabrielle, only to find her exchanging glances with someone behind him. Somehow, her demeanour seemed to have changed completely, her gaze now icy and piercing, like that of a villainous ice queen ready to freeze him.

Startled by the sudden change in atmosphere, Jindo's more pressing concern was identifying the newly arrived woman behind him. He swivelled around to investigate.

A middle-aged woman, who appeared to be an office worker, had apparently arrived mid-conversation. As Jindo looked her way, she feigned busyness, typing and staring at her monitor. However, it was evident that she was stealing glances at him, even as he watched her.

Still puzzled by the situation and looking back and forth between Gabrielle and the woman, Jindo sensed that no one would explain what was happening.

Determined to focus on his immediate priority, securing his position at Gabrielle's company, he decided to ignore the sudden chill in the air. Although Gabrielle's mood had shifted, his dedication remained steadfast.

Jindo gazed at Gabrielle, determined to demonstrate his unwavering loyalty. He was truly prepared to let her take the lead in any manner she desired. Recognising his eagerness, Gabrielle opted to put him to the test.

She returned to examining his prototypes, this time searching for any imperfections. She scrutinised every nook and cranny of the garments, eventually unearthing a flaw within the pocket of the trousers. With furrowed brows and a stern expression, she dramatically revealed the issue at hand.

"What's this?"

Her piercing gaze bore into Jindo, reminiscent of a quality control manager impossible to satisfy. Keeping his composure, Jindo attempted to respond.

"Do you mean the thread tension that wasn't…"

"THIS IS NOT GOOD."

Interrupting him, Gabrielle raised her voice. Slightly flustered by her outburst, Jindo cautiously tried to defend himself.

"Gabrielle… I think that is…"

"Non, c'est pas bien ça."

(No, this is not good.)

Again, she cut him off, shaking her head dismissively. It was a touch mortifying for Jindo as she essentially pointed out the sewing issue.

In fact, the problem was that the thread tension was not tight enough, making the pocket susceptible to damage if anyone were to use it. Meanwhile, Jindo found this a tad unfair, as the primary task of a modéliste was not to sew but to create the garment's structure.

"Excuse me, Gabrielle... are you looking for a seamstress? I thought the position was for an assistant modéliste."

Jindo cautiously raised the fundamental issue of the job interview, and Gabrielle suddenly appeared to realise the situation. A blush crept up her cheeks, and she quickly flashed an apologetic smile.

"No no, I already have my couturière (seamstress)... Yes, I'm looking for an assistant modéliste..."

Although Jindo had an inkling of what Gabrielle had tried to accomplish with her sudden critique, he was not deterred. In his mind, he was utterly committed to working for Gabrielle, no matter the circumstances. Thus, he decided to express his eagerness to the former CHANEL and Hermès employee.

"Gabrielle, please let me... The thing is, I'd like to work for you. I'd be honoured to have the opportunity to learn from you. I don't mind if you want me to be the main modéliste or the assistant... Regardless of the position, I'll give it my all..."

Jindo's voice was resolute, and he continued.

"Gabrielle, I may not have an impressive professional record like you do, but I'm really rather good... I'm confident I can prove my worth to you, and you won't be disappointed."

"…"

Gabrielle appeared flustered by Jindo's sudden, fervent plea. She then took a moment, resting her chin on her hand. She seemed pondering how to handle the situation, while the impatient applicant continued.

"Moreover, if you're planning to hire someone else as the main modéliste, I have no issue with that. I'll simply support and assist them… I'd be more than happy just to be part of your team and learn from you."

"…"

Despite Jindo's further entreaties, Gabrielle remained unimpressed, glancing at her monitor while attempting to suppress a smile. However, Jindo did not catch the moment and launched his final appeal.

"Gabrielle, of course, it's your decision, but I guarantee I'll make a significant contribution to your company. You can test me first without any paperwork and decide on my contract whenever you want. I don't mind…"

"Hm… I don't know…"

Gabrielle was still looking at her monitor, but seemingly smiling. Jindo stepped forward.

"Gabrielle please, let's have a go. I won't disappoint you, I promise."

A moment of silence passed, and Gabrielle slowly spoke up.

"I don't know Jindo, because I'm not sure how good you are…"

"That's exactly why I'm suggesting you test me first Gabrielle."

Jindo was relieved as the situation seemed to be moving forward. Meanwhile, Gabrielle still appeared to be mulling it over.

"Hm… I can see here that you've just finished your training in Paris."

"Yes."

"Then, do you not have a stagiaire (internship) requirement to complete your course?"

"Well, yes and no. The training is finished and as far as I know, for those who want to get a degree, need to fulfil their internship requirement... But in my case, as I already have a degree and work experience, I'm eager to jump into the field asap."

"Jindo, I asked because I don't know you yet. So, even if I want to test you, I'll still need some documentation."

Though Jindo had not initially planned on doing the stagiaire, he decided not to fuss over it, since the moment was an opportunity to connect with the former CHANEL professional.

"No problem at all Gabrielle. I can get the document."

"Good, then you need to bring it today because I need to cancel the other appointments."

"Gabrielle, could I bring the paper tomorrow morning? It's already late afternoon."

"No, if you don't come today, I'll be in trouble with my schedule."

Jindo found the situation a little weird. To the best of his knowledge, the stagiaire document could be filled out on the first day of work, and he could not quite grasp what she meant by her schedule.

Nonetheless, he assumed there might be something he did not know about the French employer's concerns.

"Okay Gabrielle, I'll get the paper now. I'm on my way."

Jindo hastily gathered his belongings. Then, just before exiting, he gave Gabrielle a slight nod combined with a small Asian bow, expressing his gratitude once more.

"Gabrielle, I'm truly grateful. I really appreciate it. Thank you."

Gabrielle offered no response to Jindo, and at that moment, he locked eyes with the office lady. She attempted to appear indifferent, feigning concentration on her typing.

Although Jindo found the overall situation a bit odd, he did not dwell on it. He simply assumed it might be the typical office atmosphere in this place. He then headed to his institute to obtain the document.

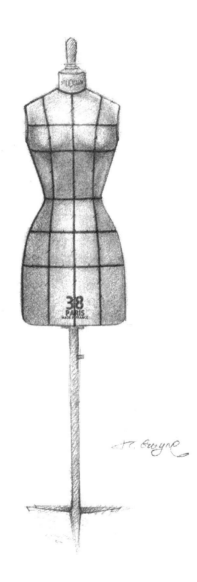

Chapter 3 : The Cave of Concealments

A few hours later…
Jindo returned swiftly with the paper in hand.

"Wow you came back fast, Jindo."

Gabrielle exclaimed, clearly delighted. She began filling out the paperwork fluently, only faltering when she reached the final section, 'rémunération'.

After a moment's pause, she scribbled down a figure and handed the document back to Jindo.

As Jindo reviewed it, he could feel Gabrielle's watchful eyes on him, along with some discreet glances exchanged with the office lady behind him. It irked him a bit, but he chose not to dwell on it. Reaching the end of the document, Jindo queried.

"Okay, Gabrielle. Everything looks fine to me, so the salary is five hundred sixty…"

"C'est normale and I actually cancelled the other good people for you, REMEMBER?"

Besides the abrupt interjection, Gabrielle's tone was rather forceful, as if she sought to silence him. Jindo tried to placate the impatient director.

"Gabrielle… I'm asking just to check the numbers because they're written in cursive."

"DE QUOI?"

Her shrill tone in her native language betrayed her tension.

"The handwritten form…"

Jindo said while mimicking a handwriting gesture.

"Ah…"

Gabrielle appeared sheepish, and Jindo calmly affirmed.

"That's just... it."

He raised and showed both his palms to indicate he did not mean to be argumentative.

"Ah… okay."

Shaking off the embarrassment, Gabrielle pressed on.

"So, we sign now?"

"Yes, please."

After signing the papers, Gabrielle smiled, a sense of relief washing over her, and seemingly exchanged a positive glance with the office lady. Jindo wondered about their silent communication but set aside his curiosity for the moment and expressed his gratitude once more for the opportunity.

The monthly salary of less than six-hundred euros was a mere pittance, but it did not bother Jindo. Instead, he was excited enough to work with the ex-CHANEL designer, eager to showcase his skills, and keen to learn from the high-profile professional.

In fact, the stagiaire salary in the French fashion sector varies, but small independent labels normally pay the minimum though it would not be the same case for a modéliste.

Now, it seemed that, for Gabrielle, she had secured an (assistant) modéliste at the minimum wage for a stagiaire, who was raring to go like a drooling dog. As for Jindo, he had the pleasure of working with someone who claimed to have been with the greatest fashion houses. Each party seemed content with their lot.

"Are you ready to come to the universe of Gabrielle?"

Gabrielle was about to give a tour, her voice tone shifting to one of delight. Her behaviour was somewhat strange, but Jindo played along, feigning excitement.

In fact, for Jindo, everything might have been acceptable since he heard that Gabrielle had worked at CHANEL and Hermès.

"Yes, please."

Passing through the door that the fedora-worn guy had entered earlier, Jindo found the path reminiscent of a cave leading into the depths. Indeed, the building was rather old, even boasting a manual lift.

Jindo was quite taken aback, unable to believe that such a rough-hewn structure existed in the heart of Paris, not in a 'well-preserved' sense, but rather 'neglected'.

Regardless, he attempted to subtly probe his suspicions.

"Gabrielle, I've never seen this sort of ancient architecture in Paris. How did you find this place?"

"I know, it's amazing, no?"

"…"

There seemed to be a slight misunderstanding of Jindo's words, but Gabrielle continued regardless.

"I think it was an industrial factory that manufactured leather goods during the war period, but I think it hasn't changed since then…"

Jindo nodded, feigning interest in his employer's story. Gabrielle carried on.

"When I first found this building, I was very happy so I made the contract right away."

"Wow, great. How did you find the property, though?"

"I found it online. Actually, the propriétaire lives in LA and she never comes here, so it's very good…"

Jindo partly understood the tenant's feeling of freedom, given the distant landlord, but meanwhile, he also could not shake the feeling that something was a bit off. Regardless, he changed the subject and continued the conversation.

"Ah, is the landlord American?"

"Yes, I think so. But her husband is French, so he comes here once a year, so it's annoying…"

Jindo could sense the genuine discontent on her face, and he cautiously delved into his somewhat suspicious inquiries.

"Why? Is he strict? Like inspecting the house condition in detail?"

"No, it's because I use the spaces that I'm not supposed to. Actually, I rented the floors only, but I also use the cave that I'm not supposed to use…"

"Cave?"

"Yes, it's like storage in French. My landlord's husband doesn't know I use it."

"Ah, but is it that serious if he finds out?"

"No, not really… He's just trying to be strict for nothing… stupid man!"

"…"

Jindo was slightly surprised by her abrupt little jibe, but meanwhile, he felt he was beginning to grasp the French director's character. He decided to chalk it up to her less advanced English. She continued.

"Anyway, I use each floor to display different layers of my creative universe, and all those unnecessary things, I just put them into the cave.

When her husband calls me to visit the house, I just clean the cave like I never use it…"

In a way, Jindo understood her reasons, but his doubts lingered nonetheless. He then broached another question.

"By the way Gabrielle, can I ask why there's no window?"

"Well, I painted the windows…"

Gabrielle spoke as if there was no issue, and Jindo cautiously proceeded.

"Haha, yes, I can see them. So, you have windows here…"

Jindo feigned amusement at Gabrielle's assertion, and she carried on.

"You know they're fake windows, though. You can't open them."

"…"

Jindo wondered if she genuinely meant it, as it seemed glaringly obvious. Then again, her earnest expression left him no choice but to play along.

"Yes, of course, Gabrielle, I won't open it, otherwise I'll get myself looking more stupid than I already am…"

"Haha, yes, be careful! They're fake, and I like it this way, haha."

"Ha… ha…"

Jindo laughed along with the eccentric director, and she continued.

"I don't want any windows in my house, by the way. I don't want people to see my space where I create my art."

"Bien sûr."

Jindo feigned a sincere understanding of the artist's preference, but meanwhile, he acknowledged that an artist might not want to reveal their work process, only the result.

However, he could not shake the feeling that this French artist still seemed to be hiding something from people. Regardless, he pondered the black painting on the walls, as it made the room quite dark.

"By the way Gabrielle, do you also prefer a dark ambience? The walls are all painted in black, and even the lighting seems a bit, not very rich… Is there any particular reason?"

"Yeah, because when it's more dark, I become more creative. It gives me some kind of mysterious energy…"

She suddenly closed her eyes for a moment, acting as if she were drawing inspiration from the air. Jindo found her somewhat spiritual in her approach. At that moment, they finally reached the atelier after the long, curvy stairs.

"Voilà!"

Gabrielle introduced the atelier, which exuded a crafty and youthful atmosphere. Vintage furniture filled the space, and graffiti paintings adorned the walls.

Four individuals were present, each appearing to have their own tasks except one; the tall fedora guy was a chapelier (hat maker), a young woman wearing black Balenciaga glasses was an assistant accessory designer, a middle-aged African man was an industrial sewing professional (seamstress), and a handsome French man was unidentifiable in his profession but just stood chatting with the others.

Jindo greeted each person with 'bonjour' and 'enchanté' in his limited French, pleased to meet his future colleagues. However, the unidentified man slightly irked Jindo's nerves, as he avoided eye contact with him but Gabrielle. It seemed that there was some issue between the two.

Initially, Jindo thought the man was just shy, perhaps unfamiliar with English or having met few Asians before. What bothered him, though, was that the man and Gabrielle exchanged glances as if arguing since Jindo had entered the place.

Jindo acted like he did not notice anything by looking elsewhere and avoiding their gaze. The situation was slightly uncomfortable, but he tried not to dwell on it. In fact, the unidentified man seemed nice, likely just shy for the moment. Moreover, the argument did not appear to be about Jindo personally. Regardless, the reason behind it remained elusive.

While the two continued their silent argument, Jindo took his time to examine the atelier more closely. He believed that, regardless of the design type, a well-organised atelier was essential for the creative execution of a brand.

As he scanned the space, he found some aspects intriguing, while others were difficult to fathom. Jindo acknowledged that a young fashion atelier might not be neat and polished yet, but in Gabrielle's case, several elements were beyond his acceptance.

There was a wonky cutting table with a severely damaged surface, propped up by a grubby, unused and seemingly broken washing machine. Various tools, including pens, rulers, and scissors, scattered about, seemingly without purpose. The ironing board was covered with unsightly spots and stains, and thread rolls were strewn everywhere, on the floor, next to the iron, under the table, on the supply shelves, and even behind fabrics. The place was simply a mess.

Despite his disappointment, Jindo tried to view the situation positively, thinking that the ex-CHANEL designer had been perhaps too busy.

He then noticed designated spaces for each component and assumed no one had just taken an interest in organising and cleaning the place yet. Some areas could be easily fixed or replaced, so he did not consider the disarray a fundamental problem.

He additionally thought that it might be unfair to expect a young director, who had achieved success in a short time with her creativity alone, to maintain a perfectly organised and professional workspace. Considering all these thoughts, Jindo did not let his impression of the atelier weigh too heavily on his mind.

As Gabrielle and the unidentified man carried on with their hushed conversation, Jindo shifted his focus to other parts of the atelier. His gaze fell upon the fitting mannequin, an object he would be working with frequently and one that could symbolise the atelier itself.

In fact, for a modéliste, inspecting a fitting mannequin in a new atelier is much like a chef checking grills in a new kitchen.

Within just a few steps, Jindo formed a strong first impression of the fitting mannequin.

It was, without question, the most grotesque specimen he had ever encountered. He wondered where on earth Gabrielle could have discovered such a monstrosity in France. Although he acknowledged Gabrielle's speciality was accessory design, he reasoned that as a garment designer now, she should have a decent, fitting mannequin.

Despite his misgivings, Jindo tried to console himself with the thought that everyone would have a different standard. He resolved to focus on learning from Gabrielle and making the most of the opportunity at hand.

Jindo then took a look at Gabrielle's pieces on hangers. Her designs predominantly featured costume-styled fashion. Although he did not find them particularly striking, he reminded himself that design would be subjective. Meanwhile, he was genuinely taken aback by a fundamental issue he noticed.

The fabric cutting was essentially wrong, with the straight (vertical) and cross (horizontal) grains reversed. Such a mistake would only be excusable for a novice, not for someone with Gabrielle's experience.

Garments made with misaligned fabric cuts may appear fine initially, but after washing, they are likely to be stretched or shrunk oddly, altering the fit over time.

Despite these concerns, Jindo could not overlook the photos on the wall featuring international celebrities, including Lady Gaga, wearing Gabrielle's pieces. Even those custom fabrics adorned with Gabrielle's initials and recognisable names, such as Disney, hinted at collaborations with global icons. This meant, regardless of his impressions, Gabrielle had evidently achieved something remarkable.

The heated exchange between Gabrielle and the unidentified man appeared to subside momentarily, but it was evident that the issue remained unresolved.

Gabrielle quickly ushered Jindo back to the office, apologising for not being able to show him the upstairs showroom due to ongoing graffiti work and the pungent fumes it produced.

Jindo was not fazed; he knew he would see it later and could glean the style from the office and atelier. Besides, he was not particularly enthralled.

Nonetheless, a small glass ceiling in the office caught his attention, and Gabrielle encouraged him to take a peek. He cast a cursory glance and feigned interest.

"It looks great."

"Well, you can't really see it properly."

Gabrielle replied, eyeing Jindo sceptically as if she could see through his polite façade.

Feeling embarrassed but unwilling to admit the truth, Jindo elaborated.

"I mean... I've never seen a wall painting in mid-process before. I didn't even know they'd be covered with vinyl. All I see is that there seem to be paintings behind the vinyl, and it's rich in multiple colours... By the way, the painter who I assume is a guy, looks quite authentic with all those tattoos..."

Jindo opted for honesty and swiftly shifted the focus to the painter to avoid conceding his inattention. His tactic seemed to work, as Gabrielle offered yet another apology.

"Yes, I'm so sorry I can't show you today. By the way, the painter is a friend of mine, and he's very good. I always ask him for my paintings, and we've worked together for a long time. He really understands my visions..."

"Great."

Jindo shot another glance at the glass ceiling, feigning interest. That was when he noticed that the painter appeared to be of Asian descent.

"Is he Asian by the way?"

"Yes, I think..."

"You… think?"

Jindo found it odd that she spoke as if she was not quite certain of her long-time friend's nationality. She seemed to read his expression.

"I think he was born here. I'm not sure. I've never asked him…"

"Ah, okay."

Jindo tried to move past the topic, as he did not intend to delve too deeply, but Gabrielle chimed in.

"I think he's from Belgique."

"Okay, great."

"I'm not really sure, though... I think he's from somewhere around there, Belgique or Pays-bas (Netherlands)…"

"Okay…"

"I'll ask him later."

"No no Gabrielle, you don't need to. I just asked because I noticed he was Asian, and... that's about it really..."

Jindo attempted to defuse the situation by raising his eyebrows and waving his hands, indicating that he did not mean anything in particular. Gabrielle continued regardless.

"Yes, well... he's not really an Asian from Asia, though..."

"Okay Gabrielle, I didn't mean anything in particular… Sorry, if my question was a bit weird..."

"No, I'm just telling you he's not an Asian from Asia."

"Okay, Gabrielle. J'ai bien compris *(I understood well)*. He's not from Asia."

"NO."

It seemed to be yet another weird outburst from Gabrielle on the subject of Asians, and Jindo opted not to comment on it. Gabrielle seemed satisfied as if she had won some sort of victory, then shot a strange glance at the office lady, seemingly celebrating her 'win'.

Regardless, the moment passed, and then Gabrielle launched into an impassioned speech about her weekend plan to finish the graffiti work. She proudly presented her vision, and Jindo played along, feigning anticipation.

Sensing the conversation dwindling, Jindo decided it was time to leave.

"I can't wait to see it Gabrielle and… I'm sorry, I think I've taken up too much of your time… You seem to have a lot to do. Maybe I should leave now so you can get back to work..."

"It's okay. I always work anyway."

"Thanks, but I think you're just being kind…"

"No, it's really okay."

" … "

Gabrielle continued standing and smiling, and an awkward silence ensued. They simply gazed at each other for a moment. It appeared Gabrielle was not ready to end the meeting and wanted to prolong it. Jindo tried to wrap things up more decisively.

"I think you're just too kind, Gabrielle. But, I don't want to take any more of your precious time, so I appreciate everything today and... I'm looking forward to seeing you next week then."

"Ah, okay..."

Finally, the welcoming session was over, and Jindo prepared to leave the office.

At that moment, he discovered the argued handsome man was standing behind the door, apparently having observed the entire scene. He was staring at Gabrielle, and she seemed embarrassed.

The office lady also looked tense, as if round two of their dispute was imminent. Jindo did not have a clue about what was transpiring, but he could sense the negative air, swiftly charging the atmosphere. He promptly made his exit.

"Au... revoir."

Chapter 4 : A Palette of Aspirations

First day…

After a revitalising morning workout, Jindo felt invigorated and ready for his first day at Gabrielle's. Since he had arrived a tad early, he decided to have a leisurely stroll around the neighbourhood, soaking up the quaint charm of the area.

Returning about a quarter of an hour before his scheduled start time, he pressed the doorbell. This time, the door swung open almost immediately, as if someone had been keenly anticipating his arrival.

There stood Gabrielle, clutching a small takeaway cup filled with a curious blend of red and green liquid, her smile warm and welcoming.

"Hello!"

Though still sporting her dusty black leggings and t-shirt, Gabrielle appeared quite refreshed. This time, Jindo could not help but notice her radiant beauty, accentuated by her now moisturised hair and luminous, blemish-free complexion.

In fact, Gabrielle cut quite a striking figure. Standing tall around at an impressive 175cm (about 5'9"), she was neither waif-like nor runway-skinny, but her slender, well-proportioned frame made it easy to believe she had once been a fitting model at LANVIN.

Upon entering the premises, Jindo discovered that not only Gabrielle, but the entire place seemed polished and revitalised. No one else appeared to have arrived yet, and Gabrielle ushered Jindo directly into her office.

"Do you want to follow me?"

"Yes, okay…"

Jindo was not quite certain why he was being led to her office, but he assumed there might be matters to discuss or paperwork to complete before commencing work.

"Voilà!"

Gabrielle exclaimed, gesturing towards her office with a flourish. She unveiled her revamped office, and it dawned on Jindo that she simply wanted to show off her latest handiwork.

As he surveyed the room, Jindo noticed that the office was immaculate and well-organised compared to the previous week. Tables and equipment were neatly arranged, and the walls now sported freshly finished graffiti murals.

Feigning interest, Jindo could sense Gabrielle's eager anticipation of his remarks.

"It's amazing, Gabrielle."

"Yes, I know."

"…"

Gabrielle appeared rather chuffed with herself, and Jindo felt compelled to linger a bit longer, indulging the weekend warrior in some well-deserved praise.

"So, did the Asian tattooed painter do this?"

"Yes, but he just painted, the design and ideas are all from me…"

Jindo detected Gabrielle's desire to emphasise her contribution, and the authentic artist continued.

"By the way, he's not Asian, I asked him and he said he's from Belgium…"

"Oh, okay…"

Jindo realised again that Gabrielle would tend to subtly differentiate between those of Asian descent born in their original countries and those born in her neighbour countries. She continued.

"He's from Antwerp."

Hearing the name of one of the most artistic cities on this planet, Jindo felt a surge of excitement but somehow chose not to dwell on it. It was likely due to his suspicion that an uncomfortable yet trivial conversation might ensue. He quickly moved on.

"Great, I love Antwerp. By the way, so that Belgian guy did all these paintings over the weekends?"

"Yes, he even stayed here."

"Stayed? You mean he worked overnight?"

"No, he slept, of course, but kept working with me for the rest of the time."

Jindo was unsure how the painter managed to sleep in the place, but as he did not know the layout of Gabrielle's upstairs, he did not dwell on it but carried on.

"Okay, anyway it looks great Gabrielle."

Jindo's gaze then swept across the office, lingering on the motley array of IT equipment occupying a fair bit of space. Each piece was black, covered in scratches, and adorned with partially peeled-off stickers. The mice and keyboards looked rather dusty, and the fans emitted desperate wheezing as if gasping for their last breaths.

Indeed, it struck Jindo as slightly odd, considering he believed that, for tomorrow's fashion, efficient IT systems could play a crucial role in fostering creativity and productivity. He also thought that such technology would be a prominent feature in the office's display, particularly in an open, guest-oriented fashion house like Gabrielle's.

Slightly curious, he felt inclined to ask.

"Gabrielle, do you use computers a lot for your designs?"

"No, I don't need to. All my designs are... in my head."

Gabrielle replied, tapping her head with her finger, a serious expression on her face.

"Ah, that's… great."

In fact, Jindo had sought to gauge her use of technology but was impressed by the self-assuredness of the gifted designer. He concluded that, as a dedicated artisan in couture, Gabrielle would not need all that tech support to prove her worth. Those devices might be there just for administrative purposes, or perhaps as relics of a bygone era.

Regardless, Jindo brushed off his unnecessary concerns, and at that moment, Gabrielle seemed eager to discuss the finished artwork gracing the walls.

"Do you like my paintings by the way?"

"Ah yes, of course."

He quickly feigned deep contemplation as though the artwork had made a profound impression on him. He surveyed the walls in a proper sense.

Featuring an array of cartoon characters, the paintings were vibrant and whimsical overall. Jindo could envision that Gabrielle's ideal empire would resemble a 'Disneyland' filled with her personal flair. However, he could not shake a certain sense of unease that emanated from the entire scene.

Set against a black backdrop, the characters were painted in bold, vivid colours. They seemed to stare at visitors with unnerving intensity, almost as if they were about to devour them like cannibals. Jindo could not help but perceive them as demonic figures donning cartoon masks.

Aside from the disconcerting atmosphere, Jindo found the concept somewhat unoriginal. Although he grasped the central idea, each element appeared to be borrowed and modified from various sources.

Even so, he acknowledged that not all creations were purely original, as they often drew inspiration from elsewhere. Bearing that in mind, he opted to praise the creator.

"They look fantastic, Gabrielle. I love the richness of your colour palette."

"Yes, I think so."

"…"

Jindo was slightly taken aback by her strong self-satisfaction, but he decided not to dwell on it.

Gabrielle then embarked on a lengthy monologue, detailing the bright, positive utopia she yearned to create. Though Jindo felt the visual representations strayed from her aspirations, he merely offered a smile and a nod along.

Meanwhile, Jindo questioned his own judgment of being so critical, harbouring all these negative vibes by himself. He scolded himself, reasoning that it was just a piece of art by the former CHANEL creator and should be appreciated for what it was. Additionally, he thought he did not fully understand her creative universe yet, so he had to experience her more to comprehend her depth of creativity.

Unaware of Jindo's internal musings, Gabrielle cheerily chatted about her ideal universe for a while, sipping her vibrant takeaway juice.

At that moment, Jindo spotted a small door in the office, seemingly leading to a lavatory, with the artwork continuing in a different theme. Somewhat desperate for a change of topic, he promptly asked.

"By the way Gabrielle, have you made any changes to the atelier?"

Jindo hoped his question would stave off another round of curation and give them an excuse to head downstairs. It was likely due to that he felt that Gabrielle would not put a stop to her art discussion unless something intervened.

"No, it's the same I think..."

"You... think?"

Jindo found her response slightly odd, but it was the moment when he had to determine whether Gabrielle herself was an eccentric character or merely her English made her come across that way. He opted for the latter for the moment, likely because he was not well-acquainted with the ex-CHANEL designer just yet. Regardless, they started to make their way downstairs.

Upon reaching the door, they encountered a massive cartoon statue partially blocking the entrance. Gabrielle warned Jindo to be cautious when opening the door. He could not fathom why she had positioned such a large, fragile object in a spot where it could easily be damaged, but he opted not to question it for the time being.

Heeding her warning, Jindo gingerly opened the door, and the pair descended the stairs. Glancing at the clock, Jindo realised there were fewer than five minutes left before the official starting time. He felt somewhat pressed for time. It was because he, in fact, had arrived early to acclimatise himself to the new work environment, but instead, he had been unexpectedly caught up in a presentation of the director's artwork.

Nonetheless, he understood that Gabrielle, the weekend warrior, was simply eager to showcase her creations. Bearing that in mind, Jindo was to focus on his objective while suppressing a wry smile at the situation.

Upon entering the atelier, Jindo cast his eyes around to envisage how he would carry out his modélisme work in the space. The atelier seemed a tad more organised compared to his previous visit, and the lights and music were already switched on in preparation for the morning.

Gabrielle assigned Jindo's workspace, and he began to settle in, unpacking his belongings. He tied his hair back and started arranging his tools on the table. His movements were fluid and practised as if he had a well-honed preference for his setup. Gabrielle observed the scene with a satisfied grin.

Like other technical professionals, modélistes place great importance on a familiar workspace, given their focus on precision and the use of specific tools. Undoubtedly, having their tools within easy reach enhances efficiency.

Having finished the preparations, Gabrielle seemed quite pleased with Jindo's eagerness to begin work. He was then about to adjust the height of the chair, and the director swiftly interjected.

"DON'T TOUCH THE LEVER, it's broken."

Jindo shot her a quizzical look, and Gabrielle explained that the chair was broken, cautioning that fiddling with it would only make matters worse. She added that she could not identify the culprit, as everyone pointed fingers at one another when the damage occurred.

"Okay, that's fine with me. I normally stand while working anyway, so no worries. I was just checking."

It was not a significant issue for Jindo, so he played it cool. At that moment, the radio chimed 9 am, and the rest of the atelier crew began to trickle in.

Jindo noticed that the handsome guy who had argued with Gabrielle last time was conspicuously absent, but he assumed he would turn up later anyway. Not dwelling on it, Jindo waited as everyone settled in.

The assistant accessory designer switched the radio to a hip-hop channel, infusing the room with energy and signalling that it was time to get down to business. As Gabrielle assigned tasks to each person, Jindo occupied himself by leafing through the lookbooks on the table, showcasing Gabrielle's previous collections. He savoured the French banter among the team members, as it made him feel truly immersed in a Parisian fashion atelier yet.

Chapter 5 : Patterns of Progress

In the realm of fashion, grading refers to the process of creating different sizes for a standard garment. Generally speaking, it is a task that demands precision and knowledge rather than creativity, as it involves dealing with numerous measurements and ensuring a proper fit across various aspects of the garment's construction.

Within the hands-on world of modélisme, grading might not be the most complex task, as it typically involves mere modifications and alterations based on specific requests. However, should any design changes or technical issues need addressing during the grading process, these matters ought to be thoroughly discussed before any work commences.

Notably, if an initial design concept or its prototype is riddled with problems, further discussions between the designer and modéliste will be necessary. In addition, it's quite common in fashion discussions to have the initial drafts and samples readily available.

After assigning tasks to each team member, Gabrielle approached Jindo and asked if he could start with a skirt grading. Whilst not the most exciting task, he was keen to take on the challenge and prove his worth to the former CHANEL designer.

Gabrielle showed him a flared skirt from one of the lookbooks, then began outlining her desired modifications. However, as she was only using a small photo in the lookbook for reference, Jindo inquired.

"Sorry Gabrielle, can we not discuss this with the constructional patterns and prototype at hand?"

"Of course!"

Gabrielle's enthusiasm spiked as she dashed behind a curtain in the corner.

Moments later, she emerged donning a headlamp, a rain poncho, and gloves. Jindo was baffled by her attire, but Gabrielle offered no explanation, merely flashing him a grin before disappearing through a metal door on the other side of the corner.

In manual fashion design, garments consist of numerous individual components, such as the body, sleeves, collar, and pockets. Each of these parts is typically patterned on paper (used to cut the fabric), and packed together without folding.

A few minutes passed, and Gabrielle returned with a large, transparent, dusty plastic bag. He could see that there were plenty of poorly folded patterns inside.

Gabrielle began to take each piece out, unfolding them one by one and placing them on the table as she searched for the ones needed for the task.

After about five minutes, she found a piece for one part and continued searching for the rest. In fact, apart from her weird way of preparing the task assignment, Jindo was rather astonished by the messy and dirty state in which the patterns were stored.

However, it was somehow the moment that he was getting used to Gabrielle's lack of professionalism. Perhaps it was because he regarded her as a 'pure artist', who had once worked at CHANEL and Hermès, and had made her prosperity in a too short time. Jindo moved on.

"Gabrielle, did the Japanese modéliste make this?"

"No, it was made by my friend."

Jindo was slightly confused since Gabrielle had mentioned that her former modéliste was a Japanese woman who had recently returned to her country. However, he decided not to dwell on it.

"Your friend?"

"Yes, he is at Balmain."

She nonchalantly answered while still searching for the remaining pieces in the dusty bag. Meanwhile, the mention of the famous brand momentarily silenced Jindo, leaving him impressed.

"Wow, so this pattern was made by a Balmain modéliste."

"No, he is not there anymore."

Jindo's confusion returned, but he remained quiet this time. Gabrielle glanced at Jindo for his silence then elaborated.

"He went to Balenciaga."

Jindo's excitement was reignited by another big name, but this time, he was more cautious not to say anything that might prompt a response from Gabrielle. It was because Jindo was likely growing weary of the context confusion that arose from her tense errors.

"Okay great Gabrielle, anyway I'm looking forward to seeing the patterns."

"WHY? He's not there anymore. He started his own company, like me."

Gabrielle unexpectedly replied, raising her pitch, and Jindo was getting irritated. This was because he felt he had not even said anything that warranted a response, yet Gabrielle kept bursting out in frustration. He decided to remain silent to avoid any further confusion or upset.

Meanwhile, Jindo considered that Gabrielle might be annoyed because she could not find what she was looking for and he had inadvertently been bothering her with his questions. He resolved to wait patiently until she had finished searching.

Regardless, Jindo was eager to see the patterns created by a modéliste who had worked at Balmain and Balenciaga. In fact, he was simply delighted to hear the names of these eminent French labels, casually mentioned as if they were local acquaintances.

In those days in Paris, it was not unusual for individual labels to have their brand-new prototypes out of the studio for promotional purposes, such as at press offices, influencers and bloggers.

In manual fashion, paper pattern pieces are typically accompanied by a file of technical sheets, which provide crucial information about the design and its construction. These sheets serve as a sort of instruction manual, akin to the leaflets that come with IKEA furniture, albeit more comprehensive.

In general, a technical folder is a standard form of communication for production matters, and indeed, it requires a significant effort to produce one.

After searching fruitlessly for the complete set of patterns, Gabrielle resumed her demonstration of the grading task. However, Jindo felt he still needed at least the minimum materials to work with, so cautiously interrupted her.

"Sorry, Gabrielle. I can see these are some of the constructional patterns, but... would it be possible to see the actual prototype? I think it'll be much easier to understand the missing pieces if I see that."

"I don't have it here."

Jindo raised an eyebrow, prompting her to elaborate, and Gabrielle continued.

"It's at the press office."

"Okay then, can I see any sort of technical folder if you have one? It's fine even with a flat drawing or sketch sheet because I just… want to know what we're talking about."

"No, I don't have them…"

Gabrielle's voice faltered, and she suddenly seemed unsure of herself. Jindo felt a pang of guilt; he had not intended to be overly demanding but had inadvertently disheartened the young, talented artist whom he yet regarded as a 'pure artist'. He attempted to reassure her.

"It's fine, Gabrielle. I understand that you've been too busy for that. I'll see what I can do, so don't worry…"

Despite his gentle tone and portrayal of a skilfully experienced individual, he felt genuinely perplexed. It was due to that it seemed the skirt was made without any form of a worksheet or even a single sketch. Regardless of the fact that she had collaborated with her friend, it was difficult for him to comprehend.

His efforts appeared to have paid off, as Gabrielle regained her confidence.

"You're right. I'm always too busy. Anyway, you can see how it looks here."

She gestured to a photo in the lookbook and resumed her explanation by finger-drawing on the small image.

"It's nothing much. We just don't have this layer anymore, but we'll attach a new layer at the back like this, then make the side longer like this."

Jindo took notes on all the points, listening attentively until the end of her explanation. Although Gabrielle's delivery was not the most eloquent, he did not raise any concerns and simply carried on.

In fact, it can be challenging for a modéliste when a designer makes a request that cannot be defined in either figures or words. It is easy to pinpoint the modéliste when things go awry afterwards. The designer could just say, 'This is not what I said'.

"Okay Gabrielle, I think I understand your points, so now… can I see the photo and patterns properly to make sure all those issues?"

"You can do it, no? It's very easy :"

Gabrielle's response came across as somewhat forceful and teasing, as though she expected Jindo to accept the challenge without fully grasping the task.

"I think I can but as I said, I need to verify if every point is feasible first."

"It's easy. It's just…"

Gabrielle launched into another round of explanation, and though Jindo noticed her request seemed to differ from the original, he was becoming accustomed to the idiosyncratic designer.

He decided not to press for clarity, but to focus on understanding her dislikes. All the while, he remained cautious about committing before examining the issues thoroughly.

"Gabrielle, I think I get all your points. But I still need to see these materials to confirm the issues… No worries, I'll let you know once I've sorted it all out."

"… okay."

Gabrielle appeared somewhat discontented, not having received the immediate affirmation she had hoped for. Jindo, however, stood his ground, unwilling to make promises he was not sure he could keep.

Examining the materials, Jindo realised that the lookbook only featured a single front-facing photo of the skirt.

"Gabrielle, do you have any other photos of the skirt by the way? The lookbook only shows the front. I need to see the back."

Gabrielle looked sheepish, prompting Jindo to soften his request.

"Gabrielle… even the original, unedited images from the photoshoot will be fine… I just want to see the skirt's design, no need to see how nice it looks…"

Although his instincts already warned him that Gabrielle might not have the photos, he asked regardless. It was that her proposed modifications to the back of the skirt left Jindo struggling to visualise the design, as the incomplete pattern pack and her verbal descriptions fell short.

"No, I don't have them. My previous assistant deleted all the photos…"

Gabrielle's unprofessional excuse surprised Jindo, and she seemed to take a moment to reminisce, shaking her head.

"She was very stupid."

Gabrielle made a grumpy face, and Jindo sensed she was gearing up for a bout of blaming session. Keen to avoid the impending rant, he quickly wrapped up the conversation, not particularly interested in hearing any more of the story.

"Okay fine, Gabrielle. I get it, no worries. Just one last question though, please... Were there any technical issues during the prototyping process?"

"No, I guess… it was… fine."

"You… guess?"

Jindo found her response weird as if she did not know about the issue or did not care. Nevertheless, he chalked it up to her poor English phrasing and decided to focus on examining the work of the ex-Balmain and Balenciaga modéliste.

Chapter 6 : Echoes in the Atelier

In the world of fashion, the true calibre of a construction plan, known as a 'pattern', is ultimately verified when a prototype is created, showcasing its exquisite shape and proportion.

After all...
The skirt pattern was a fairly standard piece of professional work, and although there appeared to be minor technical issues with the waistband, they were not insurmountable.

As for the absent pattern pieces, Jindo took the initiative and fashioned them using his common sense. On the whole, the original design and requested modifications were not terribly complicated. Jindo had anticipated witnessing the exceptional quality of a modéliste from the two esteemed fashion houses, but that was yet to be seen.

A few days later...

Jindo had finished several pieces for the grading tasks, but it soon dawned on him that Gabrielle did not seem to be inspecting his handiwork. Whenever he sought her approval, she would merely wax lyrical about his lightning-fast completion, before hastily donning that notorious helmet and poncho and dashing through the metal door.

Admittedly, the grading task was not exactly an uphill battle for Jindo, but putting up with Gabrielle was another kettle of fish. He had to bide his time during her 'searching sessions', then tidy up and restore some semblance of order to the chaos she left behind, all while enduring a full-length playback of her speech for a single enquiry. Although he tried to consider it as her standard modus operandi, he could not help but regard the process as frightfully inefficient.

Nevertheless, Jindo maintained his respect for the high-profile director, accepting her quirks as part and parcel of dealing with an 'original artist'. He reduced the frequency of his queries but cracked on with the tasks at hand. In fact, Jindo did not relish the grading missions, as he felt he was merely ticking off tasks, rather than learning and evolving.

Meanwhile, Gabrielle appeared to become increasingly chuffed with Jindo's work. This was not only because he completed tasks quickly and without a fuss, but also because he ironed out certain issues, she had deemed insurmountable. Gabrielle was pleased with his performance, and Jindo was content with the belief that his competence was being acknowledged by the former CHANEL designer.

A fortnight passed...

Jindo found himself growing closer to his fellow atelier colleagues, who appreciated his diligent work ethic. They were particularly fond of his habitual tidiness and organisational skills. They also took an interest in Jindo's assorted modélisme tools, while he, in turn, relied on their assistance to locate atelier supplies. These interactions provided opportunities for them to natter and become acquainted.

Meanwhile, Jindo maintained an air of extra politeness, likely because he wanted to show due respect to the existing members. He did not overstep any boundaries or stand out in the atelier culture. All in all, they were becoming more familiar, but a certain distance still remained.

The chapelier (hat maker), a tall French guy named Timothée from Lyon, and Jindo bonded during cigarette breaks. Although Timothée's

English was a bit ropey and Jindo's French was not much better, they shared a camaraderie as men of the same generation.

Timothée was passionate about his work and keen to learn new techniques and knowledge. Indeed, he was the one most intrigued by Jindo's modélisme tools and methods. Jindo, too, was interested in Timothée's savoir-faire, resulting in mutual respect despite the language barrier.

The assistant accessory designer, named Amélie, hailed from a small town in Western France. She worked part-time as part of an apprenticeship programme. Apparently, her institution was Chambre Syndicale de la Haute Couture, as it was often mentioned during her shift scheduling discussions with Gabrielle.

Though Amélie's passion for work did not seem as fervent as Timothée's, she was lovely to work with. She maintained her professionalism while injecting playful energy into the atelier. In fact, her presence provided a much-needed shot in the arm, as the atmosphere turned rather dull when she was away. Amélie's ability to speak English was particularly crucial for Jindo, as she was the only one in the room to whom he could ask an inquiry in detail.

Finally, there was Boubacar, the middle-aged industrial seamstress who arrived to work five minutes early, and Jindo had a brief morning chat with him each day. Originally from Africa, Boubacar had resided in France for nearly two decades. He and Jindo connected through their shared experience as non-natives and as expats since immigrants often find common ground.

With over three decades under his belt in the industry and having worked in various sectors, Boubacar was in his second year at Gabrielle's. His warmth and experience earned him the love and respect of everyone in the atelier. Amélie affectionately referred to him as 'Papa d'atelier'.

Meanwhile, Jindo could not help but wonder about the dashing man he had seen arguing with Gabrielle on his first day. Over the past few weeks, he had spotted him a handful of times as he was leaving work, but the man had never returned to the atelier.

At first, Jindo was not overly concerned, as he was preoccupied with proving his mettle to the former CHANEL designer. However, as time went on, he found it peculiar that the man only seemed to show up when the workday was over. Jindo's curiosity was piqued, but he refrained from asking anyone about him, regarding it as none of his beeswax.

One day, quite by chance, the topic arose during a conversation with Amélie. As it turned out, the mysterious, handsome man was not a member of the atelier; he had merely happened to be there on Jindo's first day. Although some questions remained unanswered, Jindo did not feel the need to pry further.

Amélie, however, continued to rabbit on about him. His name was Vincent, and he was an actor. Jindo pondered whether Vincent was involved in some sort of celebrity endorsement for Gabrielle's creation, but Amélie burst into laughter at the suggestion. She did not explicitly slate the designer director, but her words implied that no celebrity would be interested in Gabrielle's creations unless they were handsomely compensated.

Moreover, according to Amélie, Vincent was not famous or influential nor particularly keen on fashion, so he had no reason to promote Gabrielle's pieces. Even so, Amélie never revealed why Vincent frequented the company.

What struck Jindo as odd during their conversation though, was that Timothée seemed to give Amélie a subtle eye signal, as if warning her to button it. Jindo caught on and quickly changed the subject, not wanting to appear nosy or overstep his boundaries.

He was not particularly interested in the story, anyway. In fact, quite soon after the conversation, Jindo discarded the information Amélie had shared, relegating it to some manner of trash folder in his head. However, for some reason, the issue was not entirely forgotten but still dwelling in his head.

Aside from the personal quirks, everyone at the atelier was rather professional when it came to their missions. There were essentially two divisions. Timothée and Amélie usually focused on their individual tasks but shared a common workspace, so they technically belonged to the same department in the snug atelier.

In a friendly sense, they were like siblings, often bickering over trivial matters but always sticking together, even during lunch breaks. While Amélie was supposedly the junior, Timothée was not overly authoritarian and enjoyed a good bit of banter instead. Nonetheless, the pair were quite focused when it came to their assignments.

Jindo and Boubacar worked in close proximity, as a modéliste and seamstress were practically joined at the hip in a bijou atelier like Gabrielle's. Jindo admired Boubacar's wealth of industry experience and his wide array of techniques.

Though their verbal communication was not the most fluid, they found ways to convey their messages by sharing photos and using industrial sewing symbols. As a result, their collaboration grew increasingly efficient and effective over time.

In fashion production, it is often more productive to share common codes through images and illustrated symbols than through verbal explanations, as each individual's verbal expression code might differ for the same visuals.

The team members were amicable with one another, but it was only when Gabrielle was involved that tensions would rise. Although she generally seemed affable, there were frequent instances when the members argue with her.

At first, Jindo did not notice it, but as time passed, he realised they occasionally raised their voices in disagreement with Gabrielle, leaving her looking rather discomposed. Yet, after she departed the atelier, they often gossiped about her.

Although Jindo could not entirely decipher their French chatter, it was evident that they casually discussed Gabrielle's penchant for being demanding and insistent on adhering to inefficient methods within tight deadlines.

Initially, Jindo assumed it was a typical dynamic between technicians and a designer or employees and a director, but he eventually recognised that Gabrielle's inefficient working style might be a unique issue of her own.

Even so, Jindo continued to view the designer director in a favourable light, thinking she might be a tad too set in her ways. In his mind, her stubbornness could be embraced as a form of 'artistic licence'.

In fact, in those days, Jindo believed that certain artists could be obstinate in their ways, as it would be their destiny to prove their creations in their own unique manner.

On this basis, unlike the other members, Jindo never questioned Gabrielle's suggestions, even though her preferences were almost always deemed inefficient. He played the role of an excellent listener and, in a way, appeared to be rather obedient to the director. This was likely why Gabrielle, over time, seemed more at ease with Jindo, spending more time chatting with him than the other members.

Meanwhile, she appeared to take a dim view of situations when Jindo was being friendly with the other members.

One evening…

The other members had left, and Jindo was about to finalise the last bit of his work, hearing Gabrielle descending the stairs.

"Apologies for overstaying Gabrielle, I'm just about to finish up."

"No, it's okay."

She briefly glanced at Jindo's work, seemingly disinterested. Then, Jindo sensed a certain negative vibe about to emanate from her. He halted his work and regarded the director. She seemed rather miffed, already wearing a serious expression.

"Can we talk, Jindo?"

"Of course, Gabrielle."

"This afternoon, why were you laughing in the atelier?"

"Pardon?"

"I heard you laughing with Amélie."

"Ah, that's because she translated something that Timothée said in a funny way…"

"That's not good. I told you I take my work very seriously."

"No no, Gabrielle. We're working, but just laughing a bit at a little joke. That was it…"

"No! That's not good."

"Gabrielle, I was just…"

"NO! This situation never happened before."

Gabrielle cut Jindo's attempt to explain, and he became speechless, feeling remorseful for the unexpected telling-off from Gabrielle. It seemed that he had somehow disrupted the 'so-far-good' rhythm of the atelier. Believing that he had been pleasing the director with his work by then, this was quite a moment indeed.

"I'm sorry, Gabrielle. I didn't mean to… but… okay… I apologise."

Jindo wanted to explain the situation, but there was no point in raising any issues. This was probably because he thought, as the director, what she said should be the final word. He simply nodded, pulling a sincere face for the quiet apology. Gabrielle seemed to like his attitude and pressed on.

"Don't take what I say badly... I just think you're mature and very professional... For Amélie, you know she's quite young and I know she doesn't like to be here anyway... and you already know she's actually quite annoying sometimes..."

"..."

It was awkward, as Jindo felt apologetic but did not want to agree with her about Amélie being annoying. However, it was not the moment to object. He apologised once more.

"Sorry, Gabrielle."

"And Jindo, you know you're still in the test period."

"... yes, Gabrielle. I apologise again. I promise it'll never happen again…"

Gabrielle seemed rather chuffed with Jindo's submissive attitude. The Asian man seemed to be biting his tongue, and she seized the opportunity to relish her moment of authority.

"Actually, even Timothée and Boubacar… they're usually quiet. But since you came, they're laughing all the time..."

"..."

Jindo could not help but feel that Gabrielle's portrayal was a bit of a stretch. Though her shoddy English might have accounted for previous misunderstandings, this time, it seemed blatantly unfair.

In fact, Timothée and Boubacar rarely laughed, and their chuckles mostly came from their own French jokes, leaving Jindo silent due to his lack of comprehension. Moreover, Jindo laughed the least among the team members, barely making a peep. On that basis, he found it particularly vexing that Gabrielle's insinuation of him being the root of the issue.

Nonetheless, Jindo did not consider it was the right time to kick up a fuss, and then simply continued to apologise.

"Sorry, Gabrielle."

Indeed, Jindo felt that Gabrielle could not scold the other employees but him, as he was a good listener who might have come across as rather compliant.

"Jindo, from now on, come upstairs whenever you have anything to ask. Don't talk with anyone in the atelier."

"… okay."

Although Jindo did not agree with Gabrielle's rationale, he decided it was not worth stirring the pot. He simply believed that if he concentrated on his work, everything would sort itself out eventually. Taking a deep breath, he broached the subject.

"Gabrielle, I apologise once again… By the way, may I make a suggestion regarding the work?"

Gabrielle raised her eyebrows in curiosity.

"Would you mind if I organise the work on my own?"

"What do you mean?"

"Well, you usually come down, locate the patterns yourself, and explain the task in every single detail... I think it would be more efficient if you just give me a list of tasks, and then I'll organise the workload. If I need to discuss anything, I'll come upstairs and talk to you."

Jindo carefully put forth his idea, sensing that the timing was just right. Indeed, he had been mulling over this proposal for a while but had not found the opportune moment to mention it.

"Oh, that's…"

Gabrielle hesitated, evidently taken aback by his request. Her eyes darted around as she pondered the matter. Jindo suspected that his proposal would deprive her of the sessions she seemed to enjoy so much. Jindo pressed on to clarify his point.

"You're quite busy, Gabrielle. Please let me handle the nitty-gritty work while you just tell me the key points for each task as the designer and director. If you allow me to do this, I might not even have time to chat with the others. I'll be solely focused on work…"

Gabrielle seemed reluctant but started to weigh up the issue.

"But how are you going to find the patterns for each design?"

"Well, you know there's a code written on each pattern piece for every model."

"Ah…"

Jindo wondered how an ex-CHANEL designer, trained at one of the most prestigious fashion institutes in Paris, could be oblivious to such a basic industry practice. However, he brushed the thought aside for now.

"If there's anything I don't understand, I'll ask you, Gabrielle."

It appeared that the director was left with no choice, as Jindo's response made sense all around.

"… okay."

Making her face grumpy, Gabrielle begrudgingly accepted his proposal.

Chapter 7 : The Atelier's Morning Ritual

The following day…

Jindo arrived at work earlier than usual, a result of the previous evening's conversation about organising the workload on his own. As he rang the bell, he noticed that Gabrielle had been rather tardy in opening the door. Initially, he knew she was the first to arrive each morning, as she had been the one who always let him in, but something seemed to have changed.

In fact, in the first week, Gabrielle had been right behind the door, greeting Jindo with a warm 'welcome', and sipping her vibrant takeaway juice. However, starting from the second week, her presence at the entrance had waned, and the door took longer to open, sometimes leaving Jindo twiddling his thumbs for over ten minutes.

No longer did Gabrielle await him just past the threshold. Yet, he could discern the muffled clatter of hastened footsteps ascending the stairs, indicating a swift withdrawal from her fleeting obligation at the entrance.

Jindo surmised that Gabrielle, being the director, had decided the formalities were unnecessary now that he was no longer the new employee at the company. He just regarded that the director might be occupied upstairs, bustling about organising the showroom space. After all, it did not bother him much yet.

What did pique his curiosity, though, was the fact that Gabrielle had not yet unveiled the showroom. It was a bit odd, considering how she had teased its grandeur on the first day. He remembered her apology for not being able to present the space that day, as it was undergoing a graffiti paint job.

Now, with the artwork presumably complete, she had not even suggested he take a look. He recalled on the first day morning of work when she had proudly shown off her new office, a testament to her creative prowess with its curated artwork. Given that, he could not help but wonder why she had not so much as mentioned the showroom.

Nonetheless, he quickly brushed off his concerns, chalking it up to the director's busy schedule. Jindo resolved to concentrate on his own tasks and leave the insignificant worry behind.

Upon arriving at the atelier, Jindo set about preparing for the day, tying up his hair and arranging his tools. Soon, he heard footsteps on the stairs, signalling Gabrielle's arrival. As she entered, he greeted her.

This time, however, his tone was slightly different, betraying a hint of curiosity, likely stemming from the questions that had flitted through his mind that morning. She seemed to twig on his mood and volunteered an explanation.

"Sorry Jindo, I went to the gym this morning, so I was changing myself upstairs…"

"Eh?"

Jindo feigned ignorance, pretending not to grasp why she was explaining her tardiness, but indeed, he was glad to have some clarification.

"No worries, Gabrielle. I just assumed you were busy upstairs in the showroom… By the way, do you also go to the gym in the morning?"

"Yes… well, I can't go every day because I'm always busy… but I try…"

Gabrielle sounded somewhat uncertain, then lobbed the question back to Jindo.

"Do you go to the gym in the morning, too?"

"Yes, but I just do a bit of running and stretching, not much weight training…"

"That's good."

"How about you, Gabrielle?"

"Me? I… do the same… but because I'm always busy, I can't stay for long…"

"Well, I think it's great to go to the gym in the morning anyway."

As they chatted, Jindo detected a hint of insecurity in Gabrielle's speech. Regardless, he somehow found it pleasing that he and the ex-CHANEL designer shared a similar morning routine.

"By the way Gabrielle, could you give me the list of orders?"

"What list?"

"You know… the one we talked about yesterday…"

"…"

"… it's just that, if you provide me with a list of orders to produce, I'll sort the workload myself…"

"Oh, yes."

It seemed she had forgotten and was only jogged by Jindo's prompt. In fact, she had probably come downstairs to divvy up the morning tasks, an activity she appeared to enjoy whilst donning her witch attire of the poncho and headlight.

Just standing and looking at Jindo, she still seemed unaware of what to do. Jindo then gave her a facial expression that suggested he was eager to receive the list post-haste.

"Ah, okay. I'll go to the office and print it now."

"Thank you, Gabrielle."

Around fifteen minutes later…

The atelier staff began to trickle in, and Jindo found himself still awaiting Gabrielle's return. He pondered why it was taking her donkey's years to print a simple list of orders.

As he exchanged pleasantries with his colleagues, uttering 'bonjour' here and there, he heard Gabrielle clattering down the stairs, seemingly in a rush. It almost seemed as if she did not want Jindo to have the chance to natter with any of the other members.

Upon her arrival, she immediately checked if Jindo had spoken with Amélie, her gaze darting back and forth between the two. It appeared that not much had transpired between them, but Gabrielle still stood there, a piece of paper clutched in her hand. She yet seemed to ascertain whether Jindo had chatted with Amélie, and Jindo decided to address her directly.

"Is that the list of orders, Gabrielle?"

"Ah… yes…"

She replied hesitantly, and Jindo continued.

"Great, can I have a look?"

"Ah… yes…"

Still looking somewhat suspicious, Gabrielle handed the list to Jindo, and he began to scan the details. He quickly noticed that there were a fair few models to produce, but the quantity of each was rather measly. It seemed like there were only one or two pieces per model.

It was at this point that Jindo spotted the buyer's name and address at the top of the paper. It belonged to a Japanese boutique in Tokyo. Evidently, this was not the list of orders Jindo had intended to receive.

In fact, he had anticipated a comprehensive list of the total number of pieces from all buyers, not a single order list from one boutique.

He reckoned, for efficient production management, it would be more practical to manufacture items in a batch, rather than catering to individual buyers.

In those days in Paris, one of the ways that small independent labels attracted buyers from across the globe was by showcasing their collections at fashion exhibitions or fairs. Buyers would place orders after seeing and trying on sample pieces.

Jindo wanted to clarify his request but hesitated to ask Gabrielle directly. Perhaps it was due to his experience thus far, which had taught him to tread cautiously when dealing with Gabrielle; she could become easily irked out of the blue. He chose his words carefully to probe.

"Gabrielle… is the buyer… Japanese?"

"Yes, my clients are very international!"

She proudly replied with a smile.

"Great…"

Jindo then tried to get to the point step-by-step.

"Gabrielle… is this… all we need to produce? Or, have you just given me one buyer's order to begin with?"

"Um… I gave you one first."

Jindo shot the director a quizzical look, but she still seemed oblivious. He proceeded cautiously so as not to provoke the famously short-tempered director.

"As far as I think, Gabrielle… it might be more efficient if we organise all the orders first, then produce the items by model for the total quantity… After that, we can distribute the required amount to each buyer…"

"… why?"

Jindo was puzzled because he thought the reasoning was straightforward. Meanwhile, he wondered if his explanation had been unclear. He carefully elaborated further.

"It's because… I think… if we produce items by the buyer, we'll need to switch the production line frequently and repeat the same cycle for each buyer… In my opinion, that wouldn't be the most efficient process. It would be faster if we produce one item for the total quantity, and then move on to the next…"

"Hm…"

Jindo observed Gabrielle, trying to gauge if she had grasped the logic this time. She seemed to be mulling it over, but suddenly, turned to see if Amélie had been watching the exchange.

As it turned out, the accessory designer in Balenciaga shades had been quietly observing the situation from the start, appearing to understand Jindo's rationale. Gabrielle quickly switched gears, raising her voice and increasing her tempo.

"NO, I DON'T THINK SO. We do it my way. This is how we do here."

Finally, Gabrielle's irritation erupted. Although Jindo had not intended to oppose the director, this time, he did not back down as he believed the issue was worth discussing.

He was confident in his reasoning, and it seemed that Gabrielle simply had not understood the significance of the matter yet. He decided to give it one more try.

"Gabrielle, I think… my explanation wasn't very clear. What I meant was…"

"NO, I UNDERSTAND WHAT YOU SAY, but the answer is just NO!"

She snapped, and Jindo's baffled face deepened as if he found it difficult to comprehend the director's decision. He raised his eyebrows, putting his palms up, sincerely asking her to give him one more chance to explain. However, Gabrielle seized the moment.

"It's because the other buyers haven't paid for their orders yet. We're still in discussion… That's why I don't want to make items before receiving any deposit…"

Her logic made sense, but Jindo wondered why she had not mentioned that in the first place.

"Ah… okay, Gabrielle… Sorry, I wasn't aware of that…"

"YOU THINK I DON'T KNOW WHAT'S BETTER FOR PRODUCTION?"

She retorted, visibly growing more upset.

"No, Gabrielle. Of course, I never thought that way… I just wanted to suggest a more efficient way for production from my side, but I didn't know about the deposit issue… That's all…"

Gabrielle still looked disgruntled, and Jindo tried to defuse the situation.

"Gabrielle, I understand it now… I'll focus on this Japanese client's order first then."

"BAH, OUI!"

Gabrielle stormed out of the atelier, the stomping sound from the stairs clearly indicating her lingering irritation. In fact, it seemed that her anger was directed not at Jindo, but at Amélie. She had been stealing glances at the accessory designer even as she left the atelier. It had been quite a tense moment, but Jindo decided not to dwell on it and cracked on with his work.

Chapter 8 : Shadows Amidst Steam

Following Gabrielle's exit…

Jindo scrutinised the orders and categorised the models into two segments: complex and simple. He then steeled himself to venture into the mysterious metal door for the first time. He pondered if he should don the 'witch costume', though it hardly suited his tastes.

With a bit of reluctance, he decided to put them on, and Amélie started to chuckle at his appearance. She warned him that his pants and sneakers might get dirty once he entered. However, Jindo was not too concerned, assuming it would just be a slightly grubby storage area.

Opening the heavy metal door, he discovered a vast boiler room. Beyond that space, there was another dodgy-looking door, locked. Upon unlocking it, he stepped into a pitch-black space.

Once inside, he realised that the place was oppressively dark and humid. He could barely see the ground, and the headlight suddenly felt indispensable. Navigating the narrow aisle, he spotted an assortment of disused furniture pieces, some even adorned with rusty nails. Eventually, he reached the area where stocks and supplies were stored, including transparent bags of paper patterns.

Surveying the space, his instincts warned him to breathe as little as possible. The atmosphere was highly unpleasant, and the walls appeared to be covered in a sticky, steamy liquid. Jindo quickly grabbed the pattern bags and made his exit.

Upon emerging, Amélie's grin widened into peals of laughter. She appeared keen to hear his impressions of the peculiar space. Though Jindo was slightly worried about her boisterous laughter due to Gabrielle's previous warning, he brushed it aside, as Amélie's mirth seemed innocuous enough.

He quietly told her that the experience was quite shocking, emphasising that the space was the darkest he had ever encountered, akin to stepping into an ancient ground untouched for centuries.

Jindo asked Amélie how such a space could exist in central Paris, and she explained that it was typically off-limits due to the potential hazards lurking within. She then quipped that if someone were to be locked inside, they would likely never be found.

After their brief exchange, Jindo returned to his table and began to extract the patterns from the bags. He noticed that his pants and sneakers had indeed become soiled from the musty, damp area, but he did not mind too much since they could easily be cleaned.

However, the unpleasant breathing experience was still etched in his memory. He could not help but wonder why the eccentric director seemed to relish going to that place. Regardless, he set his curiosity aside and focused on his tasks.

He located the necessary materials and assessed their current state. Afterwards, he went upstairs to discuss the designer's preferences.

"Gabrielle, can I come in?"

"… yes."

Upon entering, Jindo immediately sensed Gabrielle's grumpy mood. The middle-aged office lady also appeared sullen, making the office atmosphere rather tense. Instinctively, Jindo decided to tread carefully with his words.

"Gabrielle… could I ask you about this sweater grading?"

"De quoi?"

Her tone in her native tongue was decidedly negative, and she shot Jindo a glare as if she was quite upset. Jindo proceeded cautiously.

"I mean… do you have any preferences for design changes or size normalisation?"

"It's just a sweater. It's nothing, really…"

"Ah… okay."

Jindo felt a bit embarrassed, as Gabrielle usually had plenty to say about even minor issues. This time, however, she seemed to have nothing to discuss but appeared eager to broach another subject.

"I heard you're laughing with Amélie."

"Pardon?"

"YOU, LAUGHED, with Amélie…"

She enunciated each word loudly, her tone dripping with sarcasm.

"Ah, that… well Gabrielle, I wasn't laughing but Amélie was actually… But, it was just she found my look funny with the poncho and headlamp. That's all really…"

"I told you not to talk with anyone…"

"… Gabrielle, we didn't talk much. It was just a tiny, fun moment about my appearance…"

Gabrielle did not respond to Jindo, opting to fix her gaze at her monitor instead, her grumpy demeanour unchanged. Even the office lady seemed to harbour resentment towards Jindo, and he could not fathom what the issue was, or why it had arisen. Feeling awkward, he struggled to find the right words to say.

Meanwhile, Jindo considered Gabrielle's behaviour rather disagreeable. Her attempts to isolate one person from another struck him as rather childish.

Furthermore, he was baffled by Gabrielle's apparent possessiveness towards him. Regardless, Jindo opted not to exacerbate the situation and chose to concentrate on his work.

"Gabrielle, if there's nothing particular, I'll just grade it for width and length in the conventional sense…"

"I don't care."

She snapped, and Jindo was flabbergasted by her response. While he tried to empathise with her as a young director, she was also a business owner, and her conduct seemed to stray far from even the most basic norms of professionalism.

Initially, he had attributed Gabrielle's immature behaviour as a byproduct of her being a 'pure artist', coupled with her limited English proficiency, but this time was different.

He was well aware that the ex-CHANEL designer was in a foul mood, but her actions appeared somewhat excessive. Meanwhile, he figured there was no point in making a fuss and resolved to exit the office.

"Okay, Gabrielle…"

Just as he was about to go, the brooding director pulled him back.

"You don't need to change anything. They wouldn't know anyway…"

"Pardon?"

"They ordered size thirty-six, and they haven't even seen the prototype… so actually, we don't need to do the grading because they wouldn't know anyway…"

In those days of Paris fashion, a typical sample size (prototype) for ready-to-wear (prêt-à-porter) was thirty-eight, and buyers would usually place an order based on their examination of the sample piece.

Jindo was further appalled by the director's attitude. He even wondered how the buyer could have placed an order without even seeing the sample piece, but he did not want to prolong the moment and simply wished to leave the room.

"I understood your point, Gabrielle."

As he was about to depart, Gabrielle still seemed eager to converse.

"They're Japanese anyway. We can just say it's French sizing."

"Excuse me?"

Jindo turned back to Gabrielle, and although he had always maintained his politeness towards the notorious director thus far, this time he furrowed his brow, fixing her with a stern gaze.

His reaction was likely not just due to Gabrielle's unprofessional mindset, but also his personal feeling that she was somehow belittling Asian ethnicity as a whole.

The office lady seemed to sense the tension, carefully glancing back and forth between the two individuals. There was a bit of silence, and then Gabrielle appeared to realise she had gone too far.

"You're Korean, so you know Japanese, they're quiet…"

Jindo did not reply but continued to stare at Gabrielle. He knew she was attempting to soften her words, but it simply was not working. Gabrielle was to try again.

"I mean… they just like my design and the size wouldn't be a big problem… They're buying it as a sample to display in their boutique anyway…"

Though Jindo understood her reasoning, the fundamental issue of the matter was indeed her attitude and approach, not anything else. He still did not reply and quickly brought the situation to a close, not wanting to prolong it any further.

"I understood your point, Gabrielle. I'll just refine certain lines as their measurements aren't matching precisely then move on to the next piece…"

"… okay…"

Jindo left the office, casting her a sharp look, and Gabrielle was unable to meet his eyes.

Chapter 9 : Seams of Subterfuge

In the world of fashion, it is not uncommon for initial designs to be sketched out without much thought to the technicalities. As a result, these embryonic concepts frequently undergo adjustments during the prototyping stage. Meanwhile, there are also instances where designers just change their preferences.

Regardless of the issue, what is essential is to make a note of these alterations, in order to prevent confusion for other parties. Considering the frenetic pace of the fashion industry, there can be moments when everyone is too occupied to jot down every last detail, yet still, it is better to make a note of any changes.

Days passed, and one afternoon…

Jindo was hovering outside Gabrielle's office, poised to knock for a discussion. As the door was slightly ajar, he caught a glimpse of a well-dressed lady, evidently engrossed in a rather crucial tête-à-tête with Gabrielle.

Jindo hesitated, mulling over whether he ought to pop back later, and at that moment, Gabrielle's eyes landed on him.

"Jindo! Is there something you want to ask?"

"Yes, but… I can come back later, Gabrielle."

Jindo replied hesitantly, still not wanting to intrude on their discussion.

"No no, you can come in."

Gabrielle seemed insistent, maintaining her somewhat friendly demeanour. Taking the hint, Jindo stepped inside, acknowledging the well-heeled guest with a polite nod before directing his attention towards Gabrielle.

"Gabrielle, I've noticed that this shirt collar pattern doesn't match the one in the prototype. I think it's not just the measurements but the shape as well, that seems quite different…"

"Ah, that's because I changed the design."

Gabrielle responded nonchalantly, but Jindo was somehow calm and collected. It was because, though Jindo had not seen any notation for the change on the worksheet and pattern, by this point, he was no longer surprised to encounter such omissions in Gabrielle's materials. It seemed like he had, after all, become rather well-acquainted with her somewhat lax professional standards.

"Okay Gabrielle, shall I make a pattern for this revised collar then?"

"Yes, please."

"Not a problem."

Reassuring the director with his polite demeanour, he turned to leave and Gabrielle suddenly piped up.

"Jindo! MAKE IT FINISHED BY 4 PM! I'll come down and check, and… it must be PERFECT, you know what I mean…"

Jindo felt somewhat disconcerted by Gabrielle's abrupt, authoritative tone. Her manner insinuated that his previous work had been lacking and that she would be keeping a keen eye on him this time.

Moreover, her punctilious demand, coupled with an intense stare, was an unusual display of strictness. Nonetheless, Jindo maintained a stiff upper lip and kept his cool. It was likely he did not want to create any awkwardness for the director in front of the guest.

In fact, he suspected that she was only putting on this show to flaunt her charisma to the visitor, who seemed more seasoned than her. This suspicion was bolstered by the way Gabrielle kept casting furtive glances at the well-dressed lady during their exchange.

Aware that Gabrielle cared deeply about her image in the presence of an audience, Jindo played along, improvising his response.

"Well understood, Gabrielle. I'll make it ready by 4 pm, and it's going to be good."

"Good!"

With Gabrielle's rather imperious remark ringing in his ears, Jindo exited the office, feigning nonchalance as if such displays of authority were par for the course.

Meanwhile, he found the situation rather endearing, as the young director seemed keen to showcase her mesmerising leadership to the distinguished guest.

Later, as the clock struck 4 pm in the atelier...

Jindo awaited Gabrielle, having completed the new collar and readied it for her approval. As time ticked away, he began to wonder if she was tied up with other matters. Instead of seeking her out, he remained patient, busying himself with preparations for the next piece.

When fifteen minutes had passed without any sign of Gabrielle, Jindo decided to venture to her office, suspecting that the busy director might have lost track of time.

Just as he raised his hand to knock, he overheard Gabrielle engaged in a casual conversation via speakerphone in French. Although he did not understand every word, he could tell the tone was relaxed.

With the door slightly ajar, Gabrielle caught sight of Jindo and raised her eyebrows inquisitively. He responded in a hushed voice, careful not to interrupt her call.

"Gabrielle, I was wondering if you could validate the shirt collar..."

"What shirt collar?"

She asked, her voice noticeably louder than Jindo's.

"Um… this early afternoon, we discussed that you would come down to check the shirt collar at 4 pm…"

"Me?"

"… yes…"

"Ah, yes. I remember now…"

Though Jindo found the situation a bit peculiar, considering how earnest Gabrielle had been about her promise earlier, he once again embraced the moment as part and parcel of an employee's life.

Meanwhile, Gabrielle appeared to be co-broadcasting the situation to the person on the phone, laughing and chatting, without giving Jindo any further response.

Jindo just stood there for a while, waiting for her to address him. Pretending not to eavesdrop on Gabrielle's conversation, he glanced around the office as though he were patiently awaiting her reply. Eventually, Jindo began to send her a subtle facial signal, reminding her of his presence, and Gabrielle finally noticed it.

"Oh, sorry… I'm on a very important call. I'll come down at 5 pm."

"Okay…"

Jindo replied, sceptical but compliant, and then returned to the atelier.

As 5 pm came and went…

Gabrielle still had not appeared, and Jindo decided to carry on with his task, opting not to visit her office this time.

As the clock struck 6 pm, the atelier members began to leave for the day. Hoping to get Gabrielle's validation before departing, Jindo was about to head upstairs when he heard the illustrious director coming down the staircase, bidding the departing French employees 'au revoir'. She finally arrived at the atelier.

"Sorry, I was very busy today."

"Yes, I thought so. That's why I didn't visit you at 5 pm."

"Ah… okay…"

It was clear she had likely forgotten about their appointment once again. Attempting to smooth things over, Gabrielle complimented Jindo on his work ethic.

"I think you're a very hard worker, Jindo."

"Well, I like what I do and I think I just do what I need to do."

"That's very good, Jindo."

Gabrielle smiled, evidently pleased with Jindo's attitude.

Indeed, Jindo had responded in this manner to subtly convey his dedication to work, hoping that the ex-CHANEL designer would recognise and appreciate his diligence.

"Jindo, are you normally okay with overstaying the working hours?"

"Well, I don't really mind. For me, finishing a work that I've planned is more important…"

"That's very good."

The former CHANEL designer seemed to be satisfied with Jindo's willingness to stay late and then apologised once more for her tardiness.

"I'm sorry for today. I just had many guests and phone calls."

"It's fine with me Gabrielle… By the way, you had more meetings after the lady guest this afternoon?"

"Oh, you saw her?"

Jindo found her response weird, considering she must have known.

"Um… yes, during our discussion… she was present…"

"Ah, okay… sorry, I was just too busy today."

"I understand."

Jindo reassured the director, adopting a composed expression to show his sympathy for her situation. Gabrielle offered him a grateful smile before continuing.

"She left very late though…"

"You mean the lady from this afternoon?"

"Yes."

Sensing that the employer wanted to chat about her day, the employee decided to indulge her, providing a conversation companion for the busy, and perhaps lonely, director.

"Gabrielle, who is she, by the way?"

"She's from the marketing agency I work with…"

"Oh, is that so? She looked very professional…"

"WHAT? NO! She's really annoying. She just takes money and does nothing, always making nah-nah-nah excuses… I actually asked her to come today because I'm really not happy with their service…"

Jindo listened as Gabrielle's tone shifted towards complaint. He knew he would not particularly enjoy this part of the conversation, but it was too late since he had already positioned himself as a good listener. He opted to stay neutral, nodding without interjecting.

She then expanded the topic to cover the social media individuals she worked with. Jindo, as a non-social media user, was not particularly interested but maintained the appearance of an attentive listener.

When Jindo inquired about those third-party marketing people in general, Gabrielle mentioned that most of her collaborators were simply 'influencers' or 'bloggers', with only a few from professional marketing agencies.

The social media individuals would just come to borrow her pieces for free, while the marketing professionals only appeared when they sought to increase their fees.

Jindo was not captivated by her complaints, but he ventured to ask a question.

"Gabrielle, if those influencers introduce your pieces to their followers, does it lead to many sales?"

Gabrielle suddenly shifted to look like an irate cat, voicing her disdain while fixing her gaze on Jindo.

"NO! They just want to show off with my pieces, and I have never got any orders from them or their followers. Also, they always return the pieces with a lot of damages…"

Gabrielle's frustration seemed to be at a peak, and she continued.

"But, I don't have a choice. I'm afraid of them talking about my brand badly to others…"

Her tone suddenly changed, taking on a victimised quality.

"They're just manipulating me because they think they have the power…"

Though Jindo was not a social media user, he was well aware of its influence so empathised with the director's predicament. In fact, he had more questions to ask, but held back, sensing that the beleaguered designer had reached her limit. Regardless, he gathered that Gabrielle was discontented with the marketing professionals she dealt with.

In those days in Paris, small independent labels relied on a single prototype piece for all their marketing activities. The sample would become damaged with each event, which was particularly frustrating for designers when the piece was unique.

As the clock neared 7 pm…

The pair were still in the atelier as the conversation meandered on. Jindo was eager to wrap up for the day and steered the discussion back to the original topic. He retreated a step, offering Gabrielle an unobstructed view of his work.

"So, Gabrielle, would you like to check the shirt collar for validation?"

"Ah… yes."

She seemed to recall the primary concern and quickly glanced at Jindo's work in the front.

"It's good."

Her appraisal lasted less than two seconds, and it was evident she had not examined the material properly. Regardless, Jindo continued.

"Okay then, shall I cut the fabric and finish the shirt tomorrow?"

"Yes."

Jindo felt somewhat deflated, having waited hours for those fleeting seconds of validation.

In fact, Jindo realised that Gabrielle often appeared to relish playing the role of the stern director when assigning tasks and urging him to work quickly and more, yet she never seemed particularly invested in how her directives were implemented by him.

Reflecting on days gone by, Jindo began to suspect that Gabrielle was merely possessive of him since he seemed willing to listen and comply with her every request, all whilst remaining available whenever she desired.

At that moment, they heard footsteps upstairs, as if someone were meandering around the showroom.

"Is there someone up there, Gabrielle?"

"… ah… yes… it's… my friend…"

Gabrielle looked flustered.

"Your friend?"

"… yes… I forgot I had an appointment… and she just came in because… I wasn't there…"

Jindo found Gabrielle's speech oddly stilted and suspected she might be improvising her explanation. He did not understand why she felt the need to do so.

Meanwhile, part of him wondered if it might be Vincent, the handsome French man he had often seen arriving when leaving the company. However, Jindo could not fathom why Gabrielle would not simply tell the truth or if his assumption was incorrect.

Ultimately, Jindo decided it should not be his concern and opted not to pry further, then left the work for the day.

Chapter 10 : The Fabric of Pretence

In the fashion industry, it is standard practice for fabrics and supplies to be arranged before the manufacturing process commences.

While there may be instances when they cannot be organised in a timely fashion due to logistical or supplier hiccups, it is practically unheard of for materials to be withheld simply because the designer fancies keeping them under wraps.

Days passed, and one evening in the atelier…

Jindo was in discussion with Gabrielle, about the fabric and supplies he needed for his tasks. Ordinarily, he would enlist Amélie's help during the day, but there were many occasions when she was unavailable. In those instances, Jindo would turn to Gabrielle, only to be told to wait for her to grace the atelier with her presence.

As a matter of fact, Gabrielle seemed to relish the moments when Jindo sought her out in her office, particularly when a guest was present. Whenever he requested materials, she would exclaim that they were highly expensive and unique, so she had them stashed away in a secure location. Throughout these exchanges, she would always keep a keen eye on the guest's reaction, which seemed to hold great importance for her.

Even so, Jindo, as ever, tolerated the young director's habitual ostentation. She simply wanted to give the impression to outsiders that her creations were fashioned from costly and authentic materials.

Meanwhile, on most occasions where Jindo finally received the materials from the discreet director, he would discover they were nothing to write home about, merely run-of-the-mill items.

Indeed, in Jindo's presence, she appeared to revel in playing the part of a 'treasure hunter' in the atelier, donning her witch costume of the poncho and headlamp, scouring hidden nooks for materials.

However, these antics of hers were quite vexing for Jindo, as he was ultimately the one left to tidy up the chaos she created during her little games.

So, it was on one of those evenings after working hours that Jindo found himself waiting for the notorious director in the atelier. He could have gone home at the official closing time like everyone else, but he opted to stay and secure the materials, allowing him to continue his work the following morning without delay. He did not mind the overtime, as he saw it as part of the job.

"So Gabrielle, do we buy the fabric tomorrow then?"

She chuckled, attempting to soothe the impatient modéliste.

"Not tomorrow... It's not like buying a banana from Carrefour. I need to order it from my supplier. You just need to tell me how much we need."

"We need two metres."

"ONLY TWO METRES?"

Her voice suddenly rose, her expression incredulous.

"… yes, we only need it for small bits of a few items."

Jindo felt awkward in the face of her outburst, as he had merely answered her question.

Gabrielle continued to glare at Jindo like a peeved cat, prompting him to tread lightly.

"… Gabrielle, I just answered what you asked…"

"Ah… yes…"

The irked director seemed to grasp the situation and carried on.

"Actually, we had enough but the previous intern made a lot of mistakes. That's why we don't have it anymore. She was really useless and stupid…"

Jindo sensed that the director was gearing up to launch into one of her blame-laden tirades. However, this behaviour was no longer a novelty to him. Instead, he latched onto a particular word in her statement, 'the intern'.

In the realm of manual fashion production, fabric cutting is typically a job for professionals. This is not only because it requires a certain level of finesse but also because mistakes can lead to increased costs.

At that moment, Jindo realised again that Gabrielle had never mentioned her previous Japanese modéliste or the ex-Balmain & Balenciaga modéliste among her acquaintances. When it came to her network, she tended to brag about the more recognisable names, but whenever problems cropped up in her work, she invariably pinned the blame on 'the interns'.

Jindo recalled that he was, in fact, officially an intern (stagiaire) himself, even though it had been discussed as a trial period to determine his eligibility. Despite Gabrielle's claim that she was giving him credit as an experienced individual in the field, he could not help but feel a touch of suspicion about his situation.

Nevertheless, he opted not to mention it, thinking it was not the right moment to delve into the matter. He simply moved on.

"Gabrielle, apart from this, you know we're only working on this Japanese client's order at the moment, so we don't actually have many items to produce… We have various models and sizes to make, but the volume for each is quite low…"

"YES, I KNOW. It's because we didn't receive many orders from the last season."

She abruptly shouted, fixing Jindo with a piercing gaze. Her anger flared at Jindo's frank depiction of the situation, which seemed to remind her of the company's poor business performance.

Jindo felt uneasy and cautiously inquired about the pending orders she had mentioned previously.

"Gabrielle, may I ask how it's going with the pending orders? Have they not confirmed them yet?"

"DE QUOI?"

"… the ones… you mentioned that you're still in discussion…"

"I DON'T KNOW!"

Jindo could not be sure if she meant she was unaware of the state or if she simply did not want to discuss the matter. Either way, the situation appeared as if the director was upset, and Jindo had inadvertently poked the bear.

Gabrielle's mood suddenly shifted, and she became quiet and despondent. Jindo felt sympathy for the young director, who appeared to be struggling with the business despite her hard work.

He attempted to lift the spirits of the disheartened artist.

"Gabrielle, I suppose you're taking these small-quantity assorted orders to raise your brand awareness, correct? If so, I'm sure you'll get more orders next season…"

She perked up, eager to hear more, and Jindo continued.

"You know, when I was in Italy, I used to work as a buyer and personal shopper for Asian clients, so I'm aware that they usually don't buy lesser-known brands they're not familiar with… But once they get to know the brand and find it recognisable, they start to buy it more often, and the volume increase can be quite rapid…"

The disheartened business owner seemed to listen attentively to the former Asian personal shopper.

"Really? But this Japanese boutique has bought my collection before…"

"Perhaps they just need more time…"

Gabrielle paused, mulling it over before finally smiling and speaking up.

"Yes, you're right. They don't know anything about fashion, so they need more time…"

"…"

Although Jindo found her remark a tad off the mark, he let it slide since the once disheartened designer seemed to regain her confidence by reassuring herself, that the issue lay with others rather than her own creation.

"Okay Gabrielle, shall we then focus on what needs to be done first?"

"Yes."

"Then sorry, I need to say it again, we need two metres this time please…"

Jindo gently reminded her of the necessary supply information, and she sprang back into action.

"Okay, I'll make an order tomorrow."

The awkward situation dissipated, and the two exchanged smiles. Meanwhile, Jindo grew curious about the supplier, as he was eager to know when the fabric would arrive.

"By the way Gabrielle, are the suppliers French?"

Gabrielle appeared somewhat embarrassed and hesitated for a moment before cautiously replying.

"Well… I usually use… French… or Italian…"

"That's great."

Jindo was momentarily pleased to hear that the fabrics came from the two renowned countries for their high quality. However, quickly reflecting on the materials he had dealt with at Gabrielle's thus far, he realised he never felt her fabrics to be particularly top-notch.

Taking a closer look again, he could not shake the feeling that Gabrielle's fabrics appeared somewhat subpar.

In fact, Jindo was not a textile expert, but since he often accompanied his designer mother to the local fabric market as a child, he had quite a keen eye for quality. Though not passionate about fashion back then, those childhood experiences had given him a solid grasp of fabric standards.

Meanwhile, Jindo was still self-disciplined enough to trust Gabrielle's judgment as a former CHANEL professional, thinking the lacklustre fabric's appearance might simply be due to the haphazard storage in her place.

At that moment, Gabrielle picked up a small swatch of wool fabric.

"I use a lot from Malhia KENT. You know them?"

"Ma-lee-ah… sorry I don't know them."

Gabrielle seemed positively delighted by his lack of knowledge.

"Ah, YOU DON'T KNOW THEM?"

Her tone insinuated that 'Malhia KENT' was a household name in the fashion industry, and Jindo suddenly felt rather patronised. He replied meekly in an attempt to save face.

"I saw a shop near Bastille, selling this sort of wool fabric, but I'm not sure if they are…"

"Yes, that's Malhia KENT! Ah, you know?"

Gabrielle interjected quickly, leaving Jindo feeling a bit sheepish.

"Well… I mean…"

"But you've only been to their local store, and I work with the head office."

Once again, Jindo felt her tone was condescending. However, what surprised him most at that moment was that his coincidental visit to one fabric store turned out to be relevant to the conversation.

Gabrielle continued with a self-satisfied smile on her face.

"I knew them since I was at CHANEL."

The former CHANEL designer boasted about her connections, reminding Jindo of their contrasting professional backgrounds. His voice was now subdued, and he humbly inquired.

"Ah, are they a CHANEL supplier?"

"Yes, you didn't know?"

"Pardon?"

"YOU DIDN'T KNOW?"

"… no, I didn't know…"

She seemed to relish the opportunity to provoke Jindo into admitting his ignorance once more. Jindo was irked but bit his tongue, aware that he genuinely did not know. The former CHANEL employee continued.

"You didn't see these fabrics in the CHANEL collection?"

Gabrielle continued to needle him, and Jindo's patience began to wear thin.

"Gabrielle, I've seen fabrics like this, not just in the CHANEL collection but in other collections too. But... how am I supposed to know if they're from Malia... that..."

"Malhia KENT!"

She interrupted him sharply.

"Yes, that... Mal...ia CAN'T! How am I supposed to know if they're the CHANEL supplier when I don't even know who they are? You know I'm a beginner in this sector. I'm here to learn. You know that!"

Jindo's outburst was reminiscent of a bullied dog pleading for the torment to end. She smirked, then looked him up and down with a pitying gaze.

After a brief silence, she seemed to compose herself for a grand declaration.

"Anyway, I'm special there. When you're at CHANEL, every supplier is super nice to you."

She tilted her chin upward, her expression growing haughty. Jindo cautiously inquired.

"But do you still have a good relationship with them, even though you're no longer at CHANEL?"

"DE QUOI?"

His question evidently irritated the French director, whose voice seemed to become akin to a cat hissing whenever she outburst in her native tongue. Jindo carefully elaborated.

"I mean... do they still provide you with the same level of service... though you don't work at CHANEL anymore?"

"OF COURSE! THEY KNOW ME! They know I'm doing my brand, so they offer me a special price, and even manufacture fabrics for me… Normally they don't do that to small independent designers, but I'm SPECIAL."

She was speaking rather loudly, appearing quite chuffed with herself. In a way, Jindo found her a bit full of herself, and he just wanted to pull a face at her self-satisfied demeanour.

Meanwhile, he could not deny that the jacquard fabrics in the corner, emblazoned with Gabrielle's initials, did lend credence to her claims. Jindo reminded himself once again that there was a significant gap in their professional networks and experiences. Jindo then chose to indulge the young, successful, high-profile director.

"That's amazing, Gabrielle. Good for you… For me, when I saw their fabric, I just thought they were very authentic, but I didn't know if they were a CHANEL supplier. As far as I remember, they mostly deal with wools, don't they?"

"Yes, they specialise in traditional French handmade techniques, and they never do with cheap and artificial fibres, but only NATURAL ones…"

Gabrielle proudly expounded upon her supplier's savoir-faire, which was indeed quite interesting to Jindo. Nevertheless, he wanted to return to the matter at hand.

"By the way Gabrielle, the fabrics we need this time aren't from Malhia KENT, are they?"

"What?"

She appeared to be miffed, like a disgruntled cat that had just been rudely interrupted.

It was likely because Jindo had steered the conversation away from her reminiscing about the good old days. Jindo proceeded cautiously.

"I mean, this time... we need a plain red velvet, and that won't be from Malhia KENT, correct?"

"No, they're not from Malhia KENT. I need to order them from another supplier and... they're ITALIANS that I know from CHANEL..."

Initially, she appeared rather nonplussed by Jindo's sudden change of topic, but it seemed that she quickly regained her composure and shifted gears to discuss the Italian supplier she had met at her previous company. Jindo, however, was swift in cutting to the chase.

"Okay great, so you'll contact them, and I just wait until we receive the fabric, right?"

"Ah... yes."

She appeared somewhat disconcerted by Jindo's nimble manoeuvring, but the quirky director was once again quick to change tack.

"Do other things first. You know we need to start a new collection. We're already too late."

"Pardon?"

Out of the blue, the director brought up the new project. In a way, Jindo was chuffed to bits with the update, but meanwhile, he felt a bit miffed by her tone.

It irked him because she had never mentioned it before, yet now she seemed to imply that it was delayed. Considering Jindo had not only been punctual with his tasks but also ahead of the game with his extra work, he found her implication rather unjust.

Putting personal feelings aside, Jindo was somewhat pleased that the former CHANEL designer finally appeared to acknowledge his modélisme prowess. This was due to that she was essentially entrusting him with creating a new construction for her designs.

Traditionally, in the field of modélisme, there are two types of assignments. One involves crafting a new construction, and the other entails editing or modifying existing ones.

While both necessitate a certain level of skill, the former is generally regarded as the more creative endeavour. This is because designers typically delegate a task of new construction creation to those, they have confidence in for their competence.

Jindo expressed his enthusiasm, and Gabrielle informed him that she would supply him with new designs in the upcoming week. Just like that, their evening session oddly drew to a close.

Before Jindo packed up his belongings to leave, he surveyed the current state of production. He was not exactly over the moon with it, as the majority of the pieces were still unfinished, either hanging or folded in a corner, in various stages of completion; coats missing their sleeves with the linings not attached, partially sewn layered skirts not fully assembled due to fabric shortages, sweaters lacking wristbands, and shirts without collars.

He then realised that, in fact, not a single garment had been completed in a proper sense by that point. There were always complications.

To put it bluntly, he knew that the root of the problem was Gabrielle's approach to sourcing materials. This had indeed led to frequent work switches in production.

There had been times when Jindo tried to carefully persuade the unyielding director to change her method of providing materials, but as per usual, she clung stubbornly to her inefficient practice, likely for her own reasons.

Regardless, Jindo concluded that there was no point in brooding over the issue at that moment. Instead, he opted to adopt a more positive outlook. He reasoned that it was not entirely a lost cause, as the problem stemmed from the supplies rather than the personnel. On that basis, he did not consider the situation to be an utter catastrophe yet and exited the workspace.

In smaller fashion houses that handle production as well as sampling, it is fairly common to switch production lines in various circumstances, such as when urgent requests from VIP clients arise.

However, it is not typical for production to be persistently delayed due to supply shortages, as these should normally be anticipated and accounted for in advance.

Regardless, if these production switches continue to occur, it will not only demotivate workers but also hinder overall productivity. Ultimately, the quality of the finished pieces will likely be compromised.

Chapter 11 : Fashion's New Dawn

In the realm of fashion collections, the usual protocol involves a pre-discussion before the generation of ideas; a step to set the theme and direction of the collection. However, in a boutique label where a director moonlights as the sole designer, the process often jumps directly into ideation.

On the following Monday…

Arriving at work bright and early, Jindo greeted the day, excited about the new collection. With the production of certain pieces temporarily halted, he occupied himself by updating his schedule. At that moment, Gabrielle made her entrance into the atelier.

"Morning…"

"Bonjour Gabrielle, how was your gym session this morning?"

"Ah… I didn't go."

Her reply came with a dry smile, revealing a file teeming with sketches in her hand. Jindo was pleasantly surprised since he had not expected the designer to offer fresh ideas on the very first day back at work. It seemed Gabrielle was raring to go, and Jindo was rather chuffed about the prospect of new designs.

Upon a quick glance, Jindo noticed the sketches were vibrant and rather rough around the edges, with marker strokes adding a unique touch. They seemed to be hand-drawn with the designer's personal touch, a stark contrast to the generic computerised croquis that was so prevalent nowadays.

Despite the multitude of ways to express ideas in fashion, nothing quite matches the charm of a designer's original sketch. It not only conveys the designer's concepts but also showcases their creative DNA.

Furthermore, many designers may harbour brilliant ideas, but few can express them with a cultural flair unique to them. For these talented souls, sketches alone are enough to spark curiosity about how the designs would look once realised.

Jindo was impressed by the original sketches of the ex-CHANEL designer. On closer inspection though, he realised that these were not hand-drawn, but created digitally. Gabrielle seemed to have used a digital sketch pad and stylus instead of the traditional pen and paper. This was a surprise for Jindo since he had not expected such tech-savvy finesse from someone who had seemed a traditional artisan at heart.

Indeed, Jindo was rather thrown by Gabrielle's surprising blend of skills. He had come across many talented individuals in his time, but few seemed to have a natural flair for expressing their ideas, particularly using digital tools while retaining their originality.

Although Jindo acknowledged that a manual approach often added a more authentic touch to the work, he foresaw that the future of fashion would require more instantaneous modifications and collaborations, due to the inherently dynamic nature of digital platforms.

He believed that marrying analogue and digital methods while preserving originality could be a valuable asset in the future. This made him admire Gabrielle even more, who not only had an illustrious past but also seemed to hold immense potential for the future.

Snapping out of his reverie, Jindo turned his attention back to Gabrielle's designs. She had created about ten looks and seemed rather pleased with her weekend's work. Smiling at Jindo, she launched into her presentation.

Jindo listened attentively, noting points in her demonstration that needed clarification. Indeed, initial sketches were not usually fully formed, particularly in terms of technical details, but in Gabrielle's case, she spoke with confidence about those methodological issues.

There was no problem with this, as long as it all made sense. However, Gabrielle spoke as if she had created something similar before when Jindo suspected she might have only imagined it.

Regardless, he held his questions for now, considering that the former CHANEL designer, known to be a little elusive in her explanations, might be onto something he did not fully grasp. Therefore, he kept his silence and continued studying the sheets to grasp the collection overall.

At first, Jindo noticed that Gabrielle's style range was rather broad. It spanned from sweaters to dresses, including a denim jacket adorned with laces, a custom-quilted doudoune (down jacket), a mixed fur coat, a reversed front and back shirt, formal trousers studded with pearls, a skirt featuring collaged panels with an attached leather flared panel on the side, and a separable jumpsuit with an open zip, among others. From his modélisme perspective, the pieces generally featured numerous panel cuts and an abundance of decorative accessories.

Some of the pieces echoed Gabrielle's previous collections, but many of the new styles seemed quite different. He understood that the designer might be trying to expand her repertoire, but still, he could not shake off the feeling that she was trying to portray herself as a complex designer with a vast range.

At that moment, Jindo noticed that many of her references indeed stemmed from well-known fashion codes. Indeed, the biker jacket was reminiscent of Balmain, the cropped tweed jacket echoed Dior, the doudoune brought contemporary Balenciaga to mind, the dress was Alaïa-esque, the hoodie bore similarities to Vetements, and the knit-mixed sweater was akin to Margiela's creations.

It appeared as though Gabrielle had drawn inspiration from these renowned brands and tried to infuse her own elements. Yet, to Jindo, it seemed a touch too excessive and conspicuous. Nevertheless, he bit his tongue, aware that the former CHANEL designer surely had a better grasp of fashion trends and culture.

As Gabrielle carried on with her presentation, Jindo held one of the design sheets, trying to make head or tail of it. It was a fur coat, its right sleeve adorned with a host of origami pleats while the left side sported two detachable patches of different furs. It was glaringly apparent that this was beyond his grasp. Sensing his struggle, Gabrielle teased him, a smirk playing on her lips.

"You know this, no? It's easy."

A prickling annoyance crept up on Jindo at her jibe, but he resisted conceding his inability. Instead, his little ego led him to pretend some semblance of understanding.

"Well, I haven't done anything like this before, but theoretically... I think I have an idea how to start..."

Clutching at straws to keep up his pretence, Jindo desperately rifled through his memory for any garment he had seen before bearing even a passing resemblance. He remembered a dress from last year's Paris wedding fair, a sea of origami pleats that gave it its unique shape. The designer had confessed that the dress was the fruit of 3D printing technology, something she had wrestled with for months.

This memory deflated Jindo's initial optimism. Gabrielle might have insinuated that the coat could be fashioned by hand, but he knew the reality would not be as straightforward as she implied.

Indeed, he found himself utterly at a loss for a starting point, even contemplating whether this coat might eventually be dropped from the collection. However, he remained circumspect for the moment, keeping his concerns under wraps while endeavouring to glean as much information as possible.

He then broached the subject of the overall expectations, including the total number of pieces and timelines. Gabrielle declared that there would be a minimum of sixty pieces, all due by mid-January in preparation for Paris Fashion Week.

"Okay, Gabrielle… By the way, is it the quantity you normally make per collection?"

He asked, having noted that her previous collections seemed much less extensive.

"Yes, of course. Why, you think CHANEL makes just 10 pieces for their défilé (runway)?"

As was the norm, Jindo found himself at a loss for words at the mention of the prestigious brand name. With no experience working for such big names or taking part in a runway show, he could not offer a retort. Instead, he attempted a change of topic.

"No, Gabrielle. I'm just trying to work out how I can manage the workload… By the way, are we doing runway for this collection?"

"Ah… well, that will depend on how good it is."

She seemed a touch sheepish at first, giving a rather nebulous answer. Meanwhile, Jindo found this puzzling, knowing full well that a 'runway show' would typically involve a cast of thousands and demand a hefty amount of work.

Nevertheless, given the designer's blithe dismissal of the subject, he held his doubts in check and decided not to press her further. He surmised that the director must have her own agenda and chose to move on.

"Okay Gabrielle, I'll do my best… By the way, we're going to use the existing constructional patterns, right?"

"Hm... no, I want you to make all the patterns."

"Pardon?"

Taken aback, Jindo gaped at her, then voiced his reservations about what seemed an unreasonably time-consuming decision.

"Gabrielle... I think it would save time if we used existing patterns for any similar models and spent more time on the brand-new pieces, particularly the complicated ones..."

"I don't like the previous patterns. They were all made badly."

Jindo found this weird, given her previous bragging about her previous modéliste being Japanese, and some of the other patterns were created by her friend who had worked at Balmain and Balenciaga.

Now, she seemed to be suggesting that she had never been a fan of any of their work, favouring Jindo's instead, even though he had not yet created any new patterns. Scratching his head, he pondered over this conundrum until she flashed a smile at him.

"I like your patterns better, Jindo."

Unswayed by her flattery, Jindo still sought to make sense of the situation. He picked up a design sheet to use as an example.

"So, you mean for this sweater for example... you want me to make it from scratch?"

"Yes."

"Gabrielle, I think this sweater is a classic oversized volume, so we can just use any previous construction for the base, then tape the bodice to draw this interesting asymmetric line and deconstruct it to trace each panel..."

Jindo quickly sketched out the process he believed to be the most efficient, but the director seemed less than keen to compromise.

"No, I want you to do moulage."

"Draping?"

"Why? C'est un problème?"

Her sudden switch to French was a red flag signalling her mounting impatience, but Jindo was still trying to figure out the logistics. He knew that draping would yield an exquisite form, but given the ticking clock and the projected workload, resorting to such a meticulous method for a less important piece seemed misguided.

In the world of fashion, draping is typically processed for garments that place a strong emphasis on lines or specific shapes that need constant refinement, akin to sculpting.

Still finding it a tad inefficient and unfair, Jindo felt Gabrielle's insistence was like an Italian restaurant owner insisting the chef prepare a pomodoro pasta using freshly hand-crushed tomatoes, all the while dealing with an array of more complex dishes.

After several attempts to express his concerns, Jindo found himself at an impasse with Gabrielle.

"Gabrielle, I don't mind draping, but we're producing many pieces in a short amount of time… I'm not sure if it's really necessary to drape such simple items…"

With an air of haughty confidence, Gabrielle dropped the famed label's name once again.

"In houses like CHANEL, we all do this way. I know how they do, and I'm doing exactly the same. You don't know anything about that, no? If you want to go to the luxury fashion houses like Hermès, you need to learn from how I do. YOU UNDERSTAND?"

Her stern words hung in the air, effectively muting Jindo as she underscored his lack of experience in high-end fashion. Despite nursing a head full of doubts, he decided not to poke the bear further.

Instead, he tried to broach a different subject.

"Okay, Gabrielle. I get it. By the way, I wonder if only I and Boubakah will make all those 60+ pieces?"

"..."

Gabrielle's pause hinted that she had not given this aspect much thought. After a while of silence, she responded.

"Hm... I'll hire more people."

"More people?"

"Yes, even me and my aunt will join the atelier."

"Your aunt?"

"Yes, she loves me. She's very kind and always helps me when I need an extra hand. Even since I was at school, she always helped me when I had a lot of homework to do. She actually came to help in the previous collection..."

Gabrielle seemed rather pleased about her aunt's involvement, but Jindo was left scratching his head at her vague explanation. The term 'school homework' was particularly jarring. On a brighter note, he wondered if Gabrielle's aunt was a retired couturier, perhaps one who had once graced the halls of renowned fashion houses.

Jindo eyed Gabrielle cautiously, trying to gauge if she had more to disclose about her family member, but she seemed genuinely nonchalant, blinking innocently. He realised there was no room to prod further on the subject, so he let it slide.

Meanwhile, Jindo pondered the identities of the others joining the endeavour alongside Gabrielle and her kin. Optimistically, he surmised they might hail from her professional network within the luxury fashion houses. Yet, he refrained from seeking clarification, dreading the possibility of receiving yet another embarrassing response.

He then decided to shift gears to discuss the materials and supplies for the new collection, likely prompted by his instincts urging him to confirm the details in advance.

"Gabrielle, are we ordering any fabric for sampling? For now, I can start with muslin (plain canvas) to create an initial shape, but I wonder if we'll have the actual fabrics any time soon?"

"Yes, I can order from my Italian suppliers for you."

Jindo found it strange that she stated as if she would do a favour for him, but he glossed over Gabrielle's imperfect English as he usually did.

"By the way Gabrielle, are we not going to search for any supplies in Paris?"

"WHAT? You think CHANEL visits the local fabric stores?"

"No… I suppose not…"

Jindo detected her rising tension just as the atelier members began to arrive. Aware that Gabrielle's temper tended to flare up when others were present, particularly Amélie, he suggested they continue the conversation upstairs.

Upon reaching the office, Gabrielle seemed more composed without any distractions.

"So Gabrielle, all the fabrics will come from Italy, and I need to wait, right?"

"Well, I can manufacture fabrics with Malhia KENT, but it's quite expensive because the minimum quantity is so high…"

She casually name-dropped the esteemed CHANEL fabric supplier, but Jindo found it a bit grating, now recognising it as another of her ostentatious displays.

He then contemplated whether she had any plans to conduct a general fabric hunt.

"By the way Gabrielle, do you normally go to PREMiÈRE ViSiON?"

"No, I don't have time and the ticket is too expensive…"

"…"

Jindo was surprised by her response. If she had cited time constraints or reliance on established suppliers, he would have found it reasonable. But her gripe about the ticket price struck a discordant note, particularly considering her penchant for portraying an image of lavishness.

Indeed, Jindo had asked about the renowned exhibition since it was one of the grandest fashion fairs in Europe, if not the world. To his knowledge, many major players in the global textile industry would attend the exhibition to showcase their latest products, and numerous renowned designers worldwide would visit to keep up with the latest trends in textiles and other supplies.

Regardless, he was not bothered by any of the fuss at that moment and decided to focus on the task at hand.

"Okay Gabrielle, so I should start by finding the right volumes (shapes) of the designs, right?"

"Yes."

"Then, I think we'll need some toile (muslin fabric) for draping…"

'Muslin' is a cotton fabric, used to make a mock-up version of a garment. By doing so, the right volume (shape or fit) can be studied before the actual, expensive fabric is used, preventing any costly mistakes. It is like when making a pizza, a chef might first test the recipe with simpler ones before using the best ingredients.

"We don't have any left. We need to buy more. We used it all last season."

"Okay then, do you also need to place an order for it?"

Jindo posed the question given that toile was a staple in any fashion atelier, and the more established houses typically had their own suppliers, ready to deliver at a moment's notice.

"No, it's just toile. We can get it nearby. You can go and buy it."

It seemed the former CHANEL designer was without a dedicated supplier of her own.

"Okay, should I go to Socolatex then?"

"DE QUOI?"

Her reaction was akin to a startled cat, eyes wide in surprise. Indeed, Jindo had only mentioned the boutique as he remembered that during his previous visit, a French gentleman with a ponytail had rather ostentatiously claimed that they provided top-tier toile daily to prestigious houses like Balenciaga and Christian Dior. On this basis, Jindo assumed the ex-CHANEL designer might also be a patron.

"NO! Why there? It's too expensive."

Once again, Jindo found her statement strange. She had consistently referred to the famous suppliers and Italian manufacturers she was acquainted with from her CHANEL days. Yet, when it came to loosening the purse strings, she was quite price-conscious, always going for the most budget-friendly option.

"Then... where should I go?"

"Fil deux mille, of course."

'Fil2000' is arguably one of the most frequented fashion supply stores in Paris, beloved by fashion students and independent creators alike due to its extensive assortment of reasonably priced supplies.

Regardless, the tiresome discussion had finally drawn to a close, and Jindo returned to the atelier. Upon arriving, he perused the sketches and notes once more, still pondering over Gabrielle's plan. He queried Amélie.

"Amélie, Gabrielle wants to start a new collection and she's aiming for over 60 pieces. Is that the usual number she produces per collection?"

"Je sais pas…"

(I don't know…)

Amélie's reply was curt, and she immediately returned to her work. Jindo picked up on a slightly frosty vibe from her, but shrugged it off, assuming she was simply not in the mood. He then directed the same inquiry at Timothée, but found himself confronted with a similarly chilly reception. It dawned on Jindo that their apparent absorption in their work was a deliberate effort to maintain a distance from him.

Taking a moment to reflect, Jindo formed a hypothesis. The issue might have been the perception that he and Gabrielle were growing close, particularly given this morning's events when Jindo had seemingly suggested Gabrielle go upstairs to continue their discussion. It was possible that he appeared to be intentionally excluding the atelier members in order to forge a unique bond with the director.

Uncertain of his next move, Jindo felt that voicing his thoughts on the matter would only serve to make things even more awkward. A pregnant silence fell, and he chose to redirect his attention to his work.

With the altered timetable, Jindo updated Boubacar about the production reshuffle. He was taken aback when the normally unruffled seamstress showed signs of irritation towards him. While it made sense that constant disruptions in the production line would rankle the seamstresses, Jindo found Boubacar's reaction particularly startling.

It was because he had never exhibited any signs of frustration towards Jindo before, and he was surely aware that this was not Jindo's fault or decision. Furthermore, despite Jindo always treating him with deference, the decade-long experienced seamstress was certainly well aware that a modéliste typically held a higher position in the professional hierarchy in a subtle manner.

Jindo then surmised that the atelier members might have had a bit of gossip about him during his absence upstairs. He stood there, feeling somewhat isolated.

Amélie, catching his discomfort out of the corner of her eye as she busied herself with hand-stitching, seemed to feel a pang of guilt. It was clear that she recognised Jindo as a decent individual, just trying to crack on with his work.

"Jindo, we normally don't have a plan. We just make pieces then sell them..."

With gratitude towards Amélie, Jindo was now confronted with a perplexing conundrum. Gabrielle had painted a picture of consistent collection production, yet a longstanding employee had just contradicted that notion, claiming there was never a concrete plan in place.

As minutes ticked by, the frustration and bewilderment surrounding the situation intensified for Jindo. Ultimately, he made the decision not to expend energy unravelling the mystery, instead choosing to direct his focus solely on the immediate task at hand.

Chapter 12 : Echoes of Friendship

In the afternoon...

After procuring muslin from Fil2000, Jindo was primed to embark on the first piece of the new collection. Despite Gabrielle's persistent advocacy for him to tackle the fur coat first, featuring intricate origami pleats to accentuate the sleeves, Jindo found himself in need of a contemplative pause. Having been ensnared in analogous predicaments in the past, he was keenly aware that diving in headfirst without a solid plan could culminate in a rather sticky wicket.

As he prepped the muslin for its transformation, the unmistakable echo of footsteps descending the staircase caught his attention. It was not Gabrielle's solitary footfall this time, but rather a companioned patter. She appeared, navigating her way towards Jindo, a weird grin perched upon her lips.

"Jindo, there's someone who knows you."

Still clutching the muslin, Jindo cast a glance at the director, his brow furrowing in curiosity. Obligingly, she sidestepped, unveiling the individual in her wake.

"Et voilà!"

"You..."

To Jindo's astonishment, the enigmatic visitor turned out to be Seiwa, a trusted ally from his little Parisian network. Swiftly registering Jindo's wide-eyed surprise, Seiwa moved to placate his stunned reaction.

"Oppa (An older brother in Korean), I'll explain later..."

"You'd best..."

Seiwa, a cherished comrade from Jindo's days at the fashion institute in Paris, identified as having a different sexual orientation, a detail that never encumbered their friendship. A Malaysian with a rich heritage of British Japanese and Chinese Korean ancestry, she wore her blended lineage with infectious pride.

Their commonality, both raised by grandmothers, both the offspring of designer mothers, and both alumni of English universities, created an almost immediate bond from their first encounter. Over time, their relationship evolved into a symbiosis of mischief and mutual support, their constant teasing belied by an undercurrent of genuine affection.

Jindo shook his head, a convivial grin spreading across his face. He was visibly pleased to see his 'sister', yet a trace of perceived betrayal lingered. It seemed Seiwa had been privy to Jindo's engagement with Gabrielle but had not thought to apprise him of her impending visit.

Surveying the scene, Gabrielle assessed the camaraderie between the pair. Intriguingly, Jindo seemed to command a rather dominant role in their relationship. While the two males exhibited warmth towards each other, Jindo's masculine demeanour seemed to eclipse Seiwa's feminine traits.

Recognising the dynamics at play, Gabrielle issued an abrupt warning, her countenance adopting its customary stern and grumpy expression.

"DON'T PLAY AT WORK!"

Jindo was momentarily disconcerted by Gabrielle's phrasing but swiftly chalked it up to her rudimentary English proficiency, as was his wont. He thought it a touch unjust, considering he had merely exchanged greetings with his sister, while Gabrielle had orchestrated the entire 'Guess Who?' spectacle of escorting Seiwa downstairs.

Nonetheless, Jindo refrained from voicing his objections to the director's remark. Instead, he placated her with a dash of humorous sincerity.

"Bien sûr, Madame."

His words were accompanied by an amiable smile, and he promptly returned to his draping work. Satisfied, Gabrielle maintained her stern façade, ascending the staircase with Seiwa trailing behind her.

Overall, it seemed Jindo's sister would be joining the company anytime soon, and it was, in fact, a welcome surprise for Jindo, not just because of their tight-knit bond, but also due to his conviction in the synergistic magic, they could conjure together.

Each adept in their unique disciplines, they respected and understood each other's strengths and shortcomings. Seiwa admired Jindo's craftsmanship in modélisme, while Jindo held in high regard Seiwa's prowess in digital software, a skill sharpened by her graphic design background.

Jindo would frequently rib Seiwa, jesting that her digital portfolio outshone the actual quality of her fashion creations. In response, Seiwa would endearingly dub Jindo a stubborn old mule, insisting that he had a knack for making exquisitely crafted garments appear dreadfully drab. Despite their jovial teasing, they recognised each other's expertise, continually learning from and supporting each other.

Meanwhile, Jindo experienced a trace of discomfort around his Malaysian sibling, owing to a conversation they had engaged in the previous week.

When Jindo first secured his role with Gabrielle, he had kept it under wraps. Many of his colleagues were still grappling with the job hunt, and he had no intention of appearing to be flaunting his success.

However, he had confided in Seiwa, aware that her focus was currently elsewhere. Seiwa was deeply invested in her personal projects, her job applications were infrequent and exclusively aimed at coveted labels like Maison Margiela and Acne Studios.

Now, Jindo worried that his prior descriptions may have excessively glorified Gabrielle's credentials. He had depicted Gabrielle as a distinguished alumna of the Chambre Syndicale de la Haute Couture, boasting an impressive modelling tenure at Lanvin and experiences with prestigious fashion houses including CHANEL and Hermès.

Furthermore, he had portrayed Gabrielle's fashion house as an imposing establishment nestled in the heart of Paris, claiming an entire building in the upper Marais district. He had also underscored their dedication to in-house production, each garment meticulously crafted by skilled artisans. In addition, he lauded Gabrielle's nuanced comprehension of Asian culture.

Reflecting on his words, Jindo realised he had made Gabrielle and her fashion house appear remarkably prestigious.

What particularly intrigued Seiwa, however, was his mention of Lady Gaga endorsing one of Gabrielle's pieces. Given Seiwa's deep admiration for the New York-born singer, Jindo knew this nugget of information would undoubtedly pique her interest. As expected, Seiwa humorously requested Jindo to nab the stylist's contact details of the American artist for her.

Nonetheless, Seiwa made it clear, albeit in her teasing manner, that she had no interest in working with unknown designers.

In fact, their perspectives were fundamentally divergent. Jindo advocated for starting at the bottom, regardless of age, and mastering each phase gradually. In contrast, Seiwa, despite having a comparable level of experience as Jindo, argued that she simply could not afford the time to embark on such a path. If she were to work for someone else, the brand's reputation and the company's size would be paramount.

Despite her apparent lack of interest in Gabrielle's house, it appeared that some of Jindo's tales had ignited a spark of curiosity in Seiwa.

Regardless, the day was drawing to a close, and Jindo was in the final throes of his work when he heard Gabrielle descending the stairs.

"Seiwa will be joining us from next week."

"Great."

Jindo could feel Gabrielle's trademark sternness beginning to seep in. She felt compelled to reiterate her warning.

"Jindo! Don't play at work."

Jindo glanced at Gabrielle, his expression subtly conveying his confusion at her persistent focus on this point. She repeated her warning, this time with added vehemence.

"I SAY DON'T PLAY AT WORK!"

Though he had braced himself for her inevitable bellow, Jindo remained unfazed by the repetition. With the day's end in sight, he wisely opted against engaging.

"No worries, Gabrielle."

Having mollified her, Jindo began tidying up, preparing to call it a day. However, Gabrielle, maintaining her grumpy face, was blocking his path to the stairs. Jindo looked at Gabrielle, his body language subtly asking for permission to pass. Gabrielle, however, had another warning to issue.

"Be careful, you two!"

Anticipating Gabrielle's shift into stern director mode, Jindo delicately inquired to ensure a peaceful exit.

"Gabrielle, I'm a bit confused... Have I done something wrong?"

"No, why? Did you do something wrong?"

Gabrielle retorted promptly, almost as if she was itching for an argument.

"No Gabrielle, then did Seiwa say something?"

"No, he didn't say anything. Why? Did he need to say something?"

Still swiftly volleying back responses, she squared off against Jindo, seemingly ready to spar.

"No, I'm just asking because I honestly don't understand why you're saying this to me."

"WHAT?"

Gabrielle seemed on the brink of losing her temper, her eyebrows knitted, eyes wide. Jindo proceeded with caution, aiming not to stoke the flames but to make his exit.

"I mean, Gabrielle... you already know I take my work quite seriously, and now you may know that Seiwa is also a mature individual with previous professional experiences... So, although we're good mates, when we're working, we'll be just focused as it's supposed to be..."

"YOU HAVE TO!"

"... of course Gabrielle... just to clarify, we won't be playful at work..."

"DON'T PLAY AT WORK!"

Jindo was left momentarily speechless, feeling as if Gabrielle was stuck on repeat. He had a nagging suspicion that she was simply revelling in her fantasy of playing the charismatic director that evening. However, he was not in a position to indulge in her role-play. He attempted to conclude the conversation with a logical closure.

"By the way Gabrielle, Seiwa will be working upstairs, not here in the atelier, right?"

"Yes, he'll be with me... ALL THE TIME."

"Okay, so there's nothing to worry about because he and I won't even see each other, correct?"

"…"

Gabrielle remained mum, her grumpy façade intact. But it seemed she had exhausted her repertoire to assert dominance over Jindo. She finally stepped aside, allowing him to pass. Yet, even as he made his exit, he could sense the intensity of her piercing gaze on him.

Exiting the building, Jindo promptly dialled Seiwa.

"Hey, new assistant!"

"Oppa, steady on."

Seiwa hastily tried to calm her brother as if she was controlling a drooling dog.

"I'm as calm as hell, just dying to know why someone who's only interested in big names ended up in this small, unknown enterprise…"

Jindo quipped, his words wrapped in a friendly veil of sarcasm.

"Oppa, I simply came across a job post this morning and sent an application. She called me almost immediately. Barely an hour had passed… I even forgot to customise my cover letter, but I reckon she didn't even read it. I was actually very surprised…"

"There was a job post? Ah, I think that's because we're starting a new collection this week… anyway, I don't mind you coming here mate but I can't help but wonder why a person, with so much experience and no time for anyone unknown, suddenly changed her mind and applied to this little, unknown company that no one knows about…"

Jindo continued his good-natured teasing.

"Oppa, you're annoying. Listen! I was simply browsing Fashionjobs, and I would've bypassed the job posting if you hadn't told me so much… But you did and I got intrigued by her… Despite that, I wasn't exactly raring to go, but I sent an application without any expectations and she called me almost instantly. That's all…"

"Okay okay, I get it. You don't need to justify mate. I was just teasing you as you did to me last week, remember?"

"Sorry, I didn't mean to…"

"I get it I get it, no worries."

Their playful exchange seemed to have run its course, and Seiwa resumed her account.

"By the way Oppa, it's all just weird."

"What about it?"

"I feel like Gabrielle fast-tracked me."

"Fast-tracked you?"

"Yeah, I just introduced myself and mentioned how I came to know about her company through you, then she seemed to confirm some details… and after hearing the positive points, she asked me to bring a stagiaire paper because I need a trial period…"

"Hm… my case was the same."

"Normally they don't do that, do they?"

"What? Stagiaire?"

"Well, the whole thing… For the stagiaire part to test me, I get it but bringing the document immediately was the weird part."

"I know she's a bit… impatient… maybe she just doesn't want to waste time."

Even though Jindo was itching to disclose his reservations about Gabrielle, he held back, uncertain whether it was fitting to share his uncorroborated suspicions with Seiwa. It was not merely that he did not want to circulate baseless gossip, but he also was reluctant to confess that his prior grand depictions of Gabrielle might have been somewhat overstated.

"Maybe..."

Seiwa still seemed doubtful, prompting Jindo to swiftly steer the conversation elsewhere.

"Anyway, how long is your contract for?"

"Well, it's a stagiaire Oppa, so it doesn't really matter. I actually find it annoying."

"What about it?"

"Because the job posting stated it was a temporary contract, but once we got into the nitty-gritty, Gabrielle kept hammering on about how she didn't know me, so she needed to see me in a trial period blah blah blah... I tried to argue but when she brought up your situation, that even you, with all your experience, are also on a trial period... I was at a loss for words. Because, as the older loser that you are, you obviously have more experience than I do."

"Haha, thanks but piss off."

Jindo chuckled at Seiwa's sarcastic jab, prompting her to carry on.

"Do you know what Oppa? At the end of the day, it's just her way of avoiding payment. Simple as that..."

Seiwa's voice bore a hint of irritation.

"What do you mean? You don't get paid at all?"

"She drafted the contract for two months because that's the maximum period for an unpaid internship."

"Ah, I didn't know."

"Oppa, you never know anything, but just continue working like a stupid dog."

"Once again, piss off."

Jindo let Seiwa's barb slide, and she continued.

"Oppa, did you know, if an internship extends over two months, the company is legally obligated to pay?"

Jindo decided against sharing his own situation, that he was being paid a minimal wage, knowing it would only provide fuel for his sister's teasing. The tension in Seiwa's voice was palpable as she continued.

"Anyway, I wasn't too fussed as I didn't have any long-term intentions... I was just curious to see how brilliant this former CHANEL designer is..."

"Okay okay, but there won't be much to be impressed by the way…"

"What do you mean?"

"Um… it's hard to explain. She has a bit of her own character, and it's a bit… eccentric."

Jindo gingerly hinted at his concerns, his hesitation to share more palpable.

"Oppa, actually… I sensed she was a bit odd. She asked about the nature of our relationship, and kept harping on about 'don't play at work'…"

"Ah yeah, I was going to say… because she did the same to me on the way out."

"Really? Bizarre... I think she actually brought me downstairs to gauge our relationship, and perhaps she noticed we're closer than she initially thought..."

"Okay, I get it now."

"Anyway, I don't care Oppa. All I need from her at the end of the day is her contact list of buyers, including my Lady Gaga's stylist, haha."

"Haha, good luck with that… Anyway mate, I'm glad to see you here and excited to work together."

"Thanks Oppa, me too."

Their clarifying call drew to a close, but the peculiarity of Gabrielle's conduct continued to unsettle Jindo. He tried to rationalise her actions as part of her directorial role, yet it felt distinctly odd.

Meanwhile, guilt started to seep in regarding Seiwa. He had given a casual warning about Gabrielle, the quirky ex-CHANEL designer, yet he could not dismiss his guilt for not disclosing his escalating concerns. Despite his awareness of withholding information, he was hesitant to burden Seiwa with his yet unverified suspicions.

Chapter 13 : Under the Strike's Shadow

First day of Seiwa…

As was his wont, Jindo arrived at work bright and early, promptly diving into his tasks. Having put the finishing touches on the draft constructions for a sweater and a shirt, he set them aside, awaiting the fabric's arrival, then embarked on the next piece.

At that moment, a commotion from the showroom upstairs reached his ears. It was Gabrielle, her voice escalated into what sounded like a heated argument with a man. Dismissing his curiosity, Jindo refocused on his tasks.

The atelier, usually buzzing with activity by this hour, was oddly quiet. The team was uncharacteristically tardy today.

After a tense ten minutes, Gabrielle descended, her eyes seemingly on a scan.

"Seiwa did not come yet?"

"I don't know Gabrielle. He's not here…"

Jindo replied, baffled as to why she was inquiring about Seiwa's whereabouts. However, he could sense her irritation mounting.

"Gabrielle, do you want me to call him?"

"No, you need to work. We have a lot to do. I'll call him."

Her sharp response underscored her disdain for any delay in his work.

Meanwhile, a gut feeling told Jindo that Seiwa might have overslept, a suspicion built on years of sibling understanding.

"He's not answering..."

Gabrielle ended the call, her gaze shifting to Jindo, her annoyance palpable. He could not grasp why her ire seemed partially aimed at him.

"C'est normale with him?"

"I don't know Gabrielle… perhaps, is it not because of the strike?"

"What strike?"

Her annoyance remained unabated as she poised herself to make another call.

"I think there's a strike on the metro today."

"Non, c'est pas possible."

Gabrielle muttered in her mother tongue, at which Jindo decided it was best to remain silent. Though he had been prepared to stick up for his sister, he now deemed it wise to bite his tongue.

Meanwhile, it struck him as odd that Gabrielle's fury was solely directed at Seiwa when none of the other team members had shown up either. He could not fathom her fixation on Seiwa, yet he suspected she might have pressing tasks for her new assistant on the first day. Silently, he resumed his work, hoping his sister would turn up soon.

After several unsuccessful attempts, Gabrielle finally surrendered and retreated upstairs. What unsettled Jindo, however, was her lingering, accusatory glance, as if blaming him partially for Seiwa's absence, even as she withdrew to her office.

About half an hour passed...

The team members began to trickle in, punctuating the morning with their belated arrivals. It seemed Seiwa had also arrived upstairs, but at that moment, Jindo heard an echo of a flurry of a sharp rebuke from Gabrielle, reverberating through the workspace.

While Jindo understood the director's frustration, he found it peculiar that Seiwa alone shouldered the brunt of Gabrielle's wrath. The rest of the staff slipped into their workday routines unscathed, commencing their duties leisurely over a cup of coffee.

Regardless, Jindo maintained his focus on his task, eagerly anticipating Seiwa's lunchtime tale. The morning whizzed by, and lunchtime had arrived.

The Asian siblings congregated in the foyer and prepared to venture out. Today, unlike usual, Gabrielle was ensconced on a recently placed couch near the entrance, her fingers flitting across her mobile phone. Despite her engrossment, her countenance displayed a discernible scowl. As Jindo and Seiwa exchanged their morning pleasantries, Gabrielle cast a fleeting glance their way.

Unexpectedly, the middle-aged office lady, typically an afternoon arrival, was present, standing alongside Gabrielle. As ever, her natural sullen expression was in place, and at that moment, Jindo noticed a striking resemblance between her and Gabrielle. In fact, this was the first instance Jindo had seen them side by side, both displaying sour moods. They resembled a mother-daughter duo. Nevertheless, he refrained from asking any question, readying to depart with Seiwa.

"Bon appétit, Gabrielle."

Engrossed in her phone, the irritable director offered no response. Meanwhile, Seiwa seemed downtrodden, her eagerness to leave quite evident. Without further ado, Jindo and his sister made their exit.

"You overslept, didn't you?"

"Yeah, you know Oppa..."

"Haha, it was your first day mate..."

"I know but there was a metro strike, and you know how Parisian metro can be..."

"Actually, I tried to tell Gabrielle about it, but it did not work... Anyway, she was angry?"

"Yes... but I think she overreacted..."

"Whoa whoa, hold on... you were late, mate."

"I know but there was a strike, and she didn't give me a chance to explain..."

"Yeah, I can imagine. Sometimes, she does so..."

"She ranted for like half an hour, saying no one has ever been late on their first day... and then, she started asking if all Malaysians are like this... She even mentioned that out of all the excellent candidates, she hired me, particularly because of you..."

"Me?"

"Yes, you! I'm not sure what she implied by that though... She then began harping on about all the work we have to do, blaming me for throwing off her morning routine..."

"Okay, that sounds a bit too much... but sorry mate, at the end of the day, you were late and it was your first day... so your stance in this situation wasn't that great..."

"I get that. But it was too much, really... Also, I wasn't the only one who was late..."

"Yes, I noticed..."

"I accept I messed up the first-day arrival. But it felt like she was dumping all her stress on me like she had the right to do so."

At that moment, Jindo recalled the heated exchange he had heard in the showroom and Gabrielle's subsequent venting in the atelier. However, he chose not to share this with his sister, focusing instead on boosting her morale.

"I understand… Just try not to be late again…"

"It was the bloody metro for fuck's sake."

"Calma calma, you did oversleep though… Let's not forget that part, haha. I'm actually worried you'll be late again tomorrow."

"No, I won't be late, no way… Even if I have to stay overnight, I'll be on time."

"Good good, my man."

"What?"

"Sorry, excuse-moi Madame."

"Mademoiselle!"

"Okay okay, Mademoiselle!"

"Well, that's settled then."

"By the way, I still doubt you'll be on time tomorrow, haha."

"Me too, haha."

Despite the shaky commencement, Seiwa managed to maintain punctuality for the rest of the week, and her stellar work performance coupled with her affable disposition soon managed to overturn Gabrielle's initial unfavourable perception of her.

Chapter 14 : In the Shadow of Style

One lunchtime in the following week…

As Jindo and Seiwa prepared to leave for lunch, they found Gabrielle sitting on the couch, as she had done every lunchtime since the previous week. She and the office lady had taken up a station there, like bored cats lounging in a quiet countryside garage, seemingly awaiting attention yet prone to unpredictable mood swings.

"Are you not going for lunch, Gabrielle?"

Jindo ventured although he was not particularly invested in the response.

"I don't know."

She muttered, emitting a sulky vibe that no longer surprised him. Caught in awkward silence, Jindo offered the employee's politeness.

"Okay… Bon appétit."

Gabrielle did not respond, and Jindo was about to withdraw when she suddenly spoke up.

"By the way, did you finish the combinaison (jumpsuit)?"

"No Gabrielle, I'm still working on it."

"Good. Because there's a design change…"

"Okay, do you want to talk about it now?"

"…"

Her silence spoke volumes, leaving Jindo slightly perplexed. He offered an alternative.

"Or shall I come back early from lunch?"

"No, I have an appointment in the afternoon…"

"…"

Jindo was at a loss, unsure of what Gabrielle was driving at. Meanwhile, he wondered why she would not relay her instructions to Seiwa, her assistant designer. Yet, he held his tongue, waiting for the director to elaborate.

"Where do you guys go for lunch, by the way?"

"We go to the boulangerie, just across the street."

"Ah, I know that place. It's not good."

Gabrielle's blunt critique stung a bit. Though the boulangerie was not the finest establishment, he and Seiwa had chosen it for its affordability. The Parisienne lady, however, seemed intent on offering unsolicited advice.

"I know a better one…"

"Great, can you tell us where it is?"

"… it's hard to explain…"

Jindo was on the verge of asking for the name when Gabrielle threw him a curveball.

"Actually, I was planning to go somewhere else but I can go there for you today…"

"Ah… okay."

"But remember, I don't usually lunch with my workers."

"…"

Jindo silently bristled at her choice of words. Her lunch plans reeked of a thinly veiled ploy, and he found himself regretting his initial query. Gabrielle, however, was not done yet.

"Today, I'll take it as an exception because I need to tell you about the important design change, and I don't have time in the afternoon… I'll go there for you but I'm not having lunch with you."

"… okay…"

As they prepared to leave, Gabrielle rose, a sparkle of delight in her eyes. On their way to the boulangerie, she chatted animatedly about her likes and dislikes concerning local shops and restaurants. Strangely, she had little to say about the design modifications, leading Jindo to speculate that she might simply be yearning for company. He bore her monologue with an air of patience until they reached their destination.

Despite his initial reservations, Jindo found the unexpected stroll with Gabrielle oddly charming. He appreciated the casual interaction and the director's personal tour of the street, adding a unique flavour to their Parisienne lunchtime. Yet, the office lady, who had been silently shadowing the group from the beginning with her typical grumpy mood, added a tense undertone to their outing.

Upon reaching the boulangerie…

Jindo and Seiwa purchased their sandwiches and swiftly found a quaint table in the bustling outdoor seating area. Shortly thereafter, Gabrielle emerged, scanning the crowded café for an available spot. As her gaze landed on Jindo, he ventured.

"Do you want to sit here, Gabrielle?"

"Well, I… shouldn't…"

She began, her eyes darting around the packed establishment.

"Gabrielle, please…"

"… okay…"

Her response was hesitant and reluctant as if she acquiesced solely due to Jindo's earnest plea. Jindo was then about to request an extra chair for the office lady when the woman suddenly erupted in apparent anger. She and Gabrielle exchanged heated words in French, after which the office lady huffed off, mumbling to herself.

Throughout this heated exchange, Jindo could not help but notice a striking similarity in their manner of speech. Once Gabrielle had settled down, he dared to inquire.

"Gabrielle, can I ask who she is?"

"She's my mum."

"Pardon?"

Jindo and Seiwa exchanged astonished glances.

"She's my mum. You didn't know?"

"… no, I didn't."

"She's so annoying, I want to kill her…"

"…"

Jindo was slightly taken aback by Gabrielle's blunt disregard for her mother.

"She's always following me, being miserable all the time… Because of her, people can't approach me."

"Ah… By the way Gabrielle, I really didn't know she was your mum."

"Yeah, we look so different, no?"

"…"

Jindo refrained from commenting as he thought they shared quite a resemblance, particularly when being grumpy. Oblivious to his silence, the innocent daughter changed the topic.

"How's your sandwich by the way?"

Still reeling from Gabrielle's starkly disrespectful attitude towards her mother, Jindo sought to veer the conversation towards a safer territory.

"It tastes really good. Thanks very much, Gabrielle."

Despite a slightly higher price tag than their usual fare, the sandwich was indeed a culinary delight.

"This is my favourite boulangerie in Paris."

The lonely Parisienne seemed pleased with Jindo's approval and launched into a discourse about her preferences regarding sandwiches. For someone who had claimed she did not usually lunch with her 'workers', she appeared quite content in their company. The remainder of lunch passed in the wake of her ceaseless chatter, with the Asian siblings playing the part of her audience.

From that day onward, their lunches morphed into a tacit routine. Even though no formal agreement was made, Gabrielle always seemed to contrive a new reason to join them each day, whether it involved a discussion with the modéliste or the assistant designer. Seiwa was not particularly fond of these shared meals, but they had little choice as Gabrielle seemed perpetually poised on the couch, awaiting their departure. Meanwhile, her mother, Madame Claude, curiously vanished from the scene during these lunchtime rendezvous.

At lunch another day…

Jindo and Seiwa were accompanied by Gabrielle, contemplating the director's vision for the upcoming collection. By this point, Jindo had crafted numerous preliminary constructions for the new pieces, but he was growing anxious about the arrival of fabric and supplies yet.

"Gabrielle, have you received any updates regarding the fabrics and supplies?"

"I don't know, they're not replying… They're usually busy at this time of the season so don't worry, you just focus on the construction now…"

"Okay, no problem. I just asked because, for some details of the new models, I think the construction can be more precisely made if I do some fabric tests beforehand…"

"Don't worry, I'll help you when the time comes."

"… okay, thank you."

Despite Gabrielle's reassurances, Jindo remained dubious. At that moment, he was curious about the impending runway show.

"By the way Gabrielle, you mentioned we might do a runway show for this collection…"

"Yes, we might but… why do you ask?"

"I just wonder about the schedule. Because you told me we need to make it ready by mid-January for Paris Fashion Week and it's October now. I wonder if we just make the collection ready by January, then… everything will be fine for the runway? How about the fitting with the models for example…"

"If the collection is good, I have many contacts to call and they'll organise the event for me…"

"… is that how runway shows typically operate in Paris?"

"What do you mean, Paris?"

"… isn't the show in Paris?"

"Oh, No! I cannot do it in Paris. It's expensive, and it's normally organised with invitations, made a long time in advance… Of course, in my case, I can ask them if I want but I don't like to do it in Paris."

"…"

Gabrielle's arrogance, though a common occurrence by now, still managed to irritate Jindo. Nevertheless, he continued to probe for information.

"Then, where is it going to be?"

"These days, I have many invitations from China."

"In China?"

At that moment, Jindo found himself in a whirl of confusion. Gabrielle had initially mentioned the collection should be ready for Paris Fashion Week, but now she was saying the runway would take place in China. She carried on, oblivious to Jindo's bewilderment.

"Yes, even last year, I did my runway in Chongqing."

"... okay..."

Jindo was grappling with this sudden shift in plans.

"But, as I said, the collection needs to be good first."

"So, you mean if the collection is good, you can contact your Chinese network then they'll organise a showcase for you?"

"Yes."

"Okay then, how do we know if the collection is good?"

"I decide of course. The Chinese are just event organisers. They know nothing about fashion. They just want to invite European designers to make their show look international..."

Jindo nodded, partly understanding the Asian cultural tendency of endorsing Western references to enhance their event quality.

"Okay, I get it now... By the way, does this mean, if you decide the collection is not good, we don't do runway?"

"Of course, we don't. I'm the director!"

Gabrielle retorted, as though it were the most self-evident fact in the world. She continued.

"You think all collections do défilé (runway)? A lot of collections are dropped if they are not good... Even Coco Chanel cancelled a lot of her shows just before the event... You didn't know?"

"..."

Caught off guard by her reference to the legendary fashion house, Jindo held his tongue. The ex-CHANEL designer continued.

"Well, for example, when I was at CHANEL, I made an accessory collection, and it was supposed to be presented at one big hotel event in Paris, but it was cancelled a day before because the collection wasn't good..."

"Ah... who cancelled it by the way?"

"My boss."

"Your boss? You mean Karl Lagerfeld?"

"No, he's just the icon of the brand. There was a woman, and she was officially the second after Karl, but she was the actual leader of the team..."

The ex-CHANEL designer's tone was grating and condescending, but her story was indeed fascinating to Jindo.

"Ah, so she was your boss."

"Yes, but she did nothing actually... I think she just went to her position not because of her talent, but because she knew how to manipulate people. She may be talented, but I think, once she hired me, she knew I could do what she could do... so she basically made me do everything..."

Once again, Gabrielle's arrogance rankled Jindo, but his curiosity kept him engaged in her tales.

"It sounds like you did a lot of things at CHANEL."

Jindo ventured, prompting to hear more of the story.

"YES."

Gabrielle replied, her tone curt and her expression haughty. Sensing an opportunity, Jindo prodded her further.

"So, you were practically leading the team?"

"Yes. I was managing a team of sixty people…"

"Wow!"

"Basically, I was the first assistant to Olivia, but I practically managed the whole team. EVERYBODY KNEW…"

"… ah, okay… By the way, the second boss's name was Olivia?"

"Yes, you didn't know?"

"…"

Jindo held his silence, a bit miffed by her expectation that someone unfamiliar with the inner workings of luxury fashion houses would know her former boss's name. Yet, the brand's renown made him feel somewhat contrite. Unfazed, Gabrielle carried on.

"Anyway, one of the collections we made, like days and nights for months, was cancelled, because Olivia didn't like it."

"What did she not like about it?"

Jindo asked, his curiosity piqued.

"She said the rabbit looked so sad…"

"Rabbit?"

Jindo was hooked, keen to hear more about these captivating CHANEL anecdotes. Gabrielle, always one to favour the sound of her own voice, was equally eager to share.

"Yes, the collection was about a mysterious rabbit and... we placed different jewels to make up the face. It took us two weeks just to place the little articles to make up one eye only but in the end... Olivia said she didn't like it because the rabbit looked so depressed..."

"Because she said so, the collection was cancelled the day before?"

"Yes. The collection was great actually, but I think she just hated me because I was so talented..."

"..."

Jindo refrained from commenting, allowing her to continue.

"Every time I visited her in the sauna..."

"Sauna?"

"Yes, she was always in a sauna of an expensive hotel."

"Ah, I see."

"She always didn't listen to me, being hungover every day, telling me to do a lot of her personal favours then in the end... she never thanked me or approved the work that my whole team made for weeks and months..."

"I see..."

It appeared that Gabrielle had weathered challenging times at CHANEL. She continued.

"She actually did nothing. She was always drinking at night when I visited her house to report and she was a mother of two kids but always depressed, and never took care of them... I even looked after the kids sometimes. I helped with their homework in the evening..."

The story had been interesting, but somehow, Jindo felt the former CHANEL employee was now trying to dramatise herself in it. He also knew from his experience of Gabrielle by then, that she would not possess such a nice type of warm human nature.

"Anyway, I don't want to remember all that experience now. It's quite a bad memory to me…"

"Okay, sorry that I've asked…"

"It's okay. Anyway, I want you to just focus on the new construction now, and when the time comes I'll help you and we finish the collection… and then I'll decide if we do the runway or not. Okay?"

"Yep, well understood. Everything is more than clear now."

Jindo responded succinctly, recalling that the hand-talented young artistic director might not be the most articulate in verbally. Although he acknowledged that her narratives occasionally appeared to have certain gaps, it seemed somewhat evidential and indisputable that she had a wealth of experience in the luxury French fashion sector that Jindo lacked. On that basis, he realised that he should follow the ex-CHANEL designer's lead as she might develop and adapt the plan on the fly.

Chapter 15 : A Night of Nuances

One evening, drawing the day to a close...
Jindo and Seiwa were on the cusp of departing, chattering about the prospect of a convivial gathering at their school reunion later that evening. This conversation was a continuation of a lunchtime discussion, in which Gabrielle was also present.

Seiwa was casting a scrutinising eye over her appearance, while Jindo patiently awaited her. At that moment, Gabrielle emerged from her office.

"You guys are going to that party?"

"Pardon, party?"

"The soirée you were talking about at lunch."

"Well, it's not really a party, Gabrielle. We're just catching up with a few old mates over a pint…"

"Okay, I hope you have a good evening, but may I ask you something?"

"Certainly."

"In a big fashion house like CHANEL and Hermès, it's very confidential all information inside of the company must not be mentioned outside…"

"Ah, are you talking about the new collection designs, Gabrielle?"

"Oui, well… not just that. Everything!"

Jindo comprehended the director's apprehension, though he found it slightly absurd. To his mind, at Gabrielle's place, various traits in fact fell short of professional standards. Nevertheless, he chose to respond with patience and humility.

"No worries Gabrielle, we're just going to talk about our lives in general…"

"I'm not saying you never talk about your work, but you need to be careful anyway… You know what I mean…"

"Absolutely."

In the midst of their discourse, Seiwa had finally given her reflection the nod of approval. But Gabrielle, true to form, was far from winding up her impromptu briefing.

"By the way, we have a mountain of work next week, Halloween party preparations and all…"

"Halloween party?"

In typical Gabrielle fashion, she was springing a new project on them out of the blue. Seiwa, seemingly oblivious to the conversation, had discovered a flaw in her makeup and set about correcting it. Sensing the extra moment, Gabrielle was to take her usual jab at Jindo's supposed ignorance.

"Yes, Halloween is in two weeks… Oh, you didn't know?"

Anticipating her routine, Jindo did not rise to the bait but sought to understand the specifics.

"… I'm aware of the date… By the way Gabrielle, can I ask who this party is for?"

"… it's for our VIPs."

"VIPs?"

Jindo found this peculiar. As far as he understood, VIP lists were typically reserved for brands with long-standing reputations and client relationships.

As his sister was still preoccupied with her makeup, Jindo decided to probe further into this unexpected development.

"Gabrielle, what kind of party are we talking about by the way?"

"It's just a normal Halloween party... Oh, you've never been to one?"

Again, Gabrielle aimed to jest at Jindo's alleged naivety, but he adeptly circumvented her sly dig and steered the conversation back on track.

"I mean, what are our responsibilities in terms of preparation if it's just a casual event?"

"You need to fix the past season pieces, and Seiwa needs to create invitation cards, send promotional materials on Facebook, Instagram…"

Jindo noted Gabrielle, as usual, was about to imply a sense of urgency. As Seiwa seemed engrossed in her makeup corrections, Jindo attempted to further clarify the situation.

"Okay Gabrielle, I understand Seiwa's tasks. But me, fixing the past season pieces?"

"Yes, because, in the showroom, I'll place the past stocks for sale…"

"Ah, I get it now. So, it's a party but we're basically making a little pop-up store like private sales?"

"Oui, exactement ça."

"Okay Gabrielle, does this mean the new collection will be put on hold?"

"No... well... yes..."

It appeared the director had not considered that aspect. Jindo was still dubious about her management, but Seiwa finally seemed ready to leave. Jindo made his move to exit.

"Understood well, Gabrielle."

As the Asian siblings prepared to leave, Gabrielle attempted to underscore the urgency of their upcoming tasks.

"So, you now know we have a lot to do, and we don't have much time, yes?"

"…"

"I want you to have a nice time but… please do not play much, and rest well at the weekends because next week, it'll be super busy…"

"… Gabrielle, I get it."

At the reunion…

Jindo and Seiwa were thoroughly enjoying themselves, immersed in lively exchanges with their old-school chums. These were classmates from yesteryears, a tightly-knit group still united by their shared past.

In those days at the Paris fashion institute, an assortment of unique personalities from across the globe would converge, driven by a shared passion for fashion. This naturally fostered an atmosphere of individualism and competition.

However, the class Jindo and Seiwa belonged to was an anomaly, a fact their professor often remarked upon during her three-decade tenure at the institute. Their class was a vibrant mosaic of thirty individuals representing twenty-eight different nationalities, a spectrum of ages ranging from teens to forties, and a kaleidoscope of previous professions. Their ranks included a lawyer, a restaurant chef, a NASA engineer, a gallery curator, a prodigious American Generation Z who took up sewing at four, and a delightful Puerto Rican woman who came to Paris in search of a husband and eventually relocated to Florence with her Italian fiancé. Despite the variety of characters and personalities, the class maintained a strong bond, keeping in touch even after the completion of their course, a point of pride for their tutor.

Regardless, post-graduation, some returned to their home countries, while others decided to extend their stay in Paris to further pursue their projects. This evening, the reunion was a gathering of those who had chosen to remain in the city of lights.

Jindo and Seiwa were each engrossed in their own social circles. At such events, they typically split up to mingle and catch up with their other friends.

Wrapping up the reunion...

Jindo and Seiwa were ambling back to the metro station, their steps echoing in the quiet Parisian night.

"Oppa, you do realise Gabrielle behaves rather differently around you, right?"

"What do you mean?"

"She always primping herself before speaking with you. She even inquired if you had a girlfriend,"

Seiwa revealed with a knowing smile playing on her lips, but Jindo was not still in a proper sense of understanding.

"Well, I never felt anything from her for that kind of thing... She always talks about work and she's actually quite strict with me..."

"No, I think she just wants you around all the time..."

"Really? You think so? Well, I doubt it. She always throws over her fury to me like I am her personal irritation bin..."

Jindo feigned scepticism at Seiwa's observation, but internally, he was somewhat flattered that the ex-fitting model might fancy him.

"Oppa, you really didn't notice?"

"Nope, never..."

"Even today, when we're leaving, she tried so hard to keep you there..."

"That was just about work. She just wanted to inform me about the new schedule, you saw that, you were there too."

"No, it wasn't just about that…"

"I don't know what you're talking about."

Jindo continued to act doubtful, but inside, he was secretly pleased somehow. It might be due to that it had been a while and rare in fact, to hear that a nice-looking girl would fancy him.

"Oppa, it was bloody obvious, you idiot. I'm sure she's comfortable with you."

"You really think so?"

Jindo kept prodding Seiwa for more validation.

"Duh! I already told you she asked me if you had a girlfriend."

"Haha, so what did you say?"

"I said, you don't have one… then she asked what type of girl you usually go for."

"Haha, so what did you say about that?"

Jindo seemed to be relishing the conversation.

"I said, you like French girls."

"Why did you say that?"

"I don't know… but I know for sure, you prefer Western girls over Asians."

"No, piss off. I like any girl who is attractive. It's not fair to say I don't like Asian girls…"

"No, I know you like Western girls. You act differently when you speak to them…"

"No, it's just normal because, when you talk to people from other cultural backgrounds, you talk nicer."

Jindo was manoeuvring to avoid admitting his true preference, but Seiwa's shots were hitting the mark.

"(Seiwa, mimicking Jindo) *'Different, cultural, background, blah blah blah...'* Oppa, I know you have a thing for Western girls..."

"Okay okay... let me put it this way... I tend to fancy people from different cultural backgrounds because, that way, you respect more of the difference of each one..."

"(Seiwa, mimicking Jindo) *'Respect, the difference...'* Oppa, stop it. I know the truth..."

"Well, I do admit that I'm easily attracted to Western girls, particularly the blonde ones... but that doesn't mean I don't fancy Asian girls. You know, for instance, Xiao, I'd definitely go for her..."

Jindo attempted to cite one of their Chinese acquaintances to deflect the uncomfortable truth, but Seiwa showed him no mercy.

"Wake up, loser. She's like a superstar. You'd never get a chance, even in your next life..."

"에이 씨발 (swear in Korean), my point is... I don't just fancy Western girls because they're blonde or black or any other colour that is different from me, but it's just because they have different cultural senses that fascinate me personally..."

"Keep trying, you loser..."

As Jindo scrambled to wrest control of the conversation, he deftly changed tack.

"By the way, why do you even care? You yourself prefer Western men..."

"Simply true, haha."

It appeared that Jindo had successfully redirected the sister's scrutiny back onto herself as she swiftly shifted to a different topic.

"By the way Oppa, Xiao has a new boyfriend, and he's a famous photographer from Belgium."

"Belgium?"

"Why? What's the problem?"

Somehow, Jindo was reminded of Gabrielle's long-time friend painter who did all the graffiti painting of her establishment, but ignored the memory and continued.

"No, because I suddenly recalled a painter from Antwerp but no worries... Anyway, I'm happy for her..."

"Oppa, stop pretending like you're so gentle and generous for everybody."

"Piss off, I'm naturally nice as hell and I'm being so for my dignity."

"Dignity, my arse..."

Again, Seiwa came back to rib Jindo, and Jindo tried to steer the conversation back to Gabrielle.

"Anyway, be careful with your mouth to Gabrielle!"

"Why, you don't like her?"

"No, I mean... of course, she's pretty, fit and professionally... um... I don't know... she's a bit weird anyway..."

Jindo could not complete the mention of Gabrielle's professional success, possibly due to his subconsciously existing scepticism about the ex-CHANEL designer in spite of her insider story from time to time. Seiwa continued.

"By the way Oppa, one thing I know for sure is… Gabrielle is absolutely rude, and I think that's from her mum."

"You mean, Madame Claude?"

"Yes, you have no idea how exhausting it is to spend the entire day with the pair of them…"

"Why? What's the issue?"

"I'll fill you in later. I don't want to discuss that insufferable old woman tonight."

"Okay okay…"

Jindo was curious about Seiwa's problem with Madame Claude, but he was more preoccupied with gaining clarity about Gabrielle's situation.

"Anyway, don't talk about me too much to Gabrielle…"

"Why? What's the problem? I think you could go out with her if you want. She already seems to fancy you…"

"Stop it."

"What's the matter? I know you've been lonely since your girlfriend left you…"

Seiwa tried to nudge Jindo towards Gabrielle, but Jindo remained wary.

"She didn't leave me, it was a fine farewell for both of us…"

"Fine farewell my arse… I know you've been pathetically lonely for the last 2 years, always working and drinking alone… and even masturbating all the time for sure…"

"Piss off!"

"Haha… Seize the opportunity, old man. Time's running out… Meet a pretty French girl who, for reasons beyond me, seems to fancy you… and she even owns a company in the heart of Paris…"

"... I'm not sure..."

"Don't be a pussy, you always want to show off like a man... You always say, (Seiwa, imitating Jindo) *'I want to talk like a man, think like a man, and smell like a man'*, which is disgusting by the way... but look at you now, (Seiwa, imitating Jindo) *'Um... but um... I don't know, I'm not sure...'* Just make a decision like a man!"

Despite Seiwa's teasing and abusing, Jindo was hesitant, his self-doubt creeping in.

"I mean, why would she like me? There's no reason. She's pretty, fit, and professionally successful and she's even taller than me... and I'm just like a... nobody, trying to climb the career ladder at this bloody age..."

Seiwa remained undeterred, dropping a tantalising piece of information.

"By the way, just to let you know... Gabrielle's boobs are huge..."

"What? How on earth do you know that?"

"I saw her naked photos on her iPad. She was in a posh hotel swimming pool..."

Jindo kept asking for the details, but he could not deny that he was already imagining the ex-fitting model's body in his mind. Jindo tried to prompt to bring out more information to imagine further in a snaky way.

"Really? I never thought her size would be that big though..."

"Why?"

"Because I'm a modéliste, so I can roughly tell a woman's size when I look at them..."

"Haha, modéliste my arse... you never know a woman's real size before you actually see their naked body..."

"True but... okay."

Jindo was admitting Seiwa as she just made a fair point, and it was simply a fact that she knew what she was talking about since she had seen the evidence for the case anyway.

"Why? You got a boner?"

Seiwa was gearing up to tease Jindo again.

"No, piss off."

"Haha, you got a boner!"

"No, I don't like big boobs anyway..."

Jindo tried to escape, but Seiwa seemed to be in control of the moment.

"Ah, then you prefer little tities like Francesca's?"

"What? Why do you bring up Francesca now?"

"Because you've been watching her over the whole of last year..."

"Fuck off, I didn't."

"Hey loser, I saw you, always smiling at Francesca with that stupid open mouth of yours. I even saw you looking at her tities all the time..."

Seiwa was striking Jindo with another reference, Francesca, a talented, attractive Italian girl from Rome.

"No fuck off, I really didn't..."

"(Seiwa, imitating Jindo) 'No fuck off, I really didn't...' Oppa, don't be shy, nothing wrong with that, you're a man and Francesca is pretty and fit..."

"Well, she's not just pretty and fit but also nice and kind. That's why I smiled when I talked to her because she makes that happy vibe..."

"LAME!"

"에이 씨발 (swearing in Korean)... To be fair, Francesca was always wearing that white, nearly transparent, t-shirt with no bra..."

"Ah yeah? So, you couldn't avoid the sightseeing of her tities? Because it was already see-through? Oppa, you know you're quite pathetic."

"에이 씨발, stop talking about her boobs for fuck's sake... You think because you're gay you can just talk about girl's boobs like that? Like you're so innocent?"

"Oh, my sad little Oppa... Stalking his beautiful Italian love for a year, then she finally met her tall, handsome, successful, young & rich French boyfriend then went back home with him..."

"아 짜증나네 *(So annoying)*... Let me just make it clear. For me, she's just a nice person for whom I'm happy for good..."

Jindo kept denying the truth, pretending to be a nice person, and Seiwa continued to tease him.

"Wow, how gentle and generous you are!"

"I don't like your tone."

"Why? Does that remind you of Francesca's little tities?"

"You talk more, I'll rip your mouth up!"

"Wow, I'm so scared. A pathetic loser, who wants to smell like a man, is sad because his love isn't here anymore, and now... he's trying to hurt this little, cute princess for his little fury..."

"Seriously, if you don't stop it now I'm going to reconstruct your bones..."

"Oh no... no more construction, you so passionate modéliste who knows a girl's size by just looking at them when he actually knows nothing about nothing..."

"너 진짜 뒤질래?"

(You really want to get smashed?)

"By the way, I know you work so hard just to impress Gabrielle… probably to see her tities one day, haha."

"I KILL YOU NOW!"

Just like that, the siblings' playing session was done. Coming back home, Jindo was rewinding the conversation with Seiwa.

Initially, he could not help but smile at the thought of the striking French design director harbouring feelings for him. Yet, doubt cast a shadow over his delight as he pondered whether Gabrielle could genuinely be interested in him. As he tried to recollect past interactions, uncertainty still clouded his judgement.

Meanwhile, a wave of loneliness washed over him that evening, brought on by the realisation that the girls he had admired from afar were moving on, building new, fulfilling lives with their partners. In contrast, he was merely grinding away, honouring his stagiaire contract for minimal wages, striving to prove his worth to the employer who boasted of past experiences with prestigious luxury fashion houses.

He attempted to console himself with the thought that everyone had their own circumstances, motivations, and commitments. Yet, that night, the weight of his solitude felt unusually heavy.

Nevertheless, from that day onwards, his perspective of Gabrielle began to shift. He started to view her not just as an accomplished professional who was slightly eccentric, but as a lovely French woman who might actually harbour feelings for him.

Chapter 16 : Weaving Wonders

On the following Monday...
Jindo slid into work a mere two minutes before the officially designated hour, slightly tardy by his usual standards. Upon entering, he found a trio of young French girls stationed in the entrance foyer, their anxious expressions suggesting a long wait for Gabrielle. Anticipating that the notorious director might still be in the showroom, Jindo offered a brief salutation to the girls before descending to the atelier.

One of the girls, seemingly unconcerned, was engrossed in her mobile, idly leaning against the cartoon effigy stationed near the atelier entrance. The logic behind Gabrielle's decision to position such an oversized, near Madame Tussauds-like figure in this precarious location was a mystery to Jindo. Yet, he was cognizant of her peculiar fondness for the statue, treating it almost like a treasured childhood Barbie doll.

With this in mind, he fretted over the sculpture's delicate integrity, potentially compromised under the absent-minded pressure of the young girl. Yet, he was hesitant to chide someone he had only just met. Aiming to subtly raise the girl's awareness, Jindo cautiously nudged open the door, executing an overstated glance towards the figure to ensure it remained undisturbed. His silent message seemed to hit home, and, gratefully, the girl extricated herself from the dubious object.

Chiming at 9 am from the radio...

The atelier sprung to life, the radio serving as an impromptu town crier. The familiar echo of his sister, Seiwa's, footsteps signalled her arrival upstairs, and shortly thereafter, Gabrielle's authoritative voice suffused the air as she began distributing tasks. The novice director's tone struck as unusually firm that morning, leading Jindo to ponder whether she was flexing her charismatic muscle on the greenhorns.

Engulfed in the maelstrom of rescheduling for the abruptly revised Halloween event, Jindo relayed the schedule alteration to Boubacar. The veteran seamster appeared visibly miffed by the unforeseen upheaval, expressing his vexation more candidly than Jindo had ever witnessed. While Jindo sympathised with his agitation, he found it increasingly difficult to ignore the burgeoning chasm in their rapport.

In his thought, Boubacar, boasting decades of industry experience, should have been prepared for the unpredictability inherent to a small-scale atelier. Moreover, it should have been clear to him that the decision was not Jindo's to make, but was rather a directive from Gabrielle herself.

On one hand, it could have been a ripple effect from Jindo's previous private conversations with Gabrielle, but this time, he could not dismiss the frigid undercurrent in his colleagues' demeanour.

Choosing tact over conflict, he addressed Boubacar with measured restraint.

"Boubacar, tu sais, j'ai pas décidé ça. Pourquoi tu me parles comme ça?"

(Boubacar, you know, I didn't decide this. Why do you talk to me like that?)

Jindo's default mode was to address Boubacar formally using 'vous', so his switch to the less formal 'tu', coupled with his furrowed brow, signalled his mounting tension.

After a palpable silence, Boubacar started to formulate a response. Jindo felt awkward admonishing someone of Boubacar's maturity, yet he was resolute in refuting unfounded complaints. Discerning that Boubacar would not capitulate without further remonstration, he interjected to defuse the escalating tension.

"Excuse-moi Boubacar, j'ai pas compris ce que vous parlez. En même temps, je comprends pas aussi pourquoi vous… hah (exhales)… Excuse me, I just don't understand why you keep doing this. Because you seem to be complaining that I have no idea what it is. What's the point? Gabrielle made her decision, and I'm just following her and delivering the message… hah (exhales)… Comme j'ai dit, c'est pas moi. Je suis pas content aussi, pour ces changes tous jours… You're not the only one annoyed."

His French, though not impeccable, was sincere and he wove it with English to convey his sentiments more precisely. His elevated voice resonated with genuine emotion.

Boubacar was taken aback by Jindo's rare exhibition of frustration. Their gazes locked momentarily, the usually gruff seamster silenced by Jindo's evident strain and his uncommon propensity to converse in French.

Just when the tension appeared at a crescendo, Amélie intervened, expertly disarming the smouldering confrontation. Her fluency in both languages coupled with her amiable demeanour provided a welcome relief amidst the tense face-off. With the majority endorsing the mediator's intervention, both men retreated to their respective tasks, effectively diffusing the situation.

As the morning wore on…

The atelier hummed with diligent activity, each individual engrossed in their respective responsibilities. This tranquil scene was suddenly punctuated by a cacophony from the staircase, a series of echoing thuds heralding the descent of the new French interns. Clutching an assortment of garments as though they were irreplaceable relics, the girls were tailed closely by Gabrielle, engrossed as always in her mobile phone.

Gabrielle, exuding a sense of distracted authority, briskly directed the girls to deposit the fashion pieces onto Jindo's table. She then appointed one of them to work under Amélie's guidance. It was apparent that she was swiftly designating assistant roles amongst her fresh troops. With her recruits duly assigned, Gabrielle shifted her focus to Jindo, outlining his agenda for the day.

"Jindo, as I said last Friday, we need to fix the past season pieces…"

Jindo surveyed the garments scattered across the table; his gaze superficial yet evaluative.

"Okay, is that all?"

"… of course not. I'll bring more…"

His optimism seemed to rankle her. She responded as if she were a general with a bottomless supply of soldiers to deploy. Unperturbed, Jindo attempted to structure the impending workload.

"Okay, Gabrielle… Then, are you going to bring them all now?"

"Yes."

He probed further, seeking clarity on the specifics of his assignment.

"So, I just retouch the faulty parts of these pieces, right?"

"Yes, and you need to see every single corner as there may be many damages…"

"Okay Gabrielle, one question though… Is it not more efficient to inspect the garments in the showroom, and then only bring down the pieces that need repair?"

His question seemed to perplex Gabrielle, and he pressed on with measured caution.

"It's because we don't have a big space here… Also, it'll be even better for the girls, no need to move all the pieces by running up and down between the two floors…"

As Jindo navigated his explanation, he perceived the wheels turning in Gabrielle's mind, and not in a manner he found reassuring. Gabrielle, ever vigilant of her audience, seemed perturbed by the unexpected challenge. Her cultivated persona of charismatic leadership was threatened by Jindo's seemingly arrogant suggestion; a suggestion that, in the presence of the new interns, could be misconstrued as insubordination.

Her gaze flickered nervously to the two newcomers, silently witnessing the scene. Jindo could see her pride prickling, her feathers ruffled.

"… YOU'RE SAYING MY ATELIER IS PETITE?"

Caught off-guard by her sudden outburst, Jindo scrambled to defuse the situation.

"No Gabrielle, what I'm saying is that… if we bring all the garments here there won't be a space where I can properly place out each piece to find the faulty parts… So, it's not about the atelier size, but about the space management…"

"… NO, WE NEED TO MAKE A SETTING IN THE SHOWROOM, SO WE NEED TO CLEAN UP EVERYTHING ANYWAY."

"Ah, okay…"

As ever, Jindo found himself wishing Gabrielle could simply communicate her reasoning without resorting to dramatic outbursts. Yet he shouldered part of the blame. He knew her eccentric nature, how she would roar to mask her embarrassment when her authority was questioned, especially in the presence of audiences. So, he merely nodded in silence.

Sensing Jindo's submission seemed to pacify Gabrielle. With a triumphant sweep of her gaze towards the two petrified newcomers, she regained her authoritative aura. In this revitalised spirit, she commanded them to retrieve more garments from the showroom.

Gabrielle retreated, leaving Jindo amidst the clutter of garments sprawled over his workstation. He examined them with a fair eye, finding the style not quite to his liking but careful not to pass hasty judgment. It was since style, after all, was an individual's prerogative.

Meanwhile, he was taken aback by the pitiful state of the garments, grubby and damaged beyond belief. It was not a case of flea-market wear and tear but the clear manifestation of shoddy craftsmanship in their inception.

Gabrielle had initially described these pieces as once grand, their allure later tarnished by the reckless mishandling by 'influencers' and 'bloggers'. Yet, Jindo could not ignore the glaring reality in front of him. These garments were the vestiges of poorly executed designs, right from the initial fabric cutting.

To him, they bore the hallmarks of an arrogant fashion student's work, one who habitually missed classes, lacked genuine talent, and was too obstinate to accept constructive feedback. The shoddy workmanship did not stem from a fierce dedication to a unique vision but rather from a disinclination to exert any extra effort.

This revelation ignited another ripple of scepticism regarding Gabrielle's professed tenure as an ex-CHANEL designer. Jindo had strived to give her the benefit of the doubt, acknowledging that her expertise was predominantly in accessory design. Nevertheless, the garments before him fell disappointingly short. Even so, he reminded himself he was still getting acquainted with Gabrielle, making an effort to suppress his negative impressions as he plunged into his tasks.

The garments were lamentably damaged, but a safari coat topped the list of calamities. The body of the coat was crafted from wool, while the sleeves were leather, studded generously with a multitude of metal spikes. The spikes rendered the sleeves unbearably heavy, straining the seams connecting them to the bodice to the point of fraying and near rupture.

In fact, the spike trend had seen its popularity surge a few years back, largely propelled by Christian Louboutin. Jindo could appreciate Gabrielle's nod to this trend. However, the decision to marry bulky leather sleeves with a lightweight wool bodice, supposedly sourced from Malhia KENT, was a fashion faux pas.

With a resigned sigh, he manoeuvred the coat onto the fitting mannequin, taken aback once more by its surprising heft. It reminded him of a dumbbell or the ammo boxes he had handled during his military service. While Jindo could appreciate the fashion maxim that discomfort could sometimes be overlooked in the name of style, Gabrielle's coat did not qualify. He had attempted to view Gabrielle as an artistically inclined designer who prioritised aesthetics over practicality, but this disregard for fundamental wearability crossed a line he had not foreseen.

In those days, Jindo held a belief that any design, at its core, needed to be viable. He had experienced many occasions where grand designs had been struck down by insurmountable technical issues, curtailed by time constraints and limited resources.

He was aware of the argument that an overemphasis on technicalities could potentially stifle artistic creativity. Nonetheless, he stood by the conviction that there should be a mutual understanding between designers and technicians. It seemed unfair for one party to bear the brunt of failure when faced with unfeasibility. The crux of the matter was compromised; each party should be willing to temper their capabilities and aspirations.

At this point, Jindo was becoming increasingly convinced that Gabrielle, despite her unwavering beliefs, demonstrated a scant understanding of garment design and construction.

At that moment, the weight of the safari coat toppled the mannequin. As Jindo bent to retrieve it, he heard the distinctive sound of Gabrielle's approach. Swiftly, he hoisted the coat, pretending to examine it attentively.

Accompanied by the two girls, Gabrielle arrived, her arms laden with more garments. With a careless sweep, she cleared a space on the cluttered table and laid out the newly delivered items. She turned to Jindo, her face donning a courteous smile.

"Jindo, these are my personal clothes, and I plan to sell them at this Halloween party."

"I see..."

"But, because I left them in the wardrobe for a long time, there are many parts to be retouched..."

Jindo bit back a sigh of irritation. He felt as though the director was treating him as nothing more than a 'retoucheur'. In addition, her logic also perplexed him, surely garments left untouched in a wardrobe should not present any issues.

Nonetheless, Jindo had become accustomed to Gabrielle's often bewildering rationales. Instead of countering her, he embraced this chance to lay aside the ammo-box weighted, safari coat from his hands.

"Okay Gabrielle, can I have a look?"

Spread before him were pieces from celebrated fashion houses; a skirt from CHANEL, a sweater from Lanvin, a blazer from Yves Saint Laurent, and an assortment of jeans from Balmain, among others.

At that moment, a particular detail on the CHANEL skirt caught Jindo's eye, a label stamped with 'PROTOTYPE'.

Jindo had once served as a personal shopper, traversing Europe to procure diverse items. His quest had taken him to official boutiques, private sales, outlets, warehouses, and fashion dealers. He had even ventured into select black market platforms where leaked pieces from elite labels were discreetly offered to a handpicked clientele. But even in those covert circles, he had never encountered a piece bearing a 'PROTOTYPE' stamp.

Given that this was his inaugural encounter with such a label, he was intrigued.

"Gabrielle, is it a prototype?"

"YES, I got it when I was at CHANEL."

Her response brimmed with pride.

"Gabrielle, can I ask how you got this prototype?"

"I got it from the private sale."

Although Jindo had believed he was well acquainted with the myriad of private sales scattered throughout Paris, he also knew of certain select affairs, limited to those clutching exclusive invites or the lucky employees themselves. Yet, CHANEL holding private sales was news to him. He had always known that Hermès and Louis Vuitton preferred to send their surplus stock up in smoke, but CHANEL's practice had remained an enigma. His curiosity was well and truly piqued.

"Gabrielle, is there a private sale at CHANEL?"

"Yes, but it's not for the public. It's for the EMPLOYEES…"

She emphasised the last word, raising an eyebrow suggestively, teasing him with her words. Despite the mild irritation her taunting induced, Jindo was keen to learn more.

"That's interesting. Because I didn't know CHANEL does private sales…"

"Yes, they do. But like I said, it is for the EMPLOYEES ONLY."

"…"

The hint of exclusivity in her repetition irked Jindo as if she were emphasising a divide between them. Nonetheless, it was yet another instance where Gabrielle offered a tantalising clue about her possible association with CHANEL.

There she stood, basking in her moment of self-assumed importance. She casually removed the bag slung over her shoulder.

"And, this is one of my CHANEL bags."

Jindo raised an eyebrow. The notion of the young director possessing multiple CHANEL bags was not only surprising but also intriguing. However, he struggled to understand the motive behind this theatrical display of a luxury item that was, quite frankly, more suited for a feminine audience, not Jindo. Nonetheless, she continued her show.

"This is a limited edition, there was only one piece made."

"… okay… great…"

Jindo tolerated her ostentatious display, though not without some measure of reservation. The bag did not seem to warrant such acclaim since it was rather unkempt with its exterior marred by visible wear and tear.

In part, he suspected it to be a mere prototype that Gabrielle had acquired from the private sale. The emphasis on its 'limited edition' status struck him as a feeble attempt to inflate its worth. Deciding to navigate past this unnecessary bravado, he gently steered the conversation back to the main issue at hand.

"Okay, Gabrielle… So, what is the problem with this CHANEL skirt then?"

"Eh?"

A faint blush of embarrassment tinged Gabrielle's cheeks as her moment in the spotlight was cut short. Nonetheless, she recovered quickly.

"Ah… the zipper is not working…"

Upon swift examination, Jindo ascertained that the faulty zipper was indeed beyond repair.

"Gabrielle, I think this needs to be replaced. But… I'm not sure if we can find any similar zipper to this because both the size and design look like custom-made by CHANEL, and it's not even a common type…"

"OF COURSE, it's special. It's CHANEL…"

"…"

The room was engulfed in silence. Gabrielle soaked up the astounded expressions adorning the faces of the two young French girls. Keen to curtail Gabrielle's lengthy monologue, Jindo resolved to deliver the final word.

"Gabrielle, this is something that Boubacar and I can't fix without a proper supply."

"Okay, never mind."

The conversation wrapped up as abruptly as it had started, and Gabrielle went on to pile up the other clothing items.

All bore similar problems, and Gabrielle seemed indifferent to the fact they were beyond repair. It became evident that her primary intention was merely to show off. Her audience was not Jindo, but the young French girls. She was simply using Jindo as a prop in her solo performance.

Jindo could not help but notice the quality of the other items was somewhat lacklustre as if they originated from the secondary distribution channels like outlets or private sales. In fact, having handled garments from various channels including the official boutiques, Jindo had developed a keen eye for discerning qualities of the different platforms.

In those days, the discrepancy in quality between outlet-sourced garments and boutique-bought ones was significant. Second-tier distribution items often had minor flaws like misplaced labels, buttons, or prints, or fabric irregularities like weaving stains.

While Jindo maintained his scepticism, Gabrielle seemed to relish her moment in the spotlight. Having collected her belongings, she retreated, accompanied by the girls who appeared quite impressed with the wardrobe collection of the former CHANEL employee.

As usual, Jindo felt somewhat manipulated by Gabrielle's antics, but at that moment, he had little time for contemplation as Boubacar was vying for his attention.

Chapter 17 : Tailoring Tensions

A few days passed...
Jindo was retouching one of the past season's pieces. A quilted doudoune jacket, composed of a confounding array of panels; each a different shape, combined to form a camouflage print. One could speculate on the designer's intentions, perhaps seeing it as a testament to diversity; a veritable symphony of different elements harmonising in a single garment. Nevertheless, the grand total of eighty-seven panels, crafted from nine disparate fabrics, led Jindo to question whether this truly was the only way to convey such an intent.

Stitching together variously shaped panels from an assortment of fabrics is not akin to solving a complex jigsaw puzzle. Rather, it poses a challenge far greater, fraught with the high risk of complications arising during the assembly process.

From Jindo's perspective, the jacket's style was fairly pedestrian, yet it demanded an exhaustive amount of work. The resulting piece, though laborious in its creation, failed to elicit that desired 'wow' factor. Regardless of his thoughts, Jindo reminded himself that taste would be subjective and refrained from passing further judgment.

Meanwhile, he found himself pondering the jacket's price. The estimated workload suggested that the young director would barely break even unless the jacket fetched a price in the thousands of euros. However, since Gabrielle had earlier revealed her exclusive focus on business-to-business transactions, the elusive price tag remained unknown to Jindo yet.

Regardless, the jacket demanded his attention, particularly a peculiar issue he had spotted in the form of the back side, more specifically from the shoulder to the right hem. Jindo was earnestly trying to discern the cause.

Initially, he identified that the panels around the problematic area had been improperly sewn. He proceeded to consult Boubacar, querying whether there had been any complications during the prototyping process.

"Excuse-moi, vous avez fait ça?"

(Excuse me, did you do this?)

"... oui... pourquoi?"

(... yes... why?)

Boubacar responded, albeit hesitantly, a sense of discomfort surfacing at Jindo's probing inquiry. Unperturbed, Jindo pressed on.

"Parce que c'est bizarre ici. Pourquoi il y a le pli ici?"

(Because it's strange here. Why is there a pleat here?)

"... je sais, mais il y avait beaucoup de problème dans le patron…"

(... I know, but there were many problems with the pattern…)

The seamstress appeared ill at ease, but Jindo made an attempt to assuage his concerns, clarifying that his intention was not to criticise.

"Oui, je comprends. Je vous demande, pas parce que je pense, il y a des problèmes avec votre travail, mais je veux juste trouver le problème à fixer."

(Yes, I understand. I am asking you, not because I think there is a problem with your work, but because I just want to find the problem to fix it.)

"…"

Boubacar remained discomfited. Jindo deduced that the seamstress felt compelled to defend himself, as he was not to blame for the problem at hand. Jindo continued in his attempt to offer reassurance.

"Boubacar, je comprends que c'est pas le problème avec les coutures, mais je pense que, probablement il y avait des problèmes dans la procédure de couper le tissu, ou le patron comme vous avez dit."

(Boubacar, I understand that it's not a problem with the assembly, but I think, probably there were problems from the fabric cutting or pattern as you said.)

"…"

Boubacar responded with silence, his face a portrait of displeasure.

Frequently, the relationship between a seamstress and a modéliste could be likened to that of a head nurse and a doctor. This analogy suggests that an experienced seamstress, akin to a seasoned nurse, might not appreciate unsolicited nitpicking from a modéliste, particularly when their professional experience diverges significantly.

Nonetheless, it was incumbent upon Jindo to identify the issue. The problem, he discerned, lay in the mismatch of shape and measurement across the panels. The seamstress might have taken liberties in the assembly process, a move that likely precipitated additional complications elsewhere in the piece.

Jindo set about devising a strategy to address this convoluted, albeit somewhat trivial, problem. He had little desire to invest an inordinate amount of time rectifying a single jacket when a myriad of other pieces clamoured for his attention within a rather tight timeframe.

After a bout of brainstorming, Jindo came to the realisation that the task was not as simple as fixing a single part. The interconnectedness of the issue meant that rectifying one element would inevitably lead to others requiring attention, resulting in a tedious and time-consuming process of consecutive adjustments. He concluded that even with significant effort, the outcome was far from guaranteed. Hence, he proposed a more radical solution, to replace the entire problematic zone altogether.

Jindo communicated his proposed plan of action to Boubacar, the seamstress. Boubacar, however, appeared uneasy, concerned about whether it would be acceptable to proceed without Gabrielle's stamp of approval. Jindo placated his fears, ensuring him that his suggestion would not alter Gabrielle's designs, but rather streamline the modification process.

Meanwhile, Jindo had a sneaking suspicion that should he ask the enigmatic Gabrielle for her input, she would likely not know any alternative method. Instead, he thought, she would probably insist on her own preference, a preference she might not even be entirely cognizant of.

At that moment, the sound of Gabrielle's footsteps echoed from the stairs. Boubacar's face lit up and he promptly went to meet the director as soon as she set foot in the room.

In animated French, he seemed to pour out his grievances to Gabrielle. Jindo watched, irked by what appeared to him as tattling. Gabrielle, taken aback by Boubacar's directness, nevertheless listened to him with patience.

Boubacar concluded his spiel, his eyes twinkling with anticipation for what would follow. His gaze landed on Jindo; his face was stern, yet held a trace of mirth. Gabrielle turned to Jindo with a question.

"Jindo, did you try to change my design?"

"No Gabrielle, is that what he said?"

Jindo responded, but his eyes remained locked on Boubacar. Gabrielle noticed the tension simmering between the two men and rephrased her question.

"... Boubacar just told me that you're changing my design..."

Jindo, visibly perturbed, let out a slight sigh, his gaze turning icy as he looked at Boubacar. Nevertheless, he needed to address Gabrielle first.

"Gabrielle, I didn't change your design. I just tried to replace the problematic part of the jacket as a whole, rather than fixing every single panel one by one… And I want to do it that way, just because it would be faster and more effective in my opinion."

Jindo's focus remained steadfast on Boubacar, while Gabrielle found herself playing a game of tennis with her gaze, volleying between the two men. Seeing Jindo in a state of stress for the first time, she decided not to fan the flames further.

"… okay, we'll do it your way then."

Gabrielle communicated her decision to Boubacar, who appeared displeased with the outcome. He began to remonstrate with Gabrielle, his voice escalating sharply. Gabrielle, taken aback by his sudden vehemence, looked perturbed.

Jindo, despite not fully grasping Boubacar's rapid French, felt a sense of injustice. He was of the belief that his proposed method would simply reduce the risk of unsolvable outcomes for both himself and Boubacar, nothing more, nothing less. He was confounded as to why the seamstress was so vehemently opposed to the proposal when, in his view, it was a matter not worth such contention.

On one hand, Jindo speculated that Boubacar might be getting further upset since Gabrielle appeared to be siding with the modéliste, not him. Considering their differing tenures at the company, Jindo supposed that Boubacar, being more seasoned than him, might have felt a sense of betrayal by the employer.

Meanwhile, Jindo found it increasingly difficult to stomach Boubacar's continuous bickering with the designer over such a trifling matter. It was distasteful to witness the young director being berated by her own employee. Indeed, it was not the first time that Jindo had seen members of the atelier speak harshly to Gabrielle. This time, he decided to intervene.

"Excuse-moi, Boubacar. Quel est votre problème? Why do you keep complaining about this? Let's be fair. I'm trying to make the work efficient, and now you're complaining about what? I just don't get it…"

As Jindo's tension rose, his voice became louder and his speech in the mixed languages faster. Boubacar fell silent, visibly taken aback by Jindo's interjection. The two men locked eyes as the room fell into an uncomfortable silence. Gabrielle looked flustered by the escalating tension, while the other members of the team halted their work to observe the unfolding drama. Jindo continued.

"What is it that you keep talking about to Gabrielle? Which is the part that makes you upset? I just really don't understand. Je comprends rien. Excuse-moi, Boubacar. Je comprends pas…"

Despite Boubacar's subsequent attempts to dismiss Jindo and engage Gabrielle directly, Jindo continued to interject, addressing him in a rapid blend of languages, his voice ever louder and faster than Boubacar's. The seamstress looked visibly upset but ultimately ceased his argument.

Meanwhile, during Jindo curtailing Boubacar's complaints, Gabrielle seemed increasingly impressed with the modéliste. Perhaps it was Jindo's protective zeal, reminiscent of a loyal dog guarding his owner against a boisterous stranger, that stirred her admiration.

Indeed, it seemed Boubacar had enjoyed a certain autonomy in his role by then, granting him the freedom to navigate constructional issues during the assembly process. This autonomy enabled him to solve problems in his own unique style, with nary a word of criticism or suggestion from others.

However, with Jindo's arrival, tasks now were meticulously planned and prepared, complete with instructions. The rhythm and volume of work also fell under the modéliste's purview, who even estimated the time each task would require. Undoubtedly, the seamstress resented the loss of control, leading to a deepening chasm between him and Jindo.

In this fractious dynamic, Gabrielle appeared oddly content. She seemed pleased that Jindo not only managed to keep the atelier members at bay but also stood by her side when they attempted to overpower her.

Chapter 18 : The Crating Conundrum

The following morning…

As Jindo approached the premises, he noticed six young students lingering outside the company. The group was clearly divided; two older students stood apart from the four younger ones. After confirming they were visiting Gabrielle's establishment, Jindo led them inside.

He advised them to wait for Gabrielle, who was presumably in the upstairs showroom, before descending to the atelier himself. As the radio chimed 9 am, the atelier began to fill with staff.

The upstairs area hummed with the chatter of the students, particularly the younger quartet, as they impatiently awaited Gabrielle's arrival. After an awkward ten-minute wait, the notorious director finally appeared to meet the students and promptly led the two more mature-looking ones downstairs.

Introducing them to Jindo, Gabrielle mentioned they were fashion college students who already possessed a foundational knowledge of the field.

Jindo was somewhat perplexed at the sudden influx of young students. Even more so, he pondered why he had been cast in the role of mentor when he himself was here to learn. He yearned to address these queries with Gabrielle but, observing her bustling interactions with the students, decided to hold his questions for a later time.

Without warning, Jindo found himself entwined in the unexpected responsibilities of supervising these novices. The two allocated ones, Julien and Hélène were both striking in appearance, impeccably dressed, and brimming with youthful energy. Julien claimed familiarity with constructional paper pattern work, prompting Jindo to assign him the task of copying pattern bases for the new collection. Hélène, boasting experience in fabric cutting, was instructed to prepare muslin for draping.

Their preparedness was impressive; they followed Jindo's instructions with diligence and sought clarifications on their tasks before diving into the work. It was evident that they were earnestly keen to learn and accomplish their missions.

About ten minutes later...

Gabrielle descended once again, this time with two girls in tow. One was assigned to Amélie, the other to Timothée. The girl accompanying Amélie, Mina, whom Jindo warned when she was leaning against the Madame Tussauds-like sculpture before, engrossing her mobile, was notably vivacious, bringing a burst of energy into the already bustling atelier. While Jindo could only speculate about Gabrielle's motives, he suspected she intentionally separated this lively girl from the rest.

Once Gabrielle retreated, Amélie and Timothée commenced task briefings with their respective assistants. The girl with Timothée seemed placid and perfectly comfortable working with him. In stark contrast, Mina appeared disinterested in her atelier duties. She sighed continuously and fiddled with her mobile phone, blatantly ignoring Amélie's explanation of their tasks. Upon being told to leave her phone aside while working by Amélie, she sulked in silent protest. Amélie's disdain was palpable, and Jindo sensed she was biding her time before requesting Gabrielle to replace this disinterested novice.

Several hours had elapsed...

On the brink of demonstrating the draping process with Hélène's prepared muslin, Jindo found himself under the eager gaze of the students including Hélène and Julien. Their first real-life encounter with draping work was imminent, their whispered anticipation filling the room. Jindo, feigning deep concentration on his task, took pleasure in their curiosity.

To the uninitiated, the art of draping could be a captivating spectacle. Jindo recalled his former modélisme tutor's jest about the theatrics of draping, how the process should make for a good show. The same tutor, however, was quick to stress the importance of humility in the craft. Modesty and humbleness were at the heart of her teachings.

At that moment, the bubble of the students' excitement burst with the arrival of Gabrielle. Taking in the tableau of all the newcomers riveted by Jindo's imminent demonstration, a ripple of annoyance crossed her features. She hissed at the students to return to their duties, then turned a baleful gaze on Jindo. It seemed as if she attributed the gathering to him, suspecting he had solicited this attention.

Jindo, however, read the situation differently. Gabrielle's irritation stemmed not from the lack of industry amongst the students but from the focus of their interest in him. The miffed director then posed a question to Jindo.

"Jindo, what are you doing?"

"Um... I'm... about to do draping for this skirt of the new collection?"

"Why are you doing that? Did you fix all the past season pieces?"

"... no, not yet. They're on the way..."

"I told you to repair the past season garments first..."

"... Gabrielle, I'm doing it. As you see, Boubacar is fixing the shirt, and on his left, the next two pieces are in waiting..."

"Are these three pieces the last ones?"

"No, we still have many more to go..."

"Then, why are you not fixing the rest?"

"… me? Fixing the pieces? You mean I do the sewing?"

"…"

Gabrielle looked embarrassed as Jindo seemed to have asked her an unexpected question. Jindo continued.

"Gabrielle, I don't mind sewing but we have one sewing machine… Apart from that, I don't want to give Boubacar all the pieces at once because it might be confusing for him… I'm just trying to manage the rhythm…"

"… then how long would it take to finish all the pieces?"

"… I don't know Gabrielle, but Boubacar and I are doing our best, and all will be done before the Halloween event anyway."

Though she maintained a semblance of discontent, Gabrielle seemed to acquiesce to Jindo's reasoning.

Meanwhile, Boubacar, catching snippets of the conversation and his name in Jindo's speech, seemed uneasy. His grasp of English was not comprehensive, adding to his discomfort. Gabrielle noticed his nervousness, and rather than comfort him, seemed pleased at his quiet compliance. Boubacar, usually grumbling, had now grown reticent, especially with Jindo mediating their interactions.

Flashing an odd countenance, and an unhappy smile, Gabrielle then donned her poncho and headlamp before heading into the storage area, seemingly on a retrieval mission.

Returning minutes later, she bore a dusty box that she proceeded to unload. She spread out several white cotton t-shirts adorned with cartoon characters across Jindo's already crowded workspace as if she wished to flaunt some achievement.

"These are t-shirts from my collaboration with Disneyland Paris."

Again, Jindo was confronted with tangible proof. Despite his best efforts to remain optimistic about Gabrielle, he could not deny that he had harboured many doubts about the famed designer yet. Such exhibits, however, allayed his scepticism temporarily, compelling him to engage in conversation.

"Wow, this is great... is it still in the shop at Disneyland Paris?"

"Yes, of course."

Pride radiated off the designer as Jindo pursued further.

"Great, Gabrielle... By the way, how was it to work with Disneyland? It's just such a big company."

"Hm... they're annoying because they cut the cost too much."

Gabrielle's face shifted into her customary scowl, but by now, it had lost its shock factor for Jindo. He simply continued the dialogue.

"That's surprising because I think they'll be generous as they're a big company..."

"No, they know they have the power, and they know I'll do it anyway even if I don't make any profit."

Jindo nodded, comprehending her point. It was a scenario all too familiar to young artists who would readily work for free if it meant partnering with a globally renowned entity.

At that moment, Seiwa arrived to consult with Gabrielle, and the two promptly initiated a discussion. During their conversation, the curiosity of the young girls was piqued by the array of t-shirts laid out before them. Yet, they hesitated to approach the table, possibly dreading another potential outburst from the formidable director.

Eventually, Mina bravely ventured to the table, prompting a domino effect; the rest followed suit, browsing through the t-shirts. Their faces lit up with the marvel of Disneyland prints, a sight that seemed to please Gabrielle.

After wrapping up her conversation with Seiwa, Gabrielle proudly watched the young girls admiring her collaborative work. Seiwa herself began to browse through the t-shirts and spoke up.

"Wow! Are these from your Disneyland collaboration, Gabrielle?"

"Yes."

As Gabrielle visibly revelled in her moment of pride, Seiwa continued her commentary.

"I adore Disneyland. I want to go there again."

"Oh, have you been there?"

"Yes, Madame."

"But you just went there as a visitor, no?"

"Er... yes."

Seiwa seemed perplexed, but Jindo understood that Gabrielle was merely drawing a line between her own status and Seiwa's.

"I'm a special guest there, so if you go with me, they'll treat you like a VIP."

"Really? Can we go together someday Gabrielle?"

Feigning enthusiasm, Seiwa indulged the director though Jindo could see right through the act.

"Well, I'm too busy for that..."

"Oh, that's a shame..."

Seiwa played her part perfectly, expressing faux disappointment. After this exchange, she ascended the stairs, leaving Gabrielle to bask in her moment of glory, watching the young students continue to appreciate her collaboration with the famous theme park.

As Gabrielle proudly displayed the T-shirts, Jindo's mind wandered back to a past collection's photoshoot, located in Disneyland Paris. The designer's behaviour often puzzled him, raising questions about her proclaimed high-profile status. Her fashion knowledge seemed inconsistent at times, but undeniable evidence, like the Disneyland collaboration, kept popping up. These contradictions kept his scepticism in check; the puzzle pieces of doubt were not yet fully assembled.

Regardless, the proud Disneyland collaborator proceeded to prepare a handful of the t-shirts for ironing. She intended to include them in the private sale at the Halloween event. Ever the helper, Jindo offered to iron the garments for the busy director, but she swiftly dismissed his offer, underlining that the t-shirts were a 'limited edition'. According to her, she alone could handle them without damaging their exclusive allure.

At that moment, a loud crash echoed from upstairs. It appeared that Mina had an accident on her way back from the loo. Gabrielle, abandoning her ironing midway, rushed upstairs to investigate. A stream of reprimands poured forth, even Madame Claude emerging from the office to chide the poor girl.

The mum and daughter presented a united front, chastising the girl together. Following their lead, Jindo also went upstairs to gauge the situation. Apparently, the boisterous girl had been careless while opening the door, inadvertently damaging the famous Madame Tussauds-like cartoon sculpture.

After a few minutes, the disciplinary proceedings concluded, and Mina descended, looking utterly dejected. She returned to her place without uttering a word.

Lunchtime…

Jindo and Seiwa were with Gabrielle, and the director's mood was still tainted by the morning's incident, her lingering frustration appeared to be redirected towards Jindo.

"Did you not tell the girls to be careful with the door open?"

"… me?"

"Yes, you're supposed to be a manager for the people."

"… pardon? You mean the students?"

"I told you I need a manager to look after people."

In fact, Gabrielle had never mentioned the managerial 'authority' to Jindo yet implied the managerial 'responsibility' on occasions.

"Gabrielle, I'm confused… You mean I have the authority to manage people?"

"… no, you don't have any authority, but I told you to be responsible…"

Jindo remained bemused by her statements. He could not reconcile her assertion of his supposed 'responsibility' with his lack of authority. Regardless, setting the issue aside momentarily, Jindo attempted to suggest a practical solution.

"Gabrielle, I think it'll be better if we move the sculpture somewhere else. I think the spot is too vulnerable."

"You're saying it's my fault to put it there?"

Gabrielle's countenance clouded over with irritation. Jindo hastened to pacify her.

"No no, I just meant to suggest that the piece would be safer if it weren't positioned so near the door…"

"NO! That's my brand SIGNATURE."

"…"

Jindo was bemused; the object in question was a large cartoon character toy from a popular animation series, hardly her own design. Gabrielle's claim it was 'her brand signature' left him profoundly confused.

Regardless, he realised arguing about such a tangential matter would be futile. Attempting a different approach, he once again pressed his proposal.

"Gabrielle, I was just saying that any clumsy person might break it again later."

"I'll kill them then."

"…"

Jindo was left speechless, appalled by the obstinacy of the eccentric director. Her childish refusal to entertain reason was almost laughable, but the menacing undercurrent in her tone suggested a cruel streak. The designer, reminiscent of a Cruella de Vil impersonator, was not finished.

"She was just stupid. I even burnt my exclusive Disneyland piece because of her…"

"You mean because you left the iron on the t-shirt?"

"YES. So stupid…"

"…"

Then, the director began hurling personal insults at Mina.

"It never happened before. She just had bad home education… Look at her, she's noisy, looking for wiffy (Wi-Fi) all the time for her cheap mobile phone..."

"…"

Jindo was taken aback by Gabrielle's venomous tirade. The moment she let her guard down, her inherent nature reared its ugly head; unabashedly prejudiced and alarmingly rude. Unperturbed, she continued her diatribe.

"And look at her clothes... She even comes from a banlieue (suburban)."

"Gabrielle…"

As it was going extreme, Jindo attempted to subtly intervene, fearing the conversation was veering into dangerous territory. He was conscious of the risk of others overhearing the distasteful conversation.

In fact, Jindo had heard of some Parisians being overly concerned with their prestigious central Paris postcodes, but Gabrielle's expression of her disdain was repugnantly explicit.

Nonetheless, Gabrielle, wrapped up in her vexation, was disinclined to let the matter rest.

"What? You don't know about this problem in France. She definitely comes from an immigrant family, and they probably all live together like twenty people in a stupidly small house… You don't know how many social problems those people make in this country…"

"…"

Given that Gabrielle was delving into national issues, matters he certainly held no 'authority' to engage in, Jindo remained silent. Instead, he broached another topic.

"Gabrielle, how did she come to your company by the way?"

"She's from some école, and they normally contact me if I have a place for their students… I say okay, and then they send the students. I don't have a choice…"

Gabrielle's tone suggested she perceived herself as hard done by, a sentiment Jindo found puzzling. After all, she was essentially utilising the young students as unpaid labour, delegating to them tedious, mundane tasks, and chastising them when they failed to deliver. Seeking to delve deeper, Jindo pressed further.

"Is there another option? Like not accepting the students?"

"Well, I could but I want to provide the young people with field experience…"

"…"

Jindo was left scratching his head in confusion. The reality was that Gabrielle predominantly employed the students for menial labour, such as cleaning. Moreover, her and her mother's conversations with the students were frequently laced with condescension, so palpable that even a non-French speaker could discern the tone.

Regardless, lunch came to an end, and days continued in its peculiar rhythm. With nine inhabitants crammed into the small atelier, the atmosphere teetered on the brink of pandemonium.

Chapter 19 : A Tapestry of Tensions I

A week before Halloween…
The atelier buzzed with chaotic energy, brimming over with a party of twelve individuals. The original inhabitants of the place, four team members and a quintet of students including Julien and Hélène had been infiltrated by an additional trio dispatched from her office (the studio). The notorious director justified her decision by citing a lack of space in the studio.

Jindo grappled to make sense of the situation, feeling an uncanny sense of injustice. After all, the studio harboured an equal number of students, yet two were permanently sequestered in the showroom. This fact was conveniently overlooked, and the remaining three were shoved into the atelier. Consequently, only Gabrielle, Seiwa, and Madame Claude inhabited the studio, replicating the times when students were yet to invade their space.

Eager to iron out the creases in the predicament, Jindo approached Gabrielle, only to meet with her customary irritable and stubborn demeanour. She countered with an anecdote from her time at CHANEL, claiming that her dedication to work had seen her cutting fabric on the floor due to space constraints. She skilfully wove in a dash of sarcasm, remarking that a devoted worker would always find a way, regardless of space or tool availability.

Though her point held merit, Jindo found himself sceptical about the authenticity of her personal account. However, his attempts at highlighting the difference in their situation were deftly dodged by the elusive designer who hurried out of the atelier citing her busyness.

Jindo decided not to amplify his concerns to avoid discomforting the innocent girls overhearing their exchange. However, the problem of space was ever-present. Boubacar, Amélie, and Timothée appeared undisturbed, given their designated workspaces, their only issue being the boisterous chatter of the new studio girls. Jindo found himself the solitary soul left to wrestle for a workspace amidst the mêlée.

Gabrielle initially proposed that the girls could assist the modéliste team, but Jindo struggled to find suitable tasks for them. Modélisme required a certain level of basic knowledge and the right tools; two resources scarce in Gabrielle's domain.

Nonetheless, the girls adapted well to the atelier, enjoying their tasks and exploring the new environment. An adorable detail was their collective infatuation with Timothée, characterised by hushed whispers and soft giggles. Their frequent questions to the hatmaker were nothing more than excuses to engage him in conversation. If their attention became too overwhelming, Amélie would gracefully intervene.

Despite the girls' obvious interest, Timothée was masterfully oblivious, laser-focused on his work and nonchalantly cold towards his admirers. Ironically, this seemingly aloof demeanour only intensified their attraction. Jindo found the entire tableau rather charming.

Regardless, Jindo and Boubacar were engrossed in their endeavour to revitalise past season pieces. Only a handful remained, albeit intricate or obstinate in their issues.

This afternoon, Boubacar found himself in a bind with a particular piece, mystified by Jindo's modéliste instructions.

"C'est bizarre ici… parce que ça marche pas comme ça."

(This is strange… because it cannot be done this way.)

The crux of the problem lay in the cuff of a shirt, where the seam allowance was tragically damaged. Therefore, Jindo's instructions to salvage the damaged part using the remaining seam allowance were out of the question. Quick as a flash, Jindo suggested shortening the sleeve length to procure the needed seam allowance.

Boubacar was hesitant about the idea of shortening only one sleeve. Jindo sought to reassure him, explaining that a mere centimetre would not be a significant issue for this type of oversized shirt. The precise seamstress, however, remained unconvinced. Jindo felt compelled to step in, engaging him in a private conversation.

"Boubacar, si nous voulons être précis comme ça, je pense que on a deux options. *(if we want to be that precise, we have two options.)* La première, we could raccourcir cette manche à la même façon. *(First, we could shorten this sleeve in the same fashion.)* That, I think, n'est pas really nécessaire maintenant parce que it's not comme we're making un brand-new prototype. The deuxième option could être to remplace tous les manches avec du nouveau tissu. *(The second option is to replace both sides with new fabric.)* But that, je pense, pas possible aussi parce que on n'a pas de tissu pour l'instant. *(But that, I think, is not possible either since we don't have the fabric at the moment.)* Most importantly, je pense pas si on a assez de temps for either of these solutions... *(I don't think if we have enough time for either of these options...)*"

Jindo articulated his thoughts in hushed tones, mixing two languages, keen to avoid drawing the students' attention to the compromise in professional integrity. He was not eager to highlight the shirt's initial poor craftsmanship or subsequent neglect. Furthermore, he was of the opinion that efforts were better directed towards garments with minor issues rather than those that were beyond salvation and largely soiled.

Yet, Boubacar clung to his professional principles, prompting Jindo to clarify.

"Boubacar, ne me comprenez pas mal. Je suis pas unprofessional ici mais c'est juste une chemise très grand, oversize… Les gens ont besoin de fold the sleeves to wear anyway…"

(Boubacar, don't get me wrong. I'm not being unprofessional here but it's just a piece of oversize shirt… People need to fold the sleeves to wear it anyway…)

"…"

The dedicated seamstress held his silence, face etched in disagreement. Jindo then deemed it necessary to reveal the inherent flaw in the initial production.

"Hang on…"

Armed with a measuring tape, Jindo assessed both sleeve lengths. His hypothesis was proven correct; there existed a two-centimetre discrepancy in the lengths. He demonstrated this to Boubacar.

"See? C'est differente originally… En fait, we're lucky parce que le côté problématique est le plus long. *(The problematic side is even longer.)* Donc, let's reduce it by 2cm, then it'll be the same. We're actually making it better alors…"

Jindo concluded his explanation with a wry smile, subtly infusing the moment with his customary sarcasm.

In fact, Jindo found himself grappling with the issue of juggling multiple tasks at once. He was managing six people including Boubacar, a situation which necessitated swift decision-making on his part. However, the veteran seamstress, ever the perfectionist, was stubbornly adhering to his high standards, a trait Jindo appreciated but considered impractical under the circumstances.

Since the perfectionist was still in his unsatisfied mood, Jindo took a moment to address him directly.

"Boubacar, on a pas beaucoup de temps. Je pense que c'est mieux si on concentre sur les pièces qui sont déjà dans une bonne condition, pas la pièce comme ça. Vous me comprenez?"

(Boubacar, we're pressed for time. I believe it's best if we focus on the pieces already in good condition, not ones like this. Do you understand?)

"Oui oui…"

Finally, Boubacar seemed to acquiesce to the modéliste's concern and then looked around at the five people surrounding Jindo. It seemed like the seamstress now understood Jindo's circumstances and ceased his objections.

At that moment, Jindo noticed a young blonde girl from the studio showing a keen interest in Boubacar's work. Flashing a smile at Boubacar, he inquired whether the seasoned seamstress could use her as his assistant.

Boubacar appeared to grasp what Jindo was implying and gave a composed nod of agreement. He welcomed the intrigued student to his side, outlining how she could aid him by fetching necessary couture supplies. Jindo conveyed his quiet gratitude to Boubacar, before turning his attention to the remaining studio girls, who were still idling and chattering in the confined space.

Jindo delegated them tasks of crafting accessories such as headbands and brooches, inquiring Amélie to give a demonstration. The accessory designer led them with a certain cynicism, swiftly grabbing the girls' attention.

Being typically wary of Amélie, the girls promptly ceased their frolics and plunged into the task at hand. Having sorted out this group, Jindo finally made his way to his assistant modélistes.

Julien and Hélène had been observant, noticing that Jindo was perpetually occupied, juggling Boubacar and the studio girls. Hence, they had opted not to pester him with an abundance of questions. Instead, they quietly aided the modéliste, meticulously organising materials so he could resume his work without delay.

Unlike the younger students, who appeared timid in speaking English, Julien and Hélène were quite confident. Though not exceptionally fluent, Jindo appreciated their effort, fully aware that he should be the one communicating in their native language.

Regardless, the modéliste team was diligently progressing with the new collection. Julien was crafting a paper model as per Jindo's instructions, while Hélène traced lines on muslin, following the markings from Jindo's draping work. Both of them appeared gratified with their tasks, enthusiastically declaring that they were gaining invaluable insights.

Approaching Julien, Jindo could not help but detect the lingering scent of alcohol, an echo of the previous day's indulgence. He jovially remarked that Julien's tardiness that morning was now explained, prompting a shared chuckle. Turning his attention to Hélène, he noted her concentrated effort to trace a line on the draped muslin using a Japanese ruler. Despite her lines being somewhat less than impeccable, Jindo found her endeavour endearing.

In the realm of manual modélisme, there are a variety of rulers. The two most prevalent ones are typically referred to as a Japanese ruler (aka a grading ruler) and a French ruler (aka an armhole ruler). While the Japanese variant is employed for general purposes, the French one is designed to deal with curves, like those found in necklines and armholes.

Having said that, when it comes to sketching curvy lines in draping, certain complexities arise. Some angles simply do not yield easily to the French ruler. Furthermore, many drapers want to have an overarching view of the lines they are tracing. As such, they tend to favour the Japanese ruler, even for curvy lines.

Nevertheless, sketching a curved line with a Japanese ruler calls for a certain finesse. To maintain precision, the ruler must be smoothly rotated, just a touch at a time, through deft finger movements. This method, looking somewhat suave, often impresses beginners.

Yet, arguably, it could be nothing more than showing off, as those elusive curves could indeed be traced with a French ruler.

Regardless, Jindo observed his female assistant trying to emulate his performance. Her serious expression and carefully orchestrated finger movements as she minutely twisted the ruler were somewhat endearing, though her lines still lacked sophistication.

"Hélène, you could just use a French ruler."

"Eh? Sorry, I was just..."

She looked a tad embarrassed, but Jindo was quick to assuage her concerns.

"I may be wrong, but I think you just want to precisely trace your lines by looking at what forms you are drawing. Am I correct?"

"Yes, you're right. I feel I can visualise the entire form better this way."

"I understand it, but it needs a bit of practice... It's nothing special, but still, you need practice..."

"Yes, that's why I'm trying here."

"I appreciate that Hélène, but the muslin you're tracing on, is something that we all work together... I do the draping, you trace the lines, Julien transforms it to paper, and then I rework the paper with the initial draped muslin... So, I think it'll be better if the muslin is to be clean, just for all parties to see it clearly. Does that make sense?"

"Ah sorry, I was just..."

"No need to apologise, I'm just explaining why it's important that the traced line on the draped muslin remains neat... We're a team, after all..."

"Yes, okay."

"Just practice on paper or any other leftover muslin until you feel comfortable then it'll be fine. But for now, please use the French ruler."

"Okay, Jindo."

Hélène seemed to well understand the rationale behind Jindo's words. They shared a smile of quiet agreement. Indeed, her actions were quite charming to Jindo, taking him back to his early days when he had tried to emulate his modélisme tutor.

At that moment, a sudden wave of steaming air caught Jindo's attention. Turning to locate its source, he found Gabrielle, directing a steely gaze in his direction. She appeared to have descended to collect the repaired garments, an event that Jindo did not expect. What particularly disconcerting was Gabrielle's demeanour, resembling an irate feline impersonating a fire-breathing dragon.

Eerily silent, her gaze darted between Hélène and Jindo. However, unlike previous encounters, she did not seem interested in an investigation. Swiftly and forcefully, she grabbed the completed garments from their hanger, departing without uttering a word.

Jindo was left feeling uneasy by her wrathful aura, but with no immediate solution at hand, he returned to his work.

Chapter 20 : A Tapestry of Tensions II

A few days before Halloween...

Hélène's discomfort was palpable from the start of the day, prompting Jindo's concern. He noted her trembling and perspiring, yet she showed no inclination to discuss it with him. She made frequent trips upstairs, presumably to the restroom, but Jindo refrained from prying. He suspected it was something personal.

As lunchtime approached, Hélène returned from another of her frequent trips. This time, however, signs of recent tears were evident, her eyes puffy, her face paler. Still shaking and sweating, she seemed particularly distressed, prompting Jindo to speak with caution.

"Hélène, I'm not sure what's going on, but perhaps you should talk to Gabrielle and leave work early today…"

"… I've just been to see her, and she told me to stay…"

"… you told her about your condition?"

"Yes, but she told me to stay, or I leave the work and don't come back…"

"… okay."

Jindo was aware of Gabrielle's strictness, particularly with the young female staff members, but this situation seemed different, bordering on medical concern.

Lunchtime…

Jindo was with Gabrielle.

"Gabrielle, have you heard about Hélène?"

"Yes, why?"

Merely at the mention of her name, Gabrielle's face began to contort with irritation. Treading carefully, Jindo continued.

"… I mean… she seemed not well today."

"I know, she came to see me three times this morning when I was SUPER BUSY."

"… Okay then, can I ask why she can't leave work early?"

"Why do you want to know? She asked you?"

Gabrielle maintained a piercing gaze on Jindo as he cautiously carried on.

"… no, I was just wondering about it, because I could see that she was not in a condition to work…"

Gabrielle exhaled sharply, then voiced her thoughts.

"Hah… she said she's on her period, and sometimes she has a very hard pain, and today is the day…"

"Ah…"

Jindo's suspicions were confirmed. However, he refrained from further discussion, conscious that he, being a man, lacked first-hand knowledge about the severity of such female issues. Gabrielle proceeded.

"You know girls sometimes lie about their period… just to escape from work…"

"… I think Hélène is not that type…"

Jindo gently defended his assistant, inciting Gabrielle's temper further.

"WHAT? How do you know? You only saw her less than two weeks."

"I mean, she has been doing well here as far as I saw… and I suppose she wouldn't be the type of person who would lie just to leave work early…"

"WHY ARE YOU SO PROTECTIVE OF HER?"

The irate director seemed to grow more agitated.

"… I'm not protective of her at all. I just saw her trying hard to endure the pain… but I could see that she's not in a condition to work…"

"She's just faking. I think she fancies you. I saw her smiling at you all the time…"

"…"

Jindo was left speechless as the underlying issue started becoming clear. Unabated, Gabrielle went on.

"She's too young, she needs to learn… When I was at CHANEL, I used to work day and night, and during my period, I sometimes worked without knowing it. My colleague told me that I had blood on my pants, so I changed it then got straight back to work…"

The self-proclaimed workaholic director boasted about her stint at the renowned fashion house. She continued.

"EVERYONE said, I'm a PRICELESS labour."

"Gabrielle, you're great but that's you. Hélène is still young…"

Jindo tried to argue in favour of his assistant, but Gabrielle appeared unwavering in her stance.

"She's not a child. She's over twenty years old… Just ignore her, you're a man, so you know nothing about this. She's just trying to get attention from you…"

"…"

Lunchtime passed in this fashion, with Hélène staying until the end of work hours. Jindo knew the female assistant had skipped lunch and had been physically ill several times even during the afternoon. Nonetheless, he held his tongue and offered her encouragement as she left.

"Hélène, well done today, and have a good rest."

"Merci."

A part of Jindo worried that Gabrielle might unexpectedly show up at that moment, but, fortunately, she was nowhere to be seen this time.

Chapter 21 : The Mosaic of Mystique

The day before Halloween…

Seiwa was engrossed in perfecting the showroom setting, flitting between floors from the atelier to the top floor. She orchestrated a team of five girls, showcasing an innate ability to guide them much like a little shepherd herding a flock of sheep.

This time, she descended to the atelier, fetching the Lady Gaga photo from the wall, prompting Jindo to enquire.

"Seiwa, what are you doing?"

"Gabrielle told me to put this in the showroom."

It appeared that the renowned designer intended to embellish the private sale area with a photograph of the global superstar, ensuring it was visible to shoppers.

"Okay, anyway how is it going upstairs? Is everything ready now?"

"Oppa (Jindo), I don't have time to talk. I need to finish this asap."

"Okay, calm down tiger. You still got a lot to do?"

"No, it's nearly done, but I just need to leave work on time today."

"What? You got a date?"

"Haha, you know me… Yes, I have a date. I'll tell you later…"

"Haha, okay, now I see why you dressed up nicely today."

"Excuse me? I'm always shining…"

"Okay okay, good luck."

Just like that, Seiwa wrapped up the showroom setup and exited right on time. As the other atelier members dispersed, it seemed that Jindo was the only one left behind.

He was scrutinising the work of Julien and Hélène and organising the following workday's tasks for the team, including Boubacar. Suddenly, he heard Gabrielle descending.

"Ah Jindo, you're still here. Good!"

She feigned surprise at Jindo's presence, an odd reaction since she was surely well aware that the modéliste, who functioned akin to an atelier manager at her behest, typically stayed late to review and plan for the next day. Nevertheless, she began to speak.

"I'm screwed… The DJ and beverage sponsor just cancelled their visit."

It seemed she was in a quandary concerning the catering service she had arranged. Jindo recalled the well-networked director's proud assertion that she had secured a famous DJ and numerous beverage suppliers eager to sponsor her event. Jindo probed.

"Why have they cancelled?"

"I don't know, they just called me, saying that they're not coming."

"Both of them?"

"Yes."

"Do they come from the same agency by the way?"

"…"

Caught off guard by his unexpected question, Gabrielle seemed momentarily embarrassed.

"I don't know Jindo, I'm screwed…"

True to her nature, she failed to delve into specifics, merely expressing her dismay and frustration.

"Then how are you going to deal with it?"

"I DON'T KNOW, Jindo…"

The disheartened director gave the impression of being on the verge of tears, though Jindo could not shake off the sensation of being observed. It seemed she was anticipating something from him, though he had yet to fathom what exactly she desired.

As he was still preoccupied with organising the modéliste team's workload, Gabrielle broke the silence.

"I can prepare some drinks, but I can't be at the bar as I need to welcome the guests."

Suddenly, the penny dropped for Jindo.

"Gabrielle, do you want me to be at the bar?"

"…"

She seemed pleased by his offer, though she did not respond immediately. It seemed she was expecting him to elaborate. Jindo acquiesced.

"I can be at the bar. I've never worked at a proper bar, but I used to work at a Japanese restaurant and Starbucks in London, so I know how to serve a drink if that is okay with you…"

"Really? Can you do that for me?"

"Yes, it won't be a problem."

"Oh, thank you Jindo. Thank you, you're saving my life!"

Gabrielle's countenance visibly brightened. Jindo was unfazed by the prospect of assisting the flustered director, though he pondered the other unresolved issue.

"Gabrielle, how about the DJ part then?"

"Ah, can you do that too?"

"No, sorry I don't know how to do that. I was just wondering…"

"It's okay, I can just play my SoundCloud."

"Ah… okay."

Apparently, the DJ's absence was not as catastrophic as initially feared. Nevertheless, the director's initial disappointment seemed to have evaporated.

In fact, only the studio members were rostered for the event, not those in the atelier, and they were promised the following Monday off in return. Jindo, however, did not see it as a significant issue.

The director, now visibly relaxed, engaged Jindo in conversation.

"By the way, did you see the showroom yet?"

"No Gabrielle, I haven't."

"Do you want to see it now?"

"Yes, but could you let me finish this last bit of my organisation first?"

"Ah, yes."

As Gabrielle patiently waited for the unofficial atelier manager to wrap up his work, she appeared pleased with his evident sense of responsibility towards his allocated role.

Meanwhile, Jindo could not help but feel slightly bothered by the director's impatience. She fiddled with his pair of scissors and hummed a fast-paced tune beside him. Hastening his tasks, he swiftly completed his work and they ascended to the showroom together.

Chapter 22 : Shadows of Style

En route to the showroom…
Jindo and Gabrielle ascended from the atelier, and the mistress of the house opened the portal to the showroom, revealing a passage, barely wide enough for a single individual.

Traversing the corridor led them to a curvaceous, slim staircase, likewise restrictive in its allowance for single-file movement. With Gabrielle leading the way, they finally reached the famed showroom.

"Be careful!"

Gabrielle's sudden warning jolted Jindo, causing his gaze to drop to the small section of glass flooring underfoot. Lying inconspicuously at the end of the staircase seemed almost a trap for the unwary.

Jindo, however, was more intrigued than alarmed. He connected the dots; this was the glass ceiling he had spotted in her office. A quirk of the architecture allowed visibility into the room below. It became apparent that the director wished to maintain constant, albeit indirect, surveillance over her studio. Armed with this insight, Jindo surveyed the showroom.

The walls were a riot of thematic graffiti art, offering a visual feast. Gabrielle, following her routine, proceeded to expose yet another stratum of her artistic universe. Yet, as was often the case, Jindo found the imagery oddly disconnected from her spoken narrative.

In particular, he grappled with Gabrielle's penchant for visualising her utopian ideals. While she verbalised these as radiant and positive, the scenes she manifested were somehow dark, even melancholic in a surreal way.

Regardless of how whimsy she imbued into her animated characters, they exuded a disconcerting air, an undercurrent of cannibalistic tendencies reminiscent of the office paintings. Yet, unlike the visuals in the studio which appeared to want to devour the visitor, the works here bore a subtle variation; the characters seemed poised to toy with and beguile the guest in a slightly intoxicating manner, somehow sensually.

To the untrained eye, the showroom was artistic; its composition was thoughtfully curated. However, a closer examination and a moment spent absorbing the ambience triggered an unnerving sensation in Jindo, instigating a desire to make a hasty retreat. Nevertheless, the novice visitor kept his cool, offering nothing more than rhythmic nods in sync with her narrative, all the while feigning engagement.

In fact, the showroom was a touch more generous than the studio and the atelier, yet it maintained the sealed ambience of the other floors, lacking windows and surrounded by graffiti-laden walls. Meanwhile, since the area had been designed as a private sales space, it bore no particular highlights yet.

Five racks stood in a line, the first four bearing pieces from previous collections. Most showcased the fruits of Jindo and Boubacar's recent labours; a quick review brought flashbacks of the past fortnight's intense toil and occasional friction with the seamstress.

Examining the collection as a whole, and not as items requiring repair, Jindo recognised the experimental nature of Gabrielle's designs. They did not scream 'innovation', rather they echoed the iconic styles of notable French fashion labels.

It was akin to someone attempting to replicate recognisable motifs but failing to achieve finesse due to an absence of requisite savoir-faire. In plain terms, Gabrielle's pieces were riddled with shoddy finishings, not as an artistic choice, but a reflection of incompletion.

Moreover, Gabrielle's creations were often overwhelming, teeming with too many elements within a single piece. It reminded Jindo of an overzealous chef who aimed to create a unique pizza by putting elements altogether from Hawaiian, kebab, tandoori and Margherita recipes. Worse still, it was as though the chef was incapable of perfecting even one of the borrowed dishes, betraying an all-consuming desire for recognition rather than mastery.

In fashion, there are intentionally unfinished pieces, categorised by various types such as 'raw finishing'. This method leaves fabric edges unwoven, as seen in some remarkable pieces from Martin Margiela's collection.

However, upon close inspection, these seemingly 'unfinished' details are usually completed in their own way. For instance, they might be stitched with an invisible thread to avoid future issues. This demands a certain technique, born of long-time know-how. The gap between 'a finished unfinished look' and 'an unfinished finished look' is more considerable than one might assume.

Regardless, Jindo migrated to the final row of racks. Here rested pieces from Gabrielle's personal wardrobe, the supposedly exclusive items from prominent labels. These, Jindo with his former personal shopper's insight, identified as second-line distribution, including an embossed CHANEL bag.

Jindo surmised that Gabrielle aimed to portray this particular rack as a luxury line. However, it fell short of creating the desired ambience from his standpoint. Still, he offered no critique, merely posing a question.

"Are you also selling all of these luxury items?"

"No, not all, just a few, they're just for display… Well, if somebody really wants it, I'll think about selling them but… these are very rare items…"

As she spoke, Gabrielle unhooked the CHANEL bag from the stand, the strap seeming to give her a touch of trouble, and gingerly slung it over her shoulder. Jindo acknowledged her tactic, though he was not entirely convinced of its effectiveness.

At that moment, Jindo spotted the photo of Lady Gaga that Seiwa took from the atelier, tucked discreetly behind the racks. He realised the collaborative designer had crafted a journey for her visitors; peruse her past collection, marvel at the luxury items then be confronted with the image of the global superstar. This sequence was intended to lend a certain gravitas, potentially influencing their buying decisions.

The narrative was understandable. Gabrielle hoped to portray herself as a designer formerly affiliated with high-profile labels, evidenced by her collection of 'exclusive' (seemingly prototype or faulty) items. She then transitioned into her personal label, boasting a collaboration with an international icon.

Despite Gabrielle's display strategies, what troubled Jindo most was the frankly deplorable condition of the items on show. The garments were, quite frankly, grimy. While Gabrielle had a habit of blaming influencers and bloggers for mishandling her pieces, it was no longer a matter of damaged parts that had since been mended.

Even though this was a private sale and the items could reasonably be expected to be slightly used, Jindo maintained that cleanliness would be a pivotal factor in sparking buyer interest.

In those days in fashion private sales or outlets, there were occasionally damaged items on offer. Buyers were usually willing to overlook minor faults, as long as these would not affect wearability. However, when an item was dirty, regardless of its style or uniqueness, it typically deterred potential purchasers.

Oblivious to Jindo's internal critique, Gabrielle continued her showroom tour, and it was increasingly painful for Jindo to observe the proud designer peddling her decidedly unhygienic pieces. He chose to remain silent and turned his gaze elsewhere, whereupon he discovered a large bathtub tucked into one corner.

"Wow, you have a bathtub here."

"Eh? Oh, yes, it's SPECIALLY made for me."

Caught off guard by Jindo's abrupt change of the subject at first, Gabrielle swiftly transitioned into presenting her purportedly custom-made bathtub. Jindo, feigning indifference to the ever-unique director's spiel, approached the bathtub for a closer look.

As Gabrielle prattled on about the exceptional qualities of her bathtub, Jindo quietly examined its contents. It held a selection of headbands, small clutch bags, and brooches, creations of the young interns. They were displayed much like impulse buys at the Carrefour checkout, akin to those irresistible little bags of potato crisps.

While Jindo considered this an imperfect way to display these handmade items, his main objective was to dodge Gabrielle's relentless grandiloquence. His eyes then landed on a clutter of luggage and furniture a few steps away from the bathtub, which, unsurprisingly, was also in a grubby, disordered state.

Hoping to derail Gabrielle's verbal onslaught, he posed a new question.

"Gabrielle, are these going to be on display like this tomorrow?"

"Eh? No, I'll place a stand blind and there'll also be mannequins... So, people won't see any of these..."

"Okay."

Relieved to have successfully interrupted her, Jindo quickly fired another question to pre-empt a resumption of her monologue.

"Do we have mannequins though? Because I haven't seen any."

"My friends are bringing them now."

"Your friend?"

"Yes, he owed me a lot. So, whatever I ask him he'll always do it…"

The self-claimed, well-connected director appeared to be quite pleased with herself.

At that moment, Gabrielle's phone rang.

"Oh, it's him…"

She engaged in a brief phone conversation, and it seemed her friend would be late. Hanging up, Gabrielle elaborated.

"My friend needs to go back to his office because one of his employees made a stupid mistake, so he had to deal with something urgent…"

It appeared her friend was also a business owner.

"Okay, is he also in fashion by the way?"

"No. Well… his wife is like a designer but she's not like me, she's just… no nothing really… Anyway, I actually helped them set up their own company…"

There seemed to be more to this story, but Jindo decided not to dig deeper.

Passing by 7 pm…

The delay of Gabrielle's friend's visit left her with surplus time on her hands, the time she seemed intent on spending with Jindo.

"Do you also want to see the top floor?"

"Well… okay."

Jindo responded, expressing a muted interest in her proposal.

As they manoeuvred the winding staircase, Jindo observed books standing erect on each step. The aesthetic was clear, if slightly hazardous.

Meanwhile, he discovered that the steps curled treacherously high and rather narrow. Littered with literature, it scarcely offered enough space for a firm footing. It seemed almost inevitable that an unwary foot might knock over or tread upon these bibliophilic hazards; one misplaced book could trigger a literary domino effect, books tumbling down to the ground floor in a cacophony of ruined pages.

The scene kindled in his mind the memory of the Madame Tussauds-like sculpture at the atelier door, that Mina had clumsily damaged. Regardless, cautiously trailing after Gabrielle, he noted the recurrent theme; the books bore covers stamped with the name 'CHANEL', a vast array, undoubtedly, but all fixated on the iconic designer.

For some, this might appear a meticulously curated collection. To Jindo, however, these books were mere trophies from common vintage bookshops in Paris, just another facet of Gabrielle's ostentatious decor. Still, he feigned ignorance, adopting a look of surprise.

"You have a lot of CHANEL books, Gabrielle."

"Yes, I've been collecting them since I was a child…"

The self-proclaimed collector wore her boast with pride.

"Voilà."

At that moment, they reached their destination. In her typical fashion, the proud house owner began the grand unveiling of her 'play space'. As described, it was clear this was the realm of the cartoon aficionado; character toys held court at every turn.

Directly opposite the staircase was a glass floor, reaffirming Jindo's theory about the director's penchant for overlooking her dominion, even from the highest floor.

Navigating a wide stride to avoid the voyeuristic glass panel, Jindo found, to his expectation, a glaring lack of windows on this level as well. On one hand, he attributed this to her desire for privacy. Yet, the recurrent theme of disconcertingly graphic graffiti wall murals evoking cannibalism sent a shiver of discomfort skittering up his spine.

With Gabrielle engrossed in her tour, Jindo took the opportunity to investigate the space further. A comfortable sofa, a sleek projector, and a shiny PlayStation console commanded the room's central area, indicating that this floor was designed as a sort of leisure nucleus.

Nearer to him, a shelf stood, packed with a miscellany of DVDs. His curiosity was piqued, and Jindo found his attention inexorably drawn towards this varied collection.

An aficionado of cinema, he could not resist perusing the titles. His brows knitted together as he noted the dominant genre, 'male crisis'. He recognised the titles, echoing the curriculum of a film class he had once taken at university. The shelf housed a compilation of classic movies that followed; Donnie Darko (2001), Blue Velvet (1986), Falling Down (1993), Fight Club (1999), Memento (2000) and more.

Jindo found it doubtful that this collection belonged to Gabrielle, but he refrained from voicing his suspicion yet and opened the conversation elsewhere.

"Gabrielle, I didn't expect you would have a PlayStation."

"Well, it's not really mine. My boyfriend bought me, but I don't play much... Ah! EX-boyfriend..."

Jindo discerned her emphasis on the 'EX', taking the cue that she was single now. He remembered Seiwa's assertion that Gabrielle might harbour an attraction towards him. Though he had not given it much credence by then, something in her tone made him reconsider. Oblivious to his internal deliberation, Gabrielle pointed out the PlayStation's uniqueness.

"By the way, this PlayStation is a limited edition."

"I can see that."

"Ah, you also have a PlayStation?"

"No, I have an Xbox but I know nothing about video games. I bought it myself as many people seem to have fun with it, but I just feel it's not for me... I prefer to play football with feet outside."

"Me too, I also think these video games are stupid. I just use it for Netflix."

Her dismissive remark slightly rubbed Jindo the wrong way, but he chose to let it slide.

"... I mean, if some people like it, that's great. But in my case... to be honest, I don't even have many friends to play with, so it's just not for me..."

"Ah, sorry."

"No, it's fine. Don't get me wrong. I came to France to work, and I want to work now."

"Me too. I'm also always for work, and I don't have many friends too..."

"..."

A strange bond suddenly seemed to form between them, united by a shared sense of solitude and a workaholic mindset. For a moment, they stood silently, locked in mutual understanding.

Jindo could not quite articulate it, but there was an undeniable spark of connection. As this fleeting moment began to fade, he sought a fresh topic to reignite the conversation smoothly.

In the corner, he spotted a punching bag. Its cover bore the unmistakable fabric from Gabrielle's collaboration with Disneyland Paris; the textile seemingly produced by the esteemed Malhia KENT.

"You have a punchbag here, Gabrielle."

"Yes, I made it a few years ago then all the other fashion houses copied my concept."

"..."

A silent moment passed as Jindo recalled the onslaught of boxing-themed collections a few years prior; Louis Vuitton, Gucci, and their ilk had certainly dabbled. Yet, he could not help but harbour a nagging suspicion that inspiration might have flowed the other way around. Keen to avoid a thorny discussion, he glossed over the implication.

"Anyway, it looks like a good display..."

"Well, I use it."

"You... use it?"

"Yes, because I'm a boxer."

"Pardon? You're a boxer?"

"Yes, my ex-boyfriend was a professional boxer and he trained me."

"Oh wow, how long have you been training for then?"

"Like five months?"

"..."

Chapter 23 : The Quilt of Questions

Jindo became silenced as he found it somewhat gauche for someone to claim the title of a 'boxer' after a mere five months of training. Eager to steer the conversation towards safer waters, he turned his attention towards a kitchen designed like an American bar.

"You've got a kitchen here as well. So, is this where we'll be serving drinks tomorrow?"

"Exactement."

Gabrielle responded, performing a semblance of shadowboxing in front of the punchbag. Ignorant, Jindo carried on.

"It looks like somebody can actually live here…"

"Yes, I live here."

"Pardon?"

Jindo was taken aback as he had not actually intended his remark to be taken literally. Incredulous, he pressed for more information.

"… where do you… sleep then?"

"Here."

"You mean… this sofa?"

"No, of course not. Downstairs…"

The shadow-boxer paused her bobbing and weaving, directing Jindo's gaze towards a private sale area through a little glass panel.

"… you mean... in the showroom?"

"Yes, well... it's not really a showroom though but my bedroom actually..."

Jindo still struggled to process this revelation.

"But... there was no bed in sight..."

"Oh, it's hidden in the shower."

"Shower?"

"Yes, the place where you saw all the luggage carriers..."

"Ah..."

"I have put the mattress in the shower..."

"... okay."

Gabrielle, sensing Jindo's discomfort, felt the need to elaborate.

"I always work, and this is my world, and I want to be in my creative universe all the time..."

"... okay, great."

Despite Gabrielle's attempt to portray a steadfast commitment to her art, Jindo could not shake off the perception of a somewhat self-involved individual, content to remain forever ensconced within her imaginative bubble.

Understanding dawned on him as he realised why she was always present in the showroom each morning. He began to piece together instances, like her morning tardiness, that could be attributed to late risings and morning rituals conducted while everyone else waited downstairs.

At that moment, Gabrielle received a phone call.

After a brief conversation, Gabrielle hung up, informing Jindo that her friend would be arriving at 9 pm. A glance at the clock revealed it to be around half past seven. It seemed Gabrielle had ample time to spare before her friend's arrival and was inclined to keep Jindo company for a while longer.

"Jindo, do you want to have dinner together?"

"Well… okay."

Seeing no compelling reason to refuse, Jindo accepted her invitation, content to extend his companionship.

"I'm thinking to order a Deliveroo. Are you okay with it?"

"Yes, I don't mind. Thank you."

"Is Indian okay?"

"Great."

As they settled onto the sofa after placing their order, Gabrielle offered Jindo a drink.

"Do you want a drink?"

"Thank you. That would be great."

She returned, carrying a small bottle of champagne.

"I have this, but I don't know how to open it."

"Oh, I'll do it."

Taking charge, Jindo proceeded to uncork the bottle and pour the sparkling wine into glasses. There was something in the way he went about it; a meticulousness bordering on ostentation.

In fact, when Jindo lived in England, one of his flatmates had worked at Vinopolis, London, imparting some basics about serving different types of beverages. Jindo, prone to showmanship, had seized upon these lessons and applied them with a flourish.

His approach, hand tucked behind his back, pouring the champagne in three carefully timed increments to allow the froth to settle, was reminiscent of a flamboyant Italian waiter in an upscale Milanese restaurant.

As Gabrielle watched this display with curiosity, she posed a question.

"You said you never worked at a bar, Jindo."

"No, I haven't."

"But you look like you know how to serve a drink…"

As he initiated the final pour, Jindo responded.

"Well, not really… I just learnt a little manner from my friend who is like a wine expert… But it's just a little thing, I know nothing about this culture. I'm more like a Heineken person…"

Jindo's humble brag was calculated to project an image of modesty, even while hinting at familiarity with 'high-class' culture.

Regardless, Gabrielle seemed pleased with the service and responded with a smile. The conversation continued.

"By the way Gabrielle, it looks like a limited edition of Velvet Clicquot. Is that okay if I drink it?"

"It's fine, I always receive champagne for a present anyway…"

"… okay… great."

She seemed blissfully unaware of the champagne's value, more focused on flaunting her popularity. Jindo momentarily regretted offering her an opportunity to show off, but it was time to toast.

"Tchin Tchin!"

Leaning back on the sofa with a glass of champagne, Jindo and Gabrielle began to converse more casually, the tension in the room dissipating with the clink of their glasses.

"So Gabrielle, do you like Indian food?"

"Not really… but I don't have many choices as a vegan."

"Are you? How long have you been a vegetarian?"

"Well, I'm a VEGAN, not a vegetarian."

"Ah… okay…"

Jindo felt a pang of embarrassment, sensing a ripple in Gabrielle's demeanour. In fact, the distinction between the two was not entirely clear to him.

"Sorry Gabrielle, what's the difference between a vegetarian and vegan though?"

"Well, a vegan is basically a vegetarian, but they have a stricter diet for those animal-concerned products…"

Gabrielle embarked on a small dissertation, demonstrating her knowledge with a sense of pride. Jindo nodded, indulging her fervent discourse on the topic. Deciding to keep the ball rolling, he ventured.

"Then are you a vegan since you were born, or have you changed your diet from a certain time?"

"Actually… it hasn't been long. My ex-boyfriend was a vegan, and I cooked for him every day then I also became a vegan."

"Ah okay, by the way, you cooked for him every day?"

"Yes, even during the fashion week when I was busy like crazy, I cooked for him EVERY DAY…"

While Jindo had noticed Gabrielle trying to emphasise her busy lifestyle, she seemed quite proud of her dedication to her ex-boyfriend. Over a glass of champagne, he was feeling magnanimous.

"You seemed to be a nice girlfriend to him, Gabrielle… Then, what did he do for you?"

"Nothing really, he wasn't a nice man anyway…"

"… okay."

Though it appeared there was a back story where she had been a victim, Jindo was not bothered probing further. He tried to continue the conversation by skipping the subject.

"Then why did you cook for him if I may ask?"

"Well, he was very skinny and not eating properly… so I felt bad for him."

"Ah…"

As per usual, Gabrielle kept casting herself as the damsel in the drama, and Jindo, preferring to sustain the tranquil ambience, chose to play along.

"I think you have a warm nature, Gabrielle."

"Well, I'm not sure about that, but I'm sure you're a warm person, Jindo."

"Oh no, I'm not… you don't know me yet…"

"Jindo, I know you're such a nice man…"

"… well, I'm not but… thank you…"

While responding to Gabrielle's gentle compliment, Jindo found himself a little discomforted by her intense gaze. The boundaries between professional and personal seemed to blur, yet he remained acutely aware of their work relationship, that of a director and an employee on a stagiaire contract.

In an attempt to veer the conversation onto a safer track, he enquired about Gabrielle's ex-boyfriend's profession.

"By the way Gabrielle, was your ex-boyfriend also in fashion?"

"No, he's an actor."

"Oh, wow…"

Jindo's mind instantly conjured up an image of Vincent. Various pieces of a cryptic puzzle began falling into place; the actor's ire behind Gabrielle's office door on the first day, their unexpected encounter by the entrance on the other days, and more.

The timeline, however, was slightly nebulous, but the last encounter with Vincent had barely been a week ago. Keeping his speculation hidden, he allowed Gabrielle to continue her narrative.

"He was really bad, he always wanted to take a profit from me. I always paid for all the bills, and he even lived here for free…"

"… okay…"

Jindo remained silent, his expression unreadable as he continued to piece together the disjointed puzzle. Gabrielle forged ahead with her exposition.

"He really had a bad nature. I always tried to understand him when his acting career was not going well, and his parents were separated when he was a child, so he had to make his living by himself from a young age, and he didn't even have any other family members nor many friends… I tried really hard to take care of him, but he just had so BAD HUMAN NATURE…"

"…"

Jindo refrained from commenting, prompting Gabrielle to elaborate further.

"He even fought with my PARENTS!"

"You mean, with Madame Claude?"

"Yes, even with my DAD!"

Listening to Gabrielle's portrayal of her ex-boyfriend, seemingly Vincent, as a thoroughly unpleasant character, Jindo found himself not entirely swayed. It was not that he was siding with the actor, but his encounters with Madame Claude hinted him to believe she was not one to back down from a confrontation easily.

Jindo refrained from voicing an opinion on her account, reminding himself it was but another twist in the complex tale of relationships. It was time, he decided, to navigate to safer waters.

"How did you meet him though?"

"Um… well… online…"

She seemed somewhat disconcerted by the unforeseen question; her tone noticeably less certain. Jindo continued.

"Online?"

"Well… yes."

From her reluctant response, Jindo inferred she likely met her beau on a dating platform, though she seemed reticent to use the term, possibly fearing it would undermine the credibility of her devoted relationship saga.

Her enthusiasm for discussing the topic appeared to wane, and then she steered the conversation elsewhere.

"Jindo you like boxing? I'm very good. Shook shook!"

Chapter 24 : The Unraveling Threads

The victim of digital romance was punch-motioning to Jindo, and it seemed like she wished to divert the conversation post-haste. While Jindo thought that her fisticuffs sound effects should not be produced by the rather artless mimicry of her mouth, he bit his tongue and played along.

"Gabrielle, you might hit my face soon…"

"Shook shook, don't worry Jindo, I'll do easy on you… Shook shook! Actually, I can teach you some skills…"

"Sorry, you teach me?"

"Yes."

Jindo was taken aback by the audacity of this novice pugilist, a mere five months into her training.

"Well, Gabrielle…"

"Come on, GET UP!"

Before he could marshal his thoughts, the self-believed boxer had already risen, adopting a combative stance.

"… okay…"

Jindo reluctantly stood up, and at that moment, Gabrielle immediately grabbed his shoulder and attacked him. Oddly, she attempted to demonstrate her technique, but it involved a knee kick.

Blocking her attack with his hands crossed, Jindo raised an issue.

"Gabrielle, I thought you learnt boxing. Where on earth does this knee-kick come from?"

"Eh?"

It appeared that the self-proclaimed boxing enthusiast was puzzled by his remark. Jindo clarified.

"You actually look like doing Muay Thai, even your stance looks like it…"

"Ah, you know boxing?"

"Well, I used to go to boxing clubs when I was in England and Italy, but I'm nowhere near to a professional or even a proper fine level…"

Since a little Asian guy, who was not as tall as her, was mentioning it, the uncredited Muay Thai Boxer seemed to want to test him out. She then tried to kick his thigh without any warning, and Jindo made a quick, wide backstep to avoid the attack.

"Wow, you're fast, Jindo."

In fact, it was not about Jindo's quickness but Gabrielle's slowness. Regardless, the ex-boxing club member did not say anything but tried to avoid the moment. Then again, the excited 'ninja' attempted to make another attack.

"Yap!"

Weaving towards her side, Jindo lightly motioned a bit of combination on her.

"Wow, you're so fast, Jindo!"

The slowest, five-month, home-trained, self-claimed boxer seemed to be impressed by Jindo's movement, but he was not particularly enjoying the moment since Gabrielle appeared to be not even at any level.

Jindo tried to let the complacent ninja notice his unwillingness to do this silly sparring.

"Gabrielle, do you really have to do this?"

"Jindo, I think you're very good."

"No, I'm not. Maybe I can try to defend myself if I have to, but I'm really not a level of any good…"

Jindo honestly demonstrated himself, but meanwhile, Gabrielle seemed to consider him skilful yet modest.

"No, I think you're very good Jindo."

"No, please…"

Gabrielle suddenly proceeded to run her hands over his arms and chest, which left Jindo torn between embarrassment and pleasure. It was because, in fact, it had been quite a while since Jindo had experienced the touch of a woman, and it certainly did not hurt that the woman in question was attractive and in peak physical condition.

"Wow, you have muscles, Jindo…"

"Well, Gabrielle…"

Jindo retreated to the sofa, attempting to convey shyness. Gabrielle followed him, taking a seat close by. Yet, he did not resist her touch, savouring the moment.

"I didn't know you're a boxer, Jindo."

"Gabrielle, I wouldn't call myself a boxer."

"But you're trained…"

"Well, I used to go to boxing gyms, but that hardly makes me a boxer… I enjoy boxing, and I have fun in the club, but I'm one of those who gets easily beaten up by everybody in the room… So, please don't call me a boxer, it's embarrassing…"

"No, I think you're just being modest."

She suddenly retrieved her phone, evidently wanting to share something.

"Did I show you my photos when I was modelling by the way?"

"No."

"Do you want to see it?"

"Oh, yes please."

She edged closer to Jindo, intent on viewing the photos together rather than handing her phone to him.

"It's my photo when I was modelling for L'Oréal…"

Her fingers flicked across the screen, unveiling a series of modelling shots. One provocative image, evidently a campaign for a hair product, presented a unique conundrum; although she sat primly, she was inarguably stark naked.

With each tap and swipe, her varied poses multiplied, a series of tasteful nudes unfolding on the device. Throughout this digital tour of her portfolio, Jindo's gaze busily scrutinised the model's form, framed within the modest confines of the phone screen.

Moving on, she showcased another shoot. Dressed in nothing but lingerie, she was coyly clutching a banana, her smile playful and suggestively provocative. The image looked like a risqué lingerie ad, but what captivated Jindo was the obvious professional retouching. She was, in a word, stunning.

Feigning nonchalance, he offered compliments, which she accepted with grace. However, Jindo was acutely aware of the ex-model's gradual encroachment into his personal space.

Settled to his right, Gabrielle began deftly managing her phone one-handed, leaving her left hand free to drape nonchalantly across Jindo's thigh. To add to the escalating tension, her left breast was nudging his right arm, a silent testament to her sans-bra state.

Resisting the urge to squirm, Jindo pretended to be cool, but he was, in fact, concerned about the light brown chino pants that he'd donned sans underwear. Yet, he managed to savour the moment, discarding his usual impulse to steer the conversation to safer waters.

At that moment, he noticed Gabrielle's flushed cheeks.

"Gabrielle, are you okay?"

"… eh?"

Her response was lethargic, her eyelashes fluttered lazily, reminiscent of a cat vying for its new owner's affection.

"I think your face is a bit flushed…"

"… because I think… I'm drunk…"

Gabrielle confessed with her voice unsteady. Jindo could not ignore the correlation. The more questions he asked, the more she seemed to embrace the tipsy persona.

Regardless, Jindo made no effort to escape the increasingly heated situation. Instead, he relaxed into her touch, silently inviting her advances. The inebriated belle, as she styled herself, tilted her head towards him, murmuring with a sultry undertone.

"I don't know Jindo... I feel strange…"

As ever, Jindo noticed the undertone of the moment. With a façade of cool and gentle tranquillity, his mind was a riotous arena of tactical plans, each designed to evolve the current scenario smoothly yet expeditiously.

His cautious approach, mired in the professional boundaries of being an employee, had shifted its focus to a singularly enticing objective. Taking care not to disrupt Gabrielle's leaning posture against him, Jindo made a show of sipping his champagne gingerly.

"By the way Jindo, I didn't know you had good muscles…"

"Well, I don't think mine is any good, but I do a bit of push-ups at least every day…"

"Every day?"

"Yes."

Their playful banter, while pretending to be informational, was a mere ruse to navigate the anticipatory tension between them. Keen to maintain the momentum, Jindo continued.

"Well, at the same time, I normally get muscles quite easily, particularly on my chest…"

In an act of subtle enticement, Jindo ran his hands over his chest, hoping Gabrielle would follow suit.

"Oh, really? Wow, that's good… Sorry Jindo, can I touch your chest again please?"

"Um… well… okay…"

Despite his nonchalant reply, Jindo had been fishing for exactly that reaction. When her hand graced his chest, the attention-starved man revelled in the sensation. Meanwhile, he discerned a difference in her touch this time; her index finger caressed his chest with a tantalising intensity.

A gulp caught in his throat as he sensed Gabrielle's gaze drifting towards his trousers.

Jindo's trousers, a creation of his own design, featured a distinctive detail; a double-interfaced fly-front. The rigid, substantial inner fly-front extension would, when seated, present a particular silhouette, much akin to a grandly pitched tent. This ingenious design was intended to enhance the perceived proportions of Jindo's modest endowment.

A common designer might baulk at the thought of employing such a technique for a purpose as salacious as Jindo's. However, for the curious-minded, similar effects might be observed in a particular pair of jeans from the Dsquared2 collection.

Regardless, Jindo detected Gabrielle's gaze drifting towards the unmistakable front of his trousers. At that moment, as if guided by some innate masculine instinct, Jindo knew it was time to make a move.

Reclining on the sofa was Gabrielle, with Jindo soon to occupy the upper echelon. His arms encircled the former model while he cradled her breasts, simultaneously gentle yet assertive.

Swiftly removing her T-shirt, he channelled all his affection, and sheer force of will, into his searing senses. Jindo could be likened to a parched hound, deprived of sustenance for an uncomfortable stretch of time.

For a spell, he poured his boundless affection onto the director. The self-professed inebriate appeared to relish the moment; her eyes shut, emitting a sound akin to a purring feline.

As the air in the room thickened with escalating passion, Jindo swept off the ex-lingerie model's leggings, revealing her naked body immediately, a sight unhindered by the absence of any concealing underwear.

The once patient hound, now salivating in anticipation, was on the brink of discarding his stained trousers, and at that moment, the jarring peal of the doorbell shattered the moment.

Chapter 25 : Seams of Secrets

As the doorbell echoed through the house...

Startled, Jindo and Gabrielle exchanged glances. The lady, who moments before was decidedly relaxed, seemed to be completely composed now. Simultaneously, the drooling dog of a man was hastily yanking up his trousers. Swiftly, he returned the leggings and t-shirt to the naked director and suggested he might descend to answer the door.

"Yes Jindo, please, but..."

Accepting his proposal, Gabrielle noticed the apparent stains marring the fly-front area of Jindo's pants. With a casual grace, he slid into his double-breasted long coat, buttoning it up swiftly.

"I think it'll be fine like this..."

Flashing an appreciative smile, the unclothed director nodded. The now decently clad man hurried down the curvaceous staircase. Opening the door, he was met with the sight of the Deliveroo rider.

Returning, the Indian vegetarian fare in hand, Jindo found the ex-model fully dressed back. With a chuckle, she thanked him for his efficient management of the previously delicate moment. Jindo did his best to maintain an air of nonchalance, but the pair could not suppress their laughter at the absurdity of the recent happenings.

Seated on the sofa, his coat still buttoned, they continued laughing as they set the table for dinner. The tension that had previously filled the room had dissipated, replaced by the tantalising aroma of their meal.

As they casually conversed over dinner, Gabrielle's phone chirped. She explained her friend would be arriving in five minutes and requested

Jindo's assistance in manoeuvring mannequins. He readily offered a hand, cleared the table, and readied himself for the impending arrival.

Approaching 9 pm…

The doorbell chimed, prompting them both to descend. Gabrielle welcomed the visitor, a man in a dark brown corduroy jacket. As they exchanged a customary French greeting, cheek-kissing, Gabrielle shielded the open door slightly, keeping Jindo out of view.

At that point, Jindo perceived an element of excessive politeness in the guest's behaviour. His touch travelled from her earlobe to her arm, finally crossing fingers and grasping her hand, accompanied by a laid-back, intimate tone. Observing from the shadows, Jindo found this display somewhat 'extraordinaire'.

From his experiences, Jindo had concluded that the French concept of 'skinship' tended to involve more physical contact than its Italian and English counterparts. However, this seemed beyond what he would deem appropriate in an ordinary friendship.

Suddenly, Gabrielle seemed conscious of her friend's overfamiliar greeting and shot a glance back at Jindo. Her friend then noticed the man behind the door, Gabrielle smoothly extracted her hand from his, introducing Jindo.

"This is Jindo, my new modéliste."

Caught off guard by the abrupt introduction, the friend looked to Gabrielle, clearly awaiting further explanation. Ignoring his silent query, Gabrielle turned to Jindo.

"Jindo, this is my friend, Antoine."

Antoine seemed bemused, his gaze still locked on Gabrielle. Seizing the moment, Jindo interjected.

"Enchanté, Antoine."

"… enchanté, Gin... doo…"

Gabrielle then briefly outlined Jindo's background to Antoine. Curiously, her account featured no details of his origins, focusing instead on his experience in England and Italy.

The two men exchanged pleasantries in English, with Jindo deliberately laying his unnatural British accent on thick. The handshake held a thread of quiet tension. Keen to shift the awkward moment, Jindo addressed Gabrielle.

"Gabrielle, are we going to bring the mannequins now then?"

Without skipping a beat, Gabrielle inquired about the location of Antoine's car, smoothly redirecting the conversation.

Positioned outside, the trio ventured to retrieve the mannequins. The sight of Antoine's gleaming BMW X5 awaited them, and he began to unload the lifeless forms from the spacious boot. Jindo, in turn, accepted each piece, with Gabrielle standing nearby, overseeing the operation.

In all, they transferred five mannequins, with Gabrielle instructing Jindo to temporarily house them in the entrance. The man in the buttoned-up, long coat then proceeded to lug the plastic figures inside one by one.

As Jindo manoeuvred the fourth figure, Gabrielle remained engrossed in conversation with her friend. When Jindo was handling the final mannequin, Antoine interjected.

"Jindo, is it not better to take off your coat?"

"Um... yes indeed, but um..."

Caught off guard by the poorly timed question, Jindo glanced towards Gabrielle. Their shared laughter hung in the air, and without further explanation, Jindo carried the last mannequin inside.

Antoine looked somewhat puzzled, sensing an untold story between Gabrielle and Jindo. Once the last mannequin was placed inside, Jindo stepped back out.

He patiently awaited the right moment to bid Antoine farewell but felt a shift in the BMW car owner's gaze. Despite maintaining a polite façade, Jindo could not shake the feeling of negativity creeping into Antoine's look. In turn, he offered a smug yet cynical glance to the man in the corduroy jacket, who was clinging onto Gabrielle's hands with an unshakable air of possession.

The scene was reminiscent of two dogs circling one another, not yet barking, but with a mutual understanding that they would never be friends.

Standing off to the side, Jindo heard Gabrielle ask him to go in, citing a need to discuss something with her friend. Bidding Antoine 'au revoir', Jindo retreated back inside.

As Gabrielle remained outdoors, Jindo commenced relocating the mannequins to the showroom, recalling the director's plan to use them as a stylish screen for the haphazard pile of luggage in the shower area.

In approximately ten minutes...

Returning, Gabrielle noticed the dummies had already been relocated to the showroom.

"Oh Jindo, how did you move all the mannequins so fast?"

"It's nothing really... I used to help my family boutique's window display, so I know how to carry mannequins in bulk..."

"Thank you so much Jindo, but you didn't need to do this. I was going to let the girls do it tomorrow..."

"No worries, it's fine with me."

Fashion displays incorporate a variety of mannequins. What is particular about these specific statues is their size and weight, notably larger and heavier than the fitting mannequins found in an atelier.

However, unlike the fitting mannequins, most display statues are designed to be disassembled. Those seasoned in the industry are aware that the initial step is to separate these components before transportation. This is due to the fragile nature of these plastic figures which can easily crack upon impact.

In fact, the element Jindo found most irksome when moving them to the showroom was navigating the narrow, winding staircase, the statues themselves were not an issue.

Regardless, Gabrielle appeared pleased with his endeavour. She proceeded to stage the display, dressing the mannequins. While this turn of events was somewhat unexpected for Jindo, he silently committed himself to assisting the director.

During the dressing of the mannequins...

Jindo broached a topic.

"Gabrielle, are you planning to stay here tonight?"

"... eh?"

Engrossed in perfecting the mannequin's posture, Gabrielle seemed to have missed his question. Unfazed, Jindo continued.

"I mean, are you going to sleep here tonight? Because I remember your bed is in the shower now..."

"Um... I don't know..."

Jindo, still facilitating Gabrielle's endeavours, sought an opportunity to reignite the spark of their previous intimate encounter. Gabrielle, however, remained engrossed in dressing the display.

Upon finalising the setup, Gabrielle queried.

"So Jindo, are you leaving for home now?"

"... um… yes, I... think so..."

The situation was veering away from Jindo's desires and expectations, with the prospects of a return to their earlier steamy ambience looking increasingly slim. Gabrielle continued.

"Where do you reside, by the way?"

Aware of the stereotypes Parisians might harbour regarding his suburban living arrangement, Jindo chose his words carefully.

"I reside in... the banlieue (suburbs)..."

"Where?"

The Parisienne seemed taken aback, perhaps not anticipating that the Hermès aficionado would be a suburban dweller.

"... near Bondy..."

Ordinarily, Jindo was proud of his neighbourhood, but at this moment he hesitated, subtly concerned about the perception of Bondy in those days of France.

"Ah… Bondy?"

Her tone, tinted with surprise, had a hint of jest, akin to how Italians in Milan might tease those residing in Napoli. Not to be deterred, Jindo defended his turf.

"Well, I may be wrong but if I may say… I understand there's a certain perception about Bondy, but my neighbourhood is actually quite lovely and people are so kind... It's also quite international. We have American, Portuguese, Italian, Greek, Brazilian, Chilean..."

Jindo attempted to paint a positive image of his area, contrasting with any negative stereotypes, but the Parisienne did not seem overly invested. She interrupted his spiel.

"It's okay… you're a foreigner…"

"…"

It seemed the cosmopolitan lady held certain reservations about suburban living, yet she seemed willing to acknowledge Jindo's exception. Her eyes scanned him, contemplating the man in Hermès accessories, Dolce & Gabbana sneakers, and an Armani alpaca coat, living in such a location. Intrigued, she posed another question.

"Jindo, how did you come to live in Bondy, by the way?"

"Well, when I was in Italy, I met a Korean-American painter who married a French man… When I told her I was going to Paris, she asked me if I was interested in living in a property that her husband was letting out. She said, it wasn't in central Paris but I was okay with it…"

Gabrielle remained silent, prompting the suburban dweller to continue.

"Anyway, I generally prefer living a bit away from the city centre…"

Gabrielle appeared less interested in Jindo's preferences and more curious about his living arrangements.

"Okay okay, is it a studio then?"

"No, it's a house…"

"House?"

"… yes."

"You live alone in an entire house?"

"No no, it's just one side of the floor in a house where I have my own space… including a private entrance and a little garden…"

"Garden?"

Gabrielle's interest in Jindo's dwelling seemed to pique, prompting him to further elaborate.

"Whoa whoa, Gabrielle... It may not be a typical garden that you think, it's just a little place where I can have a little tea time at a table..."

Jindo attempted to downplay his living arrangements, yet Gabrielle's interest remained, her eyes roving over his Dolce & Gabbana sneakers and Hermès rings once again.

"So Jindo, how many rooms are in your place?"

"Just two and... a living room..."

Despite Jindo's explanation, the level of ambiguity remained, and Gabrielle's curiosity was far from satisfied.

"Then how many square metres is your place then?"

"Um... as far as I know, it's about eighty something..."

"EIGHTY SQUARE METRES? Oh... c'est pas mal... *(it's not bad...)*"

Indeed, it was a rather generous space for one person. Yet Jindo refrained from disclosing that he had initially shared the space with a girlfriend, deeming it inappropriate timing for such revelations.

Chapter 26 : The Artisan's Aspiration

With an expression of pleasant surprise, Gabrielle absorbed Jindo's news, while Jindo attempted to dilute the apparent opulence attached to his dwelling.

"Gabrielle, I think if I find a place for the same amount of rental in central Paris, I may live in a very tiny studio…"

The inhabitant of Bondy strove to deconstruct the exaggerated perception of his estate, yet the Parisian lady appeared sceptical, her interest aroused to investigate more.

"Okay then, are you going to Bondy with your petite scooter now? Because it's a bit too late and Bondy is very far…"

Intriguingly, Jindo sensed she was less concerned with the time and transport logistics, but more intrigued by something else. Regardless, he provided an answer.

"Haha, of course, I'm not going to travel with this little trottinette to Bondy, which is not even a proper scooter… At the same time, it's only 10 pm, so there'll still be metro and RER…"

"Ah… you're taking RER?"

In those days of the Parisian zeitgeist, mentioning the RER often signalled a residence in the suburbs, a locale considered a distinct remove from the city's vibrancy.

Gabrielle's countenance seemed to droop slightly once more. Unfazed, Jindo continued.

"Well, in my case though, I… drive…"

"Eh? You… DRIVE?"

"… yes."

Aware that driving was an unusual mode of transport for a foreign resident whose official status as a student, Jindo tread carefully to avoid further propagating an ostentatious persona. Undeterred, Gabrielle queried again.

"How about your trottinette?"

"Well, my trottinette is just to travel from my car park to workplace because I don't like losing time… But I drive from home to Paris unless I have an appointment for a drinking session with mates…"

Ignoring the details, Gabrielle seemed to revive her interest in Jindo's eligibility for driving. She pursued the topic further.

"By the way Jindo, how can you drive in France?"

"I have a UK driving license, and I drive with it."

In fact, it was illegal to utilise a UK driving licence if one no longer resided in the UK, but this aspect eluded Jindo.

"Then, where is the car though? There aren't many parking spaces in central Paris…"

"Well, I park in Les Halles…"

The realisation hit Gabrielle, casting Jindo in a whole new light. The Parisienne seemed more intrigued by this mysterious, minimum-wage employee who claimed to own a car, which was quite unusual for many reasons.

"Jindo, is it not expensive to park in Les Halles though?"

"Well, my landlord gave me a voucher, so I only pay a little sum for now… but it's normally 175 euro per month as far as I know…"

Though Jindo tried to play it down, Gabrielle did not seem to be interested in his story but only interpreted it in her own fashion.

Her gaze softened, and she examined him anew, an Asian student from Bondy, inhabiting an unusually spacious property, decked out in an array of luxury items, his transportation a humble trottinette, yet who claimed to be a car owner who parked his vehicle in the heart of Paris. The urban lady decided to probe further.

"What car is yours though?"

Jindo detected a shift in her tone, a subtle warmth, perhaps a budding curiosity.

"It's a... small SUV..."

"What's... SUV?"

The mention of a car type stumped Gabrielle, who did not seem to have extensive knowledge about automobiles. Jindo then sought to explain in simpler terms.

"It's not a sedan... hm... okay, let me put it this way. It's like Antoine's car but mine is a bit smaller and a lot cheaper haha... Anyway, it's comfortable enough for me and I like it as it's 4x4..."

"QUART PAR QUART?"

Gabrielle did not even seem to be interested in any details mentioned, including her unawareness of the value of her friend's BMW X5, but became excited once she heard a term that she was aware of.

"Well, it's actually AWD but Gabrielle..."

"Quelle marque?"

Intercepting Jindo's breath to elaborate, Gabrielle swiftly probed for further information. Regardless, Jindo cautiously responded.

"... well, it's a little Korean marque, called Ssangyong, and I'm sure you've never heard of it... Actually, it's a small marque that frequently goes bankrupt but still survives somehow... But for me, I like the brand not just because I like their design but also because my first car was Ssangyong and I normally stick to the brand if I feel that…"

Jindo attempted to express his steadfast loyalty to the brand and his reasons, but Gabrielle appeared more interested in his car ownership, than its origin or any of his story.

"Okay okay Jindo, anyway I like quart par quart."

"… okay… do you also drive, Gabrielle?"

"No, I live in Paris and I never leave the city, so I don't need to drive… I just call an Uber or a taxi, and I've never even taken a metro or bus…"

"…"

Jindo observed Gabrielle's concerted effort to project an image of urban sophistication and a sense of exclusivity. Meanwhile, he felt somewhat irked by her emphasis on her complete lack of public transportation experience. Unperturbed, the perpetual private transport enthusiast carried on.

"But, I can drive a yacht and I also have a license… My father is a good boat driver and he taught me…"

Jindo felt a dissonance between Gabrielle's attempt to portray herself as a bastion of luxury while establishing an endearing family bond. It did not quite strike a chord with him, and he remained sceptical. Gabrielle, undeterred, sailed on with her narrative.

"Jindo, how long does it take to Bondy by the way? Because I've NEVER been there…"

Jindo found her comment slightly peculiar. He remembered her mentioning her past association with Hermès, and as far as he was aware, many of Hermès' workshops were located in Bondy. However, he chose not to dwell on it and answered her query.

"… about half an hour?"

"C'est pas mal ça."

(That's not too bad.)

Indeed, the journey from Paris to Bondy usually took more than half an hour. But Jindo's response was a subconscious attempt to imply his abode was not too distantly situated from the city. He added, with a casual air.

"Anyway, I like driving, and it may take less this time around with lighter traffic…"

As he finished his decorative words, Gabrielle threw him a curveball he had not expected at that moment.

"Jindo, do you have a spare room for me tonight? Because I don't like to sleep on a sofa because it's actually quite cold… and scary to be alone on the top floor…"

Her demeanour mirrored that of a cat on a frosty night, meowing pitifully at the outside of a window, hoping for a welcoming hearth. The senseless man, this time, immediately grasped the subtext, cautiously trying not to spook the cat while leading her towards his place.

"Well… I do have a spare room and I'm sure it's not going to be the finest condition that you have ever been to… but just from my standard, I think it can be not-too-bad…"

Jindo, the sartorially challenged, strived to understate the situation, yet his intentions were clear. Indeed, his place only had one bed, a fact he conveniently left unmentioned. He also chose to skip the detail about the lack of a sofa, for he knew Gabrielle would baulk at the offer otherwise.

"Jindo, is that really okay if I go to your place tonight?"

"Eh… yes, of course…"

Ever so cautious, Jindo did not want to scare off the former lingerie model and risk aborting their cosy tête-à-tête. Eager to keep the momentum going, yet with the utmost finesse, he proposed.

"Okay then… shall I… bring my car now?"

"Okay."

Oddly, the Parisian lady, who had claimed to have never been outside of the city, seemed to be delighted on the brink of her first romantic getaway. Unfazed, Jindo bolted towards the car park, forsaking his petite trottinette in the process.

Chapter 27 : Stitches in the Storyline

En route to the Bondy residence...

Thanks to Jindo activating the seat heater and laying out a neatly folded blanket for her, Gabrielle, who was clad solely in leggings, absent of undergarments, was soon swaddled in comforting warmth.

"Wow, you have a warm, Jindo?"

"Warm? Oh, you mean the seat heater? Yes."

"Your car is good."

"…"

Apparently, the self-claimed, quart-par-quart aficionado was no automobile connoisseur, as it was hardly the norm to praise a vehicle for the sole feature of seat warmers. Trying to offer some context, Jindo elaborated.

"Gabrielle, mine is like a fourth-hand one, and these seat heaters are quite common for any car these days… Well, compared to Antoine's though, mine is nothing really…"

Gabrielle seemed oblivious to Jindo's explanation, instead engrossed in her novel adventure out of the city confines, taking in the foreign sights and the car's interiors.

To prevent the journey from becoming a silent slog, Jindo initiated a conversation.

"By the way Gabrielle, you said you helped Antoine and his wife is also a designer…"

Having completed her perusal, Gabrielle was ready to join the conversation.

"Well, his wife is actually no one... She was an immigrant from somewhere in Eastern Europe, used to live in a big family, and I think she met Antoine then wanted to study fashion... and he paid for all her education, and now, she wanted to be a designer just after graduation... and Antoine is spending all his money for her stupid business... He actually doesn't like it at all..."

"... okay, so Antoine is actually not in fashion but investing in his wife's project?"

"Haha, it's not a project. She doesn't even have an office, but just making her stupid garment in their little apartment... Antoine is just stupid, he should invest in me, not her..."

"... okay... is she good by the way?"

"Bah, I don't know. I don't like her styles anyway..."

"Ah... I see."

Since it was evident that the self-claimed, former CHANEL designer was not in favour of the domestic designer, Jindo shifted the topic.

"What does Antoine do for a living, by the way?"

"I don't know exactly, but I think his parents gave him some parts of their business, and he also got a couple of properties in Paris..."

"Oh..."

It seemed that the X5-owner hailed from a prosperous lineage. Gabrielle added,

"You'll meet them tomorrow anyway, they're coming..."

"Ah okay, great... By the way Gabrielle, how did you come to know them? Is Antoine an old friend of yours?"

"No, I met them at a fashion event last year..."

"Last year?"

"Yes… they had no friends or guests, just stupidly standing in the event, then came to me, trying to be friendly to get some information nah nah nah… and when I saw them, I knew right away that they knew nothing about nothing… I actually taught them, from how to set up a business to make a collection…"

"…"

Indeed, Gabrielle's incessant criticism of others had ceased to surprise Jindo, although it did give him pause, given the brief period they had known each other.

"Well, I thought you two have known each other for long…"

"Eh… why?"

"Well, it just seemed so, you two looked very… friendly…"

Jindo chose to subtly hint at their previous close encounters, careful to keep his wording as neutral as possible.

"Bah, I don't know if we're close… He's annoying though, he always gossips about his wife to me… He even says because his wife is pregnant now, he doesn't have sex with her and he even doesn't want to have sex with her anymore, because he says it feels strange when he knows a baby is growing up inside and he puts his thing in…"

Jindo's mind wandered to a similar story that one of his married friends shared. As a bachelor himself, though, he could not fully comprehend the sentiment, so decided to let the conversation shift course.

"By the way Gabrielle, why is Antoine gossiping about his wife to you?"

"I don't know. He always calls me at night, saying he likes me, misses me whatever… and then he also says I'm the only one who understands him, nah nah nah…"

"... okay..."

Jindo had begun to piece together the origins of their cosy exchanges. Despite Gabrielle's stories, he could not entirely accept her version of events, remembering how the pair had greeted each other earlier.

In fact, Gabrielle had not seemed averse to Antoine's attention at all. He even speculated that had he not intruded on their intimate encounter, things might have taken a more heated turn between them. As he navigated these thoughts, Gabrielle interrupted his reverie.

"For me, we're just friends... But he always tries to cross the line..."

"I think... he likes you, simply speaking..."

"Well, it's okay he can like me, I don't care... but I don't like when he tries to kiss me, hug me... and he even tried to have SEX with me before..."

Jindo did not respond, and Gabrielle continued.

"I have many guys around me like him though, always trying to have SEX with me..."

Jindo experienced a twinge of guilt, even as he noted the emphasis she placed on the provocative word. He resolved to maintain an air of innocence, keen to alleviate the contextual nuance.

"Gabrielle, I think you don't need to take that too badly. It basically means you're sec... attractive..."

He was careful to sidestep the term 'sexy', not wanting to make his thoughts overly transparent.

"Thank you, Jindo... I'm sure you're not one of those guys..."

"..."

He still grappled with a pang of guilt even as he registered a shift in her tone. Gabrielle seemed to be adopting a more relaxed demeanour.

Without turning to look, he sensed her adjusting the knee blanket he had provided and glancing his way. After a moment, she placed her hand atop his on the gear stick.

Despite the convoluted tales, Jindo could not help but savour her touch. He neglected to shift gears even when necessary, cautious not to disrupt their intimate moment. The long-time lonely man felt his body respond to her proximity, his mind already planning how he might pursue their shared interest later that evening. They sat in companionable silence for a while, until Jindo, having minimised gear changes, finally reached his residence.

"Welcome to Bondy. This is my place…"

Chapter 28 : The Craft of Confidences

Arriving at Jindo's residence...
Before the imposing façade of the Bondy house, Jindo fished for his key while Gabrielle scanned the surroundings. The property's antiquated character was clearly visible, even under the cloak of night, and Gabrielle broke the silence.

"Your house is very old."

"Yes. My landlord told me that the house is inherited by the 3rd generation of their family…"

Jindo replied with a note of pride in his voice, about to insert the key. At that moment, a figure materialised behind the gate, and the door swung open; there stood Gregory, the landlord's cousin who resided upstairs.

"Hey, Greg."

"Hey, Jindo. How are you?"

Gregory, the de facto custodian for the landlord's absence, seemed to have locked the gate behind him and then doubled back upon hearing Jindo.

"Greg, this is Gabrielle."

"Gabrielle, this is Gregory. He's my neighbour and a big brother."

French pleasantries were exchanged between Gregory and Gabrielle, and at that moment, Jindo spotted his feline companions emerging from the garden shadows. Drawn by his familiar voice, the cats moved towards him. As he moved to pick up one of them, Gregory enlightened Gabrielle on Jindo's journey from a non-pet owner to a cat parent.

These cats, once helpless kittens, had been discovered by Gregory when they were abandoned in the garden. Already a pet parent to two cats, Gregory had proposed Jindo adopt them.

Initially hesitant, given his lack of experience with cats, Jindo had been swayed when Gregory shared that the kittens faced euthanasia at the hands of a French animal association if left unadopted. That was three months ago, and Jindo and the two cat siblings had since formed a close bond.

The conversation shifted towards Gabrielle as she started sharing tales of the cats at her parents' house and why her current residence did not permit pets. This led to discussions on her current professional life, and the Parisienne designer began to regale them with stories of her enterprise in the Marais district.

As the accomplished director revelled in her monologue, Jindo stood by, idly stroking his cat. Meanwhile, he noticed Gabrielle's habitual, ostentatious demeanour, which verged on lecturing, as though addressing someone utterly oblivious to the fashion industry.

Although Gregory's attire at that moment might not scream 'haute couture', his experience in fashion design was anything but lacklustre. A man of few words, he had honed his professions at reputed fashion houses such as Yves Saint Laurent and John Galliano and presently juggled his role as a part-time project manager for various international labels.

Despite his impressive credentials, the newly-set primary goal of the single parent was clear, being the best father possible to his daughter. This devotion may have made him appear less passionate about his work, but he certainly had no dearth of knowledge and expertise about the industry.

As Gabrielle was unaware of Gregory's background, she blissfully continued her lofty discourse. Noticing the familiar inklings of disapproval in Gregory's eyes, Jindo decided to diffuse the situation before it soured. Conveniently, the cat in Jindo's arms began to squirm restlessly, providing a perfect segue away from Gabrielle's monologue.

Although Gabrielle made an attempt to return to her soliloquy, Jindo deftly diverted the conversation by asking Gregory if he planned to retire for the night. Successfully extinguishing the tense situation, he then led Gabrielle towards his residence.

Upon entering…

Gabrielle's eyes widened at the sight of Jindo's living room. Everything was in its place, evoking a sense of order and cleanliness reminiscent of a high-end hotel.

"Jindo, do you always keep your place clean like this?"

"Well, it's a bit cleaner than normal… but yes, normally, I do tend to keep it clean since my mind is always unclean haha…"

Attempting a modest response with his personal excuse, Jindo brushed off the compliment. However, in fact, his home was a lot tidier and cleaner than usual. The previous weekend had been spent giving the place a much-needed overhaul, resulting in a fresh, revitalised environment. It was this very sense of order and cleanliness that had made him confident when Gabrielle proposed her impromptu visit.

Regardless, Gabrielle set about exploring the modest eighty-square metre house. The sparsely decorated living room held her attention only briefly before she ventured further.

Unbeknownst to her, the home lacked a sofa, housing only a single bed. Even after a cursory inspection of the bedroom, she did not question the sleeping arrangements for the night.

Her exploration culminated in Jindo's compact home studio. On entering, Gabrielle marvelled at the eclectic mix of Apple devices, a JUKI industrial sewing machine, a generously sized light table, and four fitting mannequins. The latter comprised two standard STOCKMAN forms, one each for homme and femme, and two custom models, one for dresses and the other for trousers.

In those days of France, options for fitting mannequins were somewhat limited, despite the presence of STOCKMAN, a leading industry manufacturer. The prohibitive pricing of these coveted items posed a significant barrier for many. It was a choice between an exorbitant STOCKMAN or a budget-friendly but impractical alternative. The sight of custom-made mannequins was a rarity, even online.

Gabrielle, clearly impressed, exclaimed.

"Wow, is that all yours?"

"Eh, yes…"

Caught off guard, Jindo responded with faux modesty, yet, beneath the surface, he was rather proud of his unique assortment of professional paraphernalia.

"Jindo, you also work at home?"

"Well, yes and no… It's just that I still have a lot of things that I don't know, or I'm not sure about, so when I feel limited with my imaginary simulation for certain techniques or methods, I want to test them out right away, even in the middle of the night…"

While Jindo elaborated on his exploratory approach to work, Gabrielle seemed preoccupied with something else. Her gaze landed on a corner stacked with bright orange Hermès boxes.

"Jindo, how many Hermès did you buy to get all these boxes?"

"No no, they're just boxes... When I worked as a personal shopper, I collected them and use them as storage now..."

Jindo demonstrated, opening a few boxes to reveal an assortment of supplies and stationery within. However, the visitor, seemingly disenchanted, cast a cynical eye over the array of Apple devices and sleekly attired mannequins. Jindo felt her gaze, at that juncture, was akin to a feline contemplating a tin of tuna.

Despite this, Jindo felt an urgency to expedite the scene. It was due to the fact that his ultimate intention in bringing the former lingerie model to his place was not to share his studio, but the bedroom. His damp trousers had been dried now, a circumstance he was keen to rectify at the earliest convenience.

He invited Gabrielle to freshen up with a shower. The Parisienne, however, did not seem entirely at ease. She suggested that Jindo proceed first, and he readily complied, not harbouring any objections. As he made to depart, Gabrielle queried.

"You're not going to come back late, no? Because I'll feel scared to be alone in this big place..."

"Oh okay, I'll get back fast."

Despite his plans for a swift rinse anyway, he feigned haste, giving the impression he was accelerating for her benefit. He then vanished, leaving the guest to continue her exploration of his atelier.

Having completed a whirlwind cleanse, with a generous helping of shampoo and shower gel, Jindo re-emerged. He discovered that the self-proclaimed apprehensive lady was comfortably ensconced in bed, engrossed in her mobile phone. Observing her relaxed demeanour, Jindo cautiously enquired if she was now inclined to utilise the bathroom.

The visitor demurred, still expressing her discomfort with showering in an unfamiliar locale. Remaining engrossed in her mobile, she casually mentioned her intention to shower at her place the following day.

Briefly considering whether her shower space was cluttered with luggage, Jindo asked, only to be informed by the 'Maraisienne' that she preferred to use the facilities at her exclusive gym in the district.

Indeed, it was not the most aromatic news as Jindo had detected from their earlier, suspended intimate moment, that she was rather perspired that day. However, he refrained from commenting further, prioritising not to disturb the current atmosphere.

At that moment, Gabrielle suddenly voiced up.

"Are you coming or not?"

"Eh?"

Taken aback by her forthright suggestion, Jindo feigned slight confusion, not wholly certain what she was implying. It was because no explicit arrangement had been indeed reached about sharing the bed yet.

Meanwhile, he trod lightly, wary of engaging in discussion lest the opportunity slips away. He quietly moved towards the bed, striving to act casual, an attempt that fell short of convincing. With the lights now off, he crawled into bed, met by Gabrielle who welcomed him as though they had shared a bed for years.

Jindo retained a cautious approach, taking up a modest amount of space near the centre of the bed since nothing had been still, officially decided. Gabrielle, the former lingerie model sprawling over her half of the bed, showed no intention of making more room for him. Positioning himself a safe distance from the centre, Jindo lay down, only for Gabrielle to close the distance.

"You smell nice."

As Gabrielle murmured, a modest chuckle escaped Jindo as he responded.

"Well, it's just the shampoo. My natural body smells are really bad..."

"I like it. I like Asian guy's skin, so soft..."

Jindo heard an echo of past conquests in her remark but quickly banished the unnecessary curiosity that sprung up. Instead, he found himself appreciating the proximity of the ex-lingerie model. Gabrielle drew closer, seeking the scent and touch of his skin, akin to a cat demanding a petting session.

In a fluid motion, Gabrielle draped her right leg over Jindo who was lying straight, initiating a caress from his thigh upwards. As he silently savoured the moment, he was also careful not to let her notice a condom in his pyjama pants pocket. Having overlooked the possible outcomes of their position on the bed, his hasty decision to stash a condom in his right-side pocket now caused him concern.

Her leg was now making its way past his pelvis when she detected an unmistakable hardness. She paused her exploration, an unspoken invitation for Jindo to reciprocate her earlier attention. With a swift motion, he changed their positions; no longer side by side but one atop the other.

Barely maintaining his equilibrium, Jindo delicately navigated his way atop the ex-lingerie model. This second round was considerably less impulsive than their prior encounter, a subtle dance of learnt familiarity, his oral touch tracing the contours of her body with a steady urgency that belied the throbbing ache settling into his jaw. Gabrielle sank into the sheets at his ministrations, her eyes fluttering shut in surrender, soft groans escaping her lips.

For a spell, Jindo indulged in the kaleidoscope of sensations that enveloped him, the distinct textures and nuances of a female body under his hands. His nose failed to pick up any sour notes despite Gabrielle's absence of a shower, instead, the air filled with an intoxicating cocktail of feminine pheromones that sent his senses into a delightful frenzy.

The moment was about to be in crescendo when he reached for his johnny prepared, but Gabrielle stayed his hand. She voiced her preference for the authenticity of skin-on-skin contact over the synthetic slickness of the artificial fibre.

Despite sharing her sentiments, Jindo found himself caught in a quandary. It was due to that his physical fatigue threatened to eclipse his emotional excitement, his inner enthusiast hankering for an extended session while his body flashed warning signs of a premature conclusion.

However, this was a time for action, not contemplation. Resuming his position straight into her inside, he lost himself in the tender motions, all worldly anxieties evaporating as he savoured each fleeting second. Even his staunch atheism wavered as silent prayers of gratitude were directed to divine entities for the serendipity of the moment, one that Gabrielle seemed to echo with her harmonious rhythm.

Their symphony hit an abrupt snag when pleasure threatened to overwhelm him, a sharp cramp lancing through his 'little Rambo'. The little guy had been wound up for far too long, and his overzealous anticipation seemed to be staging a rebellious mutiny. An unexpected and utterly unwelcome development, to say the least.

Astute as ever, Gabrielle picked up on the interruption, an undercurrent of embarrassment snaking its way through the ensuing silence. It was their inaugural dance of intimacy, and neither was equipped with the words to address the awkward hiccup.

Lying side by side in a contemplative silence, Jindo quickly dissected the unfolding predicament, immediate regret washing over him for his decision to forsake the rubber protection. As he grappled with this inconvenient reality, another issue crept into the forefront; one he had not anticipated, but one with significant implications nonetheless.

The revelation struck him like a bolt out of the blue. Jindo had never engaged in 'the erotic jiu-jitsu' session with a woman as statuesque as Gabrielle. Straddling her towering frame presented a unique challenge, manoeuvring her limbs into various poses, his modest arm span feeling distressingly inadequate.

His attempts to assert control over the situation only amplified the issue, her lengthy legs proving to be more of a tease than an invitation. Gabrielle's earnest attempts to assist only exacerbated matters, their synchrony seemingly thrown off kilter.

Nevertheless, their brief yet poignant liaison drew to a close, and the duo retired to sleep. Gabrielle, for all her professed discomfort with her surroundings, seemed to find a certain level of cosiness in Jindo's Bondy residence bed. She succumbed to slumber with surprising speed.

Jindo, on the other hand, grappled with this novel situation, his familiar surroundings rendered unfamiliar by the Parisienne's presence. Even so, fatigue eventually claimed him, the aching in his arms and jaw serving as a vivid reminder of their recent escapades.

Chapter 29 : Woven Whispers

At around 3 am…
Jindo woke up as he felt there was a sudden action next to him. Hearing the snore, he could see that the pretty French girl was actually quite a noisy engine even during the sleep. Supposing she might have made a little unconscious movement, he was about to go back to sleep.

At that moment, he felt she had just made another action again, and he was quite surprised by the degree. It was because her action was like somebody put high-volt electricity on her, as the motion was indeed quite wild and spectacular.

Still, in a state of surprise, Jindo witnessed a number of further movements from her. After a quick flashback, he was reminded of some freshmen he saw in the military. It was that since the training was hard and the beginners had a nervous attitude all day long, some individuals had paroxysms during sleep.

He suddenly felt pity for this struggling company owner. He then realised that this ostentatious designer might behave so because she was not treated as respectfully as she wanted to be or used to be.

Feeling pitiful for the young director, he softly put a hand on her forehead like some kind of a gentle exorcist. The lady then seemed to be calming down gradually, and looking at her for an extended moment until hearing the snore, he went back to sleep.

At 6 am…

Stirring at his customary hour, Jindo carefully extricated himself from the plush duvet's embrace, and Gabrielle roused slightly from her slumber due to his movements. Encouraging her to return to her tranquillity, he received a sleepy, serene smile in return before she drifted back to her peaceful repose.

Stepping into the kitchen, Jindo performed a quiet assessment of the breakfast provisions. As he sipped his freshly brewed coffee, he verified the presence of a satisfactory quantity of fruit and milk. Prepared for his usual morning ritual, he then quietly readied himself to step out, anticipating the fresh pastries awaiting him at the local boulangerie.

To the enlightened few, the supremacy of French pastries is an irrefutable truth. While numerous countries have replicated the French bakery experience, the originality and authenticity that emanate from the heart of France are unparalleled, regardless of the boulangerie in question.

Given his unfamiliarity with Gabrielle's breakfast routine, Jindo returned with a cornucopia of pastries; the flaky croissant, the rich pain au chocolate, the spiral escargot, the apple-stuffed chausson aux pommes, and the indulgent éclair. His return stirred the Parisienne from her cosy dreams.

"Where were you?"

"Sorry, did I wake you up? I've just been to the boulangerie."

"Why?"

"Because I didn't have any pastries left at home…"

"Okay."

With a voice still wrapped in the velvety allure of sleep, Gabrielle gifted Jindo another smile. He encouraged her to return to her warm cocoon of blankets.

"Please stay more. I'll take a shower."

"Again?"

"Pardon?"

"You had a shower yesterday."

"…"

Silence filled the room, marked by the discrepancy in hygiene standards between the two. Treading lightly to avoid offence, Jindo replied carefully.

"Gabrielle, I smell really bad when I wake up so I need to wash up…"

"Really? Come! I want to check…"

Gabrielle beckoned him closer, her request filled with gentle curiosity. Though Jindo harboured doubts about his morning state, he did not refuse.

"Gabrielle, I'm not going to be too close but…"

He moved closer to the bed, maintaining a polite distance.

"Jindo, you have to come in, so I can smell…"

Gabrielle extended an invitation, and Jindo responded with a feigned hesitation, stepping inside her domain. She began to sniff while her hands were already prepared themselves, adopting an erotic massage on his body.

Unfazed by the prospect of morning grooming with this wildcat of a lady, Jindo feigned reluctance even as he savoured the moment. His 'mini-me' appeared equally enthusiastic, bracing itself for the ensuing pandemonium.

That morning, however, Gabrielle seemed off. An unpleasant odour lingered around her, a testament to a day left unwashed. The stale hint of her morning breath was particularly distasteful to Jindo. He was all set for their upcoming intimate session, but today's preamble felt noticeably different. Although he was in fine form physically, he could not shake off an undercurrent of unaccountable unease.

Nonetheless, Jindo made the first move by going to the upper position to start, but this time, Gabrielle seemed far from submissive. She suggested they switch roles, a proposal that took him aback. Yet, shrugging off his surprise, Jindo became laid down and then the newly assertive lady began exploring his body, taking out his clothes swiftly and fluently.

Jindo relished the moment, yet he could not help but notice a departure in Gabrielle's tactics. She was less restrained, more adept, her movements teetering on the brink of the wild. As he weathered her onslaught, Jindo marvelled at her unexpected ferocity.

The self-proclaimed yacht driver seemed to revel in this exploratory session, wildly handling and raining blows on his miniature lever with gusto. He even felt heavenly with her suction power.

Yet, something about the encounter felt amiss. Gabrielle's flamboyant display seemed less like interacting and more like a showcase of her prowess. Although Jindo enjoyed the moment, he felt the session lacked reciprocal engagement. It was as if she was performing a solo DJ, intricate and wide-ranging, indifferent to her partner's reactions.

On one occasion, he even suggested she tone down her intensity, as he felt pain as though his 'mini-me' could be weeded out soon if the typhoon continued. However, Gabrielle was engrossed in her rhythm, her focus unwavering, as though she was wearing earplugs, completely absorbed in the sensitivity of the moment.

The former model continued to control the scene, bending and twisting him into various shapes, her long legs cleverly manoeuvring him. Despite the novelty, Jindo did not intervene. She seemed to have a routine, and he did not feel like disturbing it. This time, his limited endurance held out, graciously declining to call it quits prematurely. He let Gabrielle bask in her solo performance. Though the encounter lacked interaction, he savoured the morning session, finding a strange solace in it.

As the session drew to a close, Gabrielle seemed pleased with her performance and retreated. She lay back, panting heavily, as if she had been anticipating this workout since last night. A pang of empathy tugged at Jindo since he felt a twinge of sympathy for her.

Shrugging off his disquiet, Jindo eased himself off the bed, heading for a shower. At that moment, Gabrielle's voice echoed behind him.

"Where are you going?"

"Eh… to a shower?"

"What? You still want to have a shower?"

"…"

Gabrielle's question baffled him. He failed to see the connection between their recent intimacy and his need for a shower. He decided to address this confusion.

"Gabrielle, trust me I'll smell really bad if I don't…"

"No, you didn't smell no bad."

Gabrielle retorted. His standards clearly differed from hers, but Jindo held his ground.

"That's very nice of you Gabrielle, but seriously, I don't want to be smelly…"

"… okay."

Resigned to his preference, she picked up her phone, preparing to peruse her morning feed.

Fresh from the shower, Jindo asked if she wanted breakfast. The still-undressed director, engrossed in her phone, replied without looking up.

"You know I'm a vegan. I don't think you have the right food for me…"

Taken aback by her frankness, he trod carefully.

"… okay, anyway I do have some fruits and pastries if you like…"

"Are the pastries gluten-free?"

"…"

In fact, Jindo, in those days, did not even know the terminology. As this native lady quizzed him on his French pastries using a term unfamiliar to him, he felt belittled and embarrassed. He tried to ask with caution.

"Sorry Gabrielle, what is… glue-ten-free?"

"…"

She barely gave him a glance. Instead of answering, she dismissively suggested that he should help himself.

Returning to the kitchen, Jindo nonetheless asked her if she fancied some fruit or a drink. The strict vegan dismissed all his offerings, leading him to rue the morning's overzealous pastry procurement.

Shrugging off her disinterest, yet filing away the term to inquire about at the boulangerie later, he turned on the radio, preparing for a swift breakfast. At that moment, Gabrielle echoed.

"WHAT'S THAT?"

Emerging from the kitchen, half-bitten croissant in hand, Jindo asked.

"Pardon?"

"What's the musique?"

"It's the radio..."

"No, what is the music?"

"Bah... I don't know, it sounds like some classical music..."

"Can you turn that off, right now?"

"..."

Jindo adopted a quizzical expression as he failed to fathom her sudden vexation at the unknown melody, at which point she clarified.

"My ex-boyfriend was a classical music composer, and he used to listen to that kind of music every morning..."

Jindo, absorbing the information, pondered aloud.

"Ah, the boxer and actor guy was also a music composer?"

"... no, the other one..."

She momentarily halted her phone scrolling to reluctantly respond to Jindo's unexpected query. Jindo, however, did not immediately move to switch off the music, instead standing there, trying to make light conversation.

"You don't like classical music by the way?"

"Bah... I don't care..."

"Well then, can I keep it on because I..."

When Jindo attempted to illustrate his morning routine, Gabrielle shouted.

"BECAUSE HE KILLED HIMSELF!"

"Ah, right, okay, sorry..."

Being interjected by her sharp yelling with the unexpected tragic revelation, Jindo immediately dashed back into the kitchen, promptly turning off the radio. After an awkward silence, Jindo ventured out, extending his apologies.

"Sorry Gabrielle, I didn't know about your story…"

Jindo's apology fell on deaf ears as Gabrielle, the former partner of the deceased composer, already seemed to harbour resentment towards him. The naked woman was giving him her typical grumpy face, silently getting dressed. She returned to her phone, resuming her morning stroll.

Jindo retreated to the kitchen, finishing his breakfast quickly. Although he found it unjust since he did not intend to dredge up any painful memories, he still felt a pang of guilt for Gabrielle.

Emerging from the kitchen, Jindo endeavoured to act as nonchalantly as possible, making his way to throw open every window and refresh the atmosphere of the house. Suddenly, a voice bristling with irritation echoed from the adjacent room.

"WHAT ARE YOU DOING?"

"Um… opening the window…"

Jindo's response was tentative, as he failed to decipher the precise cause of her consternation.

"Why?"

"To… refresh the inside air."

"WHY?"

"…"

Her inquiry hung in the air, unanswered. A dismissive shake of her head accompanied a look of distaste directed at Jindo's rather habitual action. Despite being aware of Gabrielle's preference for her Parisian, windowless sanctuary, Jindo, this time, felt an unusual impulse to defend himself.

"Gabrielle, it's actually not that bad here. Look, we have many trees and plants in the garden. The air is quite fresh as well…"

In fact, Jindo's garden was meticulously maintained by Gregory, lending an air of tranquillity to the mornings. Yet Gabrielle, partial to her hermetically-sealed spaces, seemed to perceive the third-generation house as somewhat antiquated in the cold light of day.

Irritated with Jindo's window-opening spree, she glared at him, her fury akin to a severely vexed feline. In an attempt to alleviate the tension, Jindo ventured to steer the conversation elsewhere.

"The company will start in the afternoon today, right?"

"… but we need to leave now…"

"Pardon?"

Jindo glanced at the time, finding himself at a loss. It was barely half past seven.

"Gabrielle, do you know what time it is now?"

"YES OF COURSE I KNOW, you think my iPhone is stupid? We're already late…"

"…"

Her attention was still firmly affixed to her phone, and Jindo found himself unable to comprehend the urgency of her assertion.

Unfazed, Gabrielle began to ready herself, slipping into her sleek, black Balenciaga Speed Runner sneakers. Attempting to slow her down, Jindo interjected.

"Gabrielle, hang on… Why do we need to leave now? Can we not take a bit of time here? Because I need to…"

"WHAT? What do you need to do here, IN THIS STUPID OLD HOUSE?"

With the unexpected insult, the sprinter in the starting blocks cut him short. Jindo partly agreed that the age of the house and that there was little to attend to in the place, but meanwhile, he did not see that as a reason for their hurried departure yet. He strove to pacify the prickly lady.

"I mean... can we not have a little teatime here before we leave?"

Indicating a quaint table in the garden, Jindo's suggestion was met with a pointed narrowing of Gabrielle's eyes as she sized him up critically.

"What? Are you playing an Englishman? Do you think this is England? We don't do teatime in France... And why do you want to spend your morning by sitting in that stupid place, which is not even a garden..."

"Pardon?"

"You just have a petite space with some stupid antique table and chairs, and it even looks like your neighbour's garden, not yours..."

Gabrielle's Parisian candour once again caught him off guard. Struggling to ease the tension, Jindo tried to explain his modest proposal.

"I didn't ask to stay for a BBQ, but a tea... that doesn't practically mean to drink a cup of hot water, but to take a brief moment to get ready to start the day..."

"WELL, I'M READY..."

As she raised her eyebrows by lifting one foot of hers to show herself worn in her shoe, the remnants of sleep still clinging to them, Gabrielle seemed to take a perverse pleasure in mocking the would-be teatime participant.

Jindo returned her stare, a silence descending between them that was charged with an undercurrent of animosity. Seizing a chair from the living room, Gabrielle positioned it by the window and declared.

"Okay then, have the stupid tea now. I'll wait for you here..."

"... Gabrielle? Do you need to do this?"

"What? You said you want to have tea, then do it. I'll be here..."

This time, Jindo felt a surge of anger. It was clear that her annoyance was no longer about the work-related issues but directed towards him personally. Despite her position as his director, he felt an unprecedented indifference.

His gaze bore into her, an intensity that seemed to hint at a hitherto unseen side of Jindo. He resembled a hound that had ceased barking, ready to bite. His countenance bore no signs of mercy or his usual affability.

It did not take long for Gabrielle to pick up on the heated tension. She abruptly softened her stance, attempting to appear as innocent as possible. She bore an uncanny resemblance to a feline, exhibiting feigned docility, her eyes blinking gently in an unspoken declaration of her unwillingness to quarrel.

The air filled with a brief silence before she spoke again, choosing her words with care.

"Jindo... you know I'm a company owner and this event is important to me as I need to make sales... and I didn't want to tell you this... because you're one of my employees... but I still need to make money to give salaries and pay the rent..."

Jindo was simmering with irritation, yet his mind had swiftly grasped her reasoning. He immediately understood the entrepreneur's predicaments, chiding himself for his fleeting annoyance.

However, he could not overlook the fact that her behaviour had been less than gracious. Despite his irritation subsiding swiftly, he chose to keep this emotional shift hidden. Regaining his composure with speed, he readied his response, carefully concealing his now softer sentiments.

"Okay, I get it Gabrielle, but please get me 2 minutes. I'm not going to have tea, but I need to prepare some food for the cats..."

"Okay..."

Gabrielle attempted to steal a glance at his countenance, assessing his current state, before returning to her mobile. Jindo managed to resecure the property quickly, preparing to step outside. At that moment, Gabrielle posed her question.

"By the way Jindo, can I borrow your mannequins for today?"

"My mannequins?"

"Yes, because I think it'll be good if I put them in the atelier today... I'm sure the guests will visit the atelier, and I think your mannequins will make my stupid garments look superb..."

Jindo was disconcerted by her abrupt confession and request but simultaneously flattered by the compliments lavished upon his possessions.

"I'm not sure if..."

"There're some of my old colleagues coming, like people that I know from CHANEL and Hermès..."

She interjected by referring to the two notable labels, and Jindo was taken aback but still unsure. Gabrielle carried on regardless.

"Yes, they're coming. Look, I'm texting with them since the morning..."

Presenting her phone screen to Jindo, she seemed somewhat convincing.

"I'm sure my Hermès boss would surely come to check my working space... She's always interested in anyone's atelier..."

Although Jindo found her assertion rather odd, the mention of his dream brand still excited him. Yet, he remained unclear about the situation, and at that moment, her phone chimed with an incoming message.

"Look, it's her. She's asking…"

Gabrielle quickly flashed her screen at him, only to withdraw it abruptly to reply. She spoke up as she texted.

"I'm sure she'll be definitely impressed with your work…"

"Eh…"

Jindo remained puzzled by the sudden developments, prompting him to voice his concerns.

"By the way Gabrielle, why did you not tell me about this before?"

"Sorry I just had too many things to do, you know I'm always busy…"

Her fingers danced across the phone screen, busily typing away. A pause and then her answer floated over to him.

"Because I didn't know she was coming, but she texted me this morning…"

"Ah, okay…"

Jindo found himself swayed by the revelation as his concern was somehow moving elsewhere.

"By the way Gabrielle, I'm actually a bit worried though, because it's not my finest work that we have now. You know the majority was actually done by Hélène and Julien and… hah (exhales)…"

Jindo's words trailed off into an exhausted sigh. He was painfully aware of the imperfections in the current collection, despite his admiration for the earnest efforts of his young assistants.

Now, with the imminent arrival of VIPs from the esteemed fashion houses, he was concerned that the work's state would reflect poorly on his skills. Gabrielle, however, sought to assuage his concerns.

"You don't need to worry about that, Jindo. She'll understand it… and I'm sure she'll definitely see your fine quality… Anyway Jindo, I think it'll be better to present the pieces on your mannequins, not mine…"

As she carried on with her flurry of texts, Jindo conceded.

"Fine, but they shouldn't be displayed the way it is now…"

Without further ado, Jindo proceeded to load his four mannequins into the car, the ex-CHANEL designer watching in approval, her attention still tethered to her phone screen.

Now, Jindo set off towards Paris, and despite the morning traffic, his usual composure behind the wheel was replaced by an exhilarating dash. Gabrielle, taken aback by his uncharacteristically fervent driving, appeared to relish the thrilling ride.

Upon their arrival at the company, Jindo swiftly manoeuvred the four mannequins to the atelier. He began dissecting the existing patterns and muslins, homing in on potential issues. So engrossed was he that he lost track of time.

When the clock struck 2 pm, he was jolted back to reality by the bustle of the company staff trickling in. The non-stop, five-hour labour of intense concentration had swept him into a timeless bubble.

Chapter 30 : Silhouettes of Secrecy

The atelier came alive...

Jindo, attuned to the growing hustle and bustle, recognised Seiwa's voice drifting from the studio. She seemed to be managing last-minute alterations with the youthful girls, and as Jindo prepared to escape for a late lunch, he encountered the sister in the foyer.

"Oppa, you're here early."

"Well, I've been here since morning..."

"Since morning? What for?"

"Well… because I had… things to do…"

"What thing?"

Jindo fumbled for a response. His hesitation did not escape Seiwa's notice.

"Oppa, you're being weird."

"What? I just had to organise the atelier…"

"I feel you're hiding something…"

"I'm not hiding anything…"

"I know you're terrible at lying... what's the matter?"

"Piss off, I'm off to lunch..."

Jindo attempted to deflect, evading eye contact with Seiwa. However, she was not to be side-tracked.

"Oppa, I know you more than you do about yourself... What are you hiding from me?"

"I'm not hiding anything, you idiot..."

Jindo, seeing that Seiwa was not backing down, decided to steer the conversation elsewhere.

"Anyway, how did your date go yesterday?"

"Oh, that? It was splendid. I'm meeting him again tonight..."

"Really? Good for you. You're a bit slutty by the way…"

"No, it's for dinner tonight, you idiot."

"Okay okay… By the way, you're not staying here tonight?"

"Hell no, I'll leave right away once I finish my duty. Anyway, I hate to be with Madame Claude until then…"

"Do you still have issues with her?"

"Still? You're quite naive about her. Nobody can tolerate her... Wasn't that obvious?"

Indeed, Jindo was aware of the animosity between Seiwa and Madame Claude. He was also privy to the director's mother's notorious behaviour, particularly towards the young girls. With Seiwa, she seemed to scrutinise the assistant designer's work, finding fault where none existed.

He remembered a particular instance when Madame Claude had asked him why Seiwa was so brazen compared to his meek demeanour. Though Jindo defended his sister, he quickly discerned that Madame Claude held a general disdain for his Malaysian sister. From his vantage point, it seemed the middle-aged French woman's dislike was not rooted in Seiwa's work performance but rather, her refusal to remain docile.

In a sense, Jindo sympathised with the workers' plight, acutely aware of the director and her mother's expectation of blind obedience despite the lack of remuneration. More often than not, the two treated their employees with cruel indifference, as if they were nothing more than servants.

Jindo could not completely disregard Seiwa's grievances, yet he felt powerless in his current position. The Asian siblings had not yet broached the topic, but it seemed the issue was finally surfacing.

"Oppa, you know I came here because of the praises you sang about Gabrielle... Then later, when I told you I wanted to quit, you told me I'm too impatient always..."

Indeed, there was a time when Seiwa expressed her deep discontent with Madame Claude, even considering resigning from the unpaid internship. Jindo, however, persuaded the sister to persist until the end of her contractual term.

"Yes, I did indeed... because you always seem to quit things too early... Also, I think it's still important you stay till the end because you never know what's going to happen in the end..."

"I get your point Oppa, but Madame Claude is just so insufferable. You wouldn't know because she treats you nicely..."

In fact, Jindo had not yet encountered any issues with the notorious parent of Gabrielle.

Regardless, he decided to steer the conversation towards a less tense subject.

"Okay okay, so you're not staying late tonight anyway?"

"Definitely not... Plus, I don't even think any cute guy will come anyway, so there's no point haha..."

"Haha, okay, fair enough... By the way, you know who will be coming?"

"No, anyone famous?"

"I don't know, but Gabrielle told me that her ex-colleagues will come... like the ones from CHANEL and Hermès..."

"... really?"

Seiwa did not seem surprised but rather wore a suspicious expression.

"Oppa, I think there's something I should tell you..."

Seiwa's usual vivacity gave way to a more serious tone.

"Oppa, you know when I was sending out invitations, Gabrielle gave me a contact list and I got to communicate with some of them... and there seemed to be no one like the luxury fashion house professionals... the ones I reached out to were like normal people... like newbie influencers or just ordinary people who looked to have nothing to do with the fashion industry... It's hard to explain, but... I get a feeling that Gabrielle intentionally avoids people with experiences but somewhat inexperienced ones... I don't know how to put this..."

Seiwa paused for a moment, gathering her thoughts before continuing.

"Also, I've been handling some of her business emails and I don't know exactly what has happened before but... it seems like she has many legal cases with other brands over trademarks. There were also many reminders about unpaid balances from manufacturers..."

At that moment, the renowned director entered, returning after a four-hour absence under the pretext of a gym and shower break.

The freshly groomed lady did not waste time scrutinising the Asian siblings.

"What are you two doing here?"

"Well, I was going to lunch and just met Seiwa here..."

Gabrielle remained silent, her gaze darting suspiciously between Jindo and Seiwa.

Breaking the uncomfortable silence, Jindo asked casually, his tone hinting at his curiosity about her lengthy absence while he toiled in the atelier.

"How was your gym session by the way?"

"Eh? Ah… it was… good…"

While her typical approach was to scrutinise the siblings rigorously, Jindo was not playing the obedient employee this time. Exuding comfortable confidence, he disarmed her, and for once, she made a swift exit instead of trying to separate the pair.

Seiwa did not miss a beat.

"Oppa, she's strange…"

"Why do you say so?"

"I don't know…"

Seiwa pondered for a while before her eyes rested on Jindo. She gave him a once-over and asked.

"What happened between you two?"

"What? Nothing happened…"

Jindo found himself caught off guard by the sudden inquisition. It was not merely a guess but it felt more like a confirmation.

"Hm, something's not quite normal with you and Gabrielle… Look at you, you can't even see my face properly…"

"What are you on about, you idiot?"

"See? You're swearing… and you normally swear like that when you're embarrassed…"

With that observation, Seiwa moved closer to Jindo, trying to decipher his evasive demeanour. The gay sleuth voiced her suspicion.

"You two… slept together, didn't you? You stayed here yesterday, didn't you?"

"WHAT? No..."

Jindo responded with an expletive, still not daring to make eye contact with Seiwa.

"See see see… Oppa, I'm gay. You know I can read both sides…"

"에이 씨발, 뭔 소리야…" *(Bloody hell, what are you on about…)*

Jindo racked his brains for a way out of the predicament but drew a blank. Seiwa seemed to take Jindo's swearing in his native tongue as confirmation.

"Oppa, you really did?"

He gave a subtle nod of confirmation, trying to hush his prying sister.

"Quiet, you idiot, you're too loud… Okay okay, we did it…"

"You really did? How come? When and where? Here?"

"Shu shu shu, still too loud… not here but at my place…"

"The Bondy house? You took her there?"

"Yes, but I'll tell you later. Please… not now…"

"Wow, good for you. Somebody finally blew my Oppa's little dick…"

"Shu shu shu, you're still too loud… By the way, what do you mean by finally?"

"Well, I knew you've been pathetically lonely, always bloody working, drinking and wanking alone…"

"What? Don't be fucking rude, you dickhead."

Jindo was not in favour of prolonging the topic, but Seiwa continued to strike him regardless.

"It was the first time after your girlfriend left you, wasn't it?"

"Can you bloody shut up?"

"By the way, wow… you fucked the director."

"Shut it shut it, too loud…"

"Haha, what's wrong with that? Was it good though?"

"I'm not going to talk about my private life with you, idiot."

"You always ask me about my private life, idiot."

"It's different, mine is like a real private, and yours is just like… a one-off, online date for benefit…"

"Sod off, you loser. I always look for love that… has just not long lasted, haha… Anyway, I told you I'll meet the guy again for dinner tonight, so it's not just for the benefit this time…"

"Okay okay, I get it. Let's stop it right here…"

"Why? Oppa, good for you!"

"Stop it. I'll get going now…"

"Haha, don't be shy…"

Jindo departed, and Seiwa relentlessly teased her sheepish brother till the last step.

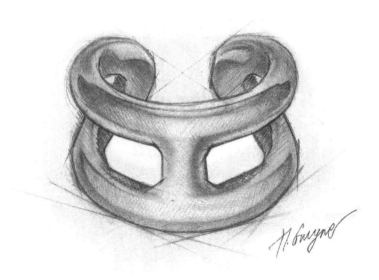

Chapter 31 : The Peacock's Parade

Passing by 5 pm…

Fresh from a respite in his personal retreat near Pont Neuf, Jindo returned and found the studio in chaos. Gabrielle, now sporting a multicoloured short leather jacket adorned with fringes, was barking orders at the scurrying studio girls. With their white t-shirts and oversized ribbon hairbands, they looked rather like rabbits being corralled by a flamboyantly plumed peacock.

Deciding the studio team had their own matters in hand, Jindo descended quietly to the atelier and found his two modéliste assistants in the place.

"What are you two up to?"

"Hi, Jindo. We just came early because we thought you might need help for the atelier setting…"

Julien responded with a sincere smile. In fact, asides from Jindo, who would be playing a bartender, the atelier staff were supposed to attend the evening event as guests.

Jindo was touched by their consideration, yet puzzled by their early arrival.

"How did you guys know I'd be here early?"

"Jindo, we know you always come early, preparing the atelier, and even leaving late…"

Again, touched by their thoughtfulness, Jindo was about to respond when Hélène noticed something unusual.

"Jindo, these mannequins are new..."

"Ah yes, they're mine... Gabrielle wanted me to... bring them for the display..."

Jindo's reply was hesitant, caught off-guard by the unexpected early arrival of his assistants. Luckily, Hélène did not probe the issue, and instead, her interest was piqued by the unique statues.

"I've not seen these custom models before..."

"Well, it's nothing special, really..."

At that moment, Julien noticed his paperwork on the table.

"Jindo, is it my work? It looks like you have changed something..."

"Yes, it's yours... I just... tidied them up a bit..."

Caught off-guard again by the sudden queries, Jindo stumbled over his words. However, Julien did not investigate further, merely acknowledging the improvement.

"It looks a lot better. Sorry for my messy drafts, Jindo..."

In fact, Julien's work often contained personal annotations. Jindo typically did not mind as he recognised, they were part of Julien's learning process. However, when it came to presenting to a third party, he believed a cleaner, more professional look would be essential.

Hélène then brought up another alteration.

"Jindo, you've even adjusted the draping... I can see you've redrawn the lines, including the axes..."

"Yes, I'm sorry... your lines were fine, but I just... polished them up a bit..."

"No, it looks more professional now. I'm sorry for my sloppy lines..."

In fact, Hélène's drafts tended to be less refined since she strove for precision, redrawing repeatedly to get it right. Jindo usually let it slide, offering occasional gentle reminders. However, for presentation purposes, he understood the importance of a neater output.

In the manual modélisme presentations, whether on paper or muslin, cleanliness is paramount. The work must be comprehensible to all parties involved. Despite some constructions being intrinsically complex, they must retain a clean appearance to effectively illustrate the journey to the final outcome.

In draping, precise axes are crucial. They serve as reference lines during fitting. Given that one of the fundamental purposes of draping is to facilitate ongoing modifications through repeated fittings, even one instance of imprecisely marked axes can jeopardise the accumulated effort.

When seasoned modélistes assess the work of potential assistants, one of the primary aspects they scrutinise is the precision and cleanliness of the work. Apart from skills and techniques, it's a reliable indicator of the candidate's basic attitude toward the work.

Over minutes, the conversation gradually became more relaxed. As they were outside of official working hours, the two assistants felt comfortable raising their queries, and Jindo interacted with them more informally.

Julien, in particular, was curious about upcoming trends in the industry.

"Jindo, I heard it's getting more important to use CAD programmes in fashion these days. Do you think it's necessary to learn?"

"I think it's not just necessary, but essential quite soon… I heard that the software developers even made a 3D programme by applying some of the flight engine technologies, to calculate a wind effect in the fabric, considering human movement… So, I think much of the modélisme work, that is required for draping, will be also done by the digital software quite soon…"

"Do you also know how to do CAD?"

"Well, unfortunately, no… I tried to learn one of the Japanese ones a long time ago but failed, as my basic modélisme knowledge wasn't enough to understand the lesson at that time… Then again, when I tried to learn 'Lectra' in Paris, I failed again, as the lesson and programme were in French. You know my French is pathetically useless…"

"Haha, no…"

"Well, I admit that I'm not a winner to be digital-friendly in this sense… Anyway, if you seriously think about becoming a modéliste in the future, I strongly advise you to learn these digital tools no matter what… I think it'll be also important for database purposes anyway…"

"Then is it not going to be the same case with you as well, Jindo?"

"Good point… For me, to be honest, I don't plan to be a permanent modéliste. Actually, my goal is to open my small, independent family boutique in Paris, then run the enterprise by hiring people… Until then, I just want to experience and learn about the industry… Playing a modéliste at the moment is because it's a kind of niche market that I can get myself to be immediately engaged in the industry and I like the work of course…"

Hélène seemed intrigued, engaging in the conversation.

"Is that why you chose to work at an independent designer's boutique like Gabrielle's?"

"Well, yes and no… Of course, I didn't come to France to work at Gabrielle's. My ideal brand is Hermès because I've had a huge respect for Hermès for a long time in many ways…"

"Oh, Hermès…"

The two assistants nodded, clearly appreciating the illustrious reputation of the label.

At that moment, the sound of footsteps echoed from the stairs, announcing the arrival of the former CHANEL designer.

"What are you guys doing here?"

"… we're just talking…"

Jindo began but trailed off, but meanwhile, Gabrielle appeared to be already irked by the modélistes gathering that seemed to be idly chatting.

"Jindo, do you not see people working upstairs?"

Jindo tried to stand up for his team.

"Gabrielle, Hélène and Julien came in early to help me, and we're just discussing what they're learning here..."

"Alors, c'est pas l'école ici…"

(Well, it's not school here…)

She snapped back, her face creased into a sour expression. Strangely enough, her gaze seemed fixed on Hélène. She only had eyes for the female assistant, causing Jindo to bring up the elephant in the room.

"Gabrielle, you know the atelier people are actually not supposed to work today…"

As the director-appointed atelier manager, Jindo felt obligated to defend his team. The irritated director, however, shot him a sharp look, clearly conveying a message for him to keep quiet. Jindo had always noticed that Gabrielle was particularly stern, even hostile, towards his female assistant.

She continued to glare at Hélène, who seemed at a loss as to how to handle the situation. Given that Hélène was standing right beside Jindo, Gabrielle appeared to be unnerved by their proximity.

"Jindo, you need to come upstairs because the drinks have arrived…"

As the evening's appointed bartender, it was his cue to move. However, Gabrielle's gaze still rested firmly on Hélène, reminding one of a territorial senior cat regarding a young newcomer in the house.

Regardless, they ascended the stairs together, ready to haul five large beverage boxes upstairs. Jindo and Julien each took one, and Hélène reached for another. At that moment, Gabrielle sharply called out to the female assistant, seemingly instructing her to assist the studio team upstairs, not Jindo.

Looking flustered, Hélène hesitated, and Jindo jumped to her defence.

"Gabrielle, you know Hélène isn't supposed to work today. She's here with us…"

Cradling the box in his arms, Jindo used his eyes to signal Julien and himself, subtly drawing attention to their unified front. Gabrielle appeared taken aback by his forthright stance. After all, this was the first time Jindo had spoken up to the director in front of the other people.

Gabrielle and Jindo found themselves locked in a silent stare-off, a newly sprouted audacity evident in Jindo; typically reserved for those who have shared an intimate encounter. Their gaze did not waver, and then Gabrielle seemed to sense the balance of power teetering towards Jindo, bolstered by his loyal assistants.

A pang of remorse struck Jindo since Gabrielle, after all, was still the director. He sought to defuse the tension.

"Gabrielle, please let Hélène help us because this is a bit too much for me and Julien to carry out…"

Ignoring his proposition, Gabrielle departed, leaving a scornful glance in her wake. Jindo, unfazed, led his team upstairs, preparing to set up the bar.

Chapter 32 : The Party's Peculiar Puzzle

A rriving at the top floor…
Having moved all beverage boxes to the kitchen, Jindo discovered a man in the corner, meticulously preparing couscous that the vegan director had ordered from a local restaurant. Jindo struck up a friendly banter, asking if the man was a restaurant employee.

However, the man's response seemed somehow frosty and haughty. He ignorantly introduced himself as the restaurant owner, not staff, and retorted whether Jindo was merely an employee.

The brusque exchange hinted at an underlying tension; the young couscous entrepreneur was evidently eager to establish a hierarchy. While initially irked, Jindo decided not to make a fuss as the man was not his superior after all. Instead, he turned his attention to preparing beverages.

As the glass arrangements fell into place, Jindo noted the couscous purveyor's lingering presence. Indeed, the food preparation had concluded a while ago, yet he seemed to be biding his time, repeatedly casting glances in Gabrielle's direction, as though waiting for an opportunity to engage her.

7 pm…

The guests started trickling in, and Seiwa appeared to have wrapped up her tasks.

"Oppa, can I have a drink?"

"You haven't left?"

"Oppa, I can't leave right away. The studio people are supposed to stay until 8 pm… Anyway, my appointment is also at 8 pm, so I'm now checking the moment to sneak out..."

"Ah, okay..."

"By the way Oppa, be careful with what I said before…"

"What? You need to be a bit specific mate…"

Seiwa glanced at Hélène and Julien flanking Jindo, opting to withhold her comment for another time.

"I'll tell you later…"

After she left, Timothée approached the bar.

"Salut, Jindo. Ça va?"

"Oui oui, très bien. Tu vas bien?"

"Oui oui, alors, c'est ma copine…"

(Yes yes, anyway, this is my girlfriend…)

Timothée introduced his Afro-French girlfriend, stylishly clad in a PVC trench coat.

Upon greeting her, Jindo enquired the chapelier about Amélie. The hatmaker shared in hushed tones that Amélie had locked horns with Madame Claude; Seiwa's assertion that the director's mother was not the easiest person to get along with seemed accurate.

Enjoying their light-hearted banter, Julien and Hélène joined in. The atelier group relished their time away from work as the party's energy swelled with an influx of guests.

After draining his glass, Timothée wandered off to mingle with others. As soon as he vacated his spot at the bar, a blue-eyed, blonde girl approached Jindo. She ordered a drink, and as Jindo prepared it, he recalled that she had been eyeing him for some time, only approaching when he was alone.

She broke the ice.

"한국분 이시죠?"

(You're Korean, right?)

"Yes, but… don't you think it's a bit strange you ask that question in Korean?"

"네?"

(Sorry?)

Jindo's dry response in English to her question in Korean seemed to catch her off-guard. Jindo had intended this, finding her somewhat overbearing. He continued in English.

"What I'm saying is… if I wasn't Korean, your question could be a bit embarrassing…"

"…"

"For example, a Japanese person might not appreciate being mistaken for Korean… not because they hate us, but because they may want to be recognised as Japanese… I hope you understand my point…"

Jindo served her the drink. Unfazed, she retorted.

"아, 근데 한국 분 인줄 알고 있었어요. 일본 사람같이 안 생기셨어요…"

(Ah, but I knew you were Korean. You don't look like a Japanese…)

"Well, the point is… it could be embarrassing if you ask a question to a person in a language that you chose, solely based on your assumption…"

The spiky bartender, hair slickly tied up, replied with a hint of a smile. Meanwhile, Jindo, for his part, was quite shocked by the blonde girl's fluidity in his native tongue.

In those days of Europe, it was not an everyday occurrence to encounter Westerners adept in Korean at a fluent level. There were those who would profess their familiarity with Korean culture, lobbying references to 'kimchi' and 'soju', but it was an exceptional rarity to meet someone who could carry a conversation, hitting all the proper notes and maintaining eye contact with the rhythm of the language.

In fact, Jindo had weathered numerous encounters with such Korean culture enthusiasts. Their conversations would often begin with a smattering of Korean phrases, and, as alcohol loosened their tongues, they would start to regard him like some cheap entertainer, ready to launch into a 'Gangnam Style' routine at the drop of a hat.

Given this context, the English-speaking Korean would bristle a touch when approached by Westerners who brazenly paraded their amateurish grasp of his mother tongue. At that moment, the French girl spoke up.

"제가 아는 한국분 들이랑 좀 다르신 것 같네요. 프랑스 사람 같으세요…"

(You seem different from Koreans that I've met. You come across as French…)

The blue-eyed, blonde girl was gently goading Jindo, refusing to make it easy for him. A perplexed expression crossed Jindo's face as he feigned misunderstanding.

"Well, which part of me looks like French? I'm a complete Korean. I can pull my trousers down and prove it if you like…"

"Haha."

Ice broken with a chuckle; they continued in friendly banter. Their exchange, now imbued with warmth, quickly progressed, revealing her deep-seated knowledge of various Asian cultures. Jindo, though still astounded by her linguistic proficiency, chose not to comment on it.

In due course, Jindo inquired about her presence at the event. She revealed that a friend, an aspiring fashion influencer, had snagged an

Instagram invite. She gestured towards her friend, now lost in the crowd, and Jindo took the opportunity to scan the room's occupants.

Observing the youthful, foreign, and seemingly fashion-novice crowd, Jindo conceded that Seiwa might have hit the nail on the head. Gabrielle, it appeared, had indeed set her sights on the inexperienced. At that moment, the girls recontinued the conversation.

"근데, 성함이…"

(By the way, what's your name?)

"Jindo."

"카카오톡 물어봐도 되나요?"

(May I ask for your KakaoTalk ID?)

"Sorry, I don't do KakaoTalk…"

Indeed, 'KakaoTalk' was a messaging application ubiquitous among Koreans, much like 'WeChat' was to the Chinese. Thus, a Korean claiming not to have it might imply a reluctance to share contact details.

She nodded, a flicker of disbelief playing across her features. The non-KakaoTalk user spoke up.

"I'll give you my phone number instead… That way, for me, is better and faster…"

She seemed to acquiesce to the unconventional Korean's preference, lending credibility to his assertion of being a non-user of the mobile messaging app.

Meanwhile, their unique conversational style drew more than a few curious glances. The blue-eyed, blonde French girl was conversing in Korean with Jindo, who replied in English. Their odd bilingual exchange was proving to be something of a spectacle.

Catching sight of this from a distance, Gabrielle made her way towards them, her multicoloured fringed jacket billowing around her. Jindo and the Korean-speaking girl were in the midst of exchanging phone numbers when Gabrielle, the tall, peacock-colourful party host, swept in.

"Jindo, the drinks are finished?"

Gabrielle's tone already carried an undercurrent of annoyance.

"Um, we still have…"

As Jindo began to check their stock, phone in hand, Gabrielle cut him off.

"Anyway, can you get some more wines from Carrefour? Ask Madame Claude for the credit card, and she's downstairs in the showroom…"

"…"

It was not hard to deduce Gabrielle's intent to pry Jindo away from the girl. Towering at more than six feet in her high heels, Gabrielle in her fringed leather jacket made quite the intimidating figure, flanked by the two mid-exchanges. The girl seemed slightly taken aback by the host's imposing presence.

Meanwhile, Jindo wanted to save her phone number before departing. He tilted his head to ask her for the rest of the phone numbers, and at that moment, Gabrielle was quick to make her displeasure known, her words striking like a hissing cat.

"Jindo, YOU NEED TO GO RIGHT NOW! More guests are coming…"

"…"

Failing to hit the save button for the girl's phone number, Jindo was about to descend via the curvy staircase when he happened upon a young girl obstructing his path. Evidently, a touch inebriated, the girl made a small movement to let him by.

No sooner had she done so, a stray kick sent one of Gabrielle's prized books, displayed so proudly on the staircase, cascading downwards. The delicate balance of the book dominos was disrupted, and they tumbled one after the other in an unfortunate sequence of events.

Jindo recalled how, at the commencement of the event, Gabrielle had warned the flock of youthful attendees about the precarious book arrangement, imploring them to tread carefully. Yet, even then, it was not wholly unexpected to witness the collapse of this literary architecture.

Startled out of her intoxicated state, the young girl turned a deep shade of embarrassment, clearly discomfited by the attention she had inadvertently drawn to herself.

Enter Madame Claude, arriving on the scene like a storm front. She subjected the mortified girl to a gaze that might as well have been a lash, compounding her distress. In this instance, Gabrielle and her domineering mother seemed in eerie harmony, making the situation increasingly unpleasant for the hapless offender.

Oddly, when Jindo attempted to share some responsibility for the unfortunate incident, Gabrielle silenced him with a severe glance, unambiguously gesturing for him to go and replenish the rapidly depleting drink supplies.

Regardless, Jindo went to purchase a box of the most budget-friendly white wine as instructed and began his return journey. On his way back, he crossed paths with Seiwa, who was on her way out.

"Oppa, I'm leaving now…"

"Oh, you're still here? It's over 9 pm…"

"I know, I'm bloody late. The old woman has been annoying as usual…"

"What happened?"

"I finished all the work that Gabrielle asked, then Madame Claude suddenly came, telling me to count sales… I did it, and it was nearly 8 pm when I was done… Then, she kept saying I miscalculated the prices of the items blah blah blah… Anyway, we counted again like four times, and it bloody turned out she's the one who miscalculated the money in her little stupid bag… She didn't even admit her mistakes, but tried to blame the young girls like they stole the money, whatever… and you know what? The kids had nothing to do with the sales, but just kept reorganising the display after people browsed… She just has such an awful human nature. So annoying… Anyway, I'm really late Oppa, I'm leaving now…"

"Okay, anyway, Gabrielle knows you're leaving, yeah?"

"I don't fucking give a shit, I already worked over hours… Anyway, they're busy forcing the poor girl to buy her stupid pieces…"

"What? They who? And who is the poor girl?"

"Gabrielle and her mum for fuck's sake Oppa, and you know, that girl, kicked the bloody stupid book dominos by accident… I think she apologised to Gabrielle like a thousand times, trying to compensate for the damages she made but Gabrielle asked her to buy her pieces instead… and now the fantastic duo of the mum and daughter are trying to upsell to the poor girl the stupid garments of Gabrielle's… The girl was even borrowing money from her friends for fuck's sake…"

"Ah, okay…"

"Anyway, you know the bloody books were set to be fallen down anyway. The poor girl was just chosen for the nightmare…"

"Okay okay, so you're leaving now?"

"Yes, wish me luck."

"Good luck."

Seiwa rushed to the metro station, and Jindo, box clutched against his chest, was about to kick the door open with his foot. At that moment, a hand, cloaked in a dark brown corduroy jacket, held it open for him.

Jindo glanced at the helper and recognised Antoine, accompanied by his pregnant wife. Their greetings, while not overly friendly, bore a sense of mutual respect in a masculine manner. Antoine introduced his wife, and Jindo greeted her.

"Enchanté, Irina."

Together, they ascended the staircase, where Jindo spotted Madame Claude in the showroom, accepting cash from the disgruntled girl. She seemed to grimace rather than smile, clearly not thrilled with her purchase, just as Seiwa had recounted. Spotting Jindo and the couple, Gabrielle hastened over to them.

Back at the bar, Jindo placed the newly purchased wines in the ice box to chill and turned his attention to pouring a drink for Irina. Gabrielle and Antoine remained near the stairs, apparently caught up in an animated rehashing of the book dominos episode.

Meanwhile, Irina and Jindo struck up a conversation at the bar.

"I heard you're doing your own brand, Irina."

"Oh, that... Well, I'm just in preparation..."

"Okay great, can I ask what type of concepts or styles you pursue?"

"Classic couture, women's wear specifically... Still very much in the experimental phase though..."

Casual as their conversation might have been, Jindo could discern that the graduate designer, Irina, was not quite as green as Gabrielle had painted her. Curiosity piqued, Jindo decided to dig a bit deeper.

"Gabrielle told me that you went straight to opening your own label after graduation... Was it not challenging?"

"Eh? No, I worked at companies for a long time... When I came to France, I went to an institute for further learning, but I worked before and even after graduation in France though it wasn't that long period..."

"Ah..."

This revelation was a bit of a curveball for Jindo. It was not at all in line with the narrative that Gabrielle had relayed the previous evening. However, he chose not to raise the discrepancy right then.

"Okay, I must have misheard then... Anyway, so you worked in France?"

"Yes. Well, I only worked at one company though... I liked the place but I just didn't extend my contract because of the pregnancy... But still, I didn't want to lose my couture sense, so I'm trying to create a small collection from home now..."

"Wow, good for you Irina... By the way, is it hard to keep being at work in France with a pregnancy? I'm wondering because Gabrielle's is the first company that I'm engaged in, so I still have no idea how things work in this country yet..."

"Well, Jindo, as I said, I've only worked once here in France, so I don't have much information either..."

"Ah okay, sorry..."

"I learned a lot from the place though..."

"That's fantastic... If you don't mind me asking, where did you work?"

"Dior."

"Pardon? Christian Dior?"

Chapter 33 : Silhouettes of Subtlety

"Pardon? Christian Dior?"

The name left Jindo momentarily dumbfounded. After all, he was under the impression that the revered French label had an infallible recruitment process, cloaked in secrecy and finesse, ensuring only the crème de la crème was selected, even for a stagiaire position.

He vividly recalled hearing such accounts, and thus his astonishment was hardly a veil since his reaction was as clear as daylight. The ex-Dior lady, modest and demure, made an attempt to downplay the revelation.

"By the way Jindo, as I said, I was merely on a temporary contract... so I wouldn't quite label myself a proper employee at Dior…"

Jindo could not help but note the stark contrast between this pregnant woman and the former CHANEL designer he was working with.

At that moment, his musings were abruptly cut short by Gabrielle's arrival at the bar.

"Jindo, I forgot to tell you we need to make a new piece of the camouflage jacket…"

"You mean, the one assembled from 87 distinct panels?"

"Oui."

No sooner had he absorbed the shock of the Dior revelation, Jindo was now confronted with a fresh predicament. He vividly recalled the painstaking retouching session on the jacket in question. Yet, in the presence of the guest, he refrained from uttering any note of dissent.

"Okay, Gabrielle… By the way, you know it'll take a bit of time."

"Why? You made it fast last time."

"Gabrielle, it was a retouch… and that was actually done with a bit of improvisation from me and Boubacar. To make a new one, it'll be a different case…"

"What are you talking about? Improvisation? You eventually changed my design?"

"… Gabrielle… you know I didn't change the design…"

With his eyes, Jindo attempted to silently convey to Gabrielle the tumultuous day of the retouching session. A day when the atelier was abuzz with the modéliste and seamstress, and Gabrielle herself was present.

However, his nonverbal plea fell on deaf ears as the always-preoccupied director was more anxious about the lack of direct acquiescence from her production manager.

In an independent fashion house, where production is kept in-house, there can occasionally be unique requests for pieces from previous collections. If materials, including fabric and patterns, are readily available, these requests will pose no issue. However, when acquiring or repairing these elements proves challenging, it invariably sparks a heated discussion before any commitments are made.

Meanwhile, Jindo, ever observant, deduced that Gabrielle's anxiety was not rooted in the practicalities of the production process. Instead, her concern appeared to be more about maintaining her image in Irina's eyes.

He was familiar with this particular modus operandi of Gabrielle's, her display of authoritative charisma when an outsider was present. Now, her vexation with the modéliste's slight objection was no different.

"Jindo, we need to make it anyway. The customer already paid the price in full…"

"Pardon?"

In boutique fashion houses operating on a made-to-order model, the payment process usually occurs in stages. A deposit is paid upfront, followed by the remaining balance before the delivery of the garment. Full upfront payments do occasionally occur, but they remain exceptions rather than the rule.

"The customer really wanted the jacket, so paid the full price. But she wants a new piece…"

Though Gabrielle relayed the case with an air of self-satisfaction, Jindo could not help but harbour doubts. Despite his recognition of the subjectivity of style preference, as a former personal shopper, he struggled to believe that anyone would be enamoured with the not-so-stellar jacket.

At that moment, a suspicion crept into his mind, the order might have come from the hapless girl who had made the unfortunate purchase.

"… Gabrielle, was it the girl in the showroom when we were coming up?"

"Yes."

An inkling of a scenario began to formulate in Jindo's mind. He surmised that Gabrielle may have coerced the young guest into buying the exorbitantly priced jacket, with the girl trying to dodge the purchase by objecting to a used piece, leading to Gabrielle's proposal of a newly-made one.

Despite these assumptions, Jindo preferred not to create any ripples in the presence of the guest.

"… okay Gabrielle, I'll see what I can do."

"Good."

The domineering director finally seemed appeased, her gaze subtly shifting towards Irina to gauge her reaction. Yet, unbeknownst to her, Jindo planned to revisit the matter at a later time.

Passing 11 pm...

Several guests began to make their exit, including Antoine, arm in arm with his expectant wife. The hulking couscous aficionado lingered, eagerly seeking an opportunity to engage Gabrielle in conversation. Madame Claude prepared to depart, her grip firm on the strap of her brown leather cross-body bag, presumably laden with the day's earnings. The top floor, now a picture of serenity, hosted a few inebriated individuals, merrily capturing selfies.

With the evening's beverages depleted, the bartender retreated to the tranquillity of the vacant studio on the ground floor. Finally off-duty, he allowed himself the luxury of sitting for the first time that night.

At that moment, the Korean-speaking, blonde girl appeared.

"진도씨, 여기 있었네요."

(Jindo, you are here.)

"Ah, yes..."

"위에서 분주해 보여서, 방해하면 안 될 것 같아서 기다렸는데, 갑자기 사라지셨더라구요... 근데, 여기 계셨네요."

(I saw you were busy up there, so didn't want to disturb you but waited... Then you suddenly disappeared, and now I find you here.)

"Sorry, I've been working since morning, so I was a bit tired..."

"네. 열심히 하시는 것 봤어요... 근데 아침부터 일 하셨다구요?"

(Yes, I saw you working hard... By the way, you worked from the morning?)

"Yes, it's a bit long story..."

Jindo let his voice trail off, a non-verbal signal of his weariness, hinting at the lengthy saga he did not wish to unravel. At that moment, he felt an intense energy from above. Lifting his gaze towards the ceiling, he spotted the multi-coloured leather jacket-clad director scrutinising the scene through the small glass panels of the upper floor.

Even with two floors between them, her piercing gaze felt uncomfortably close, as if slicing through the layers. Jindo instantly had an inkling that the peacock lady would soon descend, likely with negative implications. However, the oblivious Korean-speaking girl failed to notice and continued her conversation.

"네… 제 친구는 아까 갔는데, 저는 진도씨 한테 할말 있어서 남아 있었거든요…"

(Anyway… my friend left a while ago, but I stayed back to talk to you…)

"Okay…"

The weary man responded with little enthusiasm, but she pressed on regardless.

"다름이 아니라, 다음 주에 케이팝 좋아하는 사람들끼리 하우스 파티 하는데 진도 씨도 관심 있으시면 오시라구요…"

(Actually, there's a K-pop house party next week, and I thought you might like to come…)

"… thanks, but sorry… I'm not a K-pop person…"

Jindo was about to decline her invitation. He was not particularly enthralled by the idea of bustling parties; he would rather savour a quiet drink with a few friends in a cosy setting.

"아 근데, 케이팝 파티라고 해서 꼭 케이팝 안 좋아해도 되요. 거기 오는 사람들 다 케이팝 좋아해서 오는 사람들은 아니에요. 그냥 한국 문화에 관심있는 사람들이지…"

(Well, just because it's a K-pop party doesn't mean you have to be a fan. Not everyone there will be a die-hard K-pop follower. It's more about a shared interest in Korean culture…)

"I really appreciate your invitation, but as you may already have noticed… I don't have the… modern Korean vibe if I may say… so, there won't be much to share from me…"

Jindo was still trying to delicately sidestep the invitation, without seeming outright rude. However, the girl was surprisingly insistent.

"네. 알아요. 근데, 어딘가 모르게 진도씨는 제가 만나본 한국 사람들 중에 가장 한국인 프라이드가 강한 것 같아요. 대화하다 보면 확실히 느껴져요…"

(Yes, I understand. But somehow, I feel that you have the strongest Korean pride of all the Koreans I've met. I certainly feel it when talking with you…)

"Well, I'm not sure about that…"

Jindo was neither denying nor accepting her perception of him, when suddenly, Gabrielle made her entrance.

"What are you doing here?"

"… nothing… I'm just… resting…"

As Jindo had anticipated, Gabrielle appeared slightly perturbed. She darted a quick glance between the girl and Jindo.

"Who told you to come into my office?"

Despite her words being directed at Jindo, the undertone was undoubtedly aimed at their unexpected guest. Jindo contorted his face inquisitively, silently questioning Gabrielle's sudden acerbity.

The guest seemed to absorb the undercurrent and hastily made her exit, apologising as she left.

"Pardon, Gabrielle… 진도씨, 나중에 봬요… *(Jindo, I'll see you later…)*"

"네, 그래요."

(Okay, we do so.)

Finally, Jindo responded in his mother tongue, the foreign syllables sounding oddly provocative in the presence of the only non-Korean speaker in the room.

"What did she say?"

Rather than replying, Jindo continued to level an irked gaze at Gabrielle.

"Gabrielle…"

"What?"

In fact, it was rather odd, the way Gabrielle seemed to be embodying the role of Jindo's girlfriend. Despite their shared experiences the previous night, it was too early to conclude that any form of close relationship had formed between them.

At that moment, another persistent guest poked his head through the studio door.

"Salut…"

It was the couscous stalker, seemingly following Gabrielle. He peered into the studio, shyly seeking permission to enter. Gabrielle swiftly rearranged her features into a welcoming smile and gestured for him to come in. The pair began conversing in French, and the man's pleasure at finally engaging with the attractive host was palpable.

All the while, Gabrielle appeared to be teasing Jindo. While engaged in conversation with the guest, she would occasionally sneak a glance at Jindo, her smirk seemingly designed to provoke jealousy. However, the retired bartender, who had also moonlighted as a modéliste that morning, was too fatigued to entertain such antics.

Their conversation lingered, with Jindo seated close enough to grasp the main context, even if his grasp of French fell short of understanding every detail. The oversized guest was evidently attempting to charm Gabrielle into a post-party date, while she deftly deflected with excuses. Pointedly, she gestured towards Jindo, indicating her pre-existing plans with him.

The restaurant entrepreneur shot Jindo a surprised glance, seemingly reassessing the bartender, who evidently was not just an employee but someone of greater significance in Gabrielle's life.

The big couscous man eventually exited the studio with a look of disappointment etched on his face, leaving Jindo as the unlikely victor over the self-assured business owner. Jindo relished the moment, observing the man's departure with an air of nonchalance.

With the departure of their guest, Jindo and Gabrielle were left alone once again.

"Gabrielle, you know the couscous guy was waiting to talk to you from the beginning of the event…"

"Yes, I know. He was actually following me during the whole evening…"

"Oh, you knew? By the way, do you know him for a long time?"

"Well, I've been to his restaurants many times, but never had a proper conversation… This time, I talked about my event, and he told me he would get me a special price for his food, so I accepted the offer…"

"Okay… can I ask you how much it was though? Because I know his restaurant, and as far as I remember, it seems quite pricey there…"

"Bah… I don't know."

"You mean it was free?"

"No, it's not free of course. He told me the price but I forgot…"

"… so, you haven't paid yet…"

"Nope."

At that moment, Jindo was reminded of the overdue bill that Seiwa had mentioned earlier in the day. However, he was too weary to delve further into that particular concern. Instead, he voiced another question that had been nagging at him.

"By the way Gabrielle, did your Hermès and CHANEL colleagues come today? I forgot to ask because I was too busy…"

"Ah… yeah… they came… I think…"

Her hesitant reply caught Jindo's attention.

"You think? Does that mean you didn't see them?"

"Yes yes, I saw them… They came but left… early…"

Jindo cast a sceptical look at Gabrielle, who fumbled to justify her vagueness.

"You know my English is bad, so I said wrong… Anyway, they came but left early because it was too crowded…"

Jindo continued to regard her with a suspicious look, pressing her for more details.

"Did they visit the atelier?"

"Eh… yes… they did… my Hermès boss asked about you…"

She responded, flashing Jindo a smile. However, he remained unconvinced.

"By the way Gabrielle, when you say your Hermès boss, you mean the director of the company?"

"No no, she is… in charge… of the atelier…"

With Jindo's gaze steady on her, he articulated his next thought.

"By the way, she's your boss, but a friend?"

"Ah… well, we're… like friends… you know this is France, not Asia…"

"…"

Jindo still remained silent, his gaze unwavering. His expression veered towards the incredulous, yet with no hard evidence at hand, he could only fix a disbelieving gaze upon the ex-CHANEL designer.

He subtly tried to communicate through his stern stare, encouraging her to be honest. However, the French director seemed oblivious to his small, Asian-eyed silent plea, continuing her tale unperturbed.

"She said you have the quality…"

"…"

"Even my CHANEL friend said you're really good…"

"… Gabrielle… they said that, only after seeing the little draping works and constructional papers?"

"Yes, you know your work always looks nice and professional…"

"…"

In response to his silence, Gabrielle pressed on, feigning ignorance while subtly conveying a sense of insincerity.

"Anyway, they didn't stay long because it was too crowded… You know it was full of kids upstairs…"

Steering clear of her typical rudeness in describing her own invited guests, Jindo redirected the conversation.

"By the way Gabrielle, are they friends? Your ex-colleagues at CHANEL and Hermès…"

"Yes, they are. Normally, people in luxury fashion houses transfer between the labels… and CHANEL, Hermès and Dior are the ones at the top level, so it's common to see somebody from CHANEL to Dior, or Dior to Hermès, etc… Anyway, they know each other, through me of course…"

As Jindo pushed Gabrielle closer to the precipice, she uttered something he could not simply brush aside.

It was because Jindo recalled Gregory comparing the experience of working in high-fashion ateliers to being a footballer in the Premier League. Once someone was in, they would either stay or move within the same league, a bit like shuffling between clubs. He had also explained how these fashion houses carried a certain prestige within the industry, much like renowned football clubs, albeit less openly discussed.

Though Gabrielle's narrative aroused suspicion, her final comment mirrored insights that could only come from an industry insider. While there were numerous other aspects of Gabrielle's narrative that Jindo wanted to scrutinise, including Irina's story about her tenure at Dior, he decided to let them be for now.

His intuition suggested that any interrogation would merely result in an endless runaround with Gabrielle, who consistently dodged and deflected. Sensing his hesitation, she swiftly seized control of the conversation once more.

"By the way Jindo, we have made good sales today, though there were some annoying people, asking for a discount…"

Gabrielle shifted the conversation, leaving the unresolved matters hanging in the air. Unravelling the past could wait; Jindo decided to tag along with her new tangent.

"Okay, it's good you sold many. By the way Gabrielle, no offence… I actually wondered how come almost all the guests looked so young… I mean there's nothing wrong to be young, but I wonder if they have enough pocket money to buy your pieces…"

"Yes, you're right. They didn't have money, so annoying... Anyway, you know I placed many of the luxury label pieces from my personal wardrobe, and people bought many of them..."

"That's good."

"I'm sure they haven't even been to those luxury boutiques by themselves, so it was actually a great opportunity for them..."

"..."

Jindo simply studied her, his expression passive in the face of her dismissive tone. She evaded his gaze, busying herself with scrubbing at a small stain on the wall.

Skirting past her comment, he proceeded.

"So those luxury items were the ones that you sold mostly..."

"Yes, it's annoying, people try my pieces but never buy..."

Jindo, given his background as a personal shopper, could see the rationale but chose to stay silent. Instead, he redirected the conversation to a more pressing matter as a production manager.

"By the way Gabrielle, for the camouflage jacket, you know we don't even have the fabrics, let alone the issues with the constructions..."

"Oh, that... Don't worry about it, I took her money anyway..."

"..."

Taken aback by her nonchalance, his head was subtly shaking in disbelief. However, once again, his visual cues seemed to slip past her radar.

"Jindo, I'm really not in the mood to discuss work anymore..."

Suddenly, she moved closer, perching on Jindo's knee. Though he feigned resistance, he did not protest, instead acquiescing to her approach. The warmth of the ex-model's body against his was not unwelcome.

Chapter 34 : Intimacy's Intricate Waltz

Gabrielle leaned in to whisper in his ear; her voice sultry, claiming intoxication. Jindo, aware that she had not touched a drop of champagne that evening, did not challenge her declaration, choosing instead to savour their intimate proximity.

The echo of footsteps resonated from the stairs, signalling the departure of the remaining guests. Jindo and Gabrielle emerged to bid them farewell. A quick glance at his Apple watch told him it was nearly 1 am, prompting him to ponder the unfolding of the night ahead.

"So, Gabrielle... are you planning on staying here tonight? Or would you perhaps... consider going to my place?"

Jindo hesitated on the final query, uncertain of his odds. However, Gabrielle quickly raised her voice.

"NON, I would never go to Bondy again..."

"..."

The mild creases on Jindo's forehead deepened into friendly furrows as Gabrielle made her disdain for his suburb apparent.

"Yesterday was the first time I've been to Bondy... and I didn't like the ambience there..."

Jindo put aside his mild affront at her candid comment, choosing instead to address a discrepancy.

"By the way Gabrielle, you said you used to be at Hermès? As far as I know, most of the Hermès ateliers are located in Bondy... but you've never been to the area?"

Without missing a beat, the former CHANEL designer countered.

"Jindo, not all Hermès ateliers are in Bondy. You don't know anything about it. I think they will even open one of their workshops in Shanghai soon... Does that mean Hermès ateliers are now in Shanghai, c'est ça?"

Despite the flaw in her reasoning, Jindo found himself grappling with the revelation that his line of questioning had been perhaps too impulsive. The Shanghai venture of Hermès was indeed familiar to him, leaving him temporarily silenced.

"That's not what I meant, Gabrielle... I was just trying to say..."

"NO, STOP IT... Why do you always try to talk about Hermès with me? You know you always ask me about CHANEL and Hermès... Jindo, they're just companies, and there's nothing special there. You may be there one day, and you will understand what I'm saying now..."

Her response was smooth as if rehearsed, and Jindo was left without a retort. In a sense, her argument held water. The prospect of working for such esteemed fashion houses was admittedly appealing, silencing his budding doubts about the seemingly high-profile designer.

Deciding not to pursue the matter further, he changed the topic.

"Okay okay, Gabrielle... Anyway, you're staying here tonight then?"

"Yes, but aren't you staying with me?"

"..."

His eyebrows arched in surprise at her presumptive tone. Not one to turn down another intimate encounter with the ex-lingerie model, he trod carefully.

"By the way Gabrielle, where do we sleep? It's quite messy everywhere..."

"Well, we can make up the bed quickly."

"You mean, in the showroom?"

"Yes, I'll show you…"

With a firm grip on his hand, she led the way upstairs.

Arriving at the showroom…

Gabrielle strode into the place with an air of purpose, quickly shifting the racks aside and making way for a central space. Without missing a beat, she moved towards the shower area and began hauling out luggage carriers. Jindo watched the scene unfold, surprised at the speed at which she could bring about chaos. The state of the atelier in the mornings now made sense to him.

"Jindo, could you help me with the bed frames?"

Gabrielle requested, and he complied, carrying them out one by one. He assembled the four sections into a cohesive structure in the middle of the showroom. Next, Gabrielle beckoned him over to help lift a mattress. Turning, Jindo was met with the sight of a large, grimy mattress leaning against the wall.

Lifting it away from the wall revealed a window, a novelty in the building, and Jindo took a moment to observe it. However, the window's placement struck him as odd since it appeared to provide a clear view into the shower booth for the neighbouring building's inhabitants.

The shower area was tucked in a corner of the showroom, partially concealed from the main floor. A modestly-sized window fronted the booth, potentially turning the shower area into a live-action display for the neighbours. The peculiar arrangement intrigued Jindo, but before he could question Gabrielle, her shriek jolted him.

"AH, AH, AH, Jindo! My fingers are under the mattress. Please, lift it up…"

"Okay okay…"

Caught off guard by the sudden predicament of the seemingly hasty lady, Jindo swiftly hoisted the cumbersome mattress to free her. Together, they gradually moved the dirty furniture.

As they finally situated it on the frame, Jindo noticed a disturbing amount of blood on the mattress.

"Gabrielle, what is this blood?"

"… um…"

Her hesitation was palpable, and Jindo was still reeling.

"Is it yours?"

She appeared to be deliberating, but swiftly blurted out, seemingly flustered,

"Jindo! IT'S A LADY'S THING. You shouldn't ask about it."

"Ah okay, sorry…"

Taken aback by her explanation, Jindo chose not to question further about the unusually situated bloodstains. He surmised it was, indeed, 'a lady's thing'.

She moved to one side of the room, pressing a spot on a graffiti-painted wall. Much to his surprise, the painted door was more than mere art; it was an actual functional door. Gabrielle stepped inside and returned with a bedsheet and duvet, picked haphazardly from the cluttered floor.

In the brief moment she had left the door open, Jindo caught sight of the interior, a chaotic dressing room bursting with clothes. Sensing his astonishment, Gabrielle hastily explained, blaming her busy schedule for the disorder. Jindo, suspecting it had been a longstanding mess, decided to hold his tongue.

"Voilà!"

With the bed finally made, she stripped off her clothes and slipped into the duvet.

"Are you coming?"

Jindo was surprised by the abrupt shift in the situation, but the anticipation of seeing the former model's bare form again stirred his curiosity. He looked forward to the prospect of another intimate encounter, yet he had his own priorities.

"Gabrielle, can I take a shower?"

"What? Shower? Again? What is it with you? Are you shower-crazy or something?"

"…"

Realising their cleanliness standards were poles apart, Jindo felt the need to justify himself.

"Gabrielle, I've been sweating since morning, it would be better if I take a shower… not just for me, but for you as well."

Preoccupied with her phone, Gabrielle dismissed his concern.

"I don't understand you…"

"Gabrielle, you have no idea how bad I smell now…"

Jindo attempted to further justify his need for a shower, to which she replied offhandedly while still engrossed in her phone.

"Jindo, there's no hot water, by the way…"

"… can I ask why?"

"I didn't turn on the boiler, the energy bill in France is very expensive…"

Jindo had not considered this, as his rent covered the energy bill. He posed another question to the energy-conscious French lady.

"By the way Gabrielle, are you going to leave all the lights on like that?"

"No, you have to turn them off."

"Me?"

"Yes, I'm already in bed... naked..."

She paused her digital diversion momentarily, offering Jindo a tantalisingly cheeky smile. The anticipation tingled through him, and he knew what steps were required to advance the scene. Nevertheless, cleanliness still topped his list of priorities.

"Okay Gabrielle, I'll turn the lights off right now. But after that, I think I still need to take a shower, even with cold water..."

"Jindo! Why are you so obsessed with the shower? Is it a Korean thing? Do you guys not think about the environment?"

The self-proclaimed energy saver raised an ecological argument, and the hygiene enthusiast defended his stance.

"Gabrielle, please don't amplify the issue. It's just a shower, and I think this is not a cultural thing but personal... and I really don't think that I am the ABNORMAL case..."

His slight sarcastic undertone put an end to Gabrielle's phone browsing, and she gave him a disgruntled look.

"If you don't join me now, I won't sleep with you tonight... But if you come, I'll give you a good massage..."

Her words were accompanied by a playful yet seductive grin. Memories of their morning rendezvous flooded his mind. The promise of her touch was enough to set him in motion; he quickly ventured upstairs to extinguish the remaining lights.

Upon his return, he rapidly switched off the showroom's lights. Now the house was bathed only in soft moonlight filtering in through the shower area window.

He began to strip down, realising too late that his pyjamas were not at hand. He then kept on his trousers and t-shirt, attempting to slip into bed thus attired.

At that moment, the bare lady in the bed protested.

"Why are you still dressed?"

"… because I don't have my pyjamas…"

"My bed sheets are clean, so don't wear that."

Jindo was perplexed, considering he had witnessed her retrieve the bedsheet from the disarrayed floor of her dressing room. The memory of the bloodied mattress was still fresh. Nevertheless, he complied with the ex-model's request to maintain the mood.

Quickly divesting his clothes, he slid into bed beside her. Once he had made himself comfortable, Gabrielle placed her phone beneath the pillow and moved closer. She guided his arms around her, and Jindo did not resist her assertive manoeuvring. Even though they had only slept together once before, her actions seemed effortlessly natural.

In their intimate embrace, she whispered to him.

"I liked your kiss yesterday…"

"Eh? Well, I… liked it as well…"

Jindo blushed slightly at her openness, and Gabrielle continued.

"My ex-boyfriend never kissed me. He said I smell really bad…"

"Eh? Did he… really say that?"

"Yes, he was really bad to me…"

"Um, I think… it's more than that… It's um… actually quite rude to say it…"

Jindo responded, attempting to demonstrate empathy, yet his thoughts were wholly consumed by the intoxicating closeness of their nude forms. He vividly recalled her somewhat off-putting scent from that morning, which gave him insight into her ex-boyfriend's less-than-kind remarks.

"He also used to hit me…"

"… hit you?"

Jindo echoed distractedly, more focused on the tantalising touch of her skin against his.

"Yes, he was a really bad man…"

"Um… that's quite… shocking Gabrielle… By the way, did you not say he was a professional boxer?"

"Yes, it was really painful. He hit me here, and I got no breath…"

She guided Jindo's hand to her side, his arm brushing over her breast in the process, a touch he found undeniably enjoyable.

"Then, he always treated me like some sort of sex doll…"

"Eh… okay…"

Though engrossed in the sensations of their shared intimacy, he was slightly disconcerted when she abruptly ordered him.

"Jindo, turn turn…"

She seemed intent on reenacting a past experience. Jindo felt discomfort bubbling up as the implications became clear; she would play the male, and he would play the female.

Aiming to maintain their erotic ambience, he reluctantly turned his back to her, and Gabrielle kicked off her simulation in a harsh fashion.

"He did like, dah dah dah to me like this, every night…"

She acted out her ex-boyfriend's role, imitating aggressive sexual intercourse from behind. Jindo found himself increasingly uneasy with the situation; her forceful grip on his pelvis, the fervent, uncomfortable thrusting. Her proximity, this time, felt more invasive than intimate.

"Okay okay, I get it, Gabrielle…"

He quickly readjusted, facing her again. Gabrielle began tracing his body with her fingers, inciting a rush of desire. Despite the day's fatigue settling heavily on his body, his arousal was unyielding, standing tall with enthusiasm.

Jindo was keen on escalating the intimacy, on exploring the territory of her body, but Gabrielle halted his advancements, pushing him back down.

"NO, YOU STAY…"

As she had done that morning, she straddled him, demonstrating her mastery in the art of pleasure using hands and lips. Even though this was not Jindo's first encounter with her remarkable skill, he found himself equally impressed, lost in a realm of heavenly sensation.

After several stages of the titillating massage, the restless house host shifted onto his abdomen, prepared to enact her twerking routine. Unleashed in her familiar territory, she became more uninhibited, letting her movements grow wilder.

From his front-row perspective, Jindo revelled in the spectacle of her body in fluid motion; it was as though he was experiencing a tantalising 4D cinema adventure.

However, as Gabrielle became engrossed in her self-focused dance, Jindo found himself afforded a moment of detached observation. Under the sparse moonlight, he noticed the graffiti wall murals featuring the artist's peculiarly cannibalistic-looking cartoon characters. They seemed to watch him with an air of celebration.

A strange thought struck him since Gabrielle appeared to be the ringmaster of this bizarre circus, and he was her captive. This interpretation imbued their encounter with an eerie quality that began to unnerve him. The euphoric pleasure he was experiencing began to wane, an unexpected turn of events that served to delay the release of his mounting excitement.

Contrary to his earlier expectation of a swift climax, the sudden shift in mood meant his emotional arousal did not keep pace with his physical. Consequently, Gabrielle continued her performance, drawing out the act until the final phase. Sensing the impending culmination, Jindo alerted his partner. She deftly transitioned into the role of a practised pilot, guiding him towards a smooth landing with her hand.

However, at the critical moment, she directed the discharge onto his abdomen. Caught off guard by this unexpected manoeuvre, Jindo felt a flush of embarrassment, yet he refrained from voicing any protest to the hard-worked lady.

Following the act, he retreated to the shower to cleanse himself, while Gabrielle resumed her position in bed, nonchalantly wiping her hands on the side of the supposedly clean bedsheet.

Anticipating a frigid rinse, Jindo carefully adjusted the shower faucet, wary of triggering a rush of water. After several seconds of cautious testing, he was surprised to find warm water trickling out.

"Gabrielle, it looks like there's hot water…"

"Oh, really? That's good…"

"Did you not say you didn't put the boiler on?"

"Bah… maybe somebody turned it on…"

" "
...

Her nonchalant reply, delivered with her eyes still glued to her phone, left Jindo feeling duped once again. However, his immediate concern was to wash away the residual stickiness trickling down his torso and thigh.

As he showered beneath the oddly-placed window, he reflected on the curious conclusion to his inaugural night in Gabrielle's abode.

Chapter 35 : The Height of Intimacy

On the following morning…
Jindo woke up later than customary, possibly due to a series of restless nights. The slumbering lady beside him appeared equally fatigued, prompting him to extricate himself from the bed with the utmost discretion.

"Where are you going Jindo?"

"Sorry, did I wake you up?"

"You're not going to leave now, no? I want to have breakfast with you…"

"Okay, we do that. I'm just going out to take some fresh air…"

"Okay…"

She promptly drifted back to sleep as Jindo vacated the dwelling. Given the earliness of the hour, the city was ensconced in quietude. It seemed fitting to amble along the tranquil streets, savouring the serenity of the 2nd arrondissement, the very heart of Paris and a stone's throw away from the River Seine.

Jindo wandered towards the resplendent Cathédrale Notre-Dame de Paris, relishing the crisp morning air. His stomach rumbled, but in anticipation of the impending breakfast with Gabrielle, he restrained himself to a solitary café at a bar across the bridge, forgoing the tantalisingly fresh French pastries.

Upon his return, Gabrielle stirred but showed no immediate desire to rise. Jindo tiptoed down to the atelier, hoping not to cut short her slumber.

The atelier was a sight of sartorial disarray, fabric draping work and a plethora of construction papers littered the table. Jindo set about tidying, preparing the space for the forthcoming day of creativity.

Upon his return to the showroom, Gabrielle still engrossed in her mobile phone, asked.

"What were you doing in the atelier?"

"I just tidied up a bit…"

"Oh, that's good."

The director expressed her appreciation for Jindo's unasked cleaning service. The industrious employee, now noticeably famished, inquired.

"So, are you going to wake up soon Gabrielle?"

"It's the weekend Jindo…"

"Ah, bien sûr…"

Noting her intent to luxuriate in bed a while longer, he responded with a knowing smile and proceeded upstairs. The top floor remained a chaotic relic of the previous evening's exploits, prompting him to set to work and tidy up the space where he worked.

Indeed, the showroom and the top floor were interconnected, a stairway being the only divider. Consequently, the open-concept design allowed sounds to traverse freely between the two levels. Gabrielle's voice echoed from her resting place as Jindo's cleaning activities produced a symphony of sounds upstairs.

"Jindo, what are you doing there?"

"Eh? Just… tidying up the bar…"

"Ah, that's good…"

Once more, the director seemed gratified by his self-starting tendencies.

Jindo concluded his cleaning just as Gabrielle finally emerged from her slumber. The pouring water indicated her intention to bathe. Suddenly, a shout from below interrupted his thoughts.

"Jindo, are you coming?"

"Pardon?"

Confused, he descended the stairs to clarify.

"Gabrielle, did you ask if I come to the shower?"

"Yes."

"You mean, we take a shower together?"

"Bah, oui."

Her countenance edged with irritation at his relentless questioning, clarified her proposition. It was not a shared task of cleaning that she had in mind, but rather a private interlude in the shower cubicle.

While the prospect of a spontaneous tryst with the former lingerie model was tempting, he found himself hesitating, thanks to the residual exhaustion lingering from the morning.

Eventually, he decided to acquiesce, his decision fuelled by the awareness that the duration of their peculiar relationship remained uncertain, thereby mandating seizing every opportunity for enjoyment.

Upon entering the zone, he found Gabrielle, her skin glistening from the cascading water. The sight of her invigorated him, prompting him to swiftly discard his clothing and join her in the cubicle.

The shower space was surprisingly roomy, roughly the size of a queen-sized bed, comfortably accommodating two for a clandestine dance of intimacy.

The cubicle only featured a single showerhead, bringing Jindo in close proximity to the drenched lady. Gabrielle received him with open arms, her eyes flicking to his rather dormant little soldier.

"It's cute."

"… you mean it's a bit… small?"

"I didn't say that, but I just said it looks cute…"

"… okay, thanks…"

Jindo felt a twinge of embarrassment under her direct scrutiny. His confidence waned when it came to discussing his size, particularly in its dormant state. Her gaze still locked onto his manhood, Gabrielle voiced another inquiry.

"How often do you shave though?"

"Well, once a month on average…"

"I'm the same. Now, I haven't shaved for a long time, but I normally do…"

She then started inspecting her hair situation, which did not unsettle Jindo. However, his main concern was the open window directly opposite the shower cubicle. He kept casting glances, fearful of prying eyes from the neighbouring building.

Suddenly, Gabrielle guided Jindo's hand to her private area, instructing him on the art of a satisfying massage. He yielded to her lead, manipulating his fingers as directed. After mastering her preferred routine, he diligently worked to please her, even incorporating a little bit of personal improvisation.

Clearly enjoying herself, Gabrielle retreated to the corner, seating herself on a ledge at mid-thigh level. Though she did not vocalise her wishes, Jindo instinctively knew what was expected of him next. He knelt to face her, and she clutched his tied-up hair, as if a handle, signalling her desired course of action.

By observing her reactions, Jindo could tell she was revelling in the moment. He went above and beyond to gratify the director.

After a while, a dull ache emerged in his knees from the unforgiving tiled floor. As he rose, he noticed his little companion had stirred to life. Gabrielle immediately turned her attention to the awakened member, greeting it with familiar finesse.

Her adept handling of his 'little prince' impressed Jindo yet again. Her technique seemed infallibly potent, undeterred by time or place.

Suddenly, he perceived murmurs emanating from behind them as if from a conversation. He had been so engrossed in their intimate play that the open window had slipped his mind, only to be abruptly reminded.

"Gabrielle, can we close the window? I feel a bit uncomfortable with it…"

"No, it's okay…"

"Gabrielle, I heard some people talking…"

"No, no one is watching, just focus… you're destroying the mood…"

"… okay but Gabrielle, I can see the neighbour's living room from here, which means they can see us back…"

"Jindo, even if they do, what's the problem? The guys will be just jealous…"

"…"

The scene unfolded in such a way that Jindo found Gabrielle's comments uncannily informed as if she already had intimate knowledge of the inhabitants. His curiosities were, however, momentarily derailed as his attention was diverted by the ex-lingerie model's devoted attention to his decidedly enthused companion.

With a flicker of amusement and arousal dancing in her eyes, Gabrielle seemed to scrutinise his reaction, keenly adjusting her techniques to render him speechless.

Elegantly, she rose and pivoted, pressing her hip against his insistent arousal as though seeking the ideal spot for their connection, the 'Tsaheylu'. Despite Jindo's initial reservations about the transparencies of the moment, he soon yielded to the rhythm once they docked in harmony. His movements followed the primal instinct, the dance as old as time itself.

A snag appeared a few minutes into their heated interlude. It marked their first time exploring this intimacy while standing, and their disparity in height presented an unforeseen hurdle. As Gabrielle attempted to straighten her legs, Jindo, holding her from behind, felt her hips inch higher than was comfortable.

He suggested she bend and widen her stance, but it seemed Gabrielle had her own accustomed angle. Her long limbs seemed drawn to a particular degree, habitually retracting despite his pleas.

After several more attempts to negotiate, Jindo decided to problem-solve solo. Engaging in a silent battle for the optimum height, he ventured into various stances; elevating his own feet and even trying to coax her down with his hands on her shoulders.

The more he contorted into awkward positions, the more he fretted about the possible spectacle he presented from behind. He could only imagine he resembled a diminutive man, trying to pogo his way up to a towering lady. Despite the visual absurdity, he soldiered on, still unable to pinpoint the ideal angle.

As his stamina waned under the strain of maintaining such an unnatural posture, he grew conscious of the creeping fatigue. This toll triggered a sudden need for a tactical retreat, prompting him to swiftly disengage.

Sensing the abrupt conclusion, Gabrielle turned to investigate the root of the interruption.

"Jindo, what's the problème? T'as fini? *(You finished?)*"

"Eh… I think so…"

The disheartened man answered, but he was unable to meet her scrutinising gaze.

"Jindo, what's the matter? How do you suddenly stop like this?"

"… sorry, it was… too high…"

She regarded him with persistent disdain, refusing to accept his feeble excuse.

"No Jindo, you're too SHORT!"

This was less of an argument and more of a hiss, akin to an unforgiving feline deprived of its meal. With a swift motion, she seized a towel, leaving him behind in the booth.

Jindo wallowed in guilt, consumed by mortification and a profound sense of self-reproach. He then dutifully turned to cleanse his dejected companion. Meanwhile, Gabrielle, still evidently displeased, was drying herself off. He waited for her patiently, their only towel held hostage in her grip.

Once she had finished, she carelessly discarded the towel on the floor, proceeding to dress herself. Jindo quietly picked up the towel to dry off, then proceeded to retrieve his pants and shirt, which had been passionately cast aside earlier.

As Gabrielle sat on the bed, engrossed in her phone, Jindo hovered in the silence, his apology lingering in the air.

"Gabrielle, sorry... I'm not experienced with a tall woman like you..."

She looked at him, her countenance unforgiving, and retorted.

"Jindo, I'm not really that tall. It's just that you're too short and... small also..."

With those biting words, she shot a condemning glance towards Jindo's central part. The comment was harsh, an affront to his fragile ego.

"Gabrielle, that was a bit too much... I said sorry, and I surely didn't mean to..."

"STOP IT JINDO, it's finished anyway. Let's stop talking about it and go for brunch now..."

"... okay..."

Although still slighted, Jindo resigned to the truth in her words. He swallowed his pride and conceded, recognising the validity of her observations.

Chapter 36 : Vegan Ventures & Vexations

Passing by 11 am…
With an air of Parisian pride, Gabrielle led Jindo to their destination, an organic, vegetarian restaurant nestled within the labyrinth of the Marais district.

In those days, vegetarian establishments in Paris were not as common as nowadays; a handful existed, charging premium prices for a limited number of tables. Their scarcity made them coveted spots for the health-conscious populace.

Upon reaching the restaurant, Jindo found himself surrounded by young, creatively inclined vegetarians. Despite its inconspicuous location off the main street, the eatery seemed to be quite the local sensation, with hopeful patrons waiting patiently outside for a table.

After a brief wait, they were seated and Gabrielle swiftly placed her order without sparing a glance at the menu. Jindo scanned the petite, daily-printed menu but found the options indistinguishable. He defaulted to Gabrielle's choice of an acai bowl and avocado toast.

While he was indifferent to the flavours, his primary concern was the portion size, his appetite had been whetted since early morning. A quick glimpse at the steep prices on the menu sheet had him deciding to sample sparingly here. He reasoned that the light fare would not satiate him, and planned to indulge in a hearty meal upon returning to his Bondy residence.

As they awaited their order, Gabrielle painted a verbal portrait of the restaurant, describing it as one of her favourite vegetarian havens in Paris. Jindo feigned interest, all the while scanning neighbouring tables, assessing their servings. His intuition suggested the portions here might be on the smaller side.

Renowned vegan dishes, not requiring extensive preparation, arrived promptly. Although his earlier worries were focused solely on quantity, Jindo found himself pleasantly surprised by the visual appeal of the food set before him.

The acai bowl, a mesmerising swirl of deep purple, was adorned with an array of vibrant fresh fruits and nuts. The avocado toast was a tableau of natural colours; lush green avocado smeared on a piece of distinctively organic brown bread. It seemed as though an artist had sculpted an edible masterpiece, which inspired a sense of freshness and aesthetic appreciation in Jindo.

Regardless, they began to partake of their visually arresting vegetarian repast. Jindo, driven by gnawing hunger, devoured his petite servings in under two minutes. Gabrielle appeared somewhat shocked by his rapid dispatch of the dishes.

He continued to scrape the remnants from his acai bowl when Gabrielle asked if he found the dish that delectable. In fact, Jindo barely registered the taste, focused as he was on quelling his hunger.

Nevertheless, not wanting to appear discourteous, he told her he felt rejuvenated already. This seemed to please Gabrielle, who then embarked on a discourse extolling the virtues of vegetarianism.

As she wound down her mini-lecture, she hinted that there would be much to 'educate' him about if he were to embrace veganism. He found this slightly disconcerting, her tone suggesting she intended to orchestrate his transformation, whether he was agreeable or not.

Suddenly, Gabrielle broached a more pressing matter.

"By the way Jindo, I go to China this Friday…"

"Pardon? Suddenly?"

"Well, it was in discussion from a long time ago, but I just got confirmed last week…"

"Okay, can I ask you what it's about though?"

"It's about, there's a Chinese investor who wants to work with me, and my agent finally scheduled a meeting in Shanghai…"

"So, you're not going to be here next week?"

"No, I come back on Monday in the following week…"

"Then the rest of us will work just like normal?"

"Yes, but you need to report to me every day and night…"

"Me?"

"Yes, are you not the ATELIER MANAGER?"

"Um… well… okay…"

Jindo was accustomed to Gabrielle referring to him as the atelier manager whenever she intended to delegate additional duties. However, this time, he contemplated whether he should clarify the terms of his contract. Deciding that the timing was not quite right, he bypassed the subject and continued their dialogue.

"Anyway, good for you Gabrielle. I think China is such a huge market, and if somebody wants to make a fortune, it'll be the place…"

"Well, I'm not sure what he wants to do though… He actually has a fashion company and his wife is the designer. I think they have their local label, but he wants to launch mine in China as brand new…"

"Okay, so it's not like you're collaborating with their label, but establishing your brand independently in China, correct?"

"Yes… by the way, why would I collaborate with a Chinese label?"

"…"

The self-proclaimed ex-CHANEL designer appeared ruffled by her own misconception, and Jindo attempted to soothe the prickly femme.

"Gabrielle, I didn't say you would collaborate with their label…"

"NO, I would NEVER do that…"

"…"

As the venue swelled with an increasing throng of patrons, Gabrielle suggested they retreat to the company premises for further discourse. There were pressing matters she intended to entrust to Jindo in his role as the atelier manager.

Back at the house, they ascended to the top floor to continue their discourse over a pot of tea. On arrival, Gabrielle's brow furrowed at the sight of the unkempt space.

"Jindo, did you not clean here in the morning?"

"Pardon? I cleaned the bar only… the place I worked yesterday…"

"You cleaned the bar only? Then who cleans the rest?"

"What?"

"Jindo, you're the manager, so you also need to take care of this company…"

"Whoa whoa, Gabrielle, you keep saying I'm the manager of this company, and I actually have a lot of questions on that matter, but for now, let's make one thing clear... I don't need to do the cleaning job regardless of whatever position I'm in at this company... I normally do it by my own initiative but it's not OBLIGATOIRE..."

Jindo's gaze held Gabrielle's, ensuring the solidity of his message reached her. Gabrielle was momentarily at a loss for words.

"... okay..."

There was a tense silence that followed, an uncanny feeling, as though Gabrielle felt a sense of betrayal by Jindo's firmness. Cleaning the room by herself, Gabrielle's aura resembled that of a wild cat, poised to lash out if approached.

For a while, Gabrielle continued her solitary cleaning, with Jindo observing from a safe distance. Soon enough, however, he decided to lend a hand, though she had not asked. His assistance was noticed but went unacknowledged.

Their cleaning session continued in an uneasy silence, and at the tail end, Gabrielle decided to move a large cartoon figurine down to the showroom. Given the statue's size and weight, Jindo helped her navigate the curvy stairs with their bulky charge.

Arriving in the showroom, Gabrielle was on the cusp of positioning the unwieldy object in its assigned place when she found herself irked by the room's disorderly state. With the recent installation of the bed, the floor was in an undeniable state of disarray.

Gabrielle commenced a vigorous clean of the showroom, swearing under her breath in her native French. It appeared as though the discussion she had promised Jindo had completely slipped her mind. Jindo attempted to reboot the subject.

"Gabrielle, are you going to talk about the China project after cleaning here?"

"Ah yes... sorry..."

A subtle shift in the power dynamic between them seemed to have transpired. In fact, since the abrupt conclusion of their private tango session in the shower booth that morning, Gabrielle had maintained an air of dominance over Jindo.

This influence persisted through their cleaning endeavours on the top floor. Now, with Jindo having raised fundamental questions regarding his current presence in her house company, she seemed to realise his growing sacrifices.

Finally, she addressed him in a conciliatory tone.

"Sorry, Jindo… can we please clean here fast and have the discussion?"

Jindo responded with a slow, silent nod, and the pair resumed their cleaning. Between vacuuming, mopping, and heaving bulky objects between floors, fatigue began to creep up on him, and hunger was quick to follow.

By the time they finished cleaning, the clock had struck 4 pm, and Gabrielle proposed that they take their discussion, along with her computer, into the studio.

Upon descending to the lower floor, she set about making space for the impending meeting. However, Jindo got the distinct impression she still expected his assistance. She continuously stole glances at him while tidying alone, and yet this time, Jindo stood by passively, simply watching her.

His displeasure stemmed from the sense that she was orchestrating a situation in which he was compelled to work solo. This time, however, Jindo continued to observe the scene by merely maintaining his stance, and Gabrielle seemed to perceive his reluctance.

Gabrielle attempted to hoist several bulky files at once, only to drop them, scattering sheets haphazardly across the floor. She looked at Jindo with a helpless expression. Despite his suspicion that she might be continuing her game, Jindo saw no need to be unkind and mean until the last minute.

"Gabrielle, let me do this…"

"Okay, thank you Jindo."

Her face immediately blossomed into a triumphant grin, as if she had scored some minor victory. While Jindo could not shake off the feeling of being reeled in by her ploys once again, he decided to overlook it.

His gnawing hunger and mounting fatigue left him focused on one thing; to complete the tasks at the front and retreat home as soon as possible. Swiftly, they tidied up the studio, and at long last, settled down for their much-anticipated discussion.

Chapter 37 : Patterns of Prejudice

I n discussion…

Gabrielle was guiding Jindo through an array of photographs on Pinterest, elaborating on potential additions to their collection. Given her hectic schedule, the busy director had not the time to sketch out her thoughts. Instead, she opted to illustrate her ideas via a curated collection of images on the popular sharing platform.

Jindo was fervently jotting notes, striving to interpret Gabrielle's sartorial preferences.

In the world of fashion, designers occasionally articulate their visions through photos. Typically, it falls to the assistant designer to decipher the intricate language of fashion; the volume, preferred cuts, stitching techniques, finishings, and so on. Nevertheless, the modéliste remains the go-to for technical queries, should they arise.

Gabrielle was elaborating on several designs, and Jindo perceived similarity in one of the depicted pieces to the PVC material coat that Timothée's girlfriend had donned at the previous Halloween event.

"Gabrielle, is this coat similar to the one Timothée's girlfriend was wearing yesterday?"

"De quoi? What do you mean?"

"The PVC coat you're explaining now. It sounds like Timothée's girlfriend's yesterday…"

"Jindo, why would I make a coat that his STUPID girlfriend wore?"

"…"

Jindo found himself flustered by her unexpected sharpness. His intention was to clarify mutual understanding, but it seemed Gabrielle was repulsed by his reference, not so much for its design but due to its source. Undeterred, she continued.

"She's just a clerk at a cheap clothing store in Étienne Marcel… Why would I design a coat that the stupid black girlfriend of Timothée was wearing?"

"…"

Taken aback by Gabrielle's sudden outburst of rudeness, Jindo felt an uncomfortable jolt. He had thought Parisians were progressively embracing racial diversity, yet here was Gabrielle, clearly the exception to his perception.

Nevertheless, as the tired employee he was, he chose to remain silent and steer the conversation back on track.

"… okay, never mind. Maybe it's a completely different coat… But, just for the modélisme perspective, it's quite similar construction…"

"NO, IT'S DIFFERENT. I think you never understood my idea Jindo. Mine is like…"

She proceeded to re-illustrate her design using additional photographs. Jindo noticed subtle changes in her idea but chose to hold his tongue.

Nonetheless, there remained a dress about which Jindo needed to inquire.

"By the way Gabrielle, is this new dress going to be in the new collection too? Because it looks a bit different from the collection theme that we're doing now…"

"Oh, you're right… this dress is for me for a charity event."

"Charity event?"

"Yes, I'm invited by Fédération de la Haute Couture et de la Mode, for the Christmas charity soirée..."

The Parisian designer seemed to radiate a certain pride, and although Jindo indirectly questioned her authenticity, this moment felt genuine.

Shifting gears, Gabrielle outlined the tasks that the young French girls need to undertake during her absence. Chief among them was the creation of a Christmas tree adorned with delicate lace.

She emphasised that this colossal tree would feature at the charity event, therefore work should commence immediately given its grandeur. Thus, the atelier manager would need to ensure the diligent productivity of the young workers, guaranteeing the completion of this task, come what may.

For the modéliste team, the objective was clear; return to the pending collection, incorporating the newly added pieces.

Nearing the end of the meeting, Gabrielle's demeanour became stern, as she imparted one final directive to Jindo. Her countenance grave, she ordered him to monitor Amélie and Timothée carefully. He was to report their daily arrivals, departures, and frequency of absences from their desks.

Although Jindo understood the potential concerns of the director, he found the notion of playing informant distasteful. Gabrielle assured him there were undisclosed histories involving the French siblings, promising to explain later. Jindo remained reluctant, but for the sake of concluding the discussion, he pushed forward.

Gabrielle requested Jindo install the WeChat application on his mobile device, which would facilitate immediate communication while she was in China.

The meeting had drawn to a close around 7 pm. Jindo was feeling the effects of the long day, both fatigued and famished. Gabrielle seemed to pick up on his state.

"Jindo, are you hungry? Do you want to eat?"

Jindo's exhausted state resulted in a delayed response, to which Gabrielle promptly added.

"Do you like Thai food?"

Upon hearing this, Jindo hesitated. He had a fondness for Thai cuisine and was practically ravenous by this point. At the mere mention of food, his mouth began to water. Gabrielle went on.

"There's one near here, the restaurant is run by a gay couple, one French and one Thai. It's really good…"

In Europe at that time, when an Asian restaurant was run by mixed owners, one local and one native, the results were often stellar. They maintained the authentic flavours while infusing the locale's unique atmosphere.

Having sampled several such establishments, Jindo was intrigued. He resolved to dine there before heading home. They exited the house, making their way towards the restaurant.

As promised, it was a short journey. Upon arrival, they were greeted by a substantial queue. It was indeed a popular spot in the district. Jindo expressed his reluctance to wait, but Gabrielle reassured him that the culinary delights would be well worth the delay.

She requested from the door staff a table downstairs, revealing her familiarity with the venue. After a considerable wait, they were led to their exclusive table, some twenty minutes later.

Descending the winding staircase, Jindo found himself impressed by the setting. The passage was reminiscent of an old-world cave, but unlike Gabrielle's rustic dwelling, it was stylishly modernised.

The walls, a creamy, stone-block design, and the tables bore a hint of Baroque influence. Antique-style red candles were sporadically placed, adding a touch of vintage charm. The place was relatively sparse, with few tables peppered across the space.

This was a pleasant departure from typical Asian eateries of that era in Europe, where tables were frequently crammed into limited spaces. Jindo appreciated the ambience and, finally, they took their seats.

The French proprietor of the restaurant approached to take their order, offering Jindo and Gabrielle an extra layer of cordiality that seemed to echo the warmth usually reserved for fellow mixed-race couples.

In response to this genial welcome, Jindo, well-versed in the delights of Thai cuisine, ordered his dishes without so much as a glance at the menu. Gabrielle, a seasoned patron herself, promptly selected her preferences as well.

As they waited for their meals, Jindo savoured a bottle of Singha, while Gabrielle, as was her wont, enriched the ambience with her enchanting anecdotes. Despite the day having inadvertently elongated into a long working one, Jindo found himself blissfully unburdened of any negative experiences, thoroughly relishing the atmosphere of the charming establishment.

Gabrielle commented that the kitchen, under the helm of the Thai proprietor, ran like clockwork, an observation that was promptly validated by the swift arrival of their meals.

The dedicated herbivore was presented with vegetarian spring rolls and tofu fried rice. Jindo, on the other hand, the ardent Thai cuisine aficionado, was served chicken pad Thai and fried rice. As Gabrielle daintily picked up a spring roll to commence her meal, the ravenous Jindo dove headfirst into his dishes, voraciously devouring his food.

Delighted by the culinary feast, particularly impressed with the generous portion of chicken, Jindo was mid-bite when he detected Gabrielle's gaze upon him. Meeting her eyes, he found her expression one of mild astonishment, morphing slowly into a restrained smile. She began to speak.

"Jindo, you know when you eat meat, you also eat the animal's stress…"

"…"

Caught mid-chew, Jindo found her piercing gaze slightly disconcerting, her pitying glance making him shift uncomfortably. Unperturbed, Gabrielle continued.

"Jindo, you know animals know when they're being killed and during the moment, they fear a lot then it makes them really stressed… That means people, eating their meat, actually eat their stress and that's why those meat-eating people easily get angry all the time…"

"…"

Her words hung in the air as Jindo finished his mouthful, a frown knitting his brows in discomfort. Gabrielle did not miss a beat.

"Jindo, I'm not trying to persuade you to be a vegan, but just letting you know…"

As Jindo still tucked into his chicken, Gabrielle took it upon herself to educate him on the process of meat production. She displayed a surprisingly comprehensive knowledge of the subject, leaving Jindo torn between admiration and the desire to savour his meal.

Still, he found it prudent to withhold comment until she concluded her monologue.

"Jindo, there's actually a documentary about this on Netflix…"

A Netflix subscriber himself, Jindo asked.

"Okay, please let me know the title, and I'll check it out later…"

"When are you going to watch it?"

"Eh… I don't know. By the way Gabrielle, I'm not totally blank about this subject… I've watched Okja…"

"Ouik… jia? What is it?"

"It's a film about this issue that you're talking about? It's on Netflix too…"

"Oh, really?"

"At the same time, as far as I know, it was quite loudly premiered at Cannes Film Festival this year. There were posters everywhere in Paris, I even saw one at a bus stop in Bondy… You never heard about it?"

"No, not really. Who is the director?"

"It's Bong Joon Ho."

"Who? Is he Korean?"

"Yes."

"Ah… I've never watched Korean movies…"

Despite Gabrielle's explicit disinterest, Jindo attempted to extend the conversation, unfazed.

"Gabrielle, it's not really a Korean film though. It's an English language film…"

"…"

She merely shrugged, still looking utterly indifferent. This blatant disregard for his suggestions irked Jindo.

"Gabrielle, I'm not trying to introduce you to a Korean film, but just trying to let you know of a film that you may be interested in, for your own interest…"

"But I never heard of the director..."

Though Jindo knew that Bong Joon Ho had already achieved significant acclaim among film enthusiasts by then, he bit back the retort, acknowledging that it might seem less persuasive coming from a fellow Korean.

"Well, maybe he's not that globally famous yet like Martin Scorsese or Quentin Tarantino... but he's a great filmmaker. When I was in England, his films were often on TV..."

"Bah... I don't know."

Gabrielle's apathy stoked a spark of irritation within Jindo. It was not the film itself she disregarded, he realised, but its foreign origins. Although he did not typically flaunt nationalistic pride, her indifference felt somewhat insulting.

Nevertheless, he chose to advocate for the film's merit, not its nationality.

"Gabrielle, have you seen Snowpiercer? It's based on a French graphic novel..."

"Is it the one with Chris Evans?"

"That's the one. Tilda Swinton is also in it..."

"Oh yes, I know the movie. I watched it. Is it his film?"

"Yes, by the way, Tilda Swinton is in Okja again..."

"..."

She shrugged; her interest seemed to be piqued only by the male lead. Still, it was a start, and Jindo exhaled, relieved his references were finally hitting their mark. He decided to maintain his neutral tone.

"By the way Gabrielle, apart from the actors and directors though, to be fair, when Netflix invests in a project, and there are posters everywhere in Paris, or possibly all over France during the Cannes Film Festival, even nominated, it may not be a bad film... Don't you reckon so?"

"Hm... yes, maybe... Anyway, you want to watch that with me tonight?"

"Pardon?"

The conversation had taken an unexpected turn.

"Jindo, we can watch it together tonight. I want to watch a Korean film with a Korean."

"..."

Chapter 38 : Tears and Tensions

J indo was at a loss for words. Gabrielle still seemed oblivious to his initial intentions.

"We can watch it tonight."

"…"

Jindo silently cursed the twists and turns of their conversation. This was not the outcome he had envisioned. Tired, he sought an escape.

"Gabrielle, I think I'd better go home today. I even need to feed my cats as they must be hungry now…"

"What? Cats? You're going home because of your cats?"

Jindo recognised the flaw in his argument but pressed on regardless.

"I didn't leave much food out for them yesterday, you saw that…"

"Jindo, the CATS are more important than ME?"

As she uttered those words, her brow furrowed, and her gaze drilled into Jindo. It appeared she was once again resorting to her eccentric line of reasoning. What perplexed Jindo was her increasing tendency to address him as though he were her boyfriend.

"Jindo, they'll be fine… Cats are fine even if they don't get fed for a long time. My family had cats since I was a kid. You said you just had them for like a few months. So, you don't know anything about cats yet… Cats are not like dogs, they're always fine by just themselves…"

"…"

Silence fell over Jindo as he recognised the futility of his excuse. Scrambling for an alternative, he found his brain sluggish from the indulgence in Thai dishes and bottles of Singha.

He was reduced to staring at the domineering woman, trying to formulate a plan. At that moment, Gabrielle seized his hesitation.

"Jindo, I really want to watch that Korean movie by Boong, Jin, Neu… you talked about, you can explain to me while watching…"

"…"

Incapable of responding, Jindo could only muster an awkward smile at the absurdity of the situation.

At that moment, Gabrielle promptly settled their bill, before extending a hand towards Jindo and guiding him out of the restaurant. Though he offered sincere gratitude for her generosity, a sense of hesitance and reluctance still lingered within him. Nonetheless, he allowed himself to be led, his countenance mirroring those animals destined for the abattoir.

Arriving at the house…

Jindo was instantly hit with the stench of fresh tobacco smoke.

"Gabrielle, it smells like somebody's just smoked in the house…"

Gabrielle's eyes widened in panic. Abruptly, she ushered him back outside, and Jindo was taken aback.

"Gabrielle, what's going on?"

"I think my friend came to my house…"

Her voice was laced with anxiety, and Jindo was still in surprise.

"Your friend?"

"… yes… he sometimes just come…"

"He? Is it a man?"

"… ah… yes…"

She fluttered around like a headless chicken, prompting Jindo to a sudden suspicion.

"Is it Vincent, Gabrielle?"

His direct question left her momentarily speechless.

"... non, no... it's not him, how do you...?"

Jindo held her gaze, silently encouraging her to be truthful.

"... yes... it's Vincent..."

"One more question, Gabrielle... Is he your ex-boyfriend?"

"No, well..."

"GABRIELLE?"

Jindo fixed her with a steady gaze, prompting her silently for the truth.

"Well, um…"

Evidently uncomfortable, Gabrielle seemed embarrassed. For the first time, Jindo felt a sense of triumph at having ensnared the elusive lady in his questioning.

Maintaining his momentum, he continued.

"Gabrielle, I saw Vincent coming in, many times when I was leaving from work."

"Ah…"

She appeared frozen under his scrutiny, and Jindo maintained his intense eye contact. Eventually, she lowered her gaze, her face crumpling with the onset of tears.

"I'm so sorry Jindo…"

Her voice wavered, but Jindo remained steady, determined to see this through.

"Sorry about what, Gabrielle?"

"I… broke up with him three weeks ago, but I think he still doesn't accept it…"

Not addressing this minor discrepancy, Jindo kept his focus on the current issue.

"So Gabrielle, does he come into your house by himself?"

"… yes…"

"How come he has the key though?"

"…"

Jindo asked the questions calmly, one after another. Gabrielle, meanwhile, seemed to be sinking deeper into embarrassment.

"… I don't know Jindo, I screwed…"

Tears started streaming down her face, but Jindo remained unfazed, intent on uncovering the truth.

"You screwed? What do you mean Gabrielle?"

Refusing to break eye contact, Jindo's scrutiny seemed to trigger an escalation in Gabrielle's distress. She began to cry louder, as if desperate for a larger audience. Bystanders on the street began to take notice of the scene.

In fact, a traditional French restaurant was located adjacent to Gabrielle's place. Smokers often lingered outside, and now they were starting to observe the spectacle unfolding.

Embarrassed by the unwarranted attention, Jindo tried to address Gabrielle in a more subdued tone.

"Gabrielle, can you please make me understand what is going on? Because I haven't got any clue at the moment…"

Despite Jindo's quiet plea, Gabrielle continued to wail loudly, attracting more curious onlookers. Jindo stood stiffly beside her, his hands buried in his pants' pockets and a frown etched on his face, while it made a stark contrast as Gabrielle cried into her hands.

From an outsider's perspective, it might appear as though the semi-formal-dressed Asian man had upset the leggings-clad French girl and seemed utterly indifferent to her distress.

As the crowd drew closer, scrutinising Jindo's face, he found himself locked in a silent standoff with the onlookers. Though no words had been exchanged, Jindo could sense the crowd's misunderstanding of the situation.

Observing the spectators, Gabrielle took a deep breath and spoke up.

"It's because… when I saw you, I fancied you… then day by day when we worked together, I felt we were like a destiny… I never worked with a modéliste who understood my vision really well, and I also felt you were a very nice man…"

"…"

Jindo was rendered speechless by Gabrielle's unexpected outpouring. Unfazed, she continued her confession.

"I tried hard not to like you because you're one of my employees… but I think I already fell in love with you and I really wanted to do well with you this time… I really thought I finally met a good man that I can be with for a long time…"

"…"

Aside from Jindo being sceptical of her declaration, the situation was rapidly becoming uncomfortable. The spectators seemed to understand the nature of the exchange, offering Jindo knowing smiles in light of the romantic confession.

Meanwhile, Gabrielle continued to gauge the audience's reaction through teary eyes, causing Jindo to offer the spectators a hesitant smile in response.

Nonetheless, he did not deviate from his composed demeanour.

"Gabrielle, we talk about this later when you calm down. By the way, for now, let's sort out the problem first... So, you broke up with Vincent but he kept coming to your house, is that correct?"

"Yes."

Gabrielle halted her tears, responding with the quiet seriousness of a child reporting a schoolyard bully. The onlookers began to lose interest, dispersing gradually.

"Okay Gabrielle, do you want me to speak to him?"

His proposal seemed to startle her.

"No, no please don't do that Jindo, he's very violent, I told you his upbringing was really bad and he's got a bad temper... He even fought with my parents before, and he's also a professional boxer..."

She seemed desperate, gripping Jindo's hands in an attempt to dissuade him.

However, Jindo was undeterred. He had a gut feeling that Vincent would not pose a real threat.

"Gabrielle, I'll just go and talk to him and I think it'll be fine..."

"No, no please don't... please..."

Her grip on Jindo's hands tightened, and he could feel her trembling. Meeting her tear-filled eyes, he recognised her genuine fear.

"Jindo, please let me do it... please..."

"..."

Jindo found himself at a loss. The sight of her trembling and pleading left him uncertain.

Nevertheless, Gabrielle continued with a sense of desperation.

"Today, I'll tell him everything... I now have you and I don't want him to come to my house again..."

Despite paying attention to her impromptu speech, Jindo noticed an oddity in her words. Their relationship had never been formally addressed or agreed upon, yet she was already speaking as if they were a couple.

He was eager to clarify the specifics of their relationship, but he refrained. It felt unjust to interrogate a woman who was visibly upset, practically shaking with fear.

Jindo was still unsure about the best course of action but ultimately decided not to interfere with her personal affairs. Nevertheless, he felt concerned for Gabrielle. Despite his suspicions, there was still a chance that her claims were genuine.

"Okay Gabrielle, I'll just go back home today then... but please call me if you need any help, really, I'll come right away..."

"Thank you Jindo, thank you..."

In a show of gratitude, she planted a kiss on his cheek, as if he had just saved her life.

Although the entire situation left Jindo feeling disconcerted, he made his way home. For the remainder of the weekend, he received no news from Gabrielle. Torn between doubt and concern, he resisted the urge to contact her for an update.

Chapter 39 : Negotiations and Nuances

The following Monday…

Jindo was immersed in his usual daily tasks, executing his duties with the precision of a well-oiled machine. Throughout the day, he occasionally crossed paths with Gabrielle, yet with other employees ever present, she did not broach any subject of particular interest. At lunch, an update on the ex-boyfriend situation remained elusive, as Seiwa was also present, rendering private conversation impossible.

Despite Gabrielle's attempts to act as though their personal discourse had not transpired, a subtle change was discernible in the dynamic between the director and modéliste. Their conversations now carried a distinct undercurrent that the keen observers in the atelier could not help but notice.

With Halloween now behind them, the focus of the atelier shifted towards the new collection and the upcoming Christmas project. For several days, everyone diligently attended to their tasks without the stress of overtime. The director too appeared preoccupied with preparing her forthcoming schedule, which included meetings with various agents. Among these was a middle-aged woman from Hong Kong who was involved in the China project and resided in Paris with her French husband.

During Thursday's lunch…

Gabrielle requested Jindo's presence that evening for a call with the Chinese investor. With the investor's English far from fluent and her

Hong Kong agent unable to attend due to a pressing commitment, she asked Jindo to step in as a translator, just in case the investor reverted to Chinese.

Jindo tried to convey the linguistic disparity between Korean and Chinese, but Gabrielle seemed rather indifferent to his explanation.

In fact, Jindo suggested Seiwa might be a better fit for the task, but at the mention of Madame Claude's impending presence, the sister's little frown clearly communicated her reluctance to the brother.

Ultimately, Gabrielle entrusted Jindo with the responsibility of atelier manager and asked him, in a roundabout way, to gauge whether the investor was a trustworthy individual or a potential con artist.

After work...

As the employees trickled out, Jindo found himself alone with Gabrielle in the studio, awaiting the arrival of Madame Claude who went out for a while. The phone's sudden trill announced a call that likely signalled the imminent arrival of the senior lady.

Yet, what struck Jindo as peculiar was Gabrielle's abrupt scrutiny of his outfit after the call.

"Jindo, why are you wearing this stupid sweater today?"

"Pardon?"

"My father is coming, and I don't like your look today…"

As a matter of fact, Jindo was sporting a multicoloured, striped sweater from Sonia Rykiel, python-print trousers from Roberto Cavalli, and audacious spiked boots from Dr Martens. Despite his ensemble being somewhat avant-garde for common tastes, he deemed Gabrielle's reaction unjustified.

"Gabrielle, you didn't say anything at lunch, but why are you doing this now?"

"Because I didn't know my father was coming, but he's on his way now…"

Jindo found this particularly vexing; after all, he was an employee at a Parisian fashion house. His attire, albeit distinctive, was well within the realm of the industry's eccentricities. What puzzled him was Gabrielle's manner, which oddly hinted at her introducing a new beau to her father.

At that moment, the doorbell chimed, and her parents made their entrance. Gabrielle sprung to her father with the enthusiasm of a doting daughter, while her mother maintained a composed presence akin to a diligent secretary. It was a rather unusual sight for Jindo, who had only ever seen Madame Claude in a state of unrest.

Following the father-daughter exchange of affectionate greetings, or 'bisous bisous' as they call it, Jindo observed the scene from a distance. There was something slightly theatrical about the family's interactions, as though they were putting on a show of affection that was somewhat exaggerated.

Once the familial display concluded, the suited elderly man turned his attention to the flamboyantly dressed employee. Jindo felt a twinge of nervousness as he had just witnessed an unexpected side of the two often-cantankerous women. Yet, he managed to maintain his composure, his politeness unwavering.

When confronted face-to-face, Jindo could not help but notice the father's diminutive stature. Despite the air of confidence conveyed by his balding pate and sizable physique, there was no denying that he was rather short. Even his attempt at maintaining a proud posture by keeping his chin up could not negate his low eye level.

In fact, both parents, unlike their ex-model daughter, were somewhat vertically challenged. Regardless, the two men of Gabrielle stood face-to-face, and the father broke the silence.

"Tu parles français?"

(Do you speak French?)

"Oui, un peu..."

Despite the abrupt start to the conversation, bypassing the usual 'bonsoir' to query Jindo's local language proficiency, he felt mildly taken aback by the senior French man's tone. The high pitch of his voice was momentarily akin to a rat's squeak.

Nonetheless, Jindo maintained his decorum.

"En fait, mon parler n'est pas très bien mais je comprends mieux..."

(In fact, my speaking is not very good, but my understanding is better...)

The father's response was an indifferent shrug. Undeterred, Jindo pressed on.

"Alors, enchanté monsieur..."

(Anyway, nice to meet you, sir...)

Offering his hand for a shake, Jindo bore the politest expression he could muster. Yet, the father seemed unimpressed.

Silently examining Jindo from head to toe, he frowned slightly and shook his head, as though declaring the employee unfit for his daughter.

Slightly irked by the blatant display of arrogance, Jindo managed to hold onto his courteous demeanour, responding with a dignified lift of his eyebrows and a slight purse of his lips, withdrawing his unaccepted hand.

Casting a glance at Gabrielle for guidance, he caught her subtle frown and eye-roll that suggested his outfit was the problem. Although he still found this unjust, he conceded and decided to speak only when spoken to.

Meanwhile, the father appeared to lose interest in further conversation with Jindo. The three family members then engaged in their own discourse. Standing quietly to one side, his hands crossed in front, Jindo resembled a dutiful aide.

Listening in for a while, Jindo gleaned that they were discussing the agent from Hong Kong. Though his grasp of French was not perfect, he understood enough to recognise that they harboured some suspicions about the agent lady.

This puzzled Jindo. The Hong Kong woman, as far as he could tell, had been nothing but kind-hearted, serving Gabrielle selflessly and without seeking remuneration. This led him to a sobering conclusion; the family's nature was inherently distrustful, scrutinising anyone who crossed their path.

In a business context, Jindo's perspective was reasonable, yet he found them slightly distasteful. He had previously observed Gabrielle and Madame Claude playing the role of best friends with the lady from Hong Kong, suggesting that she was akin to a family member from a different race.

Regardless, the appointed time had arrived, and they all took their respective seats. Jindo claimed a corner chair for himself just as Gabrielle was receiving a call via WeChat. Setting it to loudspeaker mode, they all prepared to listen.

"Hellyo…"

Lifting her tone into a realm of amiable friendliness, the French designer greeted the Chinese investor. They began the conversation by referencing the Hong Kong agent, establishing common ground.

The investor's command of English was far from fluent, yet his communication skills were sufficient, clearly conveying his intentions to Gabrielle. After confirming their meeting in Shanghai, Gabrielle posed her question.

"So, you're going to pay me for my flight ticket once I arrive, yes?"

"Yes yes, I'll pay for your ticket when you come to Shanghai…"

"You know it's 2,500 euro for me and my father…"

"Yes yes, you show me the invoice and I pay you…"

"Okay, so I send you a screenshot of my payment, you give me the money, yes?"

"Yes yes, don't worry, don't worry…"

"By the way, how are you going to pay me? In euro or Chinese money?"

"I pay you in euro. Don't worry, don't worry Gabrielle…"

Listening to the overly simplistic conversation, Jindo found himself grappling with second-hand embarrassment. He flashed Gabrielle a face, gesturing with his hands, urging her to cease her relentless pursuit of the payment confirmation. In response, she shrugged her shoulders, indicating that she did not understand his apparent unease.

Turning to look at the parents, Jindo had the distinct impression he was the only one finding the situation absurd. He could not tell if the elder French couple fully grasped the English conversation, but they seemed intensely focused; faces etched in stern concentration. Jindo noted the persistent sour expressions, something of a family trademark, though it was a detail of little consequence at that moment.

The pair concluded their conversation, reaffirming the details of their Shanghai meeting. Not surprisingly, Gabrielle managed to squeeze in one last query about her flight ticket reimbursement before the call ended.

Jindo found himself questioning Gabrielle's insistence on his presence, which made even less sense when she asked for his opinion on the investor. Despite his bewilderment at his inclusion in this farcical meeting, he managed to mutter that the investor seemed to have a reasonable command of English, adding that nothing else stood out to him.

The French matriarch and patriarch joined their daughter in a serious discussion, not just about the Chinese investor but also about the agent from Hong Kong. They deliberated for a time, yet Jindo sensed that their primary concern remained the reimbursement of the flight tickets.

An incredulous smile played on his lips as he observed the consistent absurdity unfolding before him. It was then that Gabrielle caught him.

"Jindo, what are you smiling about? Is something funny?"

"… it's because… Gabrielle, I might have insufficient information at the moment, but I'm just… finding it a bit too much…"

"Too much for what?"

"I mean, do you really need to keep worrying about his payback? Is it not like you are connected with the investor via your agent? I mean… this is about a big international business project, and the Chinese investor who I reckon would be a very rich man… rich enough to take care of your little expenses… But you kept asking for the payback during the call, then you're still talking about it with your parents. Am I the only one thinking there may be more important issues to discuss about?"

As Jindo's voice gradually gained volume during his discourse, the parents viewed him with a mix of surprise and disapproval. Indeed, this was the first time Madame Claude had witnessed Jindo in a state of agitation, and she seemed eager to decipher his English. The father, on the other hand, regarded Jindo with a deeply furrowed brow, seemingly unpleased with his audacious presence.

Chapter 40 : Dinner and Disdain

Following Gabrielle's translation, her mother's response was immediate, firm in her French assertion. The father remained impassive, shaking his head dismissively, suggesting that regardless of Jindo's input, he was not a part of the 'big player's table' anyway. They exchanged words amongst themselves before Gabrielle posed a question to Jindo.

"Jindo, how do you know if he's going to pay me?"

"… Gabrielle, I think my point is not like I know he would pay back, but like I think we should discuss something more important than that… like what kind of project he or you are expecting from this collaboration, then scenarios A, B, C for instance…"

"But that is after he pays me back for my tickets…"

"…"

Jindo glanced at the parents, wondering if they were following the conversation, then surmised that the French elders agreed with Gabrielle. Not simply because she was their daughter, but because they concurred with her viewpoint.

Suddenly, Jindo had a hunch. Perhaps this family was not accustomed to repaying debts, thus their doubts about the investor's commitment to repayment mirrored their own typical behaviour. As Jindo was pondering this, Gabrielle resumed speaking.

"Jindo, 2500 euro is not small money, so it's quite important we make sure he pays back…"

"Gabrielle, I get it I get it. But enough is enough, you asked it like 5 times and I think that is more than enough…"

"But it's still important…"

Just as their debate seemed endless, Madame Claude interjected, prompting Gabrielle to translate. Upon hearing her mum's supportive comment, Gabrielle sprang back into the discussion.

"She even said it's very important to make sure the payment… C'est ça maman? *(Right, mom?)*"

"Bah, oui…"

(Oh, yes…)

"…"

Madame Claude's conviction seemed unwavering, leading Jindo to perceive the situation as increasingly ludicrous. He alternated his gaze between the mother and the daughter, just as the father suddenly interjected.

His remark was swift and high-pitched, still reminiscent of a rat's squeak, and Jindo could not grasp any of it. Yet whatever he had said appeared to amuse the two French women immensely as they erupted into laughter.

Gabrielle held back from translating her father's jibe to Jindo. The seasoned expatriate in Europe, with over a decade's experience, recognised the racial undertone behind the supposedly comedic comment about Asians. The purveyor of the 'joke', the balding man, shook his head, ready to take his leave.

Jindo was no stranger to these so-called 'friendly situations'. Unfazed and undeterred, he endeavoured to catch the eye of the French man with a smile. However, the older gentleman seemed indifferent, not sparing a glance in Jindo's direction, as though he deemed the foreigner unworthy of his attention. He shifted the conversation towards dinner plans with his daughter.

Gabrielle extended an invitation for Jindo to join them. Jindo's hesitance stemmed from a reluctance to break bread with an ignoramus.

Undeterred by his pause, Gabrielle looped her arm through Jindo's, urging him forward. The situation resembled a young woman dragging her reluctant boyfriend to a family gathering.

Regardless, they found themselves in a traditional French bar-cum-restaurant, the familiar territory where the regulars had observed Gabrielle and Jindo's public tiffs on the previous Saturday evening.

They claimed an outside table on the terrace, and after a few minutes, a server arrived to take their orders. While Gabrielle's family was still perusing the menu, Jindo requested a cheeseburger with a pint of Kronenbourg.

His choice sparked laughter amongst the French family. The father began mocking Jindo's order, imitating his accent. Jindo felt a ripple of irritation but still maintained his cool. With a grin plastered across his face, he scanned each family member one by one, subtly indicating his tolerance had its limits.

Madame Claude, attuned to the tension, interjected, suggesting Jindo try the cordon bleu burger instead. She seemed eager to engage the foreign employee in conversation, to alleviate the strain resulting from her husband's tactless humour. As Jindo braced himself to counter the French comedian, the wife appeared to play peacemaker, intent on defusing the quietly simmering tension.

In fact, Jindo harboured no particular preference for burgers, but his selection of the humble cheeseburger was a strategic one. Its attractive price point made it the least expensive option on the menu. Considering the likelihood of the parents footing the bill, Jindo did not wish to opt for a more costly dish. Furthermore, his experience suggested a cheeseburger was a reliable choice, almost guaranteed to deliver on portion size and taste, irrespective of the establishment.

Eventually, the French family arrived at their menu selections and initiated a conversation amongst themselves. Jindo sat there, savouring his lager in the warm Parisian evening, and eavesdropped as the family seemed to begin to discuss Antoine.

It was clear the parents were acquainted with their daughter's friend. However, the conversation took a gossipy turn. Though Jindo could not catch every detail, the gist of it was that Gabrielle considered Antoine a fool for funding his wife's venture.

She informed her parents that Irina was starting a collection from their petite Parisian apartment, much to Antoine's chagrin, as it had resulted in a chaotic, dust-filled environment. Her father, ever the clown, mimicked the couple, inducing laughter from the entire family.

Jindo recollected Irina downplaying her efforts, merely stating she was experimenting to discover her designer identity. He chose to stay silent, opting instead to satisfy his curiosity.

"By the way Gabrielle, did you know Irina used to be at Dior?"

"What? Who said that?"

"Irina said it when I asked… Well, she didn't say she was properly employed at the label, but just temporarily contracted once, but anyway she was at Dior. Did you know about this?"

"Jindo, she was just a couturière, not a designer…"

"Okay, but anyway she was at Dior, and you told me she just started her own label after graduation…"

"Jindo, it's nothing, anyone can go to Dior for couturière, you can even go… you want me to write a recommendation letter for you?"

"…"

Jindo was unamused by Gabrielle's facetious offer. He was acutely aware that a house as illustrious as Dior was not as Gabrielle depicted it. His French professor, a former Dior and Balenciaga employee, had emphasised their stringent and confidential recruitment process.

Nevertheless, Gabrielle raised her voice to diminish the accomplishments of the Eastern European lady. At that moment, Jindo detected an intriguing cadence in Gabrielle's speech. Whenever she gave the impression of her deep connections within the luxury fashion industry, she spoke with a rapid, overpowering fervour. This aggressive behaviour was in a way, designed to deter listeners from probing further.

Jindo watched the self-proclaimed designer with a sceptical expression. Simultaneously, he felt the piercing gaze of her father from the corner of the table. The French elder's furrowed brow and sour expression gave him the likeness of a disgruntled bulldog.

Jindo found himself locked in a silent standoff with the French hound, both seemingly ready to bark and bite back once released. At that moment, their meal arrived. Although the servers intermittently obstructed their view as they distributed the dishes, the undercurrent of tension between Jindo and the elder remained palpable.

"Bon appétit!"

Everyone dug in, and Jindo exercised impeccable table manners. His careful attention to etiquette might not have stemmed from a desire to show Gabrielle's parents utmost courtesy, but rather to prevent the French elder from finding any minute fault with him.

He painstakingly manipulated his cutlery, dissecting his burger into minuscule portions to avoid his habitual devouring while eating.

He artistically drizzled his condiments in perfect dollops for a neat appearance. Despite being capable of swallowing a burger in two minutes, he paced himself to match the tempo of his dining companions.

The French family was engrossed in their food and conversation. Eventually, Madame Claude asked Jindo about typical Korean cuisine. As he prepared to respond, he raised his palm to cover his mouth, a habit ingrained in him by his home culture to prevent any accidental splatter while speaking.

Curious, Madame Claude asked about his gesture, prompting Jindo to explain his cultural customs. The father found this amusing and, mimicking Jindo's action, elicited a chuckle from his daughter. Jindo, suppressing the impulse to spit his half-chewed cheeseburger in response, continued conversing with Madame Claude.

Upon hearing Jindo's explanation, Madame Claude lauded him with repeated 'très biens', praising his well-mannered upbringing. She even pointed out Jindo's general politeness to her husband. The elder, however, merely shrugged nonchalantly, too engrossed in his conversation with Gabrielle to pay any heed to Jindo.

Jindo appreciated Madame Claude's compliments, yet he could not shake off the suspicion that they were merely her efforts to stave off a potential dispute between him and her husband.

Soon, the conversation shifted towards Seiwa, Jindo's Malaysian sister. The woman began criticising Seiwa's arrogance, and although Jindo could not understand the specifics due to his rudimentary French, her disgruntled tone and scowl spoke volumes.

He attempted to come to Seiwa's defence, but Madame Claude overrode his objections with a torrent of rapid, loud French. Jindo realised that it was characteristic of this family to steamroll anyone daring to oppose their views. He glanced at Gabrielle, hoping she would step in and support her diligent assistant. However, she appeared more engrossed in her mobile phone.

When dinner was over, they prepared to go their separate ways. Gabrielle mentioned that she needed to pack her suitcase, while Jindo was planning to head home. Noticing that he was not headed towards the metro station, Madame Claude inquired about his transportation. At this, Gabrielle began to share details about Jindo's car and his spacious Bondy residence.

Despite numerous misconceptions being propagated, Jindo did not correct Gabrielle. He quietly listened to her narration, occasionally nodding. On hearing about Jindo's apparent affluence, Madame Claude studied him from head to toe with an impressed smile.

At this point, the ever-sour patriarch cut in, querying how Jindo had managed to own a car. Jindo explained he had purchased it from his neighbour, but the father seemed dubious and probed him further about his EU driving license.

Remaining composed, Jindo mentioned he had acquired his license while in England. Gabrielle chimed in to provide her father with a brief overview of Jindo's international stays, including his residence in Italy.

Upon hearing this, the father's grumpy countenance intensified. Reverting to his dismissive behaviour, he headed towards his car, parked conveniently in the driveway in front of the house.

The car park loomed ahead, and Jindo identified the bald French man's grey Citroën. Despite the car's noticeable age, Jindo approached, pretending to survey it closely.

He queried the vehicle's age to its owner, to which the older Frenchman proudly boasted of its enduring power despite its years. His posture mirrored his words; chin held high, voice ringing with a bolstered sense of authority. Yet Jindo merely offered a sly smile in return, standing next to Gabrielle.

An odd tension prickled the air between the two men, as the French ladies looked like silent spectators to this unfolding dance of masculinity.

In fact, Jindo was not particularly captivated by the man's car or his daughter. His aim was to needle the older man a little in response to his earlier discourtesy. Yet the joker, seemingly oblivious to his faux pas, remained oblivious.

At that moment, it suddenly dawned on Jindo, that the older man was perhaps merely playing the role of a vigilant father, seeking to guard his daughter from an unfamiliar figure. He seemed keen on showcasing himself as a formidable opponent, still capable of jousting with the younger generation.

In fact, Gabrielle's family might have struck as peculiar, given their idiosyncratic dynamics. However, their quirks were simply a part of their unique familial fabric. Despite their occasional prickliness and perceived miserliness, their affluence was undeniable.

With Gabrielle managing a business from a rented building in central Paris, and her parents both working and residing in the city's heart, they were far from inept or financially constrained.

Their behaviour might have been a coping mechanism, a survival strategy in the relentless urban jungle, much like any small family. Despite his limited knowledge of their history, Jindo sensed that they were a prosperous working-class family, not unlike his own, carrying their own distinct characteristics.

With this newfound understanding, Jindo chose not to take the evening's events to heart, quietly bringing the night to a close.

Come the next day, Gabrielle and her father departed for China.

Chapter 41 : The Seamstress's Strife

The following week...

Ever since Gabrielle's departure for China, Jindo had adopted a new routine; stopping by the French bistro adjacent to Gabrielle's to collect the keys each morning. Indeed, he had quickly become acquainted with the restaurateur due to his recent encounters, including the previous visit accompanied by members of Gabrielle's family, as well as a rather theatrical face-off with Gabrielle on the forecourt of their establishments the previous Saturday evening.

In the wake of these interactions, their morning salutations had evolved, now exuding the effortless camaraderie characteristic of Parisians embracing the birth of a new day. Their conversations, rich with the timbre of early morning Paris, were now steeped in the kind of familiarity that could only be borne from recurrent contact and shared experiences.

Regardless, as last Friday was the first day of Gabrielle's absence, it had been an exercise in organised chaos, with employees basking in the freedom of nebulous job roles. In fact, aside from Julien and Hélène, the established members including Boubacar, Amélie and Timothée, appeared somewhat ill at ease with Jindo allocating tasks.

Two months prior, these three might have regarded Jindo as merely a new employee. However, as time elapsed, they observed his increasing camaraderie with Gabrielle. Although it was not unusual for a modéliste and designer to develop a close working relationship given the nature of their roles, the trio seemed less than thrilled. There had been a palpable sense of their distancing from Jindo, further accentuated when Gabrielle and he began spending time together not only over lunch but post-work as well.

With the designer's absence, the modéliste was now acting much like the house's de facto commander. The established team had defensively circled the wagons against him. The crux of the issue lay in the fact that, while Gabrielle had consistently advised Jindo to assume responsibilities as the atelier manager, she had never formally announced his role to the team.

From Jindo's perspective, it was rather awkward; it would indeed seem peculiar if he suddenly claimed authority as the atelier manager sans an official announcement. Consequently, he often found himself invoking Gabrielle's name while delegating tasks. Yet, the trio largely dismissed him, half-ignoring his instructions.

In contrast, the newer team members seemed to accept Jindo as the interim leader, largely due to his extensive involvement in all facets of the atelier's operations.

The palpable tension between the long-standing team members and the unofficially appointed manager was not lost on Jindo. Yet, he was sanguine, believing that time and actions would ultimately lead to understanding and acceptance.

This week, he was determined to ensure that all tasks were diligently completed by each individual, spurred on by Gabrielle's less-than-pleased response to his weekend WeChat report. His resolve was steadfast, his motivation clear; to uphold the standards of the house during the director's absence.

Regardless, the atelier was now less crowded. Four interns had concluded their two-week work experience the previous Friday, leaving three teenage girls, Hélène, and Julien to complete their respective commitments.

With the two studio assistants now relocated to the atelier, Seiwa found herself alone in the studio, a solitude she cherished, particularly due to Madame Claude's absence. Consequently, the atelier had become the hub of activity in the house, bustling with its nine occupants.

Amélie, on the other hand, seemed less than thrilled to manage the three young interns. She was already overseeing Mina who had previously damaged the Madame Tussaud piece, and now she had two additional charges to guide in constructing the grand Christmas tree.

In fact, Gabrielle had confidentially requested Jindo to keep a discreet eye on Amélie's interactions with the girls, especially attentive to the kind of conversations the accessory designer had with these fledgelings. She checked with Jindo daily, probing if Amélie had uttered any comments about her to the unsuspecting interns.

However, Jindo found this clandestine request somewhat unsettling. The decorator barely seemed inclined to interact with the girls beyond work-related communication. Her preference for Timothée's company was apparent, bordering on possessiveness, as she often chided the young French girls if they tried to engage the tall fedora-adorned French guy in conversation.

In any case, Jindo discerned Amélie's particular disdain for Mina who was frequently glued to her phone yet highly sociable with her peers. He had a hunch that Amélie had been somewhat anticipating Gabrielle's absence, the harshness with which she treated the Afro-French teenager had perceptibly escalated since the director's departure. While his intuition suggested potential conflict on the horizon, his packed schedule did not yet allow him to monitor the situation closely.

As for the modéliste team, it had been divided into two projects. Boubacar and Julien were diligently working on the new collection, while Jindo and Hélène were tasked with creating Gabrielle's dress for the upcoming Christmas charity event.

In the afternoon...

Jindo and Hélène were engrossed in working on the new dress, a charming sleeveless knee-length garment in pink tweed fabric that was form-fitted at the top and delightfully flared at the bottom.

Since Gabrielle had expressed her wish for the dress to be crafted via draping, Jindo had embarked on the preparatory process that morning. With Hélène's assistance, they had conducted a fabric test, contemplated cuts, and prepared the mannequin with muslin ribboning. Now, they stood at the threshold of beginning the draping process.

As Jindo was about to secure a piece of muslin with a pin, Hélène voiced a polite yet ardent desire to try her hand at draping. It was not a wholly unexpected request. After some contemplation of the feasibility, Jindo agreed to let her tackle the fitted part of the top.

Though simpler than the flared bottom, it still held its challenges. He provided her with a quick demonstration, highlighting potential pitfalls, and then the motivated assistant plunged into her task with seriousness and gusto.

Fashion draping is an art that embraces a multitude of creative forms. When it comes to bringing these particular designs to life, the complexity can either mirror or belie the initial impression given by the design sheet. Regardless of the degree of difficulty, the draper's passion for the mission remains fundamentally vital.

As any seasoned modéliste would attest, be it a simple or complicated design, a constructional draft will be ultimately created in the end. What merits attention, however, is the enthusiastic draper's committed and sensitive touch which lends sophistication to each phase of the process. This attention to detail introduces subtle yet significant differences at each stage, cumulatively enhancing the final product's elegance and finesse.

Temporarily leaving Hélène to her independent endeavour, Jindo turned his attention to Julien. On the agenda was a crucial lesson on how to impart a task to the seamstress, a job traditionally shouldered by the main modéliste. However, with Jindo juggling the dual responsibility of overseeing Hélène, he felt it prudent to delegate this task to Julien.

One of the modéliste's significant roles was indeed maintaining a finesse in communication with the seamstress. With this in mind, Jindo painstakingly explained to Julien how to articulate the intricacies of industrial content using the appropriate vernacular.

Meanwhile, Boubacar was evidently less than thrilled about the current state of affairs. It appeared the seasoned seamstress was disgruntled at the prospect of working with Julien.

Jindo had initially thought Boubacar would appreciate the opportunity for fluid conversation in his native tongue. However, it quickly transpired that the middle-aged Afro-French man was less than enthused about having the young French guy as a constant workmate.

Jindo deftly asked for understanding, indicating his commitment to juggling his responsibilities with the modéliste team and the Christmas project. Still, Boubacar did not seem inclined to cut him any slack, grumbling discontentedly under his breath. Jindo, nonetheless, forged ahead.

In a boutique fashion house, the dynamic between the modéliste and the seamstress involves constant communication. When one party is markedly less experienced, it creates discomfort for the other. Miscommunications can give

*rise to mistakes, and more often than not, it falls to the seamstress to rectify
these errors, a situation that certainly does not lend itself to a harmonious
working environment.*

Concluding his instructions to Julien, Jindo returned his attention to
Hélène while the young French man consolidated his notes, preparing to
liaise with the seamstress. From a distance, Jindo kept an ear on Julien's
interaction with Boubakah, focusing on Hélène's progress.

After a moment, despite the palpable tension between Boubacar and
Julien, Jindo decided to hold his peace. Perhaps, he reasoned, this was
merely part of the learning curve for Julien.

However, when Boubacar's tone turned rather bitter, it did not escape
Jindo's attention. He briefly paused his work with Hélène to tune into
the French conversation behind him.

As it transpired, Boubacar was challenging Julien about his experience,
quizzing him about his accomplishments in garment-making and grilling
him about the details. The seamstress, taking an almost antagonistic
stance, told Julien that he would manage all the work himself, implying
that the intern's involvement was superfluous.

Jindo understood Boubacar's concerns but could not shake off a sense
of personal affront. The seamstress was aware that Jindo could hear him,
they were only a couple of meters apart. With a mild sigh, Jindo turned
to face Boubacar.

"Excuse-moi monsieur… Il y a un problème?"

(Excuse me sir… is there a problem?)

The tension between the modéliste and the seamstress was palpable as
they locked gazes. Jindo quickly deduced that Boubacar's antagonism
had been deliberate, a show of pent-up frustration. The intern, Julien,
appeared caught in the crossfire, his discomfort evident.

Listening to Boubacar's grievances, Jindo deduced that the seamstress's antagonism was fuelled more by spite than substance. They were working on a reversible coat with a shawl collar, a task that required creating two identical out-layers and joining them together. The issue at hand was minor; Boubacar claimed that Julien did not know about seam finishings, whether they should be open or folded.

Indeed, this issue about the seam finishings would have been quite trivial for anyone with even a smattering of experience in garment making. However, for novices, such as young interns like Julien, even the simplest of questions could be daunting when posed in a confrontational manner by seasoned professionals. The pressure could render them speechless, unable to address follow-up queries.

As Boubakah concluded his tirade, Jindo interjected.

"Boubacar, je pense que tu ne demandes pas parce que tu ne sais pas la réponse... En fait, je crois que tu fais ça pour..."

(Boubacar, I think you're not asking because you don't know the answer... In fact, I think you're doing this to...)

Boubacar cut him off, raising his voice in an apparent demonstration of his logic, though Jindo struggled to comprehend his point. He turned to Julien for assistance.

"Julien, could you translate him for me please?"

Julien, looking more nervous than ever, was caught off guard by Jindo's uncharacteristic display of annoyance. The intern hesitated.

With a sigh, Jindo pressed on.

"Julien, tell Boubakah... When making a reversible coat in wool, it's most likely to keep the inner seam finishing open. Folding it to one side would make it too bulky, and also... well, hang on, I don't bloody need to explain all this..."

Jindo paused, realising he was arguing over details he deemed trivial. He shook his head, refocusing on the crux of the issue.

"Anyway Julien, please tell him, I highly assume that he actually knows all about this… well, he actually knows more than I do… The point is, I truly think he's making this lousy situation on purpose and I bloody have no idea why he's doing this…"

Julien, translating warily while glancing between the two heated men, seemed to omit Jindo's personal commentary, focusing solely on the seam finishing issue. In response, Boubacar voiced his disagreement.

The experienced seamstress held that nothing could be definitive as every design varied. Though Boubacar was not entirely wrong in his stance, Jindo was determined to address the actual issue at hand.

"Boubacar, si je t'ai dit ça, tu me demandes la même question?"

(Boubacar, if I was the one being talked to, would you ask me the same question?)

"Bah, OUI!"

Boubakah retorted, unyielding, and Jindo, feeling his patience wear thin, made a solemn vow to the grumpy seamstress.

From that moment onwards, Jindo undertook the task of briefing Boubacar, eliminating the need for any interaction between him and Julien. Though Boubacar accepted the proposal with an ill-tempered nod, Jindo could not help but reflect on a contrasting memory.

He remembered how the Afro-French man had seemed to enjoy mentoring and working with one of the blonde female interns, the sewing novice, only a short while ago. Yet, he brushed this thought aside; what had happened was now in the past, and he still had an overwhelming array of tasks to juggle.

Chapter 42 : Threads of Mentorship

On the following day…

Hélène, after multiple corrections and revisions from the day prior, was ready to present her final draft, and Jindo was gearing up to scrutinise the muslin one last time.

"Hélène, on the whole, it looks fine now. Let's just do a bit of the final modification for the armhole lines only…"

"Are the waist and breast parts fine? Because you told me to make it fitted to the mannequin size, but Gabrielle's measurements that you wrote down here are bigger than the current draft…"

"Well, we'll handle the enlargement once I finish the skirt part… It's more effective and efficient to deal with it as a whole."

"I see… And about the armhole line, did I do something wrong?"

"No no, not at all, it's just that you've made the corner of the shoulder and armhole to be perpendicular…"

"Yes, you told me before, making that corner perpendicular is generally better…"

"Yes, you're right… But that's the case for prêt-à-porter (ready-to-wear), where many parties are engaged in the process, so the lines are better to be as simple as possible for all parties to understand… But in this case, it's custom-sized for a particular individual, and Gabrielle's got quite curvy shoulders. Plus, it's sleeveless, so with the current lines, we'll see too much space on the inside on the upper back of the shoulder…

Having said that, we can also play with the shoulder line, but that's a matter that we can consider later in the fitting stage with Gabrielle… For now, let's stick to the basics…"

As Jindo expounded on the intricacies of modélisme, he could see the bright flame of curiosity ignited within Hélène. While imparting his wisdom, he remained cautious not to reveal too much about Gabrielle's physical characteristics.

In fact, Jindo was intimately familiar with the former model's physique, having had several occasions to observe it in its purest form. Gabrielle's bust, for instance, was significantly more ample than one would surmise from her usual attire. Her standard ensemble, an oversized black cotton t-shirt sporting a large cartoonish graphic, with no bra underneath, did a remarkable job of downplaying her generous assets.

He had once taken her measurements before departing for China, but even those readings were not completely reliable. Gabrielle had insisted on not wearing a bra during the measurement session, though she claimed she would sport a slimming slip on the day of the event. This meant that those measurements need not be followed to the letter.

Moreover, Gabrielle's shoulders were unusually curvy, an attribute that made Jindo question her past as a fitting model. In his experience and knowledge, he had never seen a fitting model who would have such curvy shoulders. Despite Gabrielle's frequent claims of being a former contracted fitting model for Lanvin, Jindo had grown sceptical over time.

Models in the fashion industry served various purposes; runway models boasted statuesque figures, editorial models carried a unique and compelling aura, and catalogue models presented the relatability of everyday individuals.

Fitting models, however, regardless of being standard or plus-sized, were expected to maintain a relatively balanced silhouette, one that did not typically encompass overly curvy shoulders.

Regardless, Jindo made a point not to delve too deeply into details about Gabrielle's body; he had no intention of fuelling gossip about his personal encounters with the director.

"Anyway Hélène, as long as the armhole lines from front and back are smoothly connected with the shoulder lines linked, it'll be fine… it's just a bit less on the front and more on the back to make up the smooth flat line…"

"D'accord. J'ai bien compris."

(Got it. I well understood.)

The female assistant seemed thrilled by her newfound knowledge and appeared more driven than ever.

"By the way Jindo, can I please try the flared skirt part as well? Because I feel really on top of this draping now…"

In the realm of fashion draping, crafting a flared skirt can be considered one of the least complex tasks. The real trick, in fact, lies in perfecting the gracefully curved waistline.

Sometimes, when using computer-assisted pattern making, the emphasis is not so much on matching the sketch to an exact form but more on predetermined figures, such as the degree of flare. Yet, depending on the modéliste's expertise, the waistline's curve could be the only variable that might diverge slightly.

In couture fashion, while the amount of flare might be occasionally decided in advance, draping remains an integral step for determining the ideal waistline by visualising the shape in a three-dimensional space.

Jindo was initially reticent, but ultimately, he consented to let the female assistant undertake the task. His decision was spurred by her infectious enthusiasm and demonstrated competence, despite being her first draping attempt, she had impressively nailed the top part.

Indeed, Jindo's decision also hinged on his self-confidence. Having garnered vast experience in creating flared skirts, even winning a grand prize for one at a prestigious fashion competition in Paris the previous year, he felt supremely confident in his abilities. This meant that, even if Hélène's attempt fell short of perfection, Jindo was more than capable of smoothing out any rough edges.

Having arrived at this conclusion, Jindo gave Hélène a brief on the preliminary notes, accentuating specific points of caution, such as the correct direction for scissor cuts and a particular pinning method. The eager assistant meticulously noted down all instructions before diving headfirst into the task.

A few days later…

As Jindo returned from lunch with Seiwa, she broached a sensitive subject.

"Oppa, you seem to spend quite a lot of time with Hélène lately…"

"What do you mean? We're simply working together."

"Well, it's clear she's taken a liking to you…"

"What? Why do you always see people that way?"

"There's nothing wrong with that…"

"I'm not saying it's wrong, but you always try to put me in this kind of situation… She's just passionate and willing to learn, so I just try to let her learn as much as possible while being here…"

"Oppa, don't be silly. You're not just helping her learn. She's actually quite cute… and I know you always try to show off like a nice man to everybody... and as a matter of fact, it's not like you would reject her if she wants to fuck you..."

"Hah... fuck off you slut, I'm just nice naturally, that's it."

"Haha, alright, alright... You're a good guy, I'll give you that. But let's be honest, men aren't simply nice to women out of sheer benevolence. They always anticipate some reward or advantage, and it's the same for women too... They'll sleep with a man if he appears decent enough, and that could be some kind of desire for money, knowledge, social status, skill, network or physical attractiveness... but I can assure you, it's never just about the PERSONALITY... A personality is just like the background music of a movie, and people wouldn't go to the cinema just to listen to the background music..."

"에이 씨발, 뭔 또 개소리를 하려고 하는 거야?"

(Ah ssibal, what the hell are you about to be on about?)

"Eh? Ssibal? Kae-Soo-Lin?"

Though Seiwa did not fully grasp Jindo's native tongue, she, as a fanatic of K-drama, seemed to wonder about the words but understand the nuance. Jindo pressed on.

"So, what's your point?"

"What I'm saying is... Hélène might find you alluring, and it's clearly not for your appearance or the NICE personality..."

"아 씨발, 뭔 얘기 하나 했다..."

(Ah ssibal, now I see what you're trying to say...)

"Ssibal? Why do you keep swearing? Oppa, you need to listen to me because I know how clueless you are when it comes to reading women..."

"She's just my assistant, for fuck's sake..."

"Assistant my arse... Oppa, don't tell me you wouldn't sleep with her if she made a move."

"Woah woah, I'm not going into this game anymore."

"Listen, you idiot… She wants to be a modéliste, and while you're still honing your craft, you possess a level of competence that she might find attractive from her current position…"

"Well, it's just work-wise then…"

"Well, professional admiration can often evolve into something more personal…"

"That's not my point, you idiot. You know I'm even quite older than her, she's a bit too young…"

"What do you mean? Young? She's twenty-four…"

"… really? I thought less…"

"Well, she said she was ill when she was younger, so she had to take a few years off before going to college…"

"Okay, that makes sense then…"

"What? You actually found her attractive, but didn't say it because you're such a nice OLD man?"

"Shut it, I just noticed her determination and passion, as if she's racing to make up for lost time…"

"Well, it's rather similar to your case then…"

"What do you mean, similar to me?"

"You also delved into fashion rather late, so you've worked considerably harder than many of the younger ones… myself excluded of course, as I'm twenty-six, naturally talented as hell, still young enough to be super fresh haha…"

"Good for you, you arrogant little shit… Anyway, how did you know all this about Hélène?"

"We had a conversation during the Halloween party when you're bustling around the bar like a snack-chasing dog…"

"Why this insult all of a sudden? I always work hard, you know that…"

"Yes, I'm well aware… I probably know better than anyone how hard you work, but let's be honest. You work particularly hard at Gabrielle's, but you do that to impress Gabrielle, not yourself… You just want to make a good appeal as an employee as well as a man…"

"…"

A moment of silence ensued. Jindo could not outright deny his sister, Seiwa, who, sharp as a tack, continued unabated.

"Anyway, you fucked her on that day or maybe the other days too… But that was just compensation…"

"Compensation?"

"Yes. Do you think she would've shown such interest if she'd merely bumped into you on the street? Oppa, you have skills and experiences she needs now, and you're offering them practically for gratuite…"

"Whoa whoa, hold on there, last time you were the one who told me Gabrielle fancied me, remember?"

"Indeed, I did. So, what about it? She was, and perhaps still is… But listen Oppa, she's interested in you, not because you're a singularly extraordinary person, but because you can fulfil a variety of tasks she currently needs and there's nothing wrong with that…"

"Hang on hang on, you're really absurd…"

"Hey, idiot! Listen up! You wanted to impress her because you sought recognition from the ex-CHANEL designer as a modéliste, and at the same time, you were drawn to her ENTICING ALLURE… So now, mission accomplished, and there's nothing wrong with that…"

"…"

Somehow, Jindo was speechless and Seiwa's striking continued.

"Oppa, people are attracted to one another, and if there's an appeal, purpose, benefit, advantage, or whatever you want to call it, to be satisfied between the two parties, there's nothing wrong with that, it's the same in any relationship including gay's…"

"Good luck with your little philosophical wanking…"

"Hold on, you really need to listen to me Oppa… if you want to have a French girlfriend, it has to be someone like Hélène or Mathilde… certainly not Gabrielle, she… can be a casual friend, perhaps with benefits if you wish… but simultaneously, you might still need to do something for her like modélisme work, bartending at an event, or providing unforgettable companionship…"

"You sound like a super-dry New York bitch that I met once in London… By the way, who is Mathilde?"

"The girl from the Halloween party, speaking Korean so fluently…"

"Ah, so her name is Mathilde?"

"You didn't know her name? I saw you chatting with her at the bar…"

"Yes well, I couldn't jot down her name…"

"Why? Too occupied? Trying to impress the ex-CHANEL designer, were you?"

"Ah ssibal, BASTA così, you're too much today… What's wrong with you? Did I do something wrong to you?"

"No Oppa, I'm just trying to wake you up…"

"Wake me up?"

"Yes, you idiot… Hélène is clearly the one for you, and I'm confident if you go out with her, you guys' rhythm will be good or even better after sex… Also with Mathilde, I think she would love to have an Asian boyfriend…"

"You also talked with Mathilde?"

"Yes well, everyone adores me haha."

"…"

"Anyway Oppa, Mathilde is so absorbed in the Asian culture, and you know her Korean is actually better than yours…"

"Haha, fuck off…"

"Haha, anyway Oppa, you're thirty-two, and there's absolutely nothing wrong with a man of your age dating a twenty-four-year-old woman…"

"Whoa whoa, stop it… Enough, I'm not going to let you talk more on this, you just mind your fucking gay business…"

"What? How rude! Oppa, you really need to heed the wisdom of this smart, sexy, cutie, pretty and lovely sister of yours…"

"Get rid of the adjectives, I get your point anyway. Thanks, you little shit…"

"(Seiwa, imitating Jindo's Korean swearing) *Ehi ssibal, Kae-Soo-Lin*…"

At that moment, Jindo spotted Mina, shedding her tears at the entrance of the house.

Chapter 43 : The Atelier's Altercations

Jindo spotted the troublesome Mina, weeping pitifully at the corner of the entrance.

"Mina, what happened?"

"Amélie hit me…"

"Amélie hit you?"

"Yes, she hit me bad…"

"You mean…"

Jindo was poised to delve deeper but was abruptly cut short by a whispered interruption from Seiwa.

"Oppa, leave it… what the fuck are you going to do? It's nothing to do with you."

Jindo cast a stern glance at his overly sensible sister and scowled.

"Seiwa, it's not like I'm jumping into a situation of someone that I don't know…"

"Why? Because you're Mr Nice Guy?"

"에이 씨발, 너 진짜 뒤질래?"

(Ah ssibal, do you really want to get slapped?)

Even though Seiwa did not comprehend Jindo's Korean outburst, she could sense the mounting tension.

"Alright, suit yourself… Just remember, I didn't see any of this. Don't drag me into whatever mess you're involving yourself in later…"

"Don't you fucking worry about that… Now piss off."

"Hah… Oppa…"

"What?"

"Just leave her…"

"세이와 (Seiwa), I can't just leave her like this…"

Seiwa shook her head. Observing Jindo's chivalrous determination, she refrained from further provoking her high-strung brother and took her leave.

Straightaway, Jindo moved to confront Amélie in the atelier.

"Amélie, Mina was crying outside. Did you know that?"

"What? No!"

Amélie immediately adopted a defensive stance. Sensing her trepidation, Jindo proceeded with his questioning nonetheless.

"She said you hit her?"

"What? She came to you, saying that?"

"No, I saw her crying outside…"

"And what are you associated with this, Jindo?"

"Pardon?"

A palpable spark of tension flew between Jindo and Amélie. Until then, Jindo had maintained a polite distance from the accessory designer, but he felt it was high time to clear the air.

Amélie too felt a different charge emanating from Jindo this time around. She had witnessed his occasional tiff with the seamstress before, but this was the first time she found herself face-to-face with an irate Jindo.

After studying him for a few moments, she seemed to grasp that he was teetering on the edge, ready to blow his top. Choosing her words carefully, she dropped her tone a notch, as if not to aggravate an already growling dog.

"Jindo, I just slapped her hand once to stop when she was destroying Timothée's work…"

In fact, the episode had unfolded rather simply. The chapelier had been engaged in the process of hat-making when he decided to pause for a cigarette break, leaving the nearly-finished creation adorned with feathers.

The inquisitive apprentice, Mina, could not resist but meddle with them. As she inadvertently upset their placement and attempted to correct her blunder, Amélie struck her hand to prevent further calamity.

"Okay, so you hit her hand once then she cries like that?"

Amélie exhibited signs of irritation, not so much due to the line of questioning but more to whom the explanations were being addressed. Nevertheless, she carried on.

"I just hit the back of her hand, and she hit my hand back as for some kind of return, so I pushed her and that's it…"

Amélie then looked rather peeved at being subjected to such an inquisition. At that moment, Mina returned to the atelier, taking in the tense atmosphere. Jindo broached the subject of bringing her into the modéliste team to Amélie, who shrugged indifferently. Accepting her nonchalance as a sign of approval, Jindo directed the troublesome young girl to join him at his workspace.

By the afternoon…

It was the end of the week and Jindo had set his sights on completing Gabrielle's dress mockup in muslin. His assistant, Hélène, had put forth her final draft and it was up to Jindo to give it the green light.

Despite Hélène having done a commendable job on her first attempt, the work was not quite up to par for further progress. However, wanting to spare the diligent assistant any discouragement, Jindo suggested that they limit their alterations to the waistline.

Typically, in the construction of a flared skirt, the entire silhouette comprises two panels, front and back. Given that the waist and hip measurements between the front and back are evenly distributed, the draping on both sides tends to resemble one another, contributing to a finely finished product.

However, considering the standard French femme size thirty-eight, the only discernable difference will be found in the waistline curve. The centre back is likely to sit lower than the centre front by about 0.5-1cm.

Such subtleties are well within the understanding of an experienced modéliste adept at flat pattern making. They possess the ability to discern where and how to rectify issues without resorting to further draping manoeuvres.

With a scant two-centimetre discrepancy between the two sides of Hélène's final draft, Jindo set about adroitly positioning the muslin on the mannequin, swiftly pinning it in place.

Although this ostentatious flurry of activity was more theatrical than necessary, it seemed to emanate from a subconscious desire to display his proficiency to the novice assistant. He possibly intended to engender further trust from Hélène, whose age and infatuation were revealed to him by Seiwa not long ago. Indeed, since that disclosure, his perception of the younger assistant subconsciously seemed to have subtly transformed.

Regardless, Hélène watched his deft performance, her exclamations of awe tickling his ego. Jindo went so far as to kneel to cut the hemlines, an additional flourish that was by no means obligatory.

Once the draping was complete, the overall shape was defined, and Jindo was primed to progress to the enlargement process. At that moment, the ardent assistant proposed to take a shot at the draft herself.

With a comprehensive set of instructions at hand, Jindo yielded the task of tracing his marking points to the bright-eyed assistant.

However, he spent an inordinate amount of time informing her about the nuanced differences between French and Japanese enlargement methods. The appearing purpose was to impress the novice with his repository of knowledge, but in fact, he might intend to impress the twenty-four-year-old, cute French girl as a man. The passionate assistant though, did not notice the hidden effort from Jindo, and noted down all his instructions and promptly got down to work.

As the day drew to its close, the atelier started emptying out. Jindo was preparing to submit his daily report to the director via his iPad when Amélie happened by his table.

"Are you going to tell Gabrielle about today's happening?"

"Pardon?"

Amélie looked at Jindo with a sly grin, as though ribbing him for his role as the unofficial office snitch.

"Amélie... what are you talking about?"

"You know what I'm talking about."

With a swift flick of her middle finger, the accessory designer pushed her black Balenciaga glasses up her nose, provoking Jindo to an uncharacteristic reaction. He instantly ceased typing, rose to his feet, and faced her almost a two-centimetre distance, just like a UFC fighter's face-off.

"아이 씨발 *(What the fuck)*, what are you on about?"

"…"

Caught off guard by Jindo's unexpected assertiveness, Amélie was momentarily disconcerted. For Jindo, the situation was starkly different from his dispute with Boubacar; in Korean culture, deference towards seniors is ingrained, hence his self-restraint then. However, this altercation involved a younger, impertinent individual, whose offensive gesture prompted him to establish his dominance forthwith.

"Amélie, do you want me to report about the little catfight between you and the young stupid intern?"

"..."

Jindo's disparaging reference to Mina, with whom he had been kind and patient so far, further exacerbated Amélie's discomfort. Undeterred, he escalated his tone.

"Amélie, do I look like your bloody friend?"

"..."

"Do I look like a fucking snitch? Is it the way you've seen me so far?"

"..."

"You think I'm fucking happy to stay until late, making this stupid daily report when the director doesn't even appreciate it?"

"..."

His tirade flowed unabated, each question punctuated by the furious removal of the pinned muslin from the mannequin, a symbolic representation of his dissatisfaction.

"You think I'm happy to lead the young girls to make this stupid dress?"

"..."

His breathing grew heavy with his frustration, and at that moment, Timothée intervened.

"Ça suffit!"

(That's enough!)

In fact, tension had been quietly simmering between Amélie and Jindo all afternoon. When Mina, engaging in a boisterous conversation with other girls, cast provocative glances at Amélie, the accessory designer bit her tongue, mainly because the mischievous girl was sheltered by Jindo.

It seemed Amélie had tried to raise the tension between herself and Jindo, who had adopted the role of the house's second-in-command. Meanwhile, Jindo saw an opportunity to address the frustrations he had accumulated due to misconceptions about him.

Jindo possibly felt it was time to sound the alarm, to alert the team to his discomfort amid the escalating negativity. His patience had been worn thin by the team's indifference each time he attempted to engage them.

However, Timothée stepped in, effectively defusing the argument, only for Amélie to turn her frustration onto her brother. Jindo detected that Timothée did not fuss over Mina's bungling of his work; he merely corrected it without a fuss. Nevertheless, the tall Frenchman appeared oblivious to the simmering tension between the accessory designer and the modéliste.

The French siblings exchanged words for a bit, and just before it devolved into a family squabble, Jindo interjected, clarifying that his reports to Gabrielle only covered work-related incidents.

Their conversation began to cool, but Amélie remained perturbed. With a huff, she stormed off, her footsteps echoing on the stairwell. Timothée voiced his appreciation for Jindo's hard work, then hastily followed the angry colleague. Jindo was left with a mingling sense of regret and irritation.

In fact, the saga of atelier politics had been simmering for a while. However, Jindo had never found himself at odds with Timothée, who was, in fact, a pleasant companion during cigarette breaks. Now, it seemed an official line of conduct had been drawn, even with the chapelier, despite his attempts to stay neutral.

Jindo understood Timothée's predicament, his uncomfortable middle ground. Yet, he also recognised the chapelier's ultimate loyalty to his existing allies. This revelation made him realise the atelier might become an even lonelier place for him if the tension escalated. However, what was done was done, and there was little he could do to mend the rift. He could only press on with his duties.

Swiftly, he sent his report to the director. He mentioned the dress, now completed in muslin and ready for fabric cutting after fitting, as well as the Christmas tree, with its frame completed and awaiting lace decorations.

Chapter 44 : A Day of Disquiet

Saturday afternoon…

After a tranquil morning spent with his two cats, Jindo prepared to return to the atelier to collect his mannequins. Since he had finished the draping on his STOCKMAN, he had left his belongings at work, intending to retrieve them over the weekend.

Pulling his car into a parking spot, Jindo ventured into the French restaurant next to the building, intending to collect the keys. However, the owner informed him that the keys had already been claimed by someone. A touch of bewilderment shadowed Jindo's face, but the restaurant manager explained that they were taken by a man who regularly frequented their establishment in the evenings.

Jindo, though taken aback, did not probe further since the restaurant was buzzing with the lively chatter of Saturday afternoon patrons in central Paris. Deciding to accept the curious situation, he proceeded towards Gabrielle's place.

The door opened only after a sustained ring of the doorbell. As Jindo stepped in, he spotted Vincent.

"Bonjour…"

Jindo's greeting was doused in an undertone of surprise, clearly caught off-guard by Gabrielle's ex-boyfriend. Vincent seemed equally astonished by Jindo's sudden appearance, but his limited English vocabulary left him unable to express his confusion.

Taking the initiative, Jindo explained his purpose of the visit in slow, deliberate French. Once he understood, Vincent's expression relaxed.

Jindo commenced transferring his mannequins from the atelier to the entrance. Vincent stood awkwardly in the aisle, observing the activity. He offered to help Jindo, who expressed his gratitude but declined the assistance, as he was already handling the final piece.

At this moment, Jindo sensed an innocence in Vincent, reinforcing his perception of the actor as genuinely nice. Jindo then asked Vincent to open the door for him upon his return with the car. The introverted French actor accepted his request willingly.

On his return journey, the mannequins secure in the back of his vehicle, Jindo was tempted to ring Gabrielle and inquire about Vincent's presence. Gabrielle had adamantly insisted, just the week before, that she would forbid her ex-boyfriend from coming to her place. The situation was puzzling for Jindo.

As he navigated his thoughts, he was en route to Aéroville near Charles de Gaulle Airport. His plan involved a quick stop at the shopping complex, to collect his groceries from Auchan, followed by a visit to the Pathé cinema.

At that moment, his attention was drawn to a group of policemen stationed at the entrance of the parking lot. They seemed to be checking drivers on their way in, and, with the lot still fairly empty, it was Jindo's turn in no time.

Jindo rolled down his window as a policeman approached, requesting his driving license and vehicle registration documents. Excusing himself, he reached into the glove compartment and produced his UK driving license and a photocopy of the 'carte grise' (certificate of registration).

The officer passed these to his colleague, who retreated to their patrol car to verify the documents. As this transpired, Jindo detected an undercurrent of suspicion emanating from the officer standing before him. The man's gaze seemed to scrutinise Jindo more than necessary.

While his colleague was engaged with the documents, the officer asked Jindo about his origins, his tone hinting at his growing curiosity about Jindo's poor French language skills. Maintaining composure, Jindo explained his prior residence in England. Still, the policeman's suspicions appeared undiminished. His brow furrowed further as he frequently glanced between Jindo's face and his UK driving license.

At that moment, the second officer returned, launching into a rapid-fire string of questions. Jindo, struggling with the officer's swift French, politely requested if they could continue in English.

His encounter with the first policeman had left him feeling somewhat cornered, and Jindo instinctively decided to speak in his adoptive British accent. He hoped this might lend him some credibility in this situation where his UK driving license seemed to have sparked undue suspicion.

The second officer hesitated, seemingly uncomfortable with switching to English. He asked why Jindo was reluctant to converse in French. Choosing his words carefully, Jindo explained in his limited French that his fashion institute training in Paris had been in English, and his current employment also involved communicating primarily in English, leaving him with little opportunity to learn the local language properly.

However, this slow but somehow articulate explanation in French from Jindo caused the officer to eye him warily. He queried why Jindo was hesitant to communicate in French if he was clearly capable. Jindo gently explained that given the gravity of the situation, he wanted to avoid any potential misunderstandings.

The officer, still speaking in French, probed why Jindo appeared so nervous. Even as Jindo insisted he was not, he could feel his pulse quicken. An unsettling premonition was creeping in, suggesting something was about to go amiss. Desperate to dispel this growing tension, he cautiously switched back to English.

Jindo tentatively admitted he had not fully understood the French enquiry regarding his 'carte grise'. This sudden language switch appeared to throw the younger policeman slightly off balance, his hesitance to converse in English was palpable. Eventually, he obliged, tackling the foreign language with a thick French accent.

The officer questioned when Jindo had purchased the car, to which Jindo replied it had been about three months ago from a neighbour. On being asked about this neighbour, Jindo revealed his limited knowledge, stating he was a Korean ex-member of the French Foreign Legion. This English exchange seemed to irk the first policeman, who instructed his English-speaking colleague to translate the discussion. Once updated, the young officer informed Jindo that he may have been defrauded.

Shocked by this sudden revelation, Jindo struggled to fully comprehend the situation. His memories of the car purchase were unremarkable, the previous owner had sold the car when moving to his French girlfriend's hometown in Southern France. Moreover, he had seen the neighbour's new car, a brand Jindo himself recognised.

Still bewildered, Jindo listened as the younger officer explained that the car registration remained under the previous owner's name in their system.

As the puzzling situation escalated, another policeman arrived at the scene. The first officer briefed him, gesturing towards Jindo's UK driving license. The new arrival wasted no time in demanding confirmation from Jindo that the license was indeed his.

Instinctively picking up on the officer's rough manner of speaking, Jindo deduced this newcomer possessed an inherently aggressive nature. Striving to maintain composure, Jindo confirmed his license ownership, consciously keeping his expression as respectful as possible. Throughout this encounter, he sought out the gaze of the English-speaking officer, who seemed the least intimidating and potentially the most helpful.

The new officer decided to verify Jindo's UK driving license using his walkie-talkie. After a moment, he questioned Jindo about the UK address on the license, asking if it was his current residence.

Jindo, aware of the potential pitfall, cautiously informed the officer he was presently living in Bondy, France, avoiding direct acknowledgement of the outdated license detail. This prompted the officer to question why Jindo had not exchanged his UK license for a French one.

Feeling the pressure, Jindo's nerves began to fray. He had been under the impression that his UK license was valid across Europe. Before he could respond, the officer received a communication on his walkie-talkie. He fired a rapid question at Jindo. The sudden, rapid French query left Jindo nonplussed, and he quietly sent a pleading look towards the English-speaking officer, desperate for assistance.

Finally, the young man decided to join the conversation, translating if Jindo had ever owned any other cars. Jindo replied that he had not, apart from the current one, which triggered a hushed conversation among the three officers.

After a moment, the English-speaking officer returned, informing Jindo that two other vehicles were registered under his driving license, one in Germany, and one in the UK. He even provided the car models, to which Jindo, politely yet perplexed, professed ignorance.

Jindo proceeded to recount his history. He told of a time at university in the UK, where he had a little blue Ford KA that he sold upon graduation before relocating to London for work. Apart from that, he emphasised, he had never owned a car, only renting one annually when his family visited from Korea.

Suddenly, the arrival of two additional police cars heightened the tension. As the three incumbent officers focused on Jindo, the newly-arrived forces took up their positions, checking cars in the street. Four officers approached Jindo's vehicle, clad in intimidating armed response uniforms, one even accompanied by a sniffer dog.

Jindo felt his anxiety peak as he noticed in his side mirror that they were inspecting the back of his car. His mind conjured distressing scenarios straight from a movie scene as if they discovered illicit substances he didn't know were there.

The officers on scene briefed their new counterparts on Jindo's case, but amidst their explanation, a policewoman yelled at Jindo to exit his vehicle. Her voice, laced with authority, brought an eerie silence over the male officers.

With care and a feigned air of innocence, Jindo complied. Standing outside his car under the rain, he immediately felt the officers' gaze sweep over him. Clad in his US Army-inspired camouflage cargo pants, a plain black high-neck sweater, a snug black Prada bomber jacket and sandy-coloured Timberland boots, Jindo stood out. His man-bun only added to his distinct image.

A palpable shift hung in the air, the policemen's demeanour mirroring the growl of French Bulldogs ready to pounce on an unsuspecting, lost mongrel.

Suddenly, one of the armed response officers barked an order for Jindo to raise his arms. Jindo's grasp of French was just enough to comprehend the command, and he complied. Four officers circled Jindo, while two others, and the dog, commenced a thorough search of his car, from the backseat to boot.

Upon opening the boot, the sight of mannequins arranged in a neat row raised further questions. When questioned about their purpose, Jindo fumbled with his French in an attempt to explain the situation, a valiant effort, yet, his French language skills fell short of convincing.

In the midst of this, one officer discovered Jindo's black leather Armani Boston bag. Curiosity piqued, he peeked inside to find an assortment of modélisme tools, scissors and awls, all with a distinct vintage, rusty appearance, as if they had been employed in torture rather than fashion. They were, in fact, tools Jindo had received from his modéliste father a long time ago, and had brought to work recently for his assistants who did not have the required tools for the mission.

The English-speaking officer, though seemingly the most approachable, seemed to have little influence over the proceedings. He stood by, silent, taking direction from his colleagues. Jindo's silent pleas for assistance were directed at him, hoping he would provide the necessary linguistic lifeline.

The officers engaged in a quick huddle, after which the English-speaking officer finally seemed to have earned his moment to address the stern policewoman. He attempted to explain the situation, using Jindo's photocopy of the carte grise and UK driving license as visual aids. However, the drizzly afternoon weather had taken its toll on the paperwork, reducing its clarity.

The policewoman scrutinised the blurred documents, her face a mirror of her discontent. Suddenly, her features sharpened, and she fixed Jindo with a glare before barking out a question. The English-speaking officer quickly translated; she wanted to know if Jindo had served in the military.

Chapter 45 : Handcuffs & Misconceptions

Considering all Korean men were subject to national military service, Jindo's answer would naturally be 'yes', but he chose to remain silent for the moment.

Perhaps anticipating the situation escalating, Jindo sought to untangle the web of misunderstanding. He launched into a swift explanation in English, conscious of not letting any detail go amiss. However, his rapid, somewhat unusual British accent seemed to evade the English-speaking officer's understanding.

Closing in, the stern policewoman questioned Jindo directly in English, her words laced with a thick French accent if he was in the military. Jindo began to methodically break down the situation once more, but she cut him off if the answer is 'oui' or 'non', she demanded in a loud, uncompromising tone.

Jindo supplied her with the succinct affirmative she sought, even as he attempted to explain further. But the decision had already been made. The policewoman barked an order, and the metaphorical French bulldogs pounced.

Jindo found himself handcuffed, escorted into the backseat of his own car, flanked by two sizable officers. He called out desperately, his questions ricocheting in the car's confines, unanswered; 'pourquoi?' and 'why?'

Two additional officers occupied the front seats, and the car rumbled into motion. To Jindo's relief, the English-speaking officer occupied the passenger seat, providing a thread of hope in a perplexing situation.

Summoning his calm, Jindo asked the officer to clarify the situation. The young policeman explained that Jindo's car was registered under another name, and it did not appear to be Korean. Although he did not believe Jindo was guilty of wrongdoing, it seemed he had become an unwitting victim of fraud. He then repeated his question about the two cars registered under Jindo's UK driving license. With the solemnity of his situation heavy in his voice, Jindo reiterated his unawareness.

However, this was not sufficient to prevent their journey to the police station. There, they hoped to unravel the mystery further. The policeman then revealed a disturbing piece of information; the policewoman claimed she had seen a mugshot of someone resembling Jindo on their station's 'wanted' list, a supposed criminal of Asian descent.

Absurdity washed over Jindo. He was about to probe further when the driver intervened, instructing the English-speaking officer to cease his conversation with Jindo.

Meanwhile, although it was Jindo's debut in handcuffs, he maintained his composure, knowing his innocence. Instead of succumbing to panic, he gathered his thoughts, mentally preparing a detailed account of his predicament.

Peering at his restrained wrists, he made a concerted effort to view the situation in a positive light. After all, this would make a rather colourful story to regale friends with over dinner.

Aside from it, the reality of the handcuffs was a revelation, they were far from their cinematic counterparts. In addition to his drenched state, the icy metallic embrace was uncomfortably weighty, sinking into his wrists with an unyielding hold that seemed to tighten with each movement. Just as he was contemplating this, they arrived at the police station.

The young constable led Jindo to a stark metal bench. With one end of the handcuffs still fastened around his wrist, the other end was secured to the bench, chaining him to his uncomfortable seat before the officer vanished. Bereft of his belongings, including his mobile, Jindo was denied the chance to contact anyone. Instead, he took to studying his surroundings.

An unexpected tranquillity hung in the air for a weekend afternoon, the station seemingly deserted. The intimidating bulldogs of law enforcement were off on other pursuits, leaving Jindo alone, his one hand held hostage by the immovable handcuff.

A sudden wave of fatigue swept over him. Between the rain-soaked clothes clinging to his body and the warmth enveloping the station, sleep seemed an inviting prospect. The absence of the police and their sniffer dogs had a calming effect, allowing him to relax as he mentally fine-tuned his defence.

Having lost track of time, Jindo was jarred awake by the presence of someone standing before him. Rubbing the sleep from his eyes, he saw the assertive policewoman from before, looking down at him with a shake of her head. Jindo attempted to project an air of respectful politeness onto his face. The woman addressed him.

"Tu veux dormir ici?"

(Do you want to sleep here?)

"Non, j'ai juste…"

His stuttering response was cut short as the abrupt awakening, coupled with the sudden onslaught of nervousness, stifled his French fluency.

Just as the situation was escalating, another female officer entered the scene, inquiring about the ongoing exchange. After hearing her stony-faced colleague's side of the story, she turned her attention to Jindo, asking with measured patience.

"Do you want to speak English or French?"

"English please…"

"Why?"

"Because I believe this is a crucial moment, and I should communicate in the language I'm most comfortable with…"

With a sardonic tilt of her head, she continued in a wry tone.

"You're very good. You understand how this works."

Her gaze seemed to brim with a touch of mockery as she shook her head. Sensing the situation veering off track yet again, Jindo clung to the possibility that this might be his last opportunity to defend himself in English.

Despite the mounting desperation, he maintained his composure.

"Madame, I believe there has been a misunderstanding here…"

"Misunderstanding, huh?"

"I'm not sure what you've been told about the case, but may I present my case, please?"

"… okay, vas-y… *(go on)*"

"Thank you, Madame… So, I was on my way back from work, passing by Aéroville for some grocery shopping at Auchan… and your colleagues checked my carte gris and driving license then said, there was a problem with my documents…"

"Okay, continuer…"

"Okay thank you, Madame… Firstly, I didn't know anything about it, including the registered cars within my UK driving license. But, apart from all that, I'm just… a modéliste, working in fashion…"

"Mode-liste?"

Her unfamiliarity with the term 'modéliste' was apparent, prompting Jindo to clarify.

"Modéliste est une professionnelle qui travaille avec les stylistes dans la mode…"

(Modéliste is a professional who works with fashion designers…)

"Tu parles français?"

(You speak French?)

"…"

In the face of this recurring frustration, Jindo felt a powerful urge to express his exasperation. However, he quickly regained his calm, resetting his approach.

"Madame… I work with a designer who used to work at CHANEL. Her name is Gabrielle. If you would permit me, I could call her right now and you can verify with her…"

"…"

Her scrutinising gaze scanned him from head to toe, a look of contemplation on her face. However, her impassive countenance was inscrutable, leaving Jindo unable to predict her next move.

Eventually, she broke the silence.

"I heard you used a fake ID, and that's why you're here…"

"…"

Jindo was struck dumb by the unexpected allegation, and she pressed on.

"Why did you mention all those things… like a mode-liste? CHANEL? You work at CHANEL?"

Exhausted by the repeated misinterpretations and communication gaps, Jindo was on the verge of tears. Nevertheless, he managed to maintain his cool.

"No, Madame… I don't work at CHANEL, but I work alongside a designer who used to be at CHANEL…"

"Okay, so what? What does that have to do with your use of a fake ID?"

"…"

Feeling drained, Jindo carried on.

"By the way, Madame… may I inquire as to why you persistently assert that I used a fake ID? Because the UK driving license is indeed mine. It was issued to me when I was residing in the UK, and the name on it is my genuine name…"

"Bah, but the address is not yours…"

"… no indeed, it's not my current address but a former one. But, Madame… I was genuinely unaware that I shouldn't use the driving license if I no longer reside at that address… honestly… I truly did not know Madame. I apologise for my ignorance, but… I never misused my driving license for any other purposes…"

"That's no excuse. Using a fake ID is a serious crime in France…"

"I apologise, Madame… I genuinely didn't know…"

"You just wait here. We're yet to determine if you're telling the truth…"

"… okay, Madame…"

Jindo was teetering on the brink of surrender. He felt a deep sense of frustration growing within him. Even the handcuffs seemed to have tightened, likely due to his unconscious movement when he had been startled awake by the imposing female officer.

After a certain long while…

The English-speaking female officer returned, freeing Jindo from his handcuffs. She advised him to return home, stating they would retain his car until the case was resolved. Jindo was bursting with questions, but his sole desire was to exit the station as swiftly as possible. So, he left without uttering a word.

Navigating through three security gates requiring verification, Jindo stepped into the open air. He was unsure of his location, but that concern was far down his priority list. Without delay, he summoned an Uber, eager to distance himself from the place.

Upon hailing an Uber, Jindo promptly screenshotted his location on Google Maps, discovering he was in Villepinte. Nevertheless, he returned to his quaint abode in Bondy and made a beeline for Gregory.

Upon knocking on the door, he was greeted by Gregory's Greek girlfriend, hinting that the single father was likely spending some quality time with his significant other.

However, Jindo had an urgent matter to discuss and requested to see Gregory.

"What's up Jindo? … Are you alight?"

"I'm fine… Well, Greg… I'm actually in trouble…"

"…"

Exiting and softly closing the door behind him, Gregory seemed to pick up on Jindo's unsettled demeanour.

"What happened Jindo?"

"Er… where to start… I um… just came from the… police… 아
씨발 *(Fucking hell)*…"

Even though Jindo attempted to relay the situation calmly to Gregory,
his lone foreigner facade crumbled, allowing his pent-up anxiety to seep
through. From his heavy, shaky breaths, it was clear to Gregory that Jindo
was in a state of distress.

"Jindo, calm down… Would you prefer to discuss this back at your
place?"

"Uh… yes.. well… That might be for the best… thank you…"

Once they were comfortably ensconced in Jindo's living room, he began
to recount the day's events, starting from the beginning. Gregory listened
attentively, understanding the gravity of the situation as Jindo laid it out.
His gaze was drawn to Jindo's wrists, marred by red indentations and
minor abrasions from the handcuffs.

Gregory proceeded to shed light on some unknown facts about the
retired Korean neighbour who lived in the flat below his own. Apparently,
the ex-military man was rumoured to be some kind of secret agent in
the French Foreign Legion, and he often used different aliases, most of
which were not Korean. This might explain why one of the officers did
not believe the name was Korean, thus accusing Jindo of falsehoods.

Regardless, Gregory reassured Jindo that he would make a phone call
posthaste, and suggested he make himself a cup of tea to help calm his
nerves.

Inquiring about the location of the police station, Gregory scrutinised the
screenshot Jindo provided. Upon confirming it was indeed in Villepinte,
Gregory gave a slight nod of understanding, informing Jindo that his

misfortune was amplified due to the area's reputation for crime, making the local police particularly vigilant and tough.

Nonetheless, Gregory located the relevant office number and placed a call. After listening attentively for a few moments, he vouched for Jindo's integrity, insisting he was no criminal. He even put in a good word for the man who sold Jindo his car, a reputable figure who had served the French military honourably.

After a prolonged conversation, Gregory concluded the call and turned his attention back to Jindo to elucidate the situation. As it turned out, the police did not regard Jindo as a criminal per se; it was all a big misunderstanding. They assured Gregory that Jindo could reclaim his vehicle once the registration name issue was rectified._

Jindo queried whether the confusion was tied to his UK driving licence, to which Gregory clarified that the police had not mentioned his licence at all.

According to Gregory, the police had found Jindo's behaviour odd. His mumbling and inability to articulate himself properly during questioning had given them the impression he was concealing something.

Gregory advised Jindo to get his cousin, Michel, the actual property owner, involved when he next visited the police station. Michel would serve as a character reference for both Jindo and the retired ex-military secret agent.

Jindo still grappled with the circumstances, but Gregory counselled him to run a warm bath and unwind. As he prepared to leave, he reassured Jindo to reach out if he needed any further assistance.

Expressing gratitude towards his de facto big brother, Jindo was on the verge of retiring for the night when an incoming call from Gabrielle via WeChat disrupted his intentions.

Chapter 46 : Echoes of Exasperation

The call from WeChat…

"Hello, Gabrielle…"

"Bonjour Jindo, I have some urgent update…"

"Okay, Gabrielle… but could I call you back a bit later?"

"Why?"

"Or perhaps you could just drop me a message…"

"Why?"

"It's because… no, no worries… I'm just in the middle of something, sorry…"

Jindo tactfully tried to avoid the conversation, driven by the inherently masculine instinct to hide his vulnerability from the girl on the line.

However, his counterpart in China proved rather tenacious.

"What's happening, Jindo?"

"It's just… I just got back from a police station…"

"What? Pourquoi?"

"Because of my car registration…"

"Was it not registered?"

"… no, of course, it was registered but there was a bit of an issue with my carte grise…"

Jindo was cautious not to divulge too much about the incident, fearing he might betray his emotions.

Yet, Gabrielle seemed intent on pressing further.

"Quoi? You've been driving someone else's car?"

"No, of course not…"

"Then what's the problem? You don't have a driving license?"

"Gabrielle, you know I have a UK driving license…"

"Then what's the problème?"

"Well, I don't quite know exactly, but there seem to be some misunderstandings…"

"Okay, it's fine anyway now then, no?"

"Well, yes and no… because I got home after a couple of hours at the police station but my car is still there…"

"Ah, but you're home now. C'est bien…"

"… well, it's good that I'm home but… as a matter of fact, I was handcuffed in the process…"

"Ah, vraiment? That's not good…"

"…"

Jindo was starting to get agitated. The woman he thought he was building a relationship with seemed somewhat detached, even after he mentioned the 'handcuffs'.

"Jindo? Es-tu toujours là?"

"Yes, I'm listening…"

"What's the problem? Are you still handcuffed?"

"NO, FOR FUCK'S SAKE. I told you I'm home now, do you think I've just run away from the police station while being handcuffed?"

"Why are you shouting and swearing at me?"

Jindo recognised his emotional rise and tried to diffuse the situation.

"… sorry but, Gabrielle… can you please just leave me a message for your thing? Because I'm still… a bit not in the mood from that police station thing…"

"Well, I don't have time for texting. You can just write down what I say now…"

"… Gabrielle?"

"Quoi?"

"DID YOU NOT HEAR WHAT I SAID? Gabrielle, I've been fucking handcuffed and went to the police station in your country when I bloody don't speak your language properly and your bloody country police people fucking didn't understand my language nor give a shit actually… can you at least try to imagine how it'd have been like, even for a second?"

"…"

"Gabrielle, I'm not asking you to help me sort out the problem or whatsoever… but at least… am I wrong to be a bit sensitive after having been to a police station by being handcuffed for some stupid misunderstandings that I still have fucking no idea what they are?"

"Jindo, stop shouting, I'm your boss, you forgot that?"

"…"

At that moment, Jindo was reminded of Seiwa's words warning that Gabrielle was merely exploiting him for work.

"Gabrielle, I don't quite understand this… you seem to behave like I'm your new boyfriend… you say you think I'm a nice person, and you like me whatever, yet you constantly bring up work, always pushing for more from me under the guise of my role as ATELIER MANAGER and now... you want to emphasise that you're my boss?"

"Jindo, I didn't know it was that serious, but you still don't need to shout and swear at me..."

"Gabrielle, I'm not particularly upset about the police situation thing... I'm just trying to sort out the matter on my own... That's why I asked you to call back later or text me, remember?"

"But, I don't have time to talk later..."

"... Gabrielle... I feel you're only considering your side. Have I ever failed to accomplish what you've asked? You know I always do whatever you ask me to, regardless... and frankly, you know I'm the hardest worker in your company though earning the least salary..."

"I never asked you to work hard, you chose to do so on your own..."

"Excuse me?"

"I gave you the responsibility, but you're the one working hard to satisfy yourself..."

"MAMA BLOODY MIA... Gabrielle, I'm fucking speechless now..."

"NO, it's not fair, do you know how much I'm struggling here with my stupid dad?"

"What?"

"You don't know how annoying my father is at the moment... I really want to kill him, REALLY..."

Although Jindo was aware of Gabrielle's lamentable home education, evidenced by her patchy English, he still found her flippant 'killing parents' remark rather disturbing.

Nevertheless, he did not want to lose sight of the conversation's primary focus.

"Gabrielle, you're missing the point. We're talking about us... Don't drag your father in here..."

"NO, you must understand because I listened to you, and now, it's your turn to listen to me..."

"..."

"My dad keeps saying he's hungry when I'm super busy with sourcing and do you know how big it is in Guangzhou? And you know there's no place for vegan here, so I just eat stupid McDonald's chips all the time... and actually, I don't even have time to eat then my father stupidly follows me, taking pictures like those stupid Asian tourists in Paris, and keeps saying he's hungry..."

Jindo chose to overlook the slight dig at Asians but was taken aback by the revelation of her location.

"Gabrielle, hang on... are you in Guangzhou?"

"Oui."

"I thought you went to Shanghai for the meeting..."

"We did, and came over here yesterday for sourcing..."

"Sourcing for what by the way? The past season order?"

"Yes."

"Did you not say you ordered from your Italian suppliers?"

"Well, there was a problem so I have to get them now here..."

In fact, the atelier manager had been somehow sceptical about her past declarations regarding the supplies claimed to be ordered from Italy, as her excuses regarding the delivery date always seemed implausible.

Nevertheless, that was not the pressing issue at hand.

"Gabrielle, let me check... so you are in Guangzhou now, sourcing... then are you coming back on Monday?"

"No, that's why I called you then you shouted…"

"What?"

"You SHOUTED at me… and even SWEARING at me…"

"…"

She seemed to have entrenched herself in her position, pointing the finger at Jindo for his outburst. She continued.

"Anyway, I'm going back on Wednesday, as here it's too big to source things in a few days… and I want you to keep working on the dress by cutting fabrics then prototyping, and start decorating the tree with lace. Amélie will know what lace needs to be done first…"

"I get all that... By the way, you haven't done the fitting but you want me to cut the fabric?"

"Yes, it's a standard size anyway, so I'll fit…"

Jindo doubted her assumption even if wearing a slimming slip, and at that moment, Gabrielle was on the brink of ending the call, and Jindo was dragging her back.

"By the way Gabrielle, I saw Vincent in the house… Did you not say last week, that you were going to make sure with him, not to come anymore?"

"… what? Did you go to the house?"

Gabrielle appeared to be disconcerted, and Jindo continued.

"Yes, I did."

"Why?"

"To take my mannequins…"

"You took your mannequins?"

"Yes."

"Why?"

"It's because… they're… mine and you asked me to borrow them for the Halloween event… but since we did the draping on my mannequin as you asked… I left them during the week then was taking them back…"

"… I thought you would leave them…"

"Pardon? Why… would I leave them?"

"Because we work together…"

"Gabrielle… what do you mean? We work together. Well, we work together but…"

Jindo was utterly baffled by Gabrielle's insinuations, which left him feeling as though he had stolen her possessions.

"Jindo, are you not going to take them back ever to my house?"

"Gabrielle… I'm very confused actually. What do you mean, I take my mannequins back to your house? You know even my contract, the test period as we say… will finish soon… Did you know that?"

"… well, we can just make a new one…"

"…"

Jindo was further perplexed since Gabrielle did not even inquire whether he wanted to continue working with her. The tone was more as if she had decided it was a done deal.

Nonetheless, Jindo did not raise an issue about the contract but attempted to clarify the situation with the mannequins yet.

"Gabrielle… even if I remain with your company, are you saying that you want to continue to borrow my mannequins?"

"Borrowing?"

The lady in Guangzhou seemed unable to grasp Jindo's argument, and the temp worker remained mystified.

"Yes, because they're... MINE... Gabrielle, I'm really confused now..."

"..."

She remained silent, and Jindo found her odd behaviour baffling. It appeared as though once the mannequins entered her house, she believed them to be her property. As a matter of fact, he remembered that Antoine's mannequins were still in the showroom and had not been returned.

At that moment, Jindo did not want to lose sight of the original issue at hand.

"By the way Gabrielle, the mannequins are now at the police station in the car... and we were talking about Vincent, remember?"

"..."

She fell silent once again, seemingly at a loss for words.

"Gabrielle, are you going to explain to me or what? I even heard from the restaurant owner that he came to pick up the keys every evening..."

"..."

Jindo could discern that the French actor's ex-girlfriend was thoroughly embarrassed, but he believed it was time to assert himself.

"Gabrielle? Are you still there?"

"I can't talk to you if you keep shouting."

"Okay okay, sorry... Gabrielle, can you explain to me what's going on please?"

"... it's because he's got nowhere to go..."

"Last time you said he kept coming to your house by himself although you told him not to... and now you say he's got nowhere else to go?"

"I told you he's like an orphan, having no relatives or friends…"

"…"

At that moment, Jindo became intensely curious about the origins of her relationship with the actor.

"Gabrielle, may I ask how you two met?"

"… why?"

Jindo could detect Gabrielle's sudden defensiveness at a high level, but he pressed on regardless.

"I'm just wondering about it… before… I didn't mind it at all, and I still don't mind it by the way… but I actually met Vincent a couple of times, and even talked to him… And now, I think he didn't seem to be as a bad person as you described…"

"What? You talked to him?"

"… yes, I did… Why? Is there something that I shouldn't know?"

"NON, pas du tout."

(No, not at all.)

Jindo could sense Gabrielle's feeble attempt to hide something. Nevertheless, he persevered.

"Gabrielle, is there something you're afraid of if I get to know Vincent?"

"NO, I'M NOT AFRAID OF ANYTHING."

Her tone was akin to a child pretending to be brave when in fact she was far from it.

"Then what's going on, Gabrielle? Are you going to explain to me or not?"

"…"

"Gabrielle?"

"I can't do this conversation if you keep shouting…"

"Gabrielle… I'm not shouting and you know that…"

"YES, YOU ARE."

At that moment, Jindo realised that Gabrielle was attempting to buy time by continually pointing out unnecessary matters. He refused to be baited and remained focused.

"Gabrielle? Seriously… are you going to tell me about Vincent or not?"

Gabrielle seemed to recognise her ruse had reached a dead end and slowly began to open up.

"… okay, it's actually nothing, he told me he got nowhere else to go, so asked me if he could stay in my house until he finds a place… then I said okay because I'm not a bad person you know…"

"…"

"Jindo, it's not something serious in France…"

Gabrielle seemed to portray herself as the cool, magnanimous ex-girlfriend by invoking cultural norms, but Jindo remained focused.

"Gabrielle, I don't think this has anything to do with French culture… the question I asked is… how did you meet him?"

"…"

"Gabrielle, why do you always hide things until they're exposed?"

"I NEVER HIDE ANYTHING."

Once again, she protested like a child caught in the act, claiming innocence when clearly culpable.

"Then, what is it? Are you going to tell me or what?"

"STOP SHOUTING."

"Gabrielle, you know I'm not shouting but you are the one shouting…"

In fact, Jindo had been consciously keeping his tone calm, aware that any rise in volume, however slight, would serve as an opportunity for her to deflect blame and dodge the issue.

Nonetheless, he did not want to let this moment pass.

"Gabrielle? Are you there?"

"Yes, but Jindo, I'm not telling you like this…"

She seemed unable to come up with a suitable response, still evading the matter.

However, Jindo had not yet exhausted his patience.

"Gabrielle…"

"No Jindo, I won't discuss this further…"

At this point, Gabrielle's refusal was steadfast, and Jindo sensed he could not push her in the same direction. He decided to probe from a different angle.

"Okay then… can I ask you if he is going to be in the house even after you come back?"

"No, he said he would go to his friend's place…"

"… Gabrielle… you said he didn't have any friends…"

"I DON'T KNOW Jindo… why are you do this to me? You suddenly want to stress out the police thing to me, are you police to me?"

In addition to her deteriorating English, Jindo noted she was intent on escaping the situation at all costs, akin to a slippery fish evading capture.

She quickly moved to conclude the exchange.

"Anyway Jindo, I hope you have a nice rest for the remaining weekend, and do the work as I told you from Monday."

" ... "

Jindo had not yet replied, but she simply hung up. At that moment, Jindo noticed his two cats, observing him from a corner, their gaze mirroring the expression Seiwa would have adopted had she been present.

Chapter 47 : The Manager's Meltdown

The following Monday…

Jindo arrived at work, primed to organise the day. His primary task was to update each team member about the director's schedule changes, and just as he was formulating his plan, Amélie and Timothée walked in.

The siblings' arrival was met with a frosty reception from the accessory designer, Amélie, who did not even bother with a courteous 'Bonjour'. She sauntered past Jindo, feigning ignorance, her silence echoing loudly in the workspace.

Her brother Timothée appeared visibly uncomfortable, a manifestation of the lingering tension that sparked during the prior disagreement between Jindo and Amélie. Jindo noticed Timothée consciously averting his gaze, the awkward atmosphere signalling the commencement of an unwelcome game of strained relations.

Boubacar, the most mature individual amongst the team members, seemed aware of the brewing discontent. He gave Jindo a nonchalant, knowing glance, almost as though he had anticipated such a situation eventually unfolding.

Pushing past the palpable discomfort, Jindo informed the siblings of the updated schedule, receiving only acknowledgement from Timothée. Amélie remained obstinately unresponsive. Even when Jindo referenced Gabrielle's instructions regarding the decorative lace for the tree, she displayed wilful indifference, her ostentatious dismissal hinting at her desire for Jindo's prompt departure.

Subsequently, the remaining team members, including Mina, Hélène, and Julien, arrived, prompting Jindo to relay the revised schedule once again. Mina, oblivious to the tension between Jindo and Amélie, engaged in her usual banter with the other apprentices.

Jindo's patience this time, however, was wearing thin with Mina's chatty disposition.

He admonished her.

"Mina, when I'm speaking, you need to pay attention... You shouldn't chat with your friends during my briefing."

Jindo glowered at her like a stern watchdog, an expression that the Afro-French teenage girl had never encountered before. Mina seemed mildly perturbed, but Jindo had no intention of relenting.

Regaining his composure, Jindo resumed his instructions. Yet, Mina, oblivious to Jindo's simmering frustration, tried to restart her conversation with her peers. Jindo, teetering on the edge of tolerance, felt his irritation boiling over.

"Mina, I told you not to chat when I'm talking to you."

"I didn't say anything. You're the one, talking alone!"

Mina's defiance appeared to stoke the flames of Jindo's anger, as she met his stare with her own defiant scowl. At this, Jindo lost his cool.

"아이 씨발 *(Ah, ssibal)*, are you taking the piss or what?"

"..."

Jindo's use of the Korean expletive 'ssibal' ratcheted up the tension, akin to an irate canine baring its teeth. Mina's vivacity faltered, embarrassment colouring her features.

"I told you to listen because I'm delivering new updates from the director, and YOU SAY WHAT? I talk alone?"

In a fit of frustration, Jindo snatched a mobile phone from Mina's hand as she still seemed texting and swiping, and that left the girl frightened. Jindo continued.

"Mina, what are you? What are doing here? Do you not understand what I told you or you're just ignoring it? OR FUCKING BOTH?"

"…"

On the brink of tears, Mina found her shoulder gripped by Jindo's hand, his warning stern.

"WHOA WHOA, YOU DON'T NEED TO CRY… I didn't slap you and I didn't push you either… I was just trying to do my job and you just disturbed me for YOUR STUPID LACK OF UNDERSTANDING…"

Mina swiped Jindo's hand away, grabbed her bag, snatched back her mobile phone from Jindo's hand then fled the room in tears.

The remaining girls appeared shocked, and Jindo found himself grappling with his feelings of foolishness and exasperation. The three veteran members watched the spectacle impassively as if bearing witness to Jindo's breaking point. Their indifferent gazes seemed ready to testify against Jindo if any repercussions emerged.

Struggling with feelings of frustration and isolation, Jindo began to take deep, measured breaths, as if willing himself to regain composure. This act felt like a self-conscious performer's attempt to signal his self-annoyance to his audience.

Despite his visible struggle, no one offered a sympathetic word to the brooding figure at the centre of the storm. Resuming his duties, he calmly asked the girls to assist Amélie and moved over to the modéliste team.

His two assistants, Hélène and Julien, looked taken aback by his uncharacteristic outburst but remained professional. He instructed them to transfer the draped muslin onto the paper in preparation for cutting the fabric.

Hélène, ever careful, enquired about the absence of a fitting with Gabrielle. Jindo informed her about the schedule change due to the director's commitments. However, he found it hard to meet her gaze, feeling to have blown away a certain positive vibe with the cute, twenty-four-year-old, French girl somewhat. Julien remained unobtrusively compliant, promptly moving to prepare for his task.

Feeling unhinged by the unfolding events, Jindo maintained a low profile until Gabrielle's arrival.

Quietly passing away the days…

It was an ordinary Wednesday afternoon, and Jindo found himself meandering back from the lavatory, phone in hand, forehead knotted in consternation.

"Oppa, I had samgyupsal (pork belly in Korean) yesterday…"

Seiwa suddenly materialised in Jindo's path, but her brother's attention remained ensnared by the vexing text message on his screen.

"Oppa, I didn't call you because it was a party for ladies only…"

"Okay, no worries…"

As Jindo continued his silent battle with the cryptic text message, scarcely acknowledging Seiwa's chatter, a hint of concern tinged her features.

"Oppa, what's going on?"

"Hah… it's just… I want to take my car back from the police station asap, and I need to go with my landlord but he just texted me his flight schedule is due next week…"

"WHAT? Your car is at the police station, then your landlord… flight schedule… WHAT? Oppa, I have no idea what you're talking about…"

"It's nothing serious… It's just… there was some problem with my car registration, and I need my landlord to vouch for me but he's in the States, coming back next week…"

"Wait wait, Oppa… one detail at a time… Firstly, why is your car at the police station, and when did this happen?"

"It was last Saturday… there were policemen in the street, checking drivers on the way, just like those normal traffic uniforms… then they checked mine, saying there was a problem, then arrested me… Well, it's a bit longer and more complicated story than this, but anyway, it's a boring story that I don't even want to talk about…"

"What? You were arrested?"

"Yep, even handcuffed…"

"Oppa, why did you not tell me?"

"Tell you what? About this stupid story?"

"Yes, you idiot."

"Well, you told me you would have a little trip to Étretat at the weekend with your new boyfriend I suppose… and we didn't have lunch together for the last couple of days, as you and I had a different schedule and super-busy…"

"No, you could've called me, you idiot."

"Calling you, talking that I'm a sad little loser whose car was confiscated by the police?"

"Yes but no, that's not what I meant, you idiot… Anyway Oppa, are you okay?"

The Malaysian sister was shocked and started to worry about Jindo. The brother felt much appreciated but did not express and maintained his masculine demeanour.

"I'm fine, I'm fine, no worries... I just want to take my car back asap..."

"And you need your landlord to accompany you?"

"Yes, no worries, it'll be sorted out anyway when he comes back from LA next week..."

"LA? Your landlord is American?"

"No, he's French but married to a Korean-American woman. I suppose they're at their LA residence at the moment..."

"Okay... By the way, does Gabrielle know about this?"

"Er... yes..."

"And what did she say?"

Jindo, anticipating a sermon from Seiwa if he were to spill the truth, attempted to downplay the situation.

"Well, she didn't say anything much because I didn't really talk about it properly..."

"Oppa... WHAT THE FUCK DID SHE SAY?"

Seiwa fixed Jindo with a penetrating gaze, her brows knitted in consternation. Jindo tried to deftly sidestep the brewing storm.

"No, really... I didn't talk about it much, so she didn't say much, that's it..."

"Oppa, she knew you were handcuffed?"

Seiwa seemed genuinely concerned, and Jindo was cautious not to further unsettle his fretting sister.

"No, she didn't know that. I told you I didn't tell her much..."

"Oppa, look at me! Now tell me, she knew you were HANDCUFFED?"

Caught off guard by Seiwa's relentless questioning, Jindo, the amateur fibber, felt increasingly uneasy. He desperately improvised attempted humour to diffuse the tense atmosphere.

"Seiwa, what are you doing? Why are you doing this police thing to me? ARE YOU POLICE TO ME?"

Jindo unwittingly mimicked Gabrielle's broken English, a quote he had picked up from their conversation when she seemed nonchalant about his predicament. His light-hearted mimicry seemed to easily steer away the attention of his sister who was in fact a heavy social media addict.

"Haha, what's with this ridiculous accent? Who are you impersonating?"

"I don't know, I just felt like it..."

"Haha, you sound hilarious with that…"

"Haha, am I? ARE YOU HILARIOUS TO YOU?"

Jindo kept up the charade, even purposefully botching his grammar, in an attempt to distract Seiwa further.

"Hahaha Oppa, it sounds so stupid, just like your face…"

"DE QOUI? AM I STUPID TO ME?"

"HAHAHA."

Managing to steer the conversation to a more cheerful one, Seiwa seemed to have forgotten the earlier discussion.

However, beneath the shared laughter, Jindo's mirth was a façade. He was exasperated, his frustration directed inwardly, with no one else to blame but himself.

As the hour drew to a close, Jindo made his way back to the atelier, while Seiwa teased him about his attractive female assistant, who happened to be sporting a revealing, braless outfit that day.

The working day was nearing its end, and the notoriously punctual director was due any moment now.

Chapter 48 : The Shanghai Shadows

The doorbell trilled...

As the door swung open, the infamous and glamorous French lady, all the way from China, stood on the threshold. There were only Jindo and Gabrielle in the company, their greeting reminiscent of a couple reunited after a significant hiatus. Despite previous tiffs in their call, they embraced and exchanged cheek kisses, like an ordinary couple pining for each other's company.

Heaving her weighty trio of suitcases up to the first floor, they soon found themselves in the showroom, perched comfortably on the bed. Jindo opened a conversation.

"So, how was the meeting in Shanghai?"

"It was... good."

"..."

"Yes, it was just... good."

She seemed to keep details of her trip to herself, and Jindo switched to talk about the company work for a while.

Meanwhile, the director seemed more interested in quelling her growling stomach than discussing business affairs.

"Jindo, I'm really starving now. Because there's no vegetarian meal on the plane, I didn't eat anything during the whole flight..."

"Oh, really? They normally do have some, don't they?"

"No, they told me I should've booked the specific meal before boarding, so annoying... Next time I'll book it for sure... so stupid Chinese airlines..."

"…"

Accustomed to Gabrielle's casual jabs that occasionally tiptoed on racial commentary, Jindo refrained from responding and moved on.

"So, you want to eat here or go out?"

"Let's go out."

Despite her long-haul journey, Gabrielle seemed immune to jet lag, her energy still pulsing. The pair departed for a local Japanese restaurant, which the Parisienne championed as a popular establishment run by a native Japanese owner, not a Chinese one.

Upon arrival, they joined the bustling queue, a testament to the restaurant's appeal. Once their wait ended and they were seated, they started perusing the menu. As expected, the prices veered towards the steep end, and although Jindo adored Japanese cuisine, the salaryman with a six-hundred-euro budget opted for a modest order.

With their orders placed and their stomachs rumbling in anticipation, Jindo circled back to Gabrielle's Shanghai trip.

"So, how was the meeting? Did the investor seem decent?"

"I think he's okay and actually he looks super rich… His driver came to the airport to pick me up, and the car was like a very fancy limousine. There was even a massage function on the seat, and a screen in front, just like a business class flight…"

Having surmised the extravagant scale of Chinese wealth, Jindo was not taken aback, yet he craved further details about the project.

"So, what is it? You're going to work with him?"

"Yes, I think so… But we don't know how we're going to work together yet. I'm going back again to discuss more…"

"Ah, yeah? What for though? Was this trip not enough to see the feasibility?"

"Well, yes… But this time, he showed what he has like his company site, production and people, and I told him I'll think about it…"

"Oh, you haven't decided it yet?"

"Well, I have decided to work with him, but he told me to work in his wife's office, and I told him I would never do that…"

"Why?"

"What do you mean, why? Why would I work next to his wife? She'll copy my ideas… You know Chinese people always copy…"

"…"

Whether Jindo concurred or disagreed with her points, he refrained from voicing his opinion. Perhaps because he did not consider Gabrielle such a wellspring of revolutionary ideas, or because her show of bias came across as mildly offensive and arrogant.

He carried on regardless.

"So, what's your plan Gabrielle?"

"I asked him to make my own space on another floor, and I'll also have my own people… because if I work with her assistants, they'll copy my designs anyway…"

Pulling a face that screamed 'not-on-my-watch', the French designer seemed quite adamant about safeguarding her creative output. She continued.

"Anyway, he told me he would make my office then show it to me on the next visit…"

"Ah, that's why you're going back to check the settings?"

"Yes, but I just want to go to Guangzhou again, and I need to actually… it was too short this time…"

Jindo was thrown by her sudden mention of a different location.

"Gabrielle… a bit confused, what do you mean? You said you need to go back to see your office that the Chinese investor will prepare for you… then what? Is the office going to be in Guangzhou?"

"No, it's because I couldn't get all the sourcing from Guangzhou… it's just too big there and because of my stupid father, I couldn't really travel to the places that I had to, I already told you…"

"Sorry Gabrielle, still confused… so, what does Guangzhou have to do with your Shanghai office setting?"

"NO, WHY ARE YOU BEING SO STUPID JINDO? I'm going back to Shanghai to see my office, then passing by Guangzhou for sourcing."

Gabrielle was growing visibly frustrated, but Jindo, fresh from a recent, dramatic encounter with French law enforcement due to a similar miscommunication, seemed to be growing accustomed to this cultural nuance. He pressed on calmly.

"Gabrielle, you didn't explain that clearly… Anyway, your Guangzhou trip is for your own sourcing then, correct?"

"What do you mean, my own sourcing? It's for us, you also work with me… You're the one, always complaining like, (Gabrielle mimicking Jindo) *'Gabrielle when we will get the fabric and supplies nah nah nah'*…"

"Gabrielle, how can you…"

Just as the tension was about to mount, their food arrived, courteously served by a Japanese lady, and Gabrielle expressed for her gratitude.

"Ari-ga-to!"

With palms pressed together in the universal gesture of appreciation, Gabrielle conveyed her thanks in Japanese, while Jindo reciprocated in French.

As they began to savour their meal, Gabrielle posed a question.

"Jindo, why aren't you speaking in Japanese?"

"Pardon? Why would I speak Japanese?"

"You speak Japanese, no?"

"No... Well, I know a bit of the basic expressions as it's my neighbour's tongue, but no, I don't speak the language... Why would you think I could speak Japanese?"

"Bah, je ne sais pas *(I don't know)*... you look like you can speak Japanese with your hair..."

"My hair? Because I tied it up, like a samurai? Well, that Japanese staff will know straight that I'm not Japanese..."

"Vraiment?"

(Really?)

"Yes, Asians can generally recognise each other for their countries by looking at their eyes..."

"C'est vrai? *(Is it true?)* To me, you all look the same..."

"... WHAT?"

"Well, actually you look like a Chinese who tries to look like a Japanese..."

"Gabrielle, that's a bit insulting..."

"Why? You think Koreans look better?"

"Hah... no... I don't mind this recognition thing, but I just reckon all of us may want to look like typical people from our country, not being confused by another..."

"Okay, so you want to look like Korean?"

"Well yes of course... At the same time, I don't really mind it to be honest, because... Gabrielle, I lived in Europe for more than a decade in different countries... You think all those Europeans I met knew I was a Korean for the first time they saw me?"

"Je sais pas..."

(I don't know...)

With a nonchalant shrug, she seemed neither disturbed nor particularly interested, but Jindo carried on regardless.

"Normally, apart from those who know a bit about the Asian cultures or contents, when Westerns see Asians for the first time, the answer is normally either Japanese or Chinese..."

"Hm... yes, I think you're right. I don't have any particular image for Korean..."

With a characteristic indifference to the bemused Parisienne, Jindo carried on.

"By the way, I'm not a good representative of Korean..."

"Why?"

"I don't know... Maybe it's because, while I've lived in Europe for a long time with no proper, ongoing touch of my home country, I haven't been really updated with that Korean modernness... and I feel more and more of it as time goes on because Korea is a country evolving quite fast..."

"Okay, anyway, you look like Chinese..."

"..."

Chapter 49 : Close Cultural Confusions

J indo noticed the French woman's waning interest in his tale and steered the conversation towards what he believed would be a more engaging topic over their opulent dinner.

"Anyway, could you continue with the story about your next trip to China?"

"Oh, yes… I'm going back to Shanghai for the office thing, and will pass by Guangzhou. Actually, the Guangzhou trip is more important…"

At that moment, Jindo found himself inexplicably reminded of the incessant requests Gabrielle had made for her flight ticket reimbursement from the investor.

"By the way Gabrielle, did he pay you for the flight ticket?"

"Oh, yes. He did. He paid some in cash and some in WeChat money…"

"Great… Hang on, you have a Chinese bank account, Gabrielle?"

"Yes. I made it this time… Mr Wong helped me because last time when I was in China, I couldn't make it as the stupid Chinese banker didn't speak even a word of English…"

"…"

The notion struck Jindo as somewhat ironic, given that Gabrielle's English had been far from perfect before; Jindo had observed a marked improvement in her language proficiency, a development he modestly attributed to their daily exchanges.

In fact, Jindo had witnessed a steady and undeniable augmentation in her command of English. She was now considerably more eloquent than when he had first encountered her, even adopting into her lexicon the odd erroneous or idiosyncratic syntax that was a distinctive element of his own vernacular.

Nonetheless, what intrigued Jindo about her previous statement was the mention of her having previously visited the expansive continent.

"Gabrielle, have you been to China before?"

"Of course, because I'm INTERNATIONAL, haha."

Her self-proclaimed status as a global traveller seemed a point of pride, but Jindo, who had experience travelling to multiple countries across the continents, had an inkling that her international travel experience was likely quite limited.

In fact, he was inclined to think this trip to China was one of her few ventures abroad.

Regardless, he chose not to probe further and moved the conversation along.

"Anyway, he paid back. That's good…"

"Yes, but it's annoying… because he said he'll buy my ticket by himself from the next time… so annoying, I think he doesn't trust me…"

Her grimace was evident, but Jindo found her stance hypocritical once more. She seemed to be a person of profound mistrust herself, yet she was taken aback by the same trait in others.

Regardless, he moved the conversation forward again.

"Gabrielle, I think it's because they may have their agent or contact…"

"I don't know... Anyway, when I go back after the charity event, I'll make sure they book Air France with a vegetarian meal for my flight..."

Beyond her palpable discomfort with the Chinese investor, Jindo was caught off-guard by her spontaneous mention of her upcoming travel plans.

"Gabrielle, this upcoming one will be just after a couple of weeks from now?"

"Yes."

"By the way, if Mr Wong books your ticket, will he not find out about your Guangzhou trip?"

"I know... That's why I said it's annoying... Well, I'll just say I need to pass by Guangzhou for market research for the Shanghai project..."

Jindo now understood the root of Gabrielle's discomfort. It was largely because Mr Wong would gain insight into her itinerary if he were to handle her flight bookings.

Jindo remained sceptical about her strategy, but their dinner concluded nonetheless. Seeing that the restaurant was still bustling with patrons, he felt compelled to vacate their table promptly. He proposed continuing their discussion back at the office and approached the counter to settle the bill.

At that moment, the Japanese waiter lady asked Jindo politely,

"すみません, 日本人ですか？"

(Excuse me, are you Japanese?)

"いいえ いいえ, 私は韓口人です."

(No no, I'm Korean.)

Engaging in a brief conversation in Japanese, the two Asians caught Gabrielle's attention. The French lady seemed quite taken aback. After their fleeting exchange, Jindo and Gabrielle stepped out of the restaurant, and Gabrielle wasted no time in posing her query.

"Jindo, you speak Japanese."

"It was just a few phrases, but I wouldn't say I speak Japanese with that…"

"No, you sounded very good, just like a native…"

"Haha, no I didn't at all. Gabrielle, you don't speak Japanese. How do you know I was good?"

"Bah, I don't know. You just sounded fluent…"

"Well, I'm just fake, I'm just good at pretending with a tiny bit of knowledge…"

"Wow, that's amazing…"

"… I don't think this is something to be complimented on…"

"No, I like it."

In fact, Jindo had picked up a smattering of Japanese during his stint at a Japanese restaurant in London. Nonetheless, aware of his limitations, he had never claimed to be proficient in the language.

Meanwhile, Gabrielle seemed to take immense pride in Jindo's multilingual abilities, latching onto his arm as though asserting proprietorship over this Chinese-looking, Japanese-speaking Korean polyglot as if he were some prized pet from a British talent show.

Despite feeling a pang of guilt for letting her perceive his language skills as greater than they truly were, Jindo did not correct her. Instead, he savoured the moment, basking in the sense of worthiness it conferred upon him.

Upon their return to the residence, the globe-trotter, at last, seemed to let her guard down, inviting Jindo to join her for a spot of Netflix in her bed. Jindo harboured a slight concern for the ensuing morn, a workday, no less.

However, his anticipation for the forthcoming intimate rendezvous seemed to outweigh his pragmatic apprehensions. Subdued, he followed her into the bedroom, as Gabrielle proceeded towards the wall facing the bed.

Just as the conversation was taking an unexpected turn, Gabrielle, always unpredictable, opened a tiny door hidden in the vibrant graffiti painting on the wall. Inside lay a TV.

Making swift adjustments to the settings, she stripped down to her bare skin within seconds. Jindo, despite his increasingly frequent encounters with her sudden disrobing, strove to maintain an air of nonchalance while undressing himself.

"I didn't know there was a TV here..."

"Yes, the previous resident forgot to take it, so it's mine now, haha."

Jindo once again caught a glimpse of Gabrielle's peculiar enjoyment in acquiring others' belongings. However, that was hardly his primary concern at that moment.

He stepped out of his trousers and slipped into the bed, attempting to mask his distaste for their now routine unhygienic practice of hopping into bed without a shower, both stark naked. Attempting to tune out to hide his awkwardness, Jindo spoke up.

"Oh, it's an LG TV, by the way…"

"Eh? Is that Korean?"

"I think so…"

"I thought it was Japanese…"

"… okay…"

Uninterested in correcting her misconception, Jindo focused on settling into the bed. Gabrielle, after a few moments of indecisiveness, handed the remote control over to him. He was about to dive into the entertainment offerings when he felt Gabrielle slide closer, her body brushing against his.

"I feel like we're a married couple…"

Caught off-guard by her remark, Jindo remained silent. His attention was rather diverted to the tingling sensation of skin-to-skin contact with the former lingerie model.

"I missed you, Jindo."

Gabrielle confessed, her leg now brushing against his more intimate regions. Reacting to the stimulation, his 'mini-me' started to rouse, just like a little undressed terminator being activated.

"I really missed you, Jindo."

Guiding his hand towards her chest, Gabrielle led him to abandon the remote control. Jindo traded the uninteresting gadget for a far more appealing exploration of the female form.

Despite the salty residue on her unwashed skin, Jindo was dedicated to ensuring a mutually pleasurable experience. The faint groans Gabrielle made, reminiscent of a purring feline, affirmed he was on the right track.

With every intimate encounter, Jindo had become well-versed with the contours of Gabrielle's body, including her long, alluring legs. Although they were slightly prickly from her travels, Jindo continued his sensual ministrations with the discipline and focus of an athlete in the midst of his training regimen.

This time, Gabrielle seemed to relinquish control, allowing Jindo to dictate the pace and progression. As he moved rhythmically, akin to a 'Gangnam Style' dance on knelt, he sensed that Gabrielle was merely permitting him to do as he wished. It was not out of appreciation for his amorous efforts but rather a seeming indifference towards the current intimacy.

Jindo took charge of the moment, yet Gabrielle appeared to hum a different tune. After he finished, he cleaned her abdomen, and Gabrielle, lying supine, cast her gaze down at him.

"Did you enjoy it?"

"… yes, of course…"

"That's good…"

"…"

Jindo offered a smile in response, though he could not quite identify the reason for his warmth. He soon realised her inquiry carried a strange undertone. It felt as though a theme park owner had asked if he had enjoyed the rollercoaster ride. Regardless, Gabrielle soon succumbed to sleep, and Jindo joined her in slumber shortly after.

Chapter 50 : Authenticity's Ambiguity

The following morning…

Jindo arose early, as was his habit. He contemplated if he had enough time to return to his Bondy residence to change his clothes. He was concerned that his colleagues might notice his unchanged attire, particularly the day following Gabrielle's arrival. However, he quickly remembered his car was still at the police station, and a round trip to Bondy would not be feasible considering the time available.

Resolving to act normally around his colleagues, Jindo stepped out of the house to welcome the day. The serene Parisian morning was always a delight to witness, so he embarked on a leisurely walk around the city. This time, he extended his route to Canal Saint-Martin, pausing for a modest breakfast en route.

On his return, Jindo stopped by a shop to purchase an extravagant vegan juice, the favoured drink of the Parisian lady. Back at the company house, he approached the bed to check on Gabrielle.

Stirred by his movement, she roused, puzzled about his whereabouts. After briefly recounting his morning jaunt, he handed her the vibrant juice and headed off for a shower.

Having completed his post-coital cleansing ritual, Jindo was in the process of getting dressed when Gabrielle requested him to transport the fabrics and supplies she had procured from Guangzhou to the atelier.

With a nod of acquiescence, Jindo unzipped the trio of suitcases hailing from China, only to be met with a jarring surprise. Aside from confronting the most chaotically packed travel cases he had ever laid eyes on, he stumbled upon a plethora of counterfeit items nestled within.

"Gabrielle, what are these shoes and bags?"

"Oh that, my friends asked me…"

She replied indifferently, nonchalantly flicking through her phone in bed with the juice provided by Jindo, treating the circumstance as a mundane occurrence.

This revelation shocked Jindo on an entirely new level. The notion of the French sporting counterfeit fashion was utterly alien to him. He had observed numerous less affluent French citizens cherishing a classic Louis Vuitton bag, passed down through generations like a treasured family heirloom.

Perplexed by this startling revelation, Jindo ventured further.

"I didn't know French people wear fakes…"

"Haha, why? You think we're all rich?"

"No, I mean…"

His thought trailed off, replaced by a sudden curiosity about Gabrielle's ubiquitous black Balenciaga sneakers.

"Gabrielle, is this Balenciaga speed runner also fake?"

"Oh, yes… it doesn't look so, no?"

"…"

Caught off guard, Jindo remained silent. In fact, he had never examined her shoes until then, let alone doubted their authenticity as a self-claimed ex-CHANEL designer. Now, on closer inspection, he saw subtle hints of forgery.

In those days of fashion, Balenciaga Speed Runner sneakers were globally popular and it was one of those frequently counterfeited models. Yet, the counterfeiters' methodologies were not as sophisticated as they are today. The discrepancies were prevalent, particularly in the 'BALENCIAGA' inscription emblazoned on the front of the shoes. On these replicas, the logo was thinner, more fragile, and lacked the robust attachment found on authentic pairs.

Jindo did not respond but continued rummaging through the suitcase. To his dismay, most of the luggage space was occupied with counterfeit products rather than the necessary fabrics or supplies. It painted a peculiar image of Gabrielle, one akin to a black-market reseller.

Despite his shock at this unexpected facet of the French fashion realm, he decided to disregard Gabrielle's questionable practices, focusing on the task at hand. Gathering the salvaged materials, he descended to the atelier.

As the clock neared 8:50 am...

Jindo was busy cataloguing the new supplies and planning production for the previously halted pieces when the rest of the staff started trickling in.

Given it was the director's first-day post-hiatus, everyone seemed eager to be punctual. Jindo greeted each of the colleagues, but his effort was met with icy indifference from the accessory designer, who still breezed past him with an aloof air.

Unperturbed, Jindo was about to continue organising when he realised Mina had not yet arrived. He wondered if yesterday's incident might have deterred her, but with his modélisme assistants on hand and willing to get on their mission, he ploughed on. Nonetheless, the worry of potential negative fallout from his decision not to report the case to Gabrielle lingered.

The studio hummed to life as everyone prepped their workstations for the day. Into this industrious scene swept the infamous and unpredictable director.

After warmly greeting everyone following her lengthy absence, she set about reviewing their work. Her scrutiny first fell on the giant Christmas tree, now adorned with an initial layer of a specific lace. Her irritation was immediate and palpable; the lace used was not to her liking.

Surprisingly, Gabrielle directed her ire at Jindo, not Amélie, questioning whether he had failed to relay her instructions accurately. Jindo glanced at Amélie in response, a silent plea for support, but the accessory designer merely returned his gaze, opting to protect her own position.

Sensing the tension simmering between the two, Gabrielle decided not to probe further. She simply instructed Amélie to replace the offending lace with another, her preferred choice. Even though Jindo tried to feign normalcy, he could not help but notice the strange smile playing on Gabrielle's lips.

Next on her agenda was the chapelier, and she started to assess the hats made during her absence. Once done with Timothée, she sauntered over to Jindo's table to inspect the dress.

"It looks great, Jindo. Did you do it by draping?"

"Yes, it's done by draping…"

Jindo deliberately answered in a manner that withheld the fact that his female assistant had performed the draping. Seizing the opportunity, he quickly proposed a fitting session to Gabrielle.

"Do you want to do fitting, Gabrielle?"

"Ah, okay. Yes."

Jindo's tactic seemed successful, as the director readily acquiesced without asking any more questions. Seeing that she was wearing leggings and an oversized black t-shirt, he decided to bring up the matter of appropriate innerwear.

"Gabrielle, are you not going to wear a slim slip?"

"I think, it's okay like this, no?"

"… I think, it'll be better with the supporting innerwear…"

"Why?"

"…"

Despite Gabrielle's tendency to boast about her past as a fitting model, Jindo knew all too well that her form was no longer as effortlessly perfect as it once was.

Moreover, the figure of the recent flight passenger was noticeably bloated; a testament to the rigours of travel. Jindo had observed this first-hand during their previous night's intimate encounter, his recollection sparked by his tactile exploration during his solitary rendition of 'Gangnam Style.'

He had deftly navigated the metaphorical 'poles' of her calves and ankles, acutely aware of their uncharacteristic swell. Yet, in a display of restraint and diplomacy, he chose to hold his tongue about these less flattering observations, instead opting for gentle persuasion.

"Gabrielle, the prototype is made with a bit of extra allowance, but still… you know it's quite a fitted dress…"

"Bah… I think it'll be fine like this. Anyway, I don't have time to go upstairs and find the slim slip because I don't know where it is…"

Her words transported Jindo back to Gabrielle's riotously disorganised dressing room.

Without further ado, he pressed ahead.

"Okay, let's see then…"

Slipping into the dress from the hips, Gabrielle navigated the flare at the bottom with ease.

"Jindo, you see? It's fine…"

"… okay, we'll see…"

Jindo refrained from commenting on the snug fit around the torso. As Gabrielle guided her arms into the armholes, she requested him to zip up the back. Jindo ventured one last attempt at suggesting the supportive undergarment, only to find her patience wearing thin at his persistent questioning.

Carefully zipping up the garment, Jindo noted that the already swollen lady appeared even more so. Yet, the self-proclaimed, former-fitting model seemed delighted to have squeezed into the dress, while Jindo feared the potential for tearing.

Indeed, the prototype was sewn together using a certain type of thread, one that was sufficiently delicate to yield under the mildest strain. As prototypes are generally disassembled post-fitting, Jindo had adopted this practice he had honed at his family boutique, intended to enhance efficiency.

However, given that Gabrielle was not yet privy to this nuance, the modéliste swiftly set about evaluating the required adjustments to the garment, lest it falls to pieces prematurely.

Aside from the snug fit around her waist and bust, as anticipated, her rounded shoulders proved problematic. Jindo swiftly set about marking the area around the back shoulder, identifying a potential resolution to the issue.

As he did so, his female assistant validated his prior prediction.

"It's exactly like you said Jindo…"

"Yes, it looks so… what I'm going do now is to make a dart here, then manipulate it to be distributed to the neckline and armhole in the flat pattern…"

Not only were Jindo and Hélène physically close, but there also seemed to be an amicable rapport between them, evidenced by their shared tone of voice. The inflated lady glanced over her shoulder to regard the pair.

"What is it that was exactly like you said, Jindo?"

"Oh, it's just for the shoulder part that I told Hélène, would be the issue with a bit too much extra space…"

Chapter 51 : Accusations and Alibis

J indo's innocent expression masked his words, but Gabrielle seemed less interested in the details. She turned her gaze onto Hélène, her countenance taking on the distinct feline quality of an older cat about to pounce on an innocent kitten. The slender French assistant seemed visibly perturbed by this, as Gabrielle pivoted her inquisition back to Jindo.

"Why is there an extra space though?"

"It's just… in my experience, compared to the fitting mannequins, the majority of people have slightly curvy shoulders…"

Jindo was cautious not to utter any comment that might rile the already-swollen lady.

With an air of injured pride, the former model decided to remind them of her past.

"Jindo, you know I used to be a fitting model at Lanvin."

She delivered this statement with a glance in Hélène's direction, as though seeking to impress the young assistant with her illustrious past.

However, the non-professional female reading, modéliste replied without much thought.

"Yes, I know Gabrielle, but even some models got curvy shoulders…"

"WHAT?"

At her sudden outburst, the seams of Gabrielle's dress gave way, particularly along with the waistline around the side. The torn fabric, coupled with her black t-shirt, gave the appearance of a violently ripped-open pink Californian roll, revealing the nori seaweed within.

"… Gabrielle…"

The inflated lady, evidently exploded, yelled out.

"THE DRESS WAS TOO TIGHT LIKE STUPID. Jindo, did you respect my measurement?"

"… yes… I actually made it bigger as it's a prototype yet…"

"ARE YOU SAYING I BECAME FAT FROM CHINA?"

With that, she shoved her hands into the sizable tears at the waistline, rending the fabric all the way down to the hem. Shaking off the destroyed dress, she stormed out of the atelier without another word.

During lunch...

Jindo, Gabrielle, and Seiwa found themselves ensconced around the table, the echoes of the morning's unfortunate events still lingering palpably. Gabrielle, the still-swollen ex-fitting model, maintained an air of sullenness, her displeasure emanating like a nimbus.

Jindo, cautious and quiet due to his sister's presence, nibbled away at his sandwich. The fact that Seiwa was unaware of Gabrielle and Jindo's budding relationship lent an undercurrent of tension to the luncheon.

In the midst of this charged atmosphere, Seiwa decided to tease Jindo, a playful lilt to her words.

"Oppa, are you wearing the same outfit from yesterday?"

"… yes indeed…"

"Hélène is also wearing the same outfit today… What is it, you two were together yesterday?"

"… what?"

Caught off guard, Jindo felt a wave of embarrassment wash over him, knowing that Seiwa was bound to connect the dots about his nocturnal stay at Gabrielle's.

Seiwa, on the other hand, seemed to revel in this clandestine game. Responding to her cryptic behaviour, Jindo shot her a covert glance, his eyes asking questions his lips dared not voice.

Meanwhile, Gabrielle, her annoyance mounting by the second, opted to don a pretentious smile, aligning herself with Seiwa in this harmless jape.

"Oh, really Jindo? Are you having a relationship with Hélène?"

"…"

Jindo was left juggling the situation, flicking his gaze between the two teasing individuals, his countenance a silent plea for respite. He faced Seiwa first.

"What are you doing, Seiwa?"

"What? I'm just wondering… because you're wearing the same clothes and Hélène too…"

Seiwa, with an innocent air of feigned curiosity, appeared to be undermining the progression of Jindo's relationship with Gabrielle. Unaware of her hidden agenda, Jindo was lost in her wordplay.

"Stop it. I'm wearing the same ones because I didn't have any washed clothes at home…"

"Oppa, I know you have a lot of clothes and you do your washing every week…"

Jindo shot another warning glance at Seiwa, his silent gestures becoming more forceful. Gabrielle, however, remained engrossed in their exchange.

"Wow Jindo, GOOD LUCK with Hélène!"

Despite her cheery facade, Jindo detected an undeniable jab of sarcasm in Gabrielle's voice, prompting him to intervene, bringing the conversation to an abrupt halt.

"Haha, nice try you two... Let's go back, shall we?"

The luncheon concluded on an uncomfortable note, with Seiwa persisting in her teasing even as they vacated the premises. Jindo, perceptive as he was, could tell that Gabrielle's ire was quietly simmering beneath the surface.

In the quiet afternoon...

Jindo found himself knee-deep in re-prototyping the dress with Hélène when Seiwa summoned him to see Gabrielle. As they made their way, Seiwa swiftly outlined the situation; Gabrielle had reached out to Mina about her morning absence, and subsequently, the young Afro-French girl had turned up by afternoon, having since had a chat with Gabrielle.

Upon entering the office, Jindo found Mina perched nervously in front of Gabrielle, her tear-streaked face indicative of recent distress. Gabrielle wore an aura of stern authority, prepared to confront Jindo as a detective would a prime suspect, armed with damning evidence.

"Jindo, did you hit her?"

"Pardon?"

"She said you hit her."

"Excuse me?"

Jindo attempted to lock eyes with Mina, only to be halted by Gabrielle's sharp reprimand.

"Jindo, she didn't come today because she said she's scared of you..."

"What?"

Though Jindo acknowledged his unsavoury behaviour from the previous day, he felt the need to clarify the accusation levelled against him.

"Mina, I'm sorry about yesterday… I really am, but Mina… did I hit you?"

"Jindo, STOP IT. She said you slapped her hand then pushed her shoulders…"

At that juncture, Amélie sauntered in, seemingly in search of something within the studio. Jindo shot her a glance, but the accessory designer breezed past, displaying a studied ignorance towards the unfolding drama.

As he watched Amélie, Jindo felt compelled to defend himself.

"No, that's not true Gabrielle…"

He refrained from involving Amélie in his defence, opting instead to coax Mina into voicing the truth.

"Mina, I'm so sorry for yesterday, but did I really slap your hand and push you?"

Mina looked terrified, her gaze darting towards Amélie before settling back on her folded hands. She maintained her silence, her petite shoulders shrinking further, suggesting the onset of fresh tears. Gabrielle intervened the silence.

"Jindo, STOP TALKING TO HER!"

Seiwa, unbeknownst to Gabrielle, shot Jindo a disapproving look. Amélie, on the other hand, maintained her blissful oblivion, flipping through a file with studied indifference.

Jindo, undeterred, pushed forth.

"Gabrielle, can you just let me talk with Mina a bit?"

"NO!"

A frown threatened to mar Jindo's usually calm visage, hinting at his mounting discomfort.

At that moment, Madame Claude, the mother hen of this fashion flock, decided to participate in this troubling discourse. After a brief exchange with her daughter, Gabrielle turned back to Jindo, her mother's words translated through her.

"Ma mère said you could even get arrested for this."

"What?"

The standoff with Madame Claude left Jindo somewhat perturbed. After all, the middle-aged woman, who had previously showered him with nothing but praise for his good behaviour, now seemed to have conveniently forgotten these shared sentiments, joining forces with Gabrielle to pin him into a corner.

However, Jindo, steadfast, wanted to ascertain the truth.

"Gabrielle, before we go further, can we at least check the factual issues with Mina first?"

"No, I heard her already."

Jindo attempted to engage Mina gently in conversation.

However, the terrified young girl merely repeated her apology to Jindo.

"Mina, why are you apologising to me? You've done nothing wrong but I have... I'm the one, being so sorry to you... I sincerely apologise again for my behaviour yesterday..."

"Jindo, ARRÊTE LÀ!"

(Jindo, STOP IT!)

For a fleeting moment, Jindo felt an undercurrent of victory. Gabrielle's outburst suggested a desperate attempt to thwart Jindo's efforts to draw Mina into the discussion.

The young intern simply kept repeating her apology to Jindo, her gaze darting between Gabrielle and Madame Claude. It was clear who she was truly frightened of.

Though irked, Jindo restrained himself from pushing further. The last thing he did not want was to bring the young girl to further tears. After a tense exchange, Gabrielle dismissed Mina, asking her to return the next day. Amélie also made her exit, maintaining an aloof air, as though she had no connection to the unfolding drama.

Once Mina and Amélie had left, Jindo found himself alone with Gabrielle. Having seen Mina's fearful expression, he suspected that the Afro-French teenager had not solely pointed the finger at him.

"Gabrielle, she really said I hit her or you misheard?"

"She said she was scared of you yesterday..."

"Yes, yesterday, I get that... But she really mentioned I was the one slapping her hand and pushing her?"

"Yes."

"Really, Gabrielle?"

Jindo fixed Gabrielle with an intense stare. Clearly discomforted by his defiant stance, she tried to shift the conversation's focus.

"I don't know Jindo... But, that's not important now. The thing is, if she makes a report to her school, I'm not going to have any more interns from now... Then what? Are you going to take care of all my work?"

Despite his frustration over the unresolved facts, Jindo realised a fundamental issue needed addressing.

"By the way Gabrielle, why do I always need to deal with young pupils, not working with proper employees? You know I'm here to learn from you... I told you in the interview, remember? But I don't feel that I'm learning here but just working as a BABYSITTER every day..."

"Well then, you're doing well as a BABYSITTER for your FEMALE assistant..."

"..."

Jindo was left speechless, his gaze involuntarily shifting to his unwitting sister.

However, Seiwa merely shook her head, her focus firmly glued to her computer screen. Meanwhile, Gabrielle's gaze bore into Jindo, her silence conveying more than words ever could. He remained silent, unsure of what to say, until Gabrielle broke the awkward pause.

"Jindo, I don't want to talk about this anymore. You just go back to work, and re-make the dress with your STUPID assistant by tomorrow..."

While Jindo had intended to address what he deemed as the inexplicable aspect of Gabrielle's business, his guilt over the Hélène situation made the timing less than ideal.

To add to the turmoil, he had a lingering sense of foreboding about the likely repercussions if Gabrielle's formidable mother discovered the full extent of the situation.

The rest of the day passed without any further contention. The impending last day for all interns and the young teenage girls, including Seiwa, Hélène and Julien, was approaching.

Chapter 52 : Tangled in Tensions

The interns' final day...

Jindo was at work bright and early as was his custom, when he noticed Boubacar's conspicuous absence. When even the last of the stragglers had filed in, and the Afro-French man was yet to make an appearance, concern tickled Jindo's mind.

For Boubacar, whose punctuality rivalled Big Ben itself, tardiness was highly unusual. As the lone seamstress in Gabrielle's place, Boubacar's absence carried significant implications for garment production. Therefore, Jindo found it prudent to bring this matter to the director's attention.

"Gabrielle, Boubacar hasn't arrived yet. Do you know anything about it?"

"He called this morning, saying his son had a car accident, so he had to go to the hospital…"

"Really? Is it serious?"

"I don't know, he just told me he has to be at the hospital today…"

Although the modéliste had been distanced from the seamstress, at this particular moment, he found himself worried about his colleague. Concurrently, he perceived an undercurrent of displeasure emanating from the director.

Suspecting she might be grappling with some personal quandary, Jindo delicately broached the subject of rescheduling production.

"Gabrielle, can I ask if you know when he'll come back though?"

"I don't know, Jindo."

Her curt response validated his suspicions about her mood. Jindo attempted to defuse the tension.

"Okay... anyway, I'll put the production on hold for now then..."

"..."

The sulky director offered no response, seemingly annoyed.

"Gabrielle, is everything okay?"

"No, nothing is okay... Because Boubacar has a lot of work to do, but suddenly being absent for his stupid son..."

"Gabrielle... it's his son who had a car accident..."

"Not really, actually you know what? His son is not really his son, but some sort of his cousin or nephew from Africa that he's just taking care of..."

"..."

Silence hung in the air, thick and suffocating, and Gabrielle continued.

"You know there're a lot of African immigrants in France, who bring their whole family one by one, calling them their son or daughter nah nah nah..."

As usual, Gabrielle was making her way of racial insult about those immigrants, and Jindo did not want to make any comment but carried on.

"Okay Gabrielle, but there's nothing we can do about that... it's just an accident..."

"..."

Gabrielle remained tight-lipped, prompting Jindo to make a quiet exit from her office. Just as he was about to leave, her voice halted his departure.

"Jindo, can you sew the dress?"

Caught off guard, Jindo, who was no master of the needle and thread, expressed his uncertainty.

"Me? I'm not sure if that is a good idea…"

"Why? You can sew, no? I remember your prototypes in the interview… they were amazing quality…"

"Well, thank you Gabrielle… But I told you I actually redid that work a lot of times…"

Attempting to sidestep a task he deemed out of his depth, Jindo found Gabrielle reminding him of a past assertion.

"Jindo, I also remember you were saying you would do the sewing if needed…"

"…"

Silence. Jindo was rendered speechless as he was reminded of his past commitment.

"Jindo, I want to see that dress today..."

Reluctantly, Jindo resigned himself to the task, not wanting to rescind his earlier statement.

"Okay Gabrielle, I'll see what I can do… but please do not expect too high quality…"

"Don't worry, it's not for sale but for me anyway, just to wear at one evening event… So, it doesn't need to be the HERMÈS quality haha…"

Jindo felt an uncomfortable tickle at the back of his mind as the self-claimed ex-CHANEL designer quoted his favourite fashion brand with a sly smile.

"… okay Gabrielle, I'll do my best…"

"Good. Now, send Hélène to my office. Tell her to bring her belongings with her."

"Belongings? You mean she'll be working here today?"

"Yes."

An odd tension stretched between them, reminiscent of the undertone from the previous evening. It seemed Gabrielle's petty jealousy was still smouldering.

"Why? Is there a problem Jindo?"

"… no, Gabrielle… there's no problem…"

"Good."

Feeling as though he was losing ground, Jindo simply acquiesced to the director's command.

Back in the atelier, he instructed Hélène, the female assistant, to go to the studio. Taken aback, Hélène inquired about the situation. Jindo explained his new solo sewing assignment. Dressed in her classy, navy double-breasted blazer, she seemed hesitant but complied nonetheless.

Jindo then started assembling the infamous dress, and as predicted, errors peppered his work. With each passing minute, he grew more familiar with the manual task. As such, the morning shift whizzed by.

At lunchtime…

Jindo emerged with Seiwa, only to find Gabrielle conspicuously absent.

"Where is Gabrielle?"

"I don't know Oppa… She was off this morning, lugging around a huge suitcase."

Seiwa replied with a shrug, and suddenly, Jindo's mind was besieged with visions of those sham products Gabrielle had brought from Guangzhou. He recalled a specific case of hers, large enough to house a multitude of such faux articles. Seeking to validate his speculation, he queried further.

"Did the case have red soft cover with broken wheels?"

"Hm… yeah, it looked so."

With a rising suspicion, Jindo hypothesised Gabrielle's possible venture into peddling counterfeit goods. The trail, however, was not yet clear.

His inquiry took a more urgent turn.

"Okay, did she say where she was going to?"

"No, she didn't. She never tells me about that anyway…"

"What do you mean by she never tells you?"

"Well, she often goes out all of a sudden but never says where she goes or when she will come back… I just see those Uber receipts in her email box. C'est tout!" *(That's it!)*

Jindo, although derailed, pressed no further. Seiwa, noticing the pause, piped up.

"Anyway, none of it matters to me anymore, because it's my last day here haha."

"You look so happy to leave…"

"Of course, Oppa. Now, I don't need to see the stupid old woman anymore…"

"You mean, Madame Claude?"

"Yes, she's just the most awful human being I've ever seen in my life... Even her daughter hates her..."

"Ah yeah, I know..."

"Anyway, you still have two weeks left, don't you?"

"Yes, indeed."

"What are you going to do after this stupid place then?"

"I don't know, I have a few plans but nothing is certain for now... One thing for sure is I need to learn French..."

"Learn French? Oppa, just get a French girlfriend."

Seiwa suggested, the corners of her lips curving into a sly grin.

"Haha, I would love to but that's not something that can just happen because I want to..."

"Why do you always find a hard way?"

"What do you mean, a hard way?"

"Ask Hélène out... I think there's quite a high likeability if you ask her out..."

"Haha, how do you know that?"

"I told you she fancies you and today, we talked a lot in the studio, and I think she really seems to fancy you... I told her you don't have a girlfriend, then she looked glad..."

"Haha, how do you know all that?"

While Jindo still remained sceptical of Seiwa's melodramatic narrative, he could not deny the flicker of pleasure that sparked at the idea of the charming French girl harbouring a fondness for him.

"Oppa, I'm gay, so I have an insight into the female psyche that you don't have. I think she's wearing quite formal today because she wants to let you know she's not that young but mature enough for you…"

"Nah, you're going too far now… I like her blazer by the way, it's a bit like CELINE."

"Oppa, don't try to get away, I'm not joking. Just don't miss her this time…"

"This time?"

"Yes, last time you missed Mathilde with your stupid effort of working so hard to impress Gabrielle… This time, don't miss a cute, decent girl who you may likely have a chance with, because of your stupid laid-back attitude… Oppa, it's very rare in your life that a cute girl fancies you, isn't it?"

"Thanks, you little shit…"

"Oppa, I mean it… Hélène is the kind of girl you should meet… not the rude and arrogant French designer who insists she used to be at CHANEL…"

"You don't believe Gabrielle ever worked at CHANEL?"

"Haha, including the dubious CHANEL part, I don't believe her entirely as a person…"

Jindo found himself inclined to agree with Seiwa's scepticism about Gabrielle, having harboured his own doubts. However, what intrigued him more was Seiwa's particularly vitriolic attitude towards the director.

"By the way, since when have you started to hate Gabrielle this much?"

"Haha, yeah you already know I didn't like her… The thing is that I just felt she was an untrustful person but still okay, but it was actually this morning, I was disgusted with her…"

"What happened?"

"It's just… she didn't know it was my last day today, then when she found out, she was annoyed and gave me a lot of work like she wanted to suck my blood out till the last drop…"

Seiwa's tone turned bitter as she recollected the incident, and she pressed on.

"When I explained my incapacity to accomplish all the tasks she'd piled on me, both she and her mother went crazy… The duo is a potent combination when they try to push someone to the corner. They normally hate each other, but when it comes to a moment to attack somebody, they get united like the best union ever…"

Seiwa still appeared visibly perturbed, her breaths coming in sharp huffs, prompting Jindo to query.

"What happened? They said something bad?"

"You know the two are the most diabolical racists, and they always insult my country whenever I don't follow what they want… then today, they even insulted my parents…"

"Really?"

"Yeah, I really wanted to slap the old bitch… Actually, I wanted to smash the two of them together like BANG BANG BANG…"

The petite, delicate Malaysian sister mimicked a boxing action, causing Jindo to draw an uncanny parallel to Gabrielle's father. It seemed as if xenophobia was a shared trait in her family.

"Oppa, it's the 21st century. Who the hell do they think they are? I've never seen or heard that kind of blatant racism anywhere…"

Seiwa's mounting frustration attracted curious glances from their surroundings. The onus was on Jindo to pacify her.

"Okay okay, calma calma… I see what you mean. Anyway, today is your last day, right?"

"Yes, but I still want to slap them, bang bang!"

"Okay okay, I feel you, I feel you… Anyway, it's just a couple of hours left now so please don't ruin it. By the way, did you get Lady Gaga's stylist contact yet?"

Jindo diverted the conversation, and Seiwa, a fervent admirer of the American artist, took the bait with apparent enthusiasm.

"Oh, yes! Actually, because of the insane workload Gabrielle dumped on me, I finally gained access to her Dropbox. There I found an Excel file of the contact lists… I might've just hit the jackpot with celebrity stylists…"

"Fantastic! Did you manage to find Lady Gaga's stylist's details?"

"Not yet, I didn't have time to scour through all the names… But I do have the file now, and will check it out later at home…"

"Good on you."

"Hehe."

At the moment, a thought seemingly struck Seiwa.

"By the way, Oppa, don't forget about Hélène today… Get her phone number."

"Well, I'll see how it goes…"

"No, JUST DO IT. Don't be daft."

Just like that, their lunch break concluded. The afternoon shift whisked by rapidly, and Jindo successfully completed the assembly of the dress.

Chapter 53 : Jealousy's Jagged Edge

At 6 pm...

Gabrielle descended the stairs, accompanied by Mina and Hélène; the troublesome Afro-French teenager appeared to have come for her last moment of the internship. Seiwa was noticeably absent, and Jindo surmised that she had chosen to forgo the director's grand finale, a monologue where she was bound to be the star.

Regardless, Gabrielle was in full swing, lauding the interns for their commendable month-long work experience and delivering a seemingly interminable farewell speech.

Meanwhile, Mina seemed rather subdued, her eyes darting towards Jindo intermittently. Jindo sensed that the young girl felt a need to apologise, so he offered her a reassuring nod and a soft blink, an unspoken truce.

Behind Gabrielle, Jindo spotted Hélène clutching a petite envelope, stealing glances at him. Gabrielle continued her epic soliloquy, positioned perfectly between Hélène and Jindo, and the twenty-four-year-old French girl looked to be waiting for an opportune moment to hand over the purple letter.

Gabrielle wrapped up her speech, and Julien approached Jindo, expressing his gratitude. Farewells and good wishes were exchanged amongst the others, and as the time for Jindo and Hélène to converse approached, Gabrielle intercepted.

"Jindo, have you finished the dress?"

Jindo, with the completed garment in tow, prepared to showcase his work.

"Yes, it's done here… It's not the finest quality, but I hope it'll be okay for the event…"

"It looks good!"

Jindo was about to address Hélène, but Gabrielle interjected once more.

"Jindo, can you bring my slim slip from upstairs?"

"Your slim slip? Bah… I don't know where it is…"

"It's in the cabinet in front of the shower booth…"

With Gabrielle effectively blocking his view of Hélène, Jindo found himself reluctantly agreeing.

"Okay, but now?"

"Oui oui, maintenant maintenant *(Yes yes, now now)*… I want to try this dress now, and you don't want me to wear it without a slim slip, no?"

Gabrielle was remarkably forcing, even quoting Jindo's words from the previous fitting. Sensing that she would be unyielding regardless of his response, Jindo decided to fetch the slip promptly, darting up the winding staircase, two floors in a rush.

Arriving at the designated location, Jindo swung open the cabinet doors. It bore an uncanny resemblance to Gabrielle's laundry storage, a tumultuous ocean of unwashed garments.

He sifted through the chaos meticulously, hunting for the elusive lingerie, but it was not to be found. He extended his search to the vicinity of the shower area. The state of disarray prolonged his pursuit until, ultimately, he conceded defeat.

Upon returning to the atelier, he found Gabrielle in solitary occupancy of the space. The usual hustle and bustle had dissipated; even Hélène was conspicuously absent.

"Everybody has gone?"

"Yes."

"…"

The silence grew thick between them.

Jindo felt Gabrielle had once again led him on a fool's errand. Regardless, he felt obligated to update her.

"By the way Gabrielle, I saw the inside of the cabinet but couldn't find any slim slip there…"

"Oh, really?"

"I tried to find it in all the other places near the shower booth, but still couldn't find it…"

"Don't worry then, I maybe forgot to take it out from my dressing room…"

"…"

A wave of irritation washed over Jindo. Her casual indifference made him feel even more exploited than ever. However, he instinctively knew better than to ask about Hélène.

Quietly, he began to search for the diminutive purple envelope at his workstation. He was at it again, conducting another painstaking search. This time, he bore the air of a desperate treasure hunter. Just as he was striving to find the secret letter, Gabrielle's voice sliced through the silence.

"Are you looking for this?"

She held aloft the infamous envelope Hélène had been clutching earlier. Caught red-handed, Jindo felt a flush of embarrassment. He was rendered speechless, his eyes locked onto the envelope as if he were a dog yearning for a treat, too timid to beg.

"Hélène said it's for you, and I told her I'll deliver it to you."

"Okay… Then, are you… going to give me that now?"

Jindo ventured cautiously, but Gabrielle's response was immediate and definitive.

"NO!"

The dog's brow furrowed, still staring at the envelope, then carefully pressed on.

"Gabrielle… why?"

"Why?"

Her voice was on the rise, edging towards a crescendo as she mirrored his confusion. She repeated.

"WHY?"

Her voice peaked, eyes boring into Jindo's with the intensity of a screeching cat.

"Jindo, what are you doing? Are you and I not in some private relationship? I know we have never said to go out, but you know I like you and I thought you also like me…"

"…"

Jindo was at a loss for words.

Caught off guard, Jindo could muster no response as Gabrielle pressed on.

"Then what now? Were you planning to cheat on me? Having sex with me, then trying to have another relationship with a girl who is younger and skinnier?"

"… what do you mean by skinnier, you're also skinny Gabrielle…"

Jindo attempted to defend himself, but his argument was a feeble attempt to defuse the situation. It was clear that he was on shaky ground.

"Jindo! YOU KNOW WHAT I MEAN!"

Her gaze was the very picture of a wronged lover. Despite the odds, Jindo made another attempt to mollify her.

"Gabrielle, please calm down… It might be just a letter of appreciation…"

"N'importe quoi!"

(Bullshit!)

The French words erupted from her, a testament to her anger. Jindo still attempted to diffuse the moment.

"Gabrielle, Hélène told me she has learnt a lot from me, so it might be just a letter expressing that appreciation in a formal manner…"

"APPRECIATION? Jindo! I've already read the letter, and she put her phone number here… You think that is normal?"

Gabrielle's indignation was evident as she brandished the letter. Jindo found it impossible to meet her gaze.

The silence stretched taut between them.

"Jindo, tell me honestly… Did you have sex with Hélène while I was in China?"

"What? No Gabrielle, I think you're going too far…"

"Qui sait? *(Who knows?)* I didn't say this, but I actually noticed there was some change between you and Hélène after I came back…"

"Sorry, what change?"

"Jindo, just tell me! Did you sleep with her or not?"

"No, of course not Gabrielle…"

"I even saw you looking at her breasts yesterday when she was dressing like a PUTE *(whore)*…"

Jindo could see no escape from the spiralling conversation. He tried another approach.

"Gabrielle, you're going too far… Just think about it, if Hélène and I are already in something or have done something, which isn't true by the way, why would she give me her phone number now?"

"Je sais pas *(I don't know)*… peut-être *(maybe)* you two had sex, but didn't exchange the phone number yet…"

"Gabrielle… you know that doesn't make sense…"

"Pourquoi pas? *(Why not?)* I had sex with a lot of guys, but I never knew their phone number…"

"…"

The conversation came to a standstill.

Jindo was not exactly delighted by her candid confession but chose to remain silent.

"Jindo, you like sex so much… You even did sex to me on the day I came back from China…"

"…"

Jindo felt a pang of injustice as she brought up their recent intimate encounter as if it were entirely his doing. Still, he maintained his silence.

"Jindo, I'm really angry, and so INSULTED by you…"

"Insulted?"

"Yes, because I used to go out with an actor, a dancer, a model and a rich man… And you're not tall, handsome or anything really… but I liked you more than any other man I've ever met because I thought you were a nice person. Then what? You tried to cheat on me?"

While Gabrielle's words stung, Jindo could not help but pick up on a small detail she had omitted; she had not stated that she thought him not rich.

Regardless of this misconception, Jindo could not shake the guilt, and he tread lightly as he tried to defuse the situation.

"Sorry Gabrielle, can you please stop saying I tried to cheat on you?"

"No, you cheated on me, I know you did... I met a lot of guys before, REALLY A LOT... so I know men really well, and they always cheat..."

Gabrielle, once again, shared unnecessary details about her extensive experience with men, yet Jindo remained silent, an unsettling blend of guilt and remorse gnawing at him.

"Jindo, I'm really ANGRY now."

Jindo found himself speechless, his gaze fixed on the table. The scene almost mirrored that of a wife chastising her unfaithful husband.

Gabrielle, on the other hand, appeared to relish the scene. She had a captive audience in Jindo, who did not retaliate, rather he resembled a penitent dog accepting his reprimand.

She continued her tirade, and Jindo, for the most part, bore it silently. Eventually, her anger seemed to wane, her tone softening.

"Jindo, because I like you, I'll forgive you this time only... But, you never do this again, EVER, okay?"

"..."

"Answer me, T'AS COMPRIS? *(Do you understand?)*"

"... okay..."

With that, she tucked the purple envelope away and suggested that Jindo take his leave. The situation felt absurd, but given the emotional attachment, Jindo had personally admitted to Hélène, he decided to let it slide. Meanwhile, he was left puzzling over the nature of his relationship with Gabrielle yet.

Chapter 54 : Patterns of the Past

The following day…

Per usual, Jindo was the first to arrive at the atelier, setting the atelier for the day. His immediate task was to adjust the production schedule, as the seamstress's availability was still up in the air. As he grappled with this uncertainty, the Afro-French man, sauntered in. His usually bright demeanour was clouded by exhaustion and a touch of melancholy.

Despite the palpable tension from their recent past, Jindo greeted Boubacar with an empathetic embrace. Perhaps, he was merely happy to see him, not as a colleague, but as a fellow human navigating the ebbs and flows of life. The seasoned seamstress reciprocated the warm greeting, displaying none of his usual defensiveness.

As they settled into their respective workstations, Jindo unveiled a dress he had crafted a week prior. With an air of humility, he pointed out his perceived shortcomings. The seasoned seamstress offered complimentary remarks, highlighting that he had encountered many modélistes who could not even thread a sewing machine. Their conversation segued into a congenial chat, only interrupted by the arrival of Amélie and Timothée.

The accessory designer instantly darted towards Boubacar, affectionately embracing the papa d'atelier. Timothée's relief was evident too; his joy at seeing Boubacar return was tangible. The atelier, buzzing with this renewed camaraderie, appeared to hark back to better days. Even though a thread of tension was still discernible between the accessory designer and the modéliste, they chose to stow away their differences, at least for the time being.

After the brief reunion, everyone fell into their roles, ready to tackle the day's tasks. The atelier, absent of any pupils, hummed with professional seriousness. Each individual immersed themselves in their respective missions. With Boubacar back, Jindo delegated the remaining pieces from the previous season's order to him and focused his attention on the upcoming collection. The accessory designer was engrossed in the colossal Christmas tree project, and the chapelier, was engrossed in his solitary hat-making pursuit.

Days passed quietly, and Friday came…

Jindo had managed to finish the 22nd piece of the new collection. With no young students to mentor, he was more productive than usual, making headway on his independent tasks. The seamstress's contributions had also been significant, propelling the atelier into a productive rhythm.

Meanwhile, Jindo had been seeking an opportunity to converse with Gabrielle. With his contract ending the following week, he felt a pressing need to discuss his remaining workload. However, getting hold of the elusive director had proven challenging. She was seldom present, always tied up with commitments outside the company.

On this particular afternoon, Jindo ventured into Gabrielle's office, finding it predictably vacant. Disheartened, he stepped outside for a smoke, crossing paths with Timothée.

"Ça va, Jindo?"

(Is everything okay, Jindo?)

"Non, pas exactement…"

"Pourquoi?"

"C'est parce que je dois discuter avec Gabrielle depuis la semaine prochaine est ma dernière semaine du contrat… mais elle n'est pas dans son bureau tous jours…"

(It's because I need to discuss with Gabrielle since the next week is my last week of the contract… but she's not in her office all the time…)

"C'est pour la carte de séjour, n'est-ce pas?"

(It's for the residence permit, right?)

"Pas exactement …"

In fact, Jindo's residence permit was due for renewal only in April of the following year, so it was not an immediate concern. What troubled him more was the atelier's workload. Unsure of how Gabrielle planned to complete the collection in time, he questioned her strategy, irrespective of whether he would continue to be part of the company.

He attempted to probe Timothée about the team's past approach to managing such workload. However, his limited French hindered the conversation. Switching to slow, deliberate English, Jindo tried again.

"Timothée… in the past… how did you guys… complete… these many pieces… with just four people?"

Timothée, usually hesitant to converse in English, made a valiant effort this time.

"Bah… I don't know… mais après *(but after)* you came, les vêtements sont… prop…"

"Prop? What do you mean by that?"

"Bah… avant toi *(before you)*… we just… made vêtements… but all of them were fait *(done)* by students… comme *(like)* you see les semaines dernières *(in the past weeks)*…"

"… you mean, there was no modéliste?"

"Bah… I don't know… we had a person qui *(who)* cut the fabric with the patron *(pattern)*, but no person a créé *(has created)* the patron…"

Jindo found himself stunned. These fundamental details, hitherto unknown to him, turned his understanding on its head.

"Then, do you know where those patterns come from?"

"Bah… I don't know… Gabrielle a apporté *(has brought them)*… I think she bought sur the internet or demandé à *(asked to)* her friends… mais je sais pas *(but I don't know)*…"

"…"

Jindo fell silent, trying to piece together this unexpected revelation.

In those days, the practice of purchasing garment construction patterns online, though not widespread, was not unheard of. However, such industrial basic patterns often fell short in terms of quality.

Jindo now attempted to probe further.

"Timothée, can I ask if you know the Japanese modéliste before I came?"

"Japonais?"

"Oui."

Jindo was now to check Gabrielle's previous claims from the beginning.

"I don't know if elle… was a modéliste, but… il y avait une femme japonaise *(there was a Japanese girl)*… qui was an étudiente dans l'école française…"

"You mean, she was a language school student?"

"Bah, je crois…"

(Well, I think so…)

This additional piece of information hit Jindo like a thunderbolt, leaving him flabbergasted. Timothée registered Jindo's surprise.

"Pourquoi? Ça va, Jindo?"

Jindo met Timothée's gaze, trying to gauge if he grasped the gravity of his revelations.

However, the stylish chapelier, perpetually in his own world, seemed oblivious to Jindo's inner turmoil. Realising that further probing was futile, Jindo opted to end the conversation.

"C'est pas grave Timothée, je juste… non, c'est pas grave…"

(Never mind Timothée, I was just… no, no worries…)

Regardless, the afternoon dwindled to a close, with members trickling out one by one. Poised to make his exit, Jindo's departure was punctuated by sounds emanating from the upper floor; indicative of Gabrielle's elusive return.

Deciding to seize the moment, Jindo climbed the stairs, only to find the frenetic director in the midst of changing her attire in the showroom.

"Gabrielle, can we talk?"

"No Jindo, I need to go…"

Considering her habitual evasion of their meetings, Jindo resolved to underscore the gravity of the situation this time.

"Gabrielle, I have important things to talk about…"

"What thing?"

She questioned absently, her focus still on her clothes. Perched beside her, Jindo forged ahead.

"Well, apart from the new collection and the past season order supply shortage… do you know my contract, the test period, is finishing next week?"

"I know… But, please Jindo, can we talk about it tomorrow?"

"… Gabrielle, tomorrow is Saturday…"

"You can still come… you know I'm here all the time…"

Jindo found her assumption that an employee would willingly drop by on a weekend for a discussion, baffling. Yet, considering their peculiar relationship straddling the line between professional and personal, he bit back any protest.

He did, however, highlight his personal predicament.

"Gabrielle, I need to go to the police station tomorrow to take my car back."

"Car? What car?"

Gabrielle, engrossed in her make-up routine, seemed to draw a blank on the matter, necessitating a reminder from Jindo.

"… Gabrielle, you know my car is at the police station…"

"Really? Why? Ah, I remember… it was the day you shouted at me…"

She replied, showing little concern while applying her mascara.

"… Is that what you only recall?"

"Yes, you shouted at me like crazy when I was working so hard in China…"

"…"

Momentarily at a loss for words, Jindo was reminded of Seiwa's earlier warning; Gabrielle was ill-suited for him for various reasons.

However, keen to get the current situation straightened out, he offered.

"Gabrielle, I can come tomorrow night if you want…"

"No, I can't… I'm going to Grenoble."

"Grenoble?"

"Yes, my family has a house in Grenoble, and we sometimes go there… This Sunday, there's a birthday party for my father's friend so I leave Paris tomorrow evening…"

With her make-up impeccably done, Gabrielle turned her attention towards her vast collection of shoes, housed within a somewhat mysterious dressing room. She flung open the doors, pulling out a handful of pairs nonchalantly. The room hummed with the energy of her relentless search for the perfect pair to complement her ensemble.

Jindo observed her bustling efforts with a watchful eye, his attempts to engage her in conversation almost mirroring a domestic tableau; a patient house-husband seeking a moment of attention from his busy wife.

"By the way Gabrielle, can I ask where you're going now?"

"I'm meeting up with some old colleagues…"

"Do you mean… from CHANEL?"

Jindo's tone teetered on the edge of sarcasm, yet the preoccupied Gabrielle appeared oblivious to it.

"No Jindo, it's from Colette…"

"You mean the concept store in Saint-Honoré?"

"Yes, did you not know Colette will close permanently?"

'Colette', during its heyday, was a boutique of significance in the Parisian fashion landscape. For any aficionado in the global fashion industry, it was a touchstone, setting the pace for upcoming trends spanning not just fashion, but various other creative domains.

Aside from the iconic boutique's impending closure, what took Jindo aback was this unexpected revelation about Gabrielle's past. The news, oddly enough, lent credibility, for the first time, to the self-claimed, ex-CHANEL designer's assertion of working at a retail boutique, rather than a design studio or an atelier.

Jindo carefully probed further.

"I didn't know they were closing... By the way Gabrielle, did you use to work at Colette?"

"Yes of course, I always worked in my life..."

Gabrielle's reply, albeit misaligned with his query, gave him another opening.

"No, I mean... you worked there for long?"

"Yes, of course... Colette is like my mum, she said I'm a priceless labour..."

Jindo's face betrayed a hint of frustration. His attempts to uncover the truth behind Gabrielle's career seemed to be veering off course repeatedly.

Unfazed, he tried a different approach.

"Good for you Gabrielle... By the way, until when did you work there?"

"..."

Her flurry of activity came to a halt, sensing the motive behind his persistent questioning. A pause stretched between them, as she gathered her thoughts.

Her voice, when it broke the silence, was more measured, as though she was intent on avoiding further miscommunication.

"... it was some time ago... when I was much younger."

"..."

Chapter 55 : The Fraying Fabric of Trust

Jindo remained silent, his gaze fixated on Gabrielle. Each carefully calculated move she made, he observed. She picked her words with equal precision.

"I started working at Colette... when I was... like a teenager."

"Like a teenager?"

Jindo echoed her phrasing, this time making no effort to conceal the suspicion etched on his face. Gabrielle elaborated further.

"Yes, I worked there when I was a teenager... and I'm still... in contact with some of the colleagues there... because everybody who worked at Colette is like family. That's why they invited me to the party today although I don't work there anymore."

Her narrative seemed to solidify with every passing moment, her fluency returning. She then completed her look with the last of her accessories, and prepared to depart.

Yet, Jindo was still keen on stalling her.

"Gabrielle, I oop..."

He was silenced mid-sentence as Gabrielle pulled him into an unexpected, passionate kiss. Frozen and a little taken aback, Jindo could do little but succumb to her intense onslaught.

When she finally broke away, a playful smile dancing on her lips, she urged him to leave.

"Jindo, vas-y *(go now)*... I need to go now... I can't be late for the party..."

Attempting to rouse himself from the lingering enchantment, Jindo tried to detain her once more.

"Gabrielle, wait... Can't we chat for just a bit now?"

"No Jindo, I really need to go…"

"Well, just five mini-oop…"

Before Jindo could finish his plea, he was cut off once more. This time, Gabrielle's hand had slipped to the bulge emerging at the front of his trousers. She caressed the area provocatively, her deft hand movements triggering a slow, involuntary parting of Jindo's thighs, affording her more space to continue her bold manoeuvre.

The enigmatic puppeteer unveiled a smile, as though she found the earnest petitioner endearingly naive. Her hand began to drift towards the recesses of his privacy, occasionally tightening the grab in a teasing display of audacity.

The two were brought mere centimetres apart, and a tableau of paradoxical humour unfolded; the towering French damsel in stilettos peered down at the diminutive Asian man, sprawled wide-legged beneath her. His mouth, a slack 'O', his eyes narrowed to a semi-lidded gaze, conveyed the ecstatic tension of a roller-coaster rider on the brink of the summit.

With a dexterity borne of finesse and practice, Gabrielle manipulated Jindo's private belongings, and after carrying on this tantalising act to its peak, Jindo's slackened mouth gradually began to seal. In a heartbeat, the skilled seductress transitioned to the next stage; she let her tongue invade the closing orifice, sensuously prying it open, and traversed its inner terrain from cheek to tonsils.

Jindo, despite his established understanding of her erotic expertise, found himself awed by her novel technique and the startling length of her tongue, which seemed to flirt tantalisingly with his uvula.

After a while, Gabrielle seamlessly retreated, her python tongue withdrawn from its explorative quest. Jindo was left in a quiet aftershock of her intense invasion, gasping for breath. Gently, she led him by hand to exit the dwelling.

In quiet obedience, Jindo trailed behind. Once outside, she climbed into an Uber summoned on the way out. With a silence still cloaking him, Jindo bade her farewell, his wave and smile bearing a tinge of the unnatural.

Throughout his journey home, he remained under the residual spell of Gabrielle's 'Wingardium Leviosa'. Yet, in the throes of his recovery, he realised that he had been manipulated, once again failing to accomplish his own intentions. Resolute, he vowed to prepare a better strategy for their next encounter.

The following Monday, the last week of Jindo's contract…

The day seemed to vanish into thin air, with Gabrielle caught up in what appeared to be another one of her hectic schedules. Jindo had not laid eyes on her all day. As he was about to wrap up and depart, the illustrious director descended to the atelier.

"Jindo, are you leaving?"

"I was about to. I didn't know you were here…"

"I just came back for you, so do you want to talk to me now?"

Brimming with curiosity about her whereabouts, Jindo could not help but feel a twinge of indignation. Gabrielle, with her nonchalant demeanour, gave the impression of bestowing him with a favour.

"Gabrielle, by the way I think it isn't me who needs to bring up this topic…"

"Bah… what do you mean? Je comprends pas… *(I don't understand…)*"

Feigning ignorance, Gabrielle prompted Jindo to clarify.

"I mean, Gabrielle... my contract, the test period, finishes this week... and you haven't said any a word about it yet..."

"Bah... why do I need to?"

Gabrielle's obliviousness persisted, leaving Jindo bemused.

"Why do you need to? It's because you're the director of this company, who is supposed to manage the employee's contract and the remaining workload... in my opinion..."

"..."

Her response was silence. Gabrielle wore a quizzical expression, eager to understand more, which prompted Jindo to voice up.

"Gabrielle, I don't know what you're thinking... To be honest, I don't mind leaving here but my concern is that, how you're going to complete the past season order and also the new collection... Gabrielle, to be fair... since the last week, somehow you're barely at the company, always outside, always going out for... I don't know, party or meeting people whatever... but do you even know what piece I'm making for the new collection now?"

A growing resentment washed over Jindo, he felt burdened and neglected. In contrast, Gabrielle appeared taken aback by his outpouring.

"Jindo, are you not going to work with me?"

"Well, I don't know Gabrielle..."

In fact, Jindo had been harbouring reservations about Gabrielle and her company. He had no desire to prolong his tenure and merely wanted a quiet exit. Undeterred, Gabrielle pressed on.

"You said you wanted to work with me?"

Gabrielle was referencing Jindo's previous sentiment, prompting him to address the fundamental contention.

"Gabrielle, let's be serious… you think I'm working with you here?"

"… oui… je crois…"

(… yes… I think so…)

Gabrielle now possessed the look of a small child on the brink of losing her cherished toy. Jindo pressed on.

"You think so? How? I never felt I've worked with you for the entire time of the last three months…"

"Why? We're always together…"

"Were we? Well, I feel like I'm played by you, to be honest… Gabrielle, I came here, and started with the grading tasks, then one day, you suddenly mentioned a new collection, then I did my best to fulfil your command and preference… and then the bloody Halloween party came up, and you asked me to retouch all the past season pieces that you said damaged by those influencers and bloggers… then now again, the new collection, plus in the middle of all that, you placed me plenty of young interns that I had to take care of all day long…"

"Well, you had a nice time with one of them though…"

With a disgruntled expression, Gabrielle sought an opportunity for a jab, but this time, Jindo deftly sidestepped her barb.

"Gabrielle, don't try to bring that issue any more. You did enough…"

A steely indifference fortified Jindo's countenance, leaving Gabrielle looking flustered. Jindo continued.

"Then what now? Can you tell me why I would, or should work here?"

"…"

Gabrielle looked on the verge of tears, her lips pursed in distress.

"So you're not going to work with me, Jindo?"

"I don't know Gabrielle. You tell me... if you were me, would you work here?"

"You said you wanted to work with me in the interview, so I gave you the chance, and then you worked so hard to impress me... why do you suddenly change your mind?"

"Well, it's true but..."

Indeed, Gabrielle had not spun a tale this time; Jindo, too, remembered the moment.

Yet, a multitude of doubts concerning her, including her self-professed tenure at CHANEL, still gnawed at him. He restrained the urge to confront her, fearing it might mar the delicacy of their discourse.

Jindo opted for a subtler approach instead.

"Gabrielle, I'm not changing my words but it's been... a bit different from what I thought, working here..."

"Why? You think if you go to CHANEL or Hermès, you will work in a paradise?"

Jindo found her comment awkward since she was still speaking as though she had first-hand experience with these esteemed fashion houses.

Nevertheless, he chose to sidestep her implications and maintained his diplomatic demeanour.

"I don't know Gabrielle, maybe I'll find out one day..."

"What do you mean? You already got an offer?"

Seemingly blindsided by a possible misunderstanding of Jindo's words, Gabrielle looked genuinely taken aback. Jindo hastened to clarify.

"No Gabrielle, I haven't received any offer. You know I've been busy enough here for the last three months... What I'm saying is I'll find out my way to get there..."

"What do you mean you find out your way? You know I can get you there, but now, you need to learn..."

"..."

Jindo was at a loss about how to convey his lack of faith in her promises. After enduring his silence for a while, Gabrielle's composure crumbled.

Tears welled up, and she finally blurted out.

"You're just like the other people... you just used me and leave..."

"Excuse me? What do you mean I used you?"

"You just wanted to get information from me, then now try to leave me after you get what you wanted..."

"Gabrielle, hang on... what do you mean, I got what I wanted... I didn't get anything from working here, to be honest..."

Jindo attempted to counter her accusation, but Gabrielle, weeping, seemed more intent on airing her grievances.

"You think I didn't notice you always tried to ask me about CHANEL, Hermès and all those high fashion houses that I've been to, trying to get connections from me?"

"..."

Jindo remained silent, conceding that her accusations held a modicum of truth.

Undeterred by his silence, Gabrielle pressed on.

"People always used me and left me… Even my ex-atelier manager, who was my best friend, stole my customed Hermès Birkin bag then left… She then even went out with my ex-boyfriend who also left me alone…"

Jindo found it hard to believe that a woman, who seemed to have a penchant for knock-offs, would own a Hermès Birkin. He had no appetite for another of her personal anecdotes.

"Gabrielle, let's not talk about this…"

Jindo tried to steer the conversation back to calmer waters, but Gabrielle was relentless.

"You know she was my best friend and we worked together like a family, but one day, she started to gossip about me to everybody in the atelier, then left me by stealing all my expensive items and I became alone… Ask Timothée, he knows all about this…"

Her words came in a rush, and though Jindo was less than keen on hearing her side of the story, he could not ignore it. Something in her narrative did not add up.

"Gabrielle, you said you were left alone but Timothée was here at that time?"

"…"

Gabrielle was momentarily silenced, prompting Jindo to continue.

"As far as I heard, Timothée and Amélie are the starting members of this company, and they're still here… Gabrielle, I don't understand why you say you were left alone."

"…"

Caught in her web of inconsistencies, Gabrielle tried to regain her footing.

"No, it's a long story. You don't know anything about it…"

"Hah…"

Jindo heavily sighed, his patience waning. Seizing the moment, Gabrielle continued.

"You know my ex-boyfriend even has a share at this company?"

"Pardon?"

"Yes, he was the one, who always encouraged me to set up my own company… And I started this, not knowing anything about business… Then I'm now suffering, and he's living a fantastic life in Dubai, still having a share of my company…"

"…"

Jindo's exhaustion had reached its peak. He did not respond, merely staring at her with an air of indifference. Still, the relentless speaker forged on.

"He gave me 200 euro to establish this stupid company then I set up, and the day I moved here, he didn't come and I became alone…"

"…"

There was a silence as Jindo drained of energy and fighting off a wave of indifference, merely observed her.

Eventually, she seemed to grasp the state of the conversation and tried to conclude.

"Anyway Jindo, the thing is that you're now also leaving me, just like everybody else…"

Jindo, now thoroughly worn out, opted for a tactical shift in this wearying dance, ignoring her emotional outburst.

"Gabrielle, when did you hire the Japanese modéliste?"

"… what? What Japanese?"

She replied, caught off guard by his abrupt shift in subject.

"The previous modéliste that you told me…"

"Ah… she said she had to go back to her country."

Jindo, unflinching, held her gaze. He restated his question, annunciating each word as if etching them into stone.

"Gabrielle! Listen carefully. I asked you… WHEN, YOU, HIRED HER… WHEN?"

Gabrielle faltered under his intense scrutiny. Jindo's stern gaze, coupled with his hard tone, seemed to press her into honesty.

She returned to a more submissive demeanour, whining slightly as she spoke.

"Jindo, do you know how many people have worked here? How could I remember all of them? I think you're just trying to make your excuse to leave me…"

Jindo persisted, unabated by her attempt to divert.

"Gabrielle, she was a language school student, wasn't she?"

"… how do you… know?"

She stammered, taken aback, and then quickly added in an attempt to regain control.

"Yes, but she was a modéliste in Japan."

Undeterred, Jindo kept firing his questions.

"Gabrielle, where did you go last week with your big suitcase?"

"… what do you mean?"

"Gabrielle, did you sell all the fake items from Guangzhou?"

"… I didn't sell… it's just for… my friends…"

"So, did you give them all out, and everybody was happy?"

"… oui…"

Jindo's gaze on Gabrielle had a certain chill to it now, his mood as dry as desert sand.

Gabrielle tried to wrest back control of the conversation.

"Jindo, what are you talking about suddenly? We're talking about your leaving…"

"Hah…"

With a heavy sigh, Jindo decided he had had enough for the day. Meanwhile, he still did not want to make an unpleasant exit from Gabrielle's workplace.

"Gabrielle, let's discuss this tomorrow. I'm going home."

For once, Gabrielle did not object to Jindo's decision this time, and their peculiar conversation that evening came to an anticlimactic end.

Chapter 56 : Tears and Tensions

The following day…

Gabrielle held court in the office during the day, and Jindo, meanwhile, made himself scarce to avoid stirring the waters amidst the other employees. His objective was a peaceful departure from Gabrielle's employ, and thus he sought her out after work.

"Gabrielle, can I come in?"

"… oui…"

Her French accent lent her a calm, somehow gentle, aura. Upon entering, Jindo found her impeccably attired, her visage radiant with make-up.

Nonetheless, he disregarded her allure, focusing solely on resolving his predicament.

"Gabrielle, I'm going to be straight. I'll work as much as I can until Friday and I wish you to make a great collection."

"…"

She remained silent, her lower lip quivering, her eyes welling up as if on the brink of tears.

"So, you're leaving me, yes?"

"Gabrielle, please don't say I'm leaving you. I'm just… going my way."

"So, are you going to Hermès now?"

"Well, for numerous reasons, I don't believe I'm eligible for Hermès at this point…"

"What do you mean, not eligible? Jindo, you're very good."

"Well, I don't even speak French…"

"You do speak French, no? I think you're very cute when you speak French…"

"Thanks, but no… I seriously need to learn the language properly…"

"You can speak with me."

"Thanks… but I'll just do it in my way…"

"Do you want me to give you my Hermès contact?"

Although Jindo had ceased to place faith in her purported luxury fashion house credentials, he found himself swayed by the faint glimmer of possibility.

Still, his doubts were not entirely quelled, prompting him to probe one final time for the truth.

"Gabrielle, I'm really sorry but… did you really work at CHANEL?"

"Yes, of course… You think I LIED TO YOU?"

The self-proclaimed, ex-CHANEL designer radiated conviction, causing Jindo to be mired in uncertainty again.

"Gabrielle, please… can you tell me the truth? Were you really at CHANEL?"

"Yes, I was. Why do you not believe me?"

"Well… to be honest, I can't really believe you were at CHANEL… I really tried, I really tried hard to believe so… but, I cannot believe it, Gabrielle. Sorry…"

"You want me to show you my 'bulletin de paie *(payslip)*' when I was at CHANEL?"

Gabrielle exuded confidence that left Jindo in a state of perplexity. He opted to abandon his sceptical stance, reasoning that the notorious document would serve as a testament to her credibility, despite the potential for further confusion amidst the conundrum he found himself in.

"Okay, Gabrielle... I will believe you, but you don't need to show me the bulletin de paie..."

With Jindo's scepticism seemingly defused, Gabrielle regained her assertiveness.

"Well, you keep saying you don't believe me Jindo, so I want to show you."

"No, it's okay..."

She seemed ready to turn the tables.

"If I show you, are you not going to leave me?"

The resolute former CHANEL designer was not ready to relinquish her hold on Jindo, but he remained unwavering.

"Gabrielle... I'll go my way."

With Jindo's resolve evident, Gabrielle's expression fell, and she slipped back into melancholy.

"So, are you going to a French language school now?"

"Well, I think I'll go to the language school part-time because I need to work to have an income."

"Okay... But Jindo, I really don't understand you... because I think if you work here, you can learn French by speaking to the native French people here, also making an income... And, we can be together all the time, you can even do SEX TO ME every day..."

"..."

A pause ensued. Gabrielle's argument held merit, albeit with an awkwardly inserted sexual reference that unsettled Jindo. Beyond the linguistic faux pas, it felt as though she was propositioning him.

She forged ahead.

"Jindo, you said you want to go to Hermès, and now you don't even go there but try to go to the STUPID language school by paying money when your girlfriend is French... and you also try to work for somebody else when your girlfriend is suffering from her business situation, and there're a lot of things that you can help her with..."

Gabrielle's consistent reference to herself as his girlfriend left Jindo questioning the nature of their relationship. Nonetheless, a swift mental recap of past interactions fortified his resolution.

"Gabrielle, please let's stop right here. I'll go my way, you go yours, and we can be..."

Still uncertain how to delineate their peculiar bond, Jindo faltered, leaving an opportunity for Gabrielle to step in.

"Jindo, I'm not going to have sex with you if you leave... We're done if you leave..."

Aside from the ongoing discomfort around her sexual bargaining, Jindo was floundering, attempting to articulate his intentions with sensitivity. As he hesitated, Gabrielle seized control of the situation.

"Jindo, by the way, what's your plan? If you go to Hermès one day, you'll just work for them forever?"

"Gabrielle, I never said I would die for Hermès... It's just a brand that I admire the most in a long time. I told you about it in the interview that, I want to open my boutique one day in Paris but before then, I just want to gain experience by working at various places... and Hermès is the one that I may set as my final destination as an employee..."

"It sounds so stupid Jindo... You think, Hermès will hire people like you? Just using them and leaving one day?"

"Gabrielle, why is it that I use them? I'll work and contribute of course..."

"Jindo, you know nothing about the PARISIAN FASHION CULTURE..."

Beyond detecting a fresh wave of condescension, Jindo was intrigued by her wording.

"What exactly do you mean by Parisian fashion culture, Gabrielle?"

"You know there's some type of fashion culture in every sector... And in Paris fashion, there's a strong cultural code that I know but you know nothing about... Let me tell you Jindo, Hermès, CHANEL, or even Dior will never hire people like you..."

This Parisian designer was adept at delivering her customary offensive tirades, and Jindo felt compelled to retaliate.

"Someone like me? What do you mean, like me? You just said ten minutes ago, that I'm good enough to go to Hermès..."

"Look, you don't even know what it is...."

"Gabrielle, what is it then? You tell me..."

Feeling his patience wane, Jindo fired back in defence of his dignity.

"Gabrielle, then you think if I work here, I'll learn that bloody Parisian fashion culture?"

"I told you I'll teach you everything..."

"What bloody thing?"

"THE FASHION CULTURE INCLUDING FRENCH LANGUAGE..."

The French designer retorted as though exasperated by Jindo's perceived ignorance, and in response, he aimed to establish some fundamental points.

"Gabrielle... I'm going to make it simple. First, I'm not interested in this bloody Parisian fashion culture, whatever, but I'll make my own way anyhow... Second, even if I'm with you, we'll always speak English anyway..."

"You can speak French to me from now then... tu veux parler français *(Do you want to speak French)*?"

"Gabrielle, stop it really..."

Jindo, fatigued, heaved a heavy sigh in response to Gabrielle's stubborn refusal to compromise. He then proposed an alternative.

"Gabrielle, if you really want me to work here, how about this? I'll go to a language school, and will try to speak French with you, then work as a freelancer to help you finish the collection... how about that?"

"No, that means you're leaving..."

Shrugging dismissively, Gabrielle made it clear that she was not open to negotiation. Jindo attempted to reason with her once more.

"Why is it that I'm leaving? I'm not leaving. I'll come to work like I've done by now, but will find a time slot to go to the language school... just like Amélie does for her institute..."

"No, you're just trying to leave me..."

Manifesting her familiar sullen countenance, Gabrielle stood her ground. Jindo endeavoured to make his stance more persuasive.

"I always keep my word, you know that."

"No, you never keep your word, you said you wanted to work with me, then I gave you the chance, and now you changed your mind…"

"Don't take it that way Gabrielle, it's not fair."

"Then what? How come a man changes his word like that? I never met a man like you."

"…"

"And, freelancing means you're going to ask for big money… You have a car, STUPIDLY GIANT HOUSE…"

"Gabrielle, the car and house are not as expensive as you think… My rent is actually quite low, even the car I didn't pay much…"

"Why do I believe you Jindo? You're a liar."

"Hah…"

Battling his fatigue, Jindo ventured to set the record straight.

"Gabrielle, I just met nice people who were generous to provide me with good offers… Actually, the house thing, I helped my landlord's wife when she accidentally fell down in a café, then we connected… and somehow, I got to live in one of her husband's properties that he was renting, and she asked her husband to give me a good offer… Even for the car, I taught my neighbour how to reform some of his old clothes, so he sold his car to me at quite a low price. That's it…"

"Wow, you met so many NICE people…"

With a sarcastic shake of her head and a roll of her eyes, Gabrielle made her disbelief apparent. Jindo, however, continued unperturbed.

"I've been just lucky that I met nice and generous people…"

"Jindo, then am I not one of those nice, generous and even kind people to you?"

"…"

Jindo found himself at a loss for words. It was no secret that he held reservations about classifying Gabrielle as either 'generous' or 'kind-hearted'.

Yet, she pursued her line of inquiry.

"I'm sure you'll leave me once you find another work that pays you more… Trust me you're not the only one who used that trick."

"Trick? Don't define me like one of those people from your bad experiences…"

"No, you're a man anyway and I know men so well…"

"Hah…"

A sigh of weariness escaped Jindo's lips. He had begun to realise that attempting to reason with Gabrielle was akin to being trapped within the most exasperating of circles.

The conversation was about to take another sharp turn.

"Jindo, you know I already told the Shanghai team about you, and they're looking forward to meeting you soon but you're now screwing my plan…"

Blame was now being tossed around like a hot potato, and the drained man responded in a weary tone.

"You told them about me?"

"Yes, there was a guy from Hong Kong there, and he told me he met many great modélistes when he was working in Italy, and as an Asian, he said he was proud that there were so many Korean modélistes at many of the famous Italian fashion houses… So, I said my modéliste is also

Korean, and he also used to be in Italy, then he said he would love to meet you."

"..."

While Jindo had indeed heard of numerous Korean modélistes making strides at illustrious Italian fashion houses like Gucci, Prada, and Giorgio Armani during his time in Italy, he refrained from discussing this with Gabrielle.

Perhaps it was not his unwillingness to sound overly patriotic, but rather his desire not to acknowledge anything Gabrielle was claiming at that moment.

He, however, aimed to downplay his expertise with humility.

"By the way Gabrielle, to be fair... although I may have a bit more previous experience than other modélistes at the assistant level, I'm still like a baby who needs to learn a lot about a lot of things..."

"No, you're very good Jindo... You told me you know the Japanese method, your father's 40 years of know-hows, and now even the French way... I REMEMBER YOU SAID THAT in the interview..."

"..."

Jindo was surprised that Gabrielle, whom he had dismissed as rather forgetful, appeared to possess an uncannily precise recall of his past statements. She quoted him at the most opportune moments to bolster her preconceived notions.

Yet, he attempted to maintain his defence.

"Yes Gabrielle, you're correct, I did say that... but at that time, I just wanted to appeal myself to you like... hah..."

Abruptly, Jindo paused, taking a deep breath, feeling depleted. It seemed his instincts were hinting that no matter his efforts, this conversation was far from its conclusion.

He then endeavoured to steer the conversation in a different direction.

"Gabrielle, I think Shanghai is a big international city, and I'm sure there will be plenty of excellent modéslites there, who can make your designs so beautifully…"

"Jindo, why do you try so hard to make an excuse to leave me? Jindo, I want you and you're the best modéliste for me, and we make big money together in China."

"…"

Jindo was now too drained to formulate a response, and Gabrielle, in an emotional plea, began to shed tears.

"Jindo, I'll fail without you. I need your help…"

In response to the unceasing pleading from the distressed lady, Jindo found himself teetering on the brink of tears, stifled by the suffocating repetitiveness of this relentless cycle.

"Gabrielle, please. I really don't understand… Why me? If I didn't come here in the first place, how would you do it then? I wasn't part of your plan, was I? You said, your China project discussion had formed from a long time ago…"

"Yes, but I was never confident to do it by myself, but since you came, I become confident if I do it with you… And Jindo, I love you so much. I really love you…"

Seemingly desperate, Gabrielle appeared willing to say anything to make her plea.

However, Jindo managed to resist the temptation, endeavouring to extricate himself from the situation.

"Gabrielle, I'm really tired now and I'm sure you must be the same… For now, what I can say is that I understood all your words today but please… I want you to rethink my suggestion of freelancing because I think it's not a bad idea considering all the matters and circumstances for both of us…"

"Jindo, please…"

Her desperation painted across her face, mascara smeared, yet Jindo made his exit, albeit after a moment of hesitancy.

Chapter 57 : Movie Night Incident

On the following day, post work hours…
Just as the previous day, Jindo had managed to avoid Gabrielle throughout the day, and now he sought her out.

"Gabrielle, may I enter?"

"…"

Though met with silence, Jindo knew she was present in the office and thus walked in.

"Gabrielle, have you thought about my proposal?"

"…"

Her expression had soured considerably, and Jindo attempted to maintain a sense of normalcy.

"Gabrielle, let's sort this out professionally…"

"I don't care, FUCK YOU."

"…"

Feeling drained already, Jindo confronted her characteristic ill manners.

Nevertheless, he yearned to resolve the issue amicably.

"Gabrielle, you don't need to swear. I'm not a bad person, you know that…"

"No, you're an awful human nature. You just try to use me…"

"Using you?"

"Yes, because your suggestion is quite simple… You want to get money from me, have SEX TO ME whenever you want, and then try to meet other girls whenever you want… I even know you had SEX with the STUPID Hélène while I was in China…"

"Gabrielle…"

Rendered speechless, Jindo had no inclination to initiate a negotiation session this time.

"Why Jindo? I'm right, NO?"

"… Gabrielle… if you keep being like this, I'll just leave…"

Jindo's hand rested on the door handle, poised to exit when Gabrielle interjected.

"Okay okay, Jindo… I'll stop it."

Turning to face her again, Jindo was greeted by her smile.

"By the way Jindo, I'm hungry now, do you want to eat dinner with me?"

Although this proposition was far from his initial plans, a sense of guilt and pity nudged him to offer his time, albeit grudgingly and with an air of discomfort.

"Okay Gabrielle, what do you want to eat?"

"We eat what you want, Jindo…"

"I don't mind. Let's just eat Indian then."

"Oh, you want to be a vegetarian?"

"… no, I just know that's what you normally eat. That's why…"

"See? You're so nice and thoughtful Jindo. You care about me all the time…"

"…"

In fact, Jindo had suggested this to avoid any unnecessary fuss over what seemed trivial to him at the moment.

After ordering via Deliveroo, they ascended upstairs, with Gabrielle busy setting up the projector.

"Gabrielle, what are you doing?"

"I want to watch the Korean movie that you talked about before."

"You mean Okja?"

"Yes, that one… réalisé par Bing, Fen, Zoo… c'est ça?"

"… it's Bong Joon Ho… By the way, now?"

"Oui, maintenant…"

Nonchalantly disregarding Jindo, she continued her preparations and spoke up.

"By the way, Korean names so sound like Chinese…"

"No, it's not… You just remembered it like Chinese…"

"What? You think Koreans are better than Chinese…"

"No, that's not what I meant. I just think… no…"

Jindo cut his statement short, sensing that initiating any form of debate would likely end with her dismissing his viewpoint and him feeling drained for no valid reason.

Nevertheless, she located the film on Netflix and hit play. Somewhere along the way, they found themselves immersed in the viewing atmosphere, with Gabrielle bringing out a petite bottle of champagne.

Meanwhile, Jindo was somewhat hesitant.

"Gabrielle, I drove here today."

"It's just a glass of champagne. It's Veuve Clicquot… you like this, no?"

"Yes, but…"

While Jindo was caught in his hesitation, Gabrielle was already pouring the bubbly liquid into a glass, casually imitating Jindo's previous, showy performance with an air of relaxed humour.

Regardless, the film started, and Gabrielle continued to cater to Jindo's film aficionado side.

"Is she not the actress you like?"

"Yes, Tilda Swinton…"

"She's English, no?"

"I think she is Scottish…"

"Well, they're the same, no?"

"… I think they're different…"

Jindo ignorantly replied to the lady who seemed too dismissive to differentiate between nations. At that moment, the doorbell's chime cut through the air.

"Jindo, you get the food and I'll prepare the table…"

She darted towards the kitchen, and Jindo descended the long, curving staircase to collect their meal. Upon his return, Gabrielle greeted him with a somewhat disconcerting smile.

Ignoring the unsettled feeling, Jindo unpacked the food and they began their meal.

"Chin Chin!"

Gabrielle raised her glass for a toast, a gesture that struck Jindo as out of character. She was not one to initiate such formalities.

Nevertheless, he clinked glasses with her but set his own down untouched.

"Are you not drinking Jindo?"

"Well, I normally eat first then drink... Why?"

"It's just because I don't want this expensive champagne wasted... Because I especially bought it for you today..."

Jindo cocked an eyebrow at her odd remark.

"Gabrielle, you bought this champagne for me? Does that mean you knew I was going to be here, eating dinner with you today?"

"..."

She blushed, caught off-guard, and scrambled for an excuse.

"No, I mean I normally don't drink you know... But I bought it to drink with you."

Her response did not directly address his question, but Jindo let it slide. A lack of precision in her replies was a common occurrence.

Regardless, they proceeded with the film. Though it was Jindo's second viewing, this time, the narrative struck a different chord. Observing Okja, a creature accustomed to the serene nature, being captured and exploited for commercial representation by the callous hands of ill-natured humans, Jindo felt an inexplicable connection somehow.

As the film drew to a close and the end credits started to roll, Jindo was about to make a move to depart.

However, Gabrielle appeared reluctant to let him go.

"Jindo, I think the movie was so nice... I think Bong Hong Jong is a good réalisateur."

Rather than correcting her mispronunciation yet again, Jindo chose to keep the conversation flowing.

"Yes, he's great… At the same time, I believe this is not the best version of him yet… I think he'll be one of those really remarkable filmmakers one day…"

"Wow, is he your favourite Korean réalisateur?"

Although Jindo had the suspicion that Gabrielle was only making conversation to delay his departure, he responded courteously nonetheless.

"… no, I'm more type-classed for Park Chan Wook."

"Park, Chang, Wok? Is there any famous movie by him?"

"… Oldboy might be one that you may have heard…"

Despite Jindo's concerted effort to convey his obliviousness through both his facial expression and voice tone, an unspoken signal that he was privy to Gabrielle's intentions, she persisted in feigning ignorance, continually pressing the conversation.

"Ah, I know that movie. I loved it… It's even one of Vincent's favourites. What is his recent movie?"

"… The Handmaiden…"

"What is it about?"

"… it's about the handmaiden as it says… but there are a lot of twisting elements. Actually, it's inspired by a British novel, Fingersmith, but adapted into Korean via historical elements with Japan…"

"Ah… is it also a film for vegan?"

"…"

Clearly, Gabrielle's attention had been elsewhere during his explanation. As Jindo prepared to leave, he added one final note.

"Anyway, it's a great film. I particularly find the mise-en-scène aesthetically pleasing… I think they even got the Vulcain Prize for it from the Cannes Film Festival last year…"

"Jindo, are you not going to stay?"

Grasping his hand, a note of desperation lingered in Gabrielle's voice.

"Well, I think I need to go back home tonight…"

"I shaved today…"

"Haha, tempting… but if you give me the opportunity again next time, I'll appreciate that."

"You haven't even drunk the champagne that I bought for you…"

As the conversation seemed unending, Jindo downed his glass in one go.

"See? I drank it all… Can I go now?"

"No, there's still half left in the bottle, and you know champagne can't be kept like this. It has to be drunk all once opened…"

"Hah…"

Taking the petite bottle, Jindo gulped down the remaining liquid, finding the Veuve Clicquot still remarkably crisp.

"Okay now?"

Jindo gave her a wry smile, thinking she had exhausted her attempts to keep him there. He began his descent down the narrow winding staircase, but as he passed the showroom, a peculiar sense of dizziness overwhelmed him.

He shook his head, attempting to clear the sensation, but instead, the dizziness intensified. He reached out for the handrail, but his sight was warped as though he was peering through a kaleidoscope, causing him to repeatedly miss his grasp.

Suddenly, Gabrielle was at his side, offering her support.

"Jindo, are you okay?"

Despite her concerned words, there was an insincere undertone to her voice that gave him pause. However, in his state, he could not even muster a response, instead, he found himself leaning heavily on her to avoid a disastrous tumble down the steep spiral staircase.

She guided him to the bedroom, and before he knew it, he was drifting into oblivion, his memories fading into the ether.

Chapter 58 : The Morning's Mishap

The day before Jindo's contract finish…

Jindo found himself roused from sleep by the strident voice of a middle-aged woman. His bleary eyes fluttered open to see Madame Claude's incensed countenance looming over him, igniting a profound sense of embarrassment. Clumsily clambering out of bed, he confronted her, his consciousness yet to fully grasp his complete nudity.

Given his precarious position on the bed's edge, it only took a few moments of awkward fumbling for him to reveal his nakedness. What deepened his embarrassment was the state of his 'mini-me', standing at full attention, its orientation decidedly skyward. While a case of morning glory was not uncommon, he realised this was an abnormal level of intensity.

Unperturbed, Madame Claude locked her gaze onto Jindo's junior partner, unflinchingly observant of its bobbing dance. Gabrielle was also awake by now, choosing not to comment but merely spectate the unfolding spectacle.

Feeling an intense mortification, Jindo issued a string of apologies to the mother of the nude girl beside him before hastily retreating from the property. Reaching his car, he found himself too queasy to drive and decided to pause momentarily. Once his nausea subsided slightly, he slinked back to his humble abode in Bondy.

Upon crossing his threshold, Jindo was consumed by a sense of relief, feeling his tension melt away. Concurrently, his stomach decided to voice its disapproval, expelling remnants of the previous night's vindaloo in a vehement protest. After a bout of heaving, Jindo collapsed onto his bed, assuming the form of a defeated zombie.

His two feline companions, perplexed by his peculiar behaviour, chose to keep their distance, contrary to their usual affectionate demeanour. They surveyed him with inscrutable eyes from the room's corner.

After a while of sleep, he regained some composure, his gaze falling onto his mobile phone. He noticed a message from Gabrielle, an urgent request for a callback. A wave of hesitation washed over him, perhaps due to the lingering confusion about the morning's incident, zapping his strength to revisit the memories. His recall was foggy, fragmented at the descent of the winding staircase.

Nonetheless, he mustered enough to return her call.

"Gabrielle, is everything okay?"

"Well, no… you know my mother was angry…"

"…"

Her words abandoned him as he found himself mired in the storm of Madame Claude's wrath.

"Don't worry Jindo, she's angry not because I've slept with you but because we're still sleeping when it's nearly the work hour…"

"Ah…"

Jindo exhaled a breath he had not realised he was holding, readying himself to probe the past night's mysteries.

"Gabrielle, about yesterday…"

"It's okay. She's just a mom, and I'm her only daughter, so she's a bit too sensitive sometimes… Anyway, she likes you, and you know that…"

Gabrielle's words tumbled out in a rapid-fire manner, hardly affording Jindo the opportunity to chime in.

"Okay but Gabrielle, I actually…"

"She said, your body was cute though…"

Once again, Gabrielle cut him off with her unyielding pace, subtly diverting him from voicing his thoughts. She pressed on.

"She said you're very healthy haha…"

Gabrielle's laughter punctuated her words, heightening Jindo's discomfort. He attempted to redirect the dialogue away from the embarrassing topic.

"Gabrielle, can we not talk about this?"

"What? It's a compliment…"

"… okay, but I'll appreciate it if you stop talking about this."

"I SAY WHAT I WANT."

The fiercely independent French girl dismissively brushed off Jindo's plea. He felt ill at ease to counter her at this moment, possibly because he sensed a temporary power imbalance in their interaction.

He fell silent, letting her proceed.

"Anyway Jindo, you have a rest today and come tomorrow…"

She swiftly hung up, and despite their contract negotiations being incomplete and his impending final day, Jindo found himself harbouring pessimistic expectations about the future outcome.

Meanwhile, he still had no recollection of the previous evening but fostered suspicions about the champagne. He momentarily contemplated ringing back Gabrielle to inquire, but his intuition cautioned him that she would unlikely confess to any foul play.

Jindo decided on a soothing bath, hoping it would help jog his memory about yesterday's happenings. To his surprise, he discovered his 'mini-me' still standing to attention as if under the influence of a counterfeit Viagra.

Having partaken in several bouts of self-pleasure to quell the unwavering arousal, he finally managed to resolve the issue. Subsequently, he spent some time pondering his situation, concluding that, regardless of the circumstances, it was imperative to extricate himself from Gabrielle's entanglement.

Chapter 59 : The Last Weave

The final day of Jindo's contract...
Arriving at the atelier with the early morning dew, Jindo dove straight into his tasks. His cohorts, intrigued by his sudden absence the day prior, were pacified by a terse explanation of food poisoning.

With the exception of Timothée, the team remained oblivious to the impending end of Jindo's tenure. He chose to share this news at the last minute of the working day. The frostiness in Amélie's demeanour towards Jindo seemed to thaw, and she wished him well. Boubacar, too, boosted his spirits with a few well-chosen words. However, the chapelier maintained an odd silence, observing Jindo with an enigmatic expression.

Bidding his farewells to the atelier, Jindo ventured towards Gabrielle's. Upon arrival, he discovered the presence of Madame Claude, seated in close proximity to her daughter. The older woman bore a disconcerting expression as if he were in her debt.

Undeterred by the intimidation, Jindo was resolute in bringing his chapter at Gabrielle's to a close. Although offered a seat, he chose to remain standing; a silent assertion of his intent to depart post-haste following his say.

"Gabrielle, I thank you for everything so far, and I wish you the best of luck with your collection..."

Gabrielle appeared taken aback by Jindo's forthrightness, but quickly composed herself, seemingly not prepared to let him off easily.

"Jindo, was it fun that you played me?"

"Pardon?"

"STOP SAYING PARDON. You always say pardon when you try to win time... Jindo, you know what I mean..."

"No Gabrielle, what are you talking about?"

Jindo, although taken aback, managed to maintain composure and sought clarification.

"Hah, you came here, desperately asked for a job, then worked so hard to appeal yourself to me, then after you got what you wanted, you're trying to leave without taking any responsibility..."

"Responsibility? I don't know what you're talking about, Gabrielle."

Despite detecting her recurring tactic of self-victimisation, Jindo retained his oblivious stance, steadfastly disregarding her accusations. Gabrielle appeared flustered by his nonchalance, then broached another grievance.

"You even enjoyed having SEX TO ME whenever you wanted..."

This time, Gabrielle's self-declared victimhood took an angle Jindo had somewhat anticipated. However, the presence of her mother in the same room elevated his anxiety levels.

Unsurprisingly, Madame Claude seemed to latch onto the contentious dialogue, her frown deepening. Jindo decided to issue a warning.

"Gabrielle, I'm not going to let you talk like this anymore... I had sex to you? Gabrielle! WE HAD SEX TOGETHER, not like I DID IT BY MYSELF."

"NO, you always CREATED THE SITUATION."

"What do you mean I created the situation?"

"I still remember you made me drunk, then took me to your stupid house in Bondy, then did SEX TO ME..."

"..."

Jindo was momentarily silenced by this unforeseen turn of events. He had indeed anticipated Gabrielle bringing up the recent evening, providing him with the opportunity to confront the questionable champagne incident.

However, the current accusations necessitated immediate attention. He decided to defer the champagne issue, opting instead to address the current contention assertively.

"Gabrielle, that night, as far as I remember, we had a pleasant moment in this house before continuing the session in my place... You mentioned that there was no place for you to sleep here. Am I mistaken?"

Jindo's tone was unwavering, but Gabrielle mirrored his staunchness. This evening, a tangible icy tension had settled between them, indicating that neither party was willing to back down.

"You're wrong, Jindo. Why do I not have a place to sleep? My parents have a house in Paris. I can just go there, and it's not far like the STUPID Bondy from here..."

Jindo felt a surge of fatigue. His instincts told him that this conversation was set to be an uphill battle.

Nevertheless, Gabrielle proceeded with her accusations.

"Also, you made me drink that day then I got drunk... I never drink alcohol because I get drunk easily. You can ask my mom about that..."

With that, Gabrielle gestured towards Madame Claude, who was already shooting malevolent glances at Jindo. The middle-aged woman appeared ready to leap into the discussion and probe her daughter further.

"Gabrielle, you don't need to bring your mum in..."

Jindo made an effort to ward off Gabrielle from enmeshing her mother further into the conversation, but his protests were to no avail. Despite his objections, Gabrielle disclosed the nitty-gritty to her mother, who could only converse in French. The older woman offered a terse 'non' in response to her daughter's account.

"See, she says I never drink alcohol…"

Emboldened by her mother's backing, Gabrielle's confidence appeared to burgeon, much to Jindo's dismay. He felt a tinge of unease as her mother, an impenetrable fortress in his view, took an active part in the ongoing dispute.

The middle-aged Frenchwoman leaned towards Gabrielle, her facial expression indicating a keen desire to grasp every spoken word henceforth.

Yet, Jindo maintained his stance, unswerving.

"Gabrielle, this is unfair. You know we've even done it on the other days, and I'm sure you enjoyed some of those days… SO, PLEASE STOP SAYING like I did it on my own…"

Jindo strove to broach the topic without descending into obscenity, but Gabrielle appeared to turn a deaf ear.

"Jindo, you're not getting this at all… The thing is that whatever happened, I was fine because I liked you and I thought you liked me. That's why I had sex with you WITH PLEASURE… But, let's be fair. You enjoyed it more than I did because you looked always so happy to suck my body like a starving dog…"

"…"

As she delivered this unabashed description, Gabrielle emulated Jindo's actions, causing him discomfort under the disdainful gaze of her mother.

"Gabrielle, stop it."

"You did like this, no?"

Unmoved by his plea, Gabrielle continued her vivid pantomime with her tongue, mimicking Jindo's action during their intimate moment.

Jindo responded with a weary shake of his head, desperate to extricate himself from this surreal nightmare.

Gabrielle swiftly broached another subject.

"Even yesterday, you were drunk and did it again."

Seizing the opportunity, Jindo latched onto this newly introduced subject matter.

"Well said Gabrielle... Actually, I was going to ask you about it. Gabrielle, please tell me honestly... you put something in the champagne, didn't you?"

"What do you mean?"

With an instant switch to an ingenue's guise, feigning shock, she portrayed ignorance.

However, Jindo was not fooled; he had the distinct impression that she had braced herself for this confrontation.

"Gabrielle, seriously... you put something there, didn't you? Because I would never get drunk by just a small bottle of champagne that was even half left and also... my... thing..."

Jindo felt a pinch of embarrassment; the frank mention of his private anatomy was something he wished to avoid in front of Madame Claude.

Caught in his hesitance, Gabrielle found an opening.

"What thing are you talking about?"

"My... MINI... ME..."

A look of vexation crossed Jindo's face as he gestured subtly, indicating with a downward glance.

Catching his signal, she responded with a chuckle.

"Mini... you? Ah, haha, yes, it's mini..."

"That's not the point. What I'm trying to say is… my mini-me was even aroused for a long time without my intention…"

"I don't know what you're talking about Jindo. All I know is you drank the champagne in one shot then got yourself drunk then did sex to me…"

"아, 씨발 미치겠네 *(This is getting me nuts)*. Because you…"

Jindo vented in his native Korean, exasperated beyond measure. As he paused, contemplating the situation and his part in it, Gabrielle struck again.

"No one asked you to drink like that, Jindo… I just wanted to stay with you more, but you tried to leave so fast and it was the only thing I could do, asking you to drink the expensive champagne that I BOUGHT FOR YOU…"

Her voice quivered as she teetered on the edge of tears, adding an emotional tinge to the unfolding drama. Watching the spectacle, Madame Claude's countenance soured, despite the language barrier.

However, Jindo dedicated himself to remaining unswayed, his face a mask of calm indifference, prepared to weather Gabrielle's emotional storm.

"Gabrielle, please don't cry. Cry after we get this situation sorted…"

Despite his blunt interjection, Gabrielle's emotional upheaval did not falter. Jindo quickly veered the conversation to safer grounds.

"Gabrielle, can you please tell me what happened yesterday?"

His prompt interruption halted her tearful narrative, and Gabrielle composed herself to respond.

"You got drunk, then I helped you lay on the bed, but you suddenly started to do sex to me… I didn't mind having sex with you because I like you but yesterday you were trying sex me VERY BAD…"

Madame Claude's discomfiture was growing palpable, each mention of the term 'sex' causing a visible wince. Jindo, eager to ease the tension, continued the conversation.

"Okay, so we did it yesterday..."

"Yes, you even finished onto all over my bed sheet, so I had to clean the disgusting thing when you already fell asleep..."

"..."

Though Jindo had unravelled the sequence of events, he found himself at a loss for words. His memory failed him, and there appeared to be solid evidence that endorsed Gabrielle's account.

Simultaneously, an incensed middle-aged woman, likely having painted a vivid tableau in her mind with the trigger words 'champagne' and 'sex', trained a blazing stare on Jindo. Her daughter, a known teetotaller, was on the brink of tears.

The mother of the victimised girl embarked on a tirade directed at Jindo, her anger pouring out in rapid French. Jindo was unable to grasp her words, yet the essence was clear enough. He did not ask Gabrielle to intervene, but a tearful Gabrielle translated nonetheless.

"She says she's very disappointed in you... She never thought of you that way. She thought you were well-educated, polite, sincere, hard-working, intelligent, and fashionable... She thought you were a GENTLEMAN."

"..."

There were countless rebuttals Jindo longed to voice, but instead, he held the gaze of the two French women, his breaths coming in measured cycles, as though trying to steer this unfolding drama towards closure, yet unsure how to navigate.

Chapter 60 : Echoes of the Endgame

At that moment, the doorbell chimed, and the enraged mother moved to answer it. The visitor's distinctive, rat-squeaking voice was instantly recognisable to Jindo.

The patriarch of the family walked into the room, his eyes landing on his teary-eyed daughter. The short, bald man shot a murderous glance at Jindo, who, rather than displaying fear, merely sighed, his gut sinking at the prospect of what was to come.

The mother relayed the circumstances to her spouse, her words lost on Jindo as they sped past in heated French. Nevertheless, Jindo did not need to understand the language to recognise her animated facial expressions painted him in a damning light.

As she vented, the father's glare seared into Jindo, seemingly deliberating over the most fitting form of punishment once the whole story was unveiled. Jindo, trapped in this surreal scenario, continued to heave silent sighs.

Suddenly, Seiwa's earlier statement sprung to mind, the belief that Gabrielle and Madame Claude, though typically at odds, united seamlessly when cornering an adversary. Now, it seemed the father had also entered the fray.

Jindo turned his gaze towards Gabrielle. Through her tear-streaked face, she appeared to comprehend his silent rebuke, his eyes broadcasting his knowledge of her deceptive game. Still, she sustained her performance, playing the victim to her father who was preparing to question her.

The father's voice, squeaky and incomprehensible in French, seemed to cross-examine Gabrielle's account. Gabrielle, usually relishing in drawn-out explanations, now responded tersely, resembling a cowed victim on the stand.

Jindo remained a bystander, allowing them to stage their drama. Despite the turmoil, his resolve to vacate the premises by nightfall remained unwavering.

When the grilling session concluded, the father muttered a few sharp words to his wife and daughter. Gabrielle, in turn, translated.

"My father said we can just CALL THE POLICE."

Caught off guard by this audacious proposal, Jindo nevertheless maintained his composure.

"Gabrielle, I actually want to laugh at all of this but..."

He was cut short as Gabrielle pre-emptively translated his initial words to her father. The irate father lunged at Jindo, clutching his throat. With the elderly French man grabbing the scruff of his neck, the impassive Asian man refrained from retaliating against him yet.

Instead, he locked eyes with him before swivelling his gaze back to Gabrielle.

"Gabrielle, you don't need to translate for me right now. Please just listen to me until the end and then translate."

As usual, her face creased into a scowl and she shrugged, feigning indifference to his words. Regardless, Jindo pressed on.

"Gabrielle, let's be reasonable... you know I'm not a bad person, but you constantly fabricate situations where you're the victim..."

Once again, Gabrielle interjected, defending herself.

"Jindo, what do you mean, I FABRICATE... why are you always trying to make me a bad person?"

Ignoring her deflection, Jindo noticed her dramatics intensifying, her father's presence seemingly emboldening her. He shook his head in revulsion.

All of a sudden, Jindo felt a firmer grip as the father inadvertently tightened his hold, inflicting a jolt of pain. Jindo swiftly countered with a wrist-twist, causing the older man to tumble onto the floor, clutching his wrist and wincing in pain. The two French women rushed to his aid, Gabrielle still in tears and Madame Claude berating Jindo.

Unintentionally having caused injury, Jindo found himself painted as the aggressor. Swallowing his embarrassment, he knelt beside the two women to inspect the older man's wrist, only to be shoved onto the floor by the indignant daughter.

Feeling a pang of guilt, Jindo issued a flurry of apologies that fell on deaf ears. As Madame Claude reached for her phone, presumably to make a call, panic set in.

"Gabrielle, who is she calling?"

"I don't know... POLICE peut-être *(maybe)*..."

His anxiety escalated, and his lack of French skills rendered him powerless. Thinking on his feet, Jindo plucked the phone from Madame Claude's grasp.

Once he confirmed that she was indeed placing a call, he saw Madame Claude lunging to retrieve her phone. Jindo evaded her grasp, which provoked Gabrielle to join in. The father, despite his aching wrist, became part of this ludicrous jujitsu-esque skirmish unfolding on the floor.

Eventually, Jindo managed to extricate himself from the fracas and stand upright. Gabrielle attempted to snatch her mobile phone from her desk, but Jindo was quicker, spiriting it away. The situation devolved into a frenzied spectacle, their jujitsu contest continuing upright.

"Gabrielle, what the hell are we doing?"

"You're the one who took our phones away, Jindo."

"Because you guys were going to call the police."

Still struggling for the phone retrieval, their conversation continued.

"And what are you afraid of, Jindo?"

"I'm not afraid of anything, but I can see what's going to happen..."

"We're not calling the police but an ambulance..."

"Yes, you do. You were going to call the police."

Jindo, more sceptical than ever, attempted to seize control of the situation.

"Gabrielle, let's sort this out finely, shall we? Let's get out everything into the air... you weren't happy because I was leaving, were you?"

"What are you talking about, Jindo? You just used me and then tried to leave..."

Responding thus, she persisted in trying to retrieve her phone from Jindo.

"Okay, fine fine. Gabrielle, let me put it this way... I never meant to use you. I'm sorry if it came across that way, but I have to say it was an absolute pleasure to be with you, including our private moments. I still remember all those moments fondly... However, to be completely honest, you were right that I was tempted to be introduced to high-fashion houses through your connections but I never intended to play you... I'm sorry if things appeared differently... I really am sorry..."

Jindo's tone was desperate, but the French family seemed to be engrossed in their own conversation. It dawned on Jindo that they were attempting to use his father's phone, which had run out of charge.

When Gabrielle tried to go out of the office, Jindo swiftly positioned himself before the door, blocking her exit with a distinctly disgruntled expression and demeanour.

"에이 씨발, 제말 말 좀 끝까지 좀 들어라…"

(For fuck's sake, please listen to me till the end…)

Jindo exploded in his mother tongue. The Asian man, sporting a black Prada puffer vest and his hair tied back, clutching two phones, resembled a bouncer barring anyone from leaving the premises.

Meanwhile, Jindo was unsure whether Gabrielle was trying to secure the office phone in the foyer or enlist assistance from outside. Regardless of her intentions, he knew he needed to intervene, as either outcome would put him at a disadvantage.

Preparing to continue his appeal, he noticed the French parents engrossed in another conversation. Jindo realised he needed to capture their attention.

"Mama and Papa… je pense que toutes les choses aujourd'hui sont juste… tout de mal compréhensions…"

(Mum and Papa… I think everything that happened today is just all misunderstanding…)

Jindo, clearly agitated, struggled to articulate his thoughts, the language barrier only adding to his growing anxiety. His speech, a chaotic blend of Italian and French all of a sudden, filled the room with tension.

"Mama and Papa, 'io'… ah… je suis… 'mi piace' ta femme, ah, fille… et 'io voglio' être avec ta fille, mais il y avait une grande mal compréhension 'oggi'… 'però' maintenant, je pense que c'est peut-être juste normale 'come coppia'… 'Voglio laborare' ici et 'non so perché adesso la situazione sia diventata così'…"

(Mum and Papa, I… ah… I like your girl, ah, daughter… and I want to be with your daughter, but there has been a big misunderstanding today…

but now... I think that it's perhaps just normal as a couple... I want to work here and I don't know why the situation happened like this so far...)

His desperate plea, littered with the erratic language switch, made it all the more poignant. His primary concern was clear; to prevent the French family from involving the authorities.

It appeared that his linguistic cocktail caught the attention of the older couple. Encouraged, Jindo shifted his gaze back to Gabrielle.

"Gabrielle, I want to be with you, and I also want to work with you... and I admit that I was going to leave this place because, to be completely honest, I was suspicious about your CHANEL career..."

"You're saying you were only with me because I was at CHANEL?"

"... no, that's not what I meant..."

Exhausted from the emotional turmoil and linguistic gymnastics, Jindo felt drained. Despite his dwindling trust in the self-proclaimed, ex-CHANEL designer, he was desperate to end the conflict. Without giving much thought, he turned to Gabrielle again.

"Gabrielle, you're beautiful and..."

Abruptly realising that the parents had resumed their private discussion, Jindo felt the urgency to reclaim their attention.

"Mama et Papa, ta fille est très belle et... 'Mi piace molto... Guarda, ho habitato in Inghilterra, in Italia et' now I live in France but your daughter... ta fille est la plus belle femme ever and I always felt intimidated to be with her because elle est trop belle pour moi... 'ecco perché'... I tried to leave... mais now I get everything understood... tutto est bene... ho capito... je comprends..."

(Mama and Papa, your daughter is very beautiful and... I like her a lot... Actually, I lived in England, Italia and now in France but your daughter... she's the most beautiful girl I ever saw and I always felt intimidated to be with her because she's too pretty for me... that's why... I

tried to leave… but now I get everything understood… and everything is fine with me… I get it… I get it…)

Notwithstanding his seemingly reckless wordplay aimed at diffusing the situation and drawing the attention of the French family, Jindo's linguistic finesse was undeniably impressive.

His image transformed from an ostensible instigator into a distinctly Europeanised Asian gentleman, marked by heavy brows and dramatic facial expressions.

Despite the seemingly arbitrary nature of his extended discourse, it successfully thawed the frosty ambiance, prompting Gabrielle to reclaim her mobile phone.

"Jindo, give me my phone back."

"…"

Reluctantly, he handed over the phone. Gabrielle's following question echoed in the room.

"So, you agree that you played on me, but now want to continue to work with me?"

Humiliated and frustrated, Jindo met her gaze, her raised eyebrows showing her resilience. Jindo replied.

"… yes."

"Are you staying tonight?"

"… okay."

With that, the French family members left the room, their chatter fading into the distance. Left alone in the office, Jindo's gaze fell on the graffiti painting adorning the wall. He studied the cannibalistic animated characters, a bizarre reflection of Gabrielle's artistic universe. Little did he know, his stay at Gabrielle's would extend far beyond his initial anticipation.

About the Author

H. Gwyne is a debut novelist from Korea, whose work draws on a rich tapestry of multicultural experiences accumulated over a decade of residencies in England, Italy, and France. His narrative style is distinctive, occasionally weaving English, French, Italian, and Korean languages into an immersive reading experience.

Gwyne's narratives, set against the vibrant backdrop of the fashion industry, showcase his adept use of humour and satire to challenge cultural stereotypes and perceptions. His unique perspectives, shaped by his former roles as a personal shopper and modéliste, and his current position as a co-managing director of a small local family boutique in Korea, permeate his writing.

Despite the demanding duties and tasks associated with managing his family-run boutique, which specialises in tailored women's wear, Gwyne remains steadfastly dedicated to his passion for writing. He seizes every opportunity to develop his craft.

Looking ahead, Gwyne's ambitions are twofold: nurturing his burgeoning writing career and expanding his family's fashion business. With his eyes set on Paris for the future, he is eager to learn, open to advice, and ready to embrace opportunities in the publishing world. His humorous narratives, steeped in cultural insights, are his unique offering to readers worldwide.

Website: http://www.maison-h-gwyne.com

Email: contact@maison-h-gwyne.com

Instagram: @maisonhgwyne

Pinterest: @maisonhgwyne

Youtube: @maisonhgwyne

TikTok: @maisonhgwyne

Acknowledgement

I am compelled to acknowledge a number of individuals who have offered their unwavering support and assistance throughout this journey.

To Mike, I extend my deepest gratitude for your understanding of my ambition and for your companionship on this path. Our weekly discussions over the past year have not only helped to form my identity as a writer, but also instilled in me a deep sense of pride in my craft.

To Diana, I offer my thanks for your exceptional illustrations. Whilst our collaboration was initially rooted in fashion, you embraced the challenge of designing for my book design, a venture beyond your accustomed domain. Your understanding, creativity, and invaluable contributions are sincerely appreciated.

To Kwangsoo, your support has been a cornerstone in this journey. Despite my limited availability, your regular visits to my atelier, often involving drives of over two hours, and your continual encouragement for my ambitious endeavour, have served as a constant source of strength.

To Joshua, the seeds of this novel project were sown through your inspiring words. In spite of the many events and obstacles we encountered – before, during, and even after the pandemic – your consistent encouragement and support have been instrumental, for which I am immensely grateful.

To those who provided encouragement and feedback in times of self-doubt, I convey my heartfelt thanks: Anna, Christopher, Eleanor, Giulia, Ivan, Laurent, Melissa, and Vivienne.

To my family, I express my profound gratitude for your unwavering, tacit support. Despite not fully understanding my sudden aspiration to write a novel, or the increasing amount of time I devoted to it, often resulting in my absence from family events, your unquestioning encouragement and belief in my pursuit of happiness are deeply appreciated.

Published by **ATELIER H**.

ISBN: 9791198584816 (Paperback)

ISBN: 9791198584809 (EPUB)

ISBN: 9791198584830 (Audiobook)

First Edition: Dec 2023

Printed in the United Kingdom.